Book 2 in the Davina + Quinn Series

Love's Promises

Deborah Armstrong

ISBN paperback: 978-0-9950945-8-1
ISBN eBook: 978-0-9950945-9-8
ISBN audio: 978-1-989747-00-1

This is a work of fiction.
Names, characters, places and incidents either are the product
of the author's imagination or are used fictitiously,
and any resemblance to any actual persons, living or dead, events,
or locales is entirely coincidental.

This book was printed in the United States of America.

Cover, interior and eBook conversion:
Rebecca Finkel, FPGD.com

To order additional copies of this book, contact:
Terrahill Publishing
www.DeborahArmstrong.ca/Terrahill-Publishing/
Orders@DeborahArmstrong.ca

this book is dedicated to

my husband Philip,

who made me promises many years ago

and kept every one of them.

I am forever yours

author's note

Love's Promises was first published in 2013. It is the continuation of Davina and Quinn's love story. I believed they had more to tell and that my readers would agree.

With the second edition of *Love's Promises*, I've made minor improvements to the writing. I have grown as a writer and learned more about the romance genre. Although I consider Davina and Quinn's stories romance, they also belong to the women's fiction genre. My novels deal with love and family. They also have suspense, and some might say they touch on the spiritual. Although, to me, the spiritual is the love connection we have for each other.

Davina and Quinn are very special to me, and I feel honoured that they've chosen me to tell their story. I hope you enjoy their continuing love story as I enjoy writing it for you.

Prologue

Guy Tremblant sat across from his brother-in-law in the backseat of the French ambassador's limousine. His gaze focused on the tarmac as he watched the movement of the various airport service vehicles. It wouldn't be hard to escape on one. He had used this scenario in one of his movies. *Patience.*

The French movie director had a gift for playing out a scene in his mind, knowing how everything would look before filming it. He could see every angle, knowing which would best show what needed to be seen and hide the action's mechanics. This gift made him one of the top action genre directors in the business.

"Guy!" his brother-in-law Jean-Luc barked at him. Why Guy refused to accept the seriousness of the situation was inconceivable to him.

"Oui," Guy said as he tore his gaze away from the tarmac. His skin tingled from the anticipation of his escape, but he kept his voice dull, not wanting to give himself away. "You were saying?"

"I've called in every favour from the American government and our own. There will be no more privileges for you. Once you are on that plane, you cannot return to the United States. You are to stay in France and make a life with Marie. Do you understand?"

Guy stared at his wife's brother. He was a smart man, as evidenced by his position as French ambassador to the United States. He was cultured and highly respected—a tribute to his French upbringing and family's wealth. However, the poor man had no idea what it was like to have the flame of unfulfilled love burning in his heart. He had no idea what it was like to love a beautiful woman, only to have her snatched away by another man, one who was unworthy of her love. Guy tried to explain it once, but his words fell on deaf ears. No one cared for his reasoning, including the police, the judge, or the court-appointed psychiatrist. They all thought that Guy Tremblant was delusional, out of touch with reality.

Guy smiled as he thought of Davina Stuart. She wanted him, but her husband, Quinn Thomas, stood in her way. She didn't want to be married to him, Hollywood's beloved movie star. He couldn't give her what Guy could give her, what he had promised her.

"Attempted murder is a serious charge, Guy," Jean Luc said roughly, embarrassed that a member of his family committed such a heinous crime.

"It was simple assault, brother, nothing more." Guy sighed, bored with this never-ending recrimination. "He survived, didn't he?"

"You hit him over the head repeatedly with a steel pipe! You tried to kill the man! All for what? His wife? What about Marie?"

Guy waved off Jean Luc's questions casually. His marriage to Marie had been dead for years. It was a mutual understanding that they would stay married. Money and position always won out over divorce. "Marie understands."

"Then you are one lucky man, Guy. I've known wives who would kill for less."

"Talking about your indiscretions now?" Guy knew he had his brother-in-law. Infidelity was one thing, but when it involved prostitutes and bondage? "Thank you for the ride, Jean Luc. I can walk to the plane from here."

"I gave my word that I would escort you to the plane. That was the condition of your release into the French government's custody," Jean Luc said coolly.

"The plane is right there," Guy said as he nodded towards it. "Where else can I go?" Guy held out his hand to him. "Thank you, Jean Luc. I appreciate all that you have done. Don't worry. I won't cause you any further embarrassment." Without waiting for a reply, Guy Tremblant exited the limousine and headed towards the private jet.

He timed it perfectly. As he approached the stairs to the jet, a baggage cart drove by, briefly blocking Jean Luc's view. In a split second, Guy Tremblant was on the baggage cart heading towards the terminal.

Minutes later, as Jean Luc learned that his brother-in-law had not boarded the jet, Guy Tremblant walked through the airport's service gates, heading back to New York City. This time, there would be no stopping him. Davina Stuart would be his.

XO XO XO

Maggie Templeton sat in front of her stone fireplace, its heat almost burning her skin, yet she still shivered. She pulled her shawl around her shoulders, protecting herself from the cold, but there was no cold except for what she saw in her mind—the cold of darkness.

"No," she cried out softly.

She hadn't noticed her husband entering the room until he sat beside her and wrapped his arm around her waist.

"Another nightmare?" he asked. Concern filled his voice. His wife had been plagued by nightmares every night for the last week.

"No," she answered as she pressed her fingers against her temples. "It's happening, Charlie. The darkness is coming."

"How do you know?"

She turned to look at him. "I can feel it. It's so damned cold."

Charlie wiped away her tears. "You still don't know what it is?"

"No." Maggie's voice was soft as a whisper, as though voicing her vision would give the darkness power. "But it's coming for Davi. It's closer now, almost touching her."

Charlie pulled his wife in tight and kissed the top of her head. "I know this is difficult for you, knowing that something is going to happen to Davi, but you know it's going to work out. Your psychic told you so. Didn't she say that light will follow?"

"What if she's wrong? Do you know how this is killing me, knowing that the cards show something happening to my best friend and the only way to help her is to say nothing to her? What do I say when she comes back from her honeymoon? Tell me what to do, Charlie."

"Be there for her, love. That's all you can do."

one

A warm breeze blew off the Caribbean Sea onto the hot white sands of Palm Beach, Aruba. Davi Stuart Thomas lazed on the chaise lounge, enjoying the sun's heat and the distant sound of the waves crashing against the shore. She peered through her sunglasses at the cloudless blue sky. *This is nice, very nice.*

Davi looked over at her dozing husband, Hollywood heartthrob Quinn Thomas. She shuddered at the thought of how he had narrowly survived an attack by Guy Tremblant, a crazed director, only weeks ago. The short stubble on his head and the red bandana covering his surgical scars were the only visible reminders of the attack. She sighed as she looked upon his face. He was so gorgeous, even without his trademark thick shaggy brown hair, that he still made her heart skip a beat.

Davi reached for the crossword puzzle book lying across Quinn's chest. It was her book. Ever since she introduced Quinn to her beloved pastime, she competed with him to finish a puzzle.

"What are you doing?" Quinn asked as he gently grabbed her wrist.

"I'm reclaiming what is mine." She smiled sweetly at him. "I'd like to finish one puzzle before you finish the book."

Quinn pulled Davi on top of him and kissed her. His famous blue bedroom eyes sparkled. Davi always melted when he looked at her that way.

"It's later," he purred as his hands caressed her backside.

"Later? We had later an hour ago, and if I remember correctly, it was where you are lying right now."

"Then we'll move. I'll come over to your place if you don't mind." Quinn nodded towards Davi's chaise lounge.

"No. It has to be someplace different. It's our honeymoon, Quinn. No repetition in twenty-four hours, remember? It has to be a different place or position every time. It's an unwritten rule."

"Your unwritten rules come up at the strangest times. It's a good thing I have a vivid imagination."

Without hesitating, Quinn stood up and gathered Davi in his arms. Davi clasped her hands behind his neck as Quinn started to run out of their private patio towards the sea. She laughed as her husband of one month splashed into the warm water, the waves crashing against his legs. Quinn stopped when the water reached his chest and began to kiss his laughing bride. Davi's legs wrapped around Quinn's waist. She could feel his erection press against her. Quinn pulled aside the crotch of her bikini bottoms. Davi moaned as she felt his hardness push into her. His hands held her buttocks as he moved inside her. He was in total control.

Davi looked at Quinn and smiled. She kissed him softly on the mouth. "I love you."

Quinn smiled back at her. "Hold on tight. Some big waves are coming. I'd hate to lose you before we finish."

Davi held on tight just as a wave crashed against her back. Quinn jumped up to avoid the wave hitting him in the face. Davi laughed. As soon as Quinn set down, another wave crashed into them. Quinn's six foot, three-inch height kept his head above water, and that was all. Davi went under for a few seconds. When she finally surfaced, she was gasping for air.

"Quinn, you're crazy! I hope you're almost done," she sputtered. "I don't want to drown over five minutes of lovemaking."

"Only five minutes?"

"I know you can do it in five. Do your best, stud." Davi kissed him again. This time, it was a long and tender kiss.

The waves crashed over them. Davi held on tight as his thrusts increased. Quinn's moan vibrated through Davi as his mouth covered hers. Quinn released her from her kiss and smiled at her.

Quinn ignored the cameras aimed at them. He'd seen the paparazzi camped out on the beach, by the pool, and at the gym, poorly disguised as tourists. Quinn was used to them, a price he had to pay when he became famous. Davi, on the other hand, was new to this. He had no idea how she'd react if she knew that her every move was being recorded. That's why Quinn went deep with her into the water. The paparazzi might be able to guess what they were doing, but there was no way he'd help them take a good picture.

The newlyweds held on to each other as they enjoyed the waves. Quinn was supposed to be keeping his head protected from the sun and water, something he forgot about as they played together. As the couple walked out of the sea, Quinn took the bandana off his head and wrung out the water. Davi made a careful inspection of his incision, running her hand carefully over his head. It was healing well. Soon his hair would hide the scars.

Quinn looked at his watch. It was three o'clock, time for his afternoon workout. He spent two hours at the hotel's gym every afternoon, then Davi would join him for a walk on the beach.

They held hands as they walked to their villa. It had one bedroom with a king-sized bed, a large living room with a kitchen, and the bathroom had a Jacuzzi bath and shower. Off the front of the villa was a secluded patio, just perfect for honeymooners. Quinn and Davi made regular use of the privacy it offered.

Quinn stripped as he entered the private patio and hung up his shorts to dry. Davi sighed as she gazed at his naked body—his broad chest, rippled abs, strong arms, and muscled legs. Everything about him called out to her.

Quinn reached for Davi and pulled her into his bear hug. "This body is only for you, love. You know that," he murmured as he kissed the top of her head.

She smiled, no longer embarrassed at feeling like a lovestruck teenager around him. "I know. I still can't help admiring you."

"I don't have to go to the gym right now. I'd be happy to stay and keep you company."

"Quinn, we just made love."

"It's our honeymoon. I want to do it again, and I can tell that you want it, too. It's your turn."

Quinn put his finger under her chin, tilting her face up towards him. His blue eyes sizzled as he put his mouth on hers and kissed her. His hand pressed against her lower spine as he pulled her in close. Quinn was giving Davi her kiss. She moaned as her body pressed against his. Her legs weakened as she felt a tingle move up her legs to her belly.

Quinn kept up the pressure, his kiss pulling Davi in. Soon she moaned her release, soft and low. He picked her up and carried her to the bedroom. He laid her on the bed and undressed her slowly.

His finger traced along Davi's tan lines. She trembled at his touch, closing her eyes as she enjoyed the sensation. She parted her lips and ran her tongue over them, waiting for Quinn's kiss. Quinn's kiss was soft. Davi wanted more. She wrapped her arms around his neck and pulled him in tight. Her mouth devoured his. They kissed for a long time as Davi refused to release him. She lifted her hips and used her legs to keep him tight on top of her.

Quinn managed to push himself up from Davi as he gasped for air. His gaze burned into hers as she smiled at him.

"You drive me crazy," he moaned. "I want all of you. Now."

"What's taking you so long?" Her eyes still held his gaze, daring him to take her.

The telephone rang. Both Quinn and Davi stopped, not having heard their hotel phone ring since their arrival over two weeks ago. They both stared at the phone.

"You'd better get it, Quinn. It could be important."

Quinn swore as he reached for the phone. "Hello," he grumbled.

"Quinn. Hi, it's Luke. You weren't busy, were you?" The voice of Quinn's best friend and manager was cheerful.

"I'm on my honeymoon, Luke. Of course, I'm busy. This better be good."

He rolled off Davi and sat on the edge of the bed. Davi kneeled behind him, hugging him around his chest. She kissed a trail down his neck then across his shoulders.

"Your cell phone goes straight to voice mail."

"As I said, I'm on my honeymoon. You have twenty seconds to talk. Then I'm hanging up."

Luke laughed, enjoying the knowledge that he had interrupted his only client on his honeymoon. "Olivia called. She wants you to be her guest on her live show in two days."

"Why does she want me? Did she say?"

"Do you not read a newspaper or listen to the news while you're away? You and Davi are everywhere. So much has happened to the two of you that everyone wants to talk to you. *Lovestruck* is releasing. It's time to promote it, or have you forgotten? You've just wrapped up *Untitled*, and the director tried to kill you. You've married Davi, and you're still Hollywood's number one heartthrob. Your getting married didn't change that at all. In fact, it boosted your ratings."

"None of that matters," Quinn said through gritted teeth as he felt Davi's nails scrape across his balls then along his hardened cock. "Davi's my only concern right now. So if you'll excuse me, I have something more important to do than listen to your news report. I'll phone you when we get home. Bye, Luke." He ended the call.

In one fluid motion, Quinn turned around and had Davi on her back against the bed. She laughed as her husband pinned her arms above her head and covered her with hot kisses.

"You are bad, Davi Thomas. Did anyone ever tell you that?" he said against her neck, his breath warm against her salty skin.

"Only you, Quinn Thomas," she teased. "Got a problem with it?"

"Never."

Davi didn't ask Quinn about the phone call. She heard both sides of the conversation. She didn't mind being his excuse for turning down Olivia. The rest of the world could wait as far as she was concerned. They had both waited too long for this honeymoon, and no one was going to interfere with it.

"You said you wanted all of me now. Anytime you're ready, Mr. Hollywood Heartthrob."

"That's lover to you. There's no Hollywood in the bedroom. Not for you."

Davi caught him with her legs around his waist and pulled him in tight against her. Davi didn't want foreplay this time. She wanted him.

"In a hurry?" Quinn asked as his lips brushed against hers. "I could do this all day. I love kissing you and doing this—"

Davi moaned as Quinn entered her slowly, filling her. His thrusts were slow and deliberate. Davi longed to touch him, to run her hands down his back, then grab onto his perfect ass and hold him tight to her. She pulled against his grasp, but he held on tight.

"Something different," he murmured. "Your rules, remember?"

Davi moaned again as his hot kisses trailed down her neck to her breasts. She didn't mean this. She didn't want to be held down. The thought never crossed her mind. What made him think—she lost her train of thought as Quinn's tongue flicked her nipple, and then his teeth scraped across its sensitive tip.

"Quinn," she breathed.

"We haven't done this before," he said as his attention moved to her other breast. "What's it like not being able to touch me, to dig your fingernails into my back? I know how you love to do that to me."

"You like it, too," she cried out as she felt herself nearing orgasm. Her hips writhed underneath him, moving to his slow and deliberate thrusts. Her nipples tingled from his hot kisses and expert tongue.

"I like this, too. Giving you pleasure. You're so hot, so wet."

The phone rang.

Quinn ignored it as his lips moved over Davi's mouth. Their tongues mated as he kissed her hard. His thrusts increased as Davi cried her release into his mouth. He took her cries greedily as they heightened his pleasure. Everything about her filled his senses—her taste, her smell, the feel of her body as it trembled beneath him. More. He wanted more of her.

The phone continued to ring.

Quinn cursed against her lips. "Ignore it. It will stop."

"Answer it, Quinn. It will be Luke," Davi said as she fought to regain her senses.

Quinn released Davi's hands then picked up the receiver. "What?" he yelled into the phone.

"I didn't interrupt you again, did I?" Luke laughed. "I'm so sorry, man, but Olivia really wants you. She won't take no for an answer."

"Luke, I've got another week left of honeymoon time. I'm not leaving."

"What time zone are you in? You've got two days left before you're scheduled to be back here."

"Really?" Quinn acted surprised. "Where has the time gone?" He leaned down and kissed Davi, knowing what he'd been doing with his time.

"Olivia wants only you and no one else. You're the show. That's why she wants you back early. You know she doesn't beg, but I'm pretty sure she's close to doing that."

"I'll have to talk it over with Davi. I'll only do it with her approval."

"What?" Luke asked, dumbfounded.

"Hold on. I'm going to talk with Davi."

Quinn put the receiver down on the bedside table. He nuzzled Davi's neck. His breath was hot against her skin. "Olivia wants to interview me in two days."

"I heard." She moaned from underneath him, still tingling from her orgasm.

"We'd have to go home tomorrow," he said as his kisses moved down her neck to her collarbone. "I'll only do it if you say yes."

Davi ran her nails up his back, stopping at his shoulders. Her legs wrapped around his waist, pulling him in tight once again.

"It means cutting our honeymoon short." Quinn kissed a line to her left breast. His tongue laved and flicked her nipple.

"By one day."

"By one day," he said into her breast. "It means one less moonlit walk on the beach, one less day of making love under the stars, one less—"

Quinn felt her tighten around him. He clenched his teeth, forcing down a groan. It took every ounce of self-control to reach for the receiver and speak into it.

"Luke, the answer's no. Now fuck off." He slammed the receiver back into the phone.

Davi pulled Quinn down to her and held on tight. Quinn moaned as her sexual hunger devoured him. She was insatiable. He pumped away furiously as Davi held on to him. Her teeth nipped his ear lobe as her nails dug deeper into his back. Another moan escaped from Quinn. Quinn tensed with one final thrust and let his orgasm shudder through him before he collapsed onto Davi's body.

Quinn rolled off Davi, pulling her on top of him. His arms held her. His fingers reached up to her head, stroking her long brunette hair as they lay quietly for several moments.

"What are you thinking?" he asked her as her head rested on his chest.

"I'm glad you said no."

"Why?"

"I'm not ready to give you back to Hollywood. I don't want to go home yet."

"I feel the same way. I'm not ready for this to end. We have a lot to catch up on, including hot, mind-blowing sex."

Davi smiled. No matter how much she tried, she couldn't convince him that there was no time lost. They had met when they were supposed to meet—not one day sooner or one day later than their destined time.

"I wouldn't have left Ross for you. We met when we were supposed to. Let it go."

"How do you know what I'm thinking?" Quinn asked with amusement.

"I know you." Davi knew he thought of the years they spent apart. It was time neither of them could have changed. She had been married to Ross for twenty-five years, most of it happily until he cheated on her. They raised a family and ran a successful farm together. Then Ross died unexpectedly. Davi wrote a book to help her deal with her grief, and two years later, the book was being made into a movie with Quinn cast to play her son. A chance meeting on an airplane and Quinn was immediately in love with Davi. Davi only wanted a fantasy night filled with hot sex. Her heart was closed to love. Then Quinn made her open her heart. After a whirlwind romance, she was pregnant, and then they married. Their life together couldn't have started any sooner than it did. She pushed herself up from Quinn's chest. "Tell me I'm wrong."

He smiled at her. "You know you're never wrong." He lifted his head and kissed her.

"You have to go. Your gym buddies will be wondering what has happened to you."

Quinn groaned as Davi rolled off him and let him get out of bed. She watched him as he dressed in shorts and a T-shirt. He sat on the edge of the bed and tied his sneakers.

"Will I see you in a couple of hours?" he asked as he turned to give her a good-bye kiss.

"Yes."

"I'll be waiting for you."

XO XO XO

Davi walked off to the bathroom and started the shower. She loved her ice-cold showers—a luxury she could only enjoy when Quinn didn't join her. He didn't like having his manhood shrink, and his lips turn blue, although he was getting used to a cooler temperature. Davi

appreciated his attempt to compromise with her. She stood under
the cold shower, letting the water run through her hair as she soaped
her body.

She wasn't ready to go home. The feeling of foreboding was so
unlike her. She loved being on the farm with her family and her cows,
which she lovingly called the Ladies. She'd never been away from home
this long before, but something in the pit of her stomach made her
feel that going home wasn't a good idea, not yet anyway.

Davi didn't usually have feelings of foreboding. The last time was
just before she met Quinn. She wondered what she was doing taking
a flight to LA when she should be at home with her family. However,
Maggie, her best friend, read her tarot cards and told her she'd find
love and success on her trip. She had to go. The cards were right. Davi
wished she could have her cards read now. She needed to know why
she felt this way.

Davi turned off the shower and towelled herself dry. After she
dressed, she went to her bedside table and pulled out a pen and old
leather-bound book from the top drawer. She walked over to the kitchen
table, sat down, and then opened the journal to the first blank page,
about three-quarters of the way into the book. With beautiful pen-
manship, she wrote, "The Knight's Adventure at Sea."

She was writing for Quinn. It was to be his Christmas present.
The book was a collection of short stories in which he was the knight,
and she was his fair lady whom he rescued. He fought dragons, wizards,
witches, and barbarians for her. Davi wanted to show Quinn how
much she saw him as her hero.

Quinn longed to be Davi's hero. She knew how much it bothered
him that he was powerless to intervene when Guy Tremblant tried
to kidnap her on their wedding day. Jake Goodman, Quinn's head of
security, came to her rescue. He convinced Guy that he was on his

side, and then with one quick left hook, Guy was on the floor, and Davi was back in Quinn's arms. Davi didn't want a hero. She wanted her husband alive and well. She didn't care about how it looked to others. Quinn did the right thing by letting Jake rescue her.

Suddenly, without warning, a few days later, at a red carpet event in New York City, Guy Tremblant attacked Quinn. Quinn spent over a week in the hospital recovering from a fractured skull. Davi was terrified of losing Quinn. Her only comfort was in knowing that Guy Tremblant was locked away in a psychiatric ward somewhere far away. She hoped he'd never see the light of day.

Davi spent her hour writing. The story flowed through her quickly. She had plenty of time to gather her thoughts to write them. Spending most of the day sunbathing gave her that opportunity. When Quinn wanted to make love, "honeymoon sex," he called it, she made mental notes for the love scenes she would write later for her handsome knight. She wondered if Quinn would realize her motive behind the unwritten rule for their honeymoon lovemaking—a different place or position every time. She needed the material for her stories.

XO XO XO

Davi made her way to the gym situated across one end of the large swimming pool. The wall was all glass, giving everyone outside a look at who was working out, and everyone inside could watch the sunbathers by the pool. Davi knew more people enjoyed looking into the gym than looking out from it today. Every time Quinn went to the gym, his workout became one of the resort's major attractions. Women would line up their chaise lounges to face the gym to watch Quinn as he pumped iron. The bravest tried to pretend to work out in the gym while their eyes were on Quinn. Quinn didn't mind. Once he turned on his music and started his workout, he tuned out everyone around him. He was in his own world.

Davi could overhear the women's comments about Quinn as she passed by them on her way to the gym entrance. Most of them spoke freely about their fantasies of him. Davi was past being embarrassed about what she heard—it was all part of the package that came with being married to him. As she walked into the gym, she noticed Quinn speaking with a few men, giving them advice on using the weights. A few women watched Quinn's workout as well. They stood back, a safe distance from the weights, as they watched the men.

Quinn's eyes lit up when he saw her. He finished his conversation with the men and then put his weights on the shelf.

"Hey, Davi, is it that time already? How many crosswords did you finish without me?" He winked at her.

"One," she answered. "I could have stayed to do another, but I knew you'd be worried about me. Two hours seem to be the most you can handle without your ball and chain."

Quinn hugged her tight against his sweaty body. "I would die without my ball and chain. We both know how true that is, Davi. Don't ever let me go," he whispered in her ear.

Davi felt the energy flow between them. She pushed away gently and smiled at him. "We have an audience. Are you going to talk to your fans now or later?"

Quinn looked over at the group of women. "I can do it now. I'm finished here."

Quinn towelled off as best he could, and then Davi handed him a clean T-shirt from her beach bag. Davi could hear the women sigh as they watched.

"How do I look?"

"Like the heartthrob who just finished a workout—sexy and gorgeous. Be careful, husband, don't break too many hearts."

Davi stood back while Quinn turned and smiled at the group. His Hollywood charm turned on immediately.

"Hello, ladies, enjoying your workout?" Quinn asked as he approached them.

Davi could hear them giggle with delight as they had their pictures taken with him. Davi leaned against a machine as she waited for Quinn to talk to every one of them. She didn't mind sharing him with his fans. She knew that he was hers and only hers. When Quinn finished with them, he turned his attention back to her.

He held out his hand to Davi. "Let's go."

Davi took his hand and walked out of the gym with him. She could feel everyone's eyes on them. She wondered if she would ever get used to this constant attention.

Quinn led Davi down to the beach. He pulled off his sneakers and dropped them into Davi's beach bag. He then took the bag in one hand and wrapped his free arm around her waist. They walked in silence for a few minutes before he spoke.

"I called Luke."

"Did you apologize to him for telling him to fuck off?" Davi asked with a chuckle.

Quinn smirked, ignoring her question. "He sent me my schedule for the next two weeks. We're fully booked."

Davi stopped instantly. "What do you mean by 'we'?"

"Our tour, the press junkets, premieres, talk shows, the whole gamut."

"That's your job, not mine. After New York, I swore that I'd never be a part of that again."

"Please," Quinn begged, gazing into her eyes. "Two weeks. That's it."

Davi couldn't resist his eyes, and he knew it. "You promised."

"Everyone wants to see you."

"I want to see my kids," she replied.

"You will. We'll fly home after Chicago and spend the weekend with them, then start the tour."

"Chicago." Davi mulled over the word. Olivia was in Chicago. "You're doing her show?"

They hadn't broken their connection. Quinn smiled as he cupped her face in his hand. Davi leaned into its soft warmth.

"We leave tomorrow morning."

"What about one more moonlit walk on the beach and making love in the sand?"

"We have plenty of time, love, to do everything I promised you."

"You made a lot of promises, Quinn."

"Don't worry. I intend to keep all of them."

two

"Ready?" Quinn asked as he opened the door to their waiting taxi.

Davi slid into the backseat, followed by Quinn. She closed her eyes. Davi never rode well in the backseat of a car unless it was a limo. She chuckled at the realization.

"What's so funny?"

"I miss your limo. I don't feel sick when I'm in it."

"Be sure to tell Jake. He would like to hear that."

Check-in was fast at the airport. Quinn and Davi passed through customs then headed to the departure lounge.

"Quinn, we have to stop and get some snacks and magazines. I won't last five hours on the plane without some junk food."

"They feed you on the plane, you know," Quinn teased. "You didn't have junk food with you when I first met you."

"I did have it with me. It's just that I had other things to do to keep my mind off flying. But now that we're married, that novelty has worn off, and I need my junk food."

Without warning, Quinn stopped and pulled her close to face him. "Did you just call me a novelty?" His eyes gazed deeply into hers.

Davi knees weakened. She had no resistance to his baby blues. "No, you were not the novelty. It was sitting beside you and fantasizing about having mind-blowing sex with you that was the novelty. Chewing on a piece of licorice didn't seem appropriate at that time. Now it does."

"Why is that?" His gaze still held hers, and a smile tugged at the corners of his mouth.

She smiled. "You're not a fantasy for me anymore. I get mind-blowing sex all the time."

"I'm glad you think so," Quinn said before he kissed her softly on the mouth.

Davi headed towards the gift shop with Quinn trailing behind her. She saw the magazine covers first. Luke was right. Photographs of Quinn and Davi featured on every one of them. Davi reached for the first one. Guy Tremblant's attack on Quinn was the headline. Yesterday's news. Davi didn't want to relive that memory.

The next magazine made Davi stop in her tracks. The front cover had pictures of their honeymoon. She grabbed the magazine and opened it quickly, finding the article in the centre of the magazine. They were all close-ups of them—sunbathing on the beach, working out at the gym, having an intimate candlelit dinner for two, and more.

Davi closed the magazine and then turned to face Quinn. "You knew about the photographers, didn't you?" she demanded, keeping her voice low.

"Yes. Is there a bad shot of you?" he teased, trying to make light of the situation.

"They have a picture of us having sex, Quinn," she said through gritted teeth. "You knew, and you still had sex with me in public?"

Quinn took the magazine from her and found the offensive picture. He smiled when he recognized when it had taken place.

"If I remember correctly, and I always do, we were seventy feet from shore, and the water was just below your shoulder. No one could see a thing."

"The point is you knew," Davi said, fighting back the tears of embarrassment.

"I made sure you were never in a compromising position, love. I'd never let that happen." Quinn looked over her shoulder and saw a magazine that was sure to make her smile. He reached for it. "Here, read this. I'm sure we're not having sex in this one."

Davi looked at the cover. *Vanity Fair* had published their wedding pictures. The magazine's head photographer took their wedding photos, including ones of Davi with her beloved cows.

"You're not off the hook," she said as she reached for a copy of every celebrity magazine on the shelf. "Not until I see every last picture of us in these damned magazines."

Davi made her purchase, including licorice, gum, chocolates, and a bottle of water. Quinn stood back and watched her in amazement. He didn't add anything to her pile.

"Do you always buy that much junk?" he asked with disbelief.

"Humour me. Maybe I'll share."

Their flight to Miami was uneventful. Quinn plugged into his cell phone and listened to music while reading a script Luke insisted he take with him on his honeymoon. Davi spent the first hour reading her magazines. She stewed in silence as she read the fabricated reports about her—how she had used some spell to cause Quinn to fall in love with her and then used that magic to keep Quinn alive while recovering from Guy Tremblant's brutal assault. It wasn't magic. It was love, plain and simple. Did she have to scream at the top of her lungs that Quinn pursued her and that she was not a cougar? How many times had she told him that she was too old for him? Fifteen years was a big difference in age, but not to Quinn. Now Davi didn't see anything wrong with the age difference either. *Get over it, people.* She jammed the last of the celebrity magazines into her bag.

She saved the *Vanity Fair* issue for last. Realizing that she hadn't seen this photograph, she stared at the cover for the longest time.

Davi and Quinn gazed into each other's eyes as though they were the only two people in the world. *That's how it felt.* Inside the magazine were pictures of Quinn, Quinn and Davi, and Davi by herself. Davi sighed at every photo. It was a beautiful photo spread.

She hesitated before reading the article, knowing she'd be devastated if it matched the other magazines' falsehoods. The interview with the photographer came first. He explained the reason for the black and white photos and the use of the cows as background. He loved Quinn's idea and gave him full credit for suggesting it to him. He said Davi and Quinn glowed when they were together in front of the camera and that he would like to photograph them again.

The primary interview was with Quinn. Davi didn't know when he gave it, but then he didn't tell her everything. He liked to surprise her.

He talked about how the two of them met and how it was love at first sight. "I looked down and saw this incredible pair of legs, and then I followed them up to find this beautiful woman sitting beside me. She was busy reading, ignoring me, but I didn't mind. It gave me time to take in every inch of her and fall in love. Every day I find something new to love about her. There is no better way to begin my day and to end it than to have this amazing woman next to me."

When asked to compare his style of romance on the silver screen to his love life with Davi, Quinn replied, "You'll have to ask her. I don't kiss and tell, but I know she does." Davi's mouth dropped open as she read the words. Davi turned to look at Quinn, then swatted him with the magazine.

"What?" he asked in surprise as he pulled out his earphones. "Did you find more pictures of us having sex?"

"No." She then read the two lines aloud to him.

"I didn't think they'd use that. But it's good." He gave her a wide grin. "You can't be mad at that. It's true. You talk about me all the time."

"I told your female friends about you once, but to tell the whole world that I talk about you like that, well, it's . . ."

"It's normal. Women do that. You even told me so."

"You make it sound like I brag about you."

"But you did, and I don't mind one bit." Quinn winked at her.

Davi gasped as Quinn's full meaning hit her. "You used me! You bragged about the fact that I bragged about you. You were a peacock in that sentence. Your tail was full out for everyone to see!"

"But who is going to see it, love? I fanned my tail for you only. I doubt many will get the double meaning. You're the writer. I said it for you." Quinn leaned over and kissed Davi's forehead. "You know I don't care what other women think about me. You're the only one that matters."

"Olivia's going to hit you with this one, lover. Be prepared. Of all the magazines I read, this is the one that she's going to use, and it's not just because of the pretty pictures."

Davi put the magazine away and fished her cell phone from her bag. She put her earphones on, started her music, and then reclined her seat. She would tune him out and let him think about what he'd done. Davi was asleep in five minutes.

Davi felt a tickle on her cheek. She kept her eyes closed as she raised her hand to touch the source of the tickle. Her hand cupped Quinn's face and then pulled him towards her and gave him a soft kiss.

"Are you still mad at me?"

Davi opened her eyes as she removed her earphones. "No. I wasn't mad at you, only slightly miffed. What's happening?"

"We're landing in fifteen minutes, sleeping beauty. It's time to wake up."

Davi looked at her watch. She'd been out for four hours. "I needed that," she said as she glanced at the script on Quinn's lap. "So how is the script? Is it any good?"

"I'll have to give it some serious thought. I can't say yes to it right away."

"Why?"

Quinn's eyes sparkled with mischief. "You may not want me to do it."

Davi knew that look. It meant he wanted to play. "Are you the romantic lead?"

"Yes."

"Is there sex in it?"

Quinn's eyebrows arched as he feigned surprise. Davi always asked about sex. He answered lustily, "Yes."

"How many partners do you have?"

"Only one that matters."

"Lots of nudity?"

"Most likely."

"Mostly hers, I hope."

"I thought you liked my ass," Quinn teased.

"That's all I'm willing to share. Your package is mine, Quinn Thomas. No one gets to see that on the silver screen."

"What if it makes the movie?"

"If seeing your penis on the silver screen makes the movie, then I suggest that you give it a pass. You don't need that kind of publicity."

"It's supposed to be a blockbuster movie. The book has sold millions of copies. Women are going crazy knowing it's becoming a film."

Davi looked down at Quinn's lap and read the title page of the script. "No! You've got to be kidding."

"What? You don't think I can do it?"

"It's not that," Davi said, moving closer to whisper in his ear. "You're much better than that book hero. What he does in the bedroom…"

"Yes?"

"It would be misleading your fans. You're much better than that."

XO XO XO

The airplane landed and taxied to the arrivals gate in good time. Quinn took both of their bags and led Davi through customs and to their next departure gate. They had over an hour before boarding their connecting flight.

"Let's get something to eat."

Quinn was familiar with Miami's airport. He led Davi to a sports bar. It wasn't too busy for them to find a table. Quinn ordered for them both—two cheeseburgers, salads, chocolate milk, and ginger ale.

Davi chuckled. "You ordered for me. In hunter mode again, I see." She called him Quinn the Hunter since he was always hunting for her, making sure she was eating now that it was for two.

"You haven't eaten a nutritional meal all day. Licorice and chocolate don't cut it for healthy eating. You need protein, veggies, and milk. I'm not going to have you collapse when we land in Chicago. And besides, they serve delicious burgers here."

"Where don't they serve delicious burgers?" she asked with amusement. Quinn had a penchant for burgers. "Thank you for looking after me."

"You're welcome."

"Did you get any sleep at all? You look tired."

"I will sleep on our flight to Chicago. I wanted to make sure you got settled first, and I had to get that script read." Quinn glanced at the television screen behind the bar. "We're heading into a snowstorm."

"Wonderful," Davi replied with a groan. 'Does that mean there'll be turbulence?

Quinn answered with a shrug. "Let's go."

XO XO XO

Quinn fell asleep shortly after takeoff. Davi was thankful for the executive business class seats. Quinn could stretch out his six foot three length, and Davi liked the privacy and the quiet.

Davi startled. The plane shook while the fasten seat belt sign flashed.

The pilot made an announcement. "Ladies and gentlemen, we're encountering some turbulence as we approach Chicago. It's being hit by a major snowstorm right now. We may have to delay our arrival time, but I'll keep you posted. In the meantime, please stay in your seats and fasten your seat belts. Thank you."

Quinn slept soundly while the plane continued to shake.

We could die in a crash, and he'd never know it. Davi took his hand in hers. *That would be the way to go.* She closed her eyes and rested her head against the headrest.

Thirty minutes later, the pilot made an announcement. "Ladies and gentlemen, this turbulence will be with us the rest of the flight. There is only one available landing strip, so we will be circling Chicago until we can land. Please remain seated with your seatbelts fastened."

Davi felt a warm hand on the side of her cheek. She turned her head to look at Quinn.

"You've been missing out on all the fun."

"You should have woken me."

"So you could do what? Watch me be sick to my stomach?" Davi shook her head. "No, thank you. I didn't need an audience for that."

"What can I do to help?"

"Can you hold me and make it go away?"

"I can try. Come here." Quinn opened his arms to her.

Davi cuddled into his chest and closed her eyes. "Talk to me and take my mind off my stomach."

"What would you like me to talk to you about?"

"Tell me about the script you read and don't leave out any details. I want to know everything."

"Everything?"

"You know—how many scenes they expect you to show off your perfect ass and more. There's only so much of you I'm willing to share."

three

Quinn's cell phone rang. It was nine o'clock in the morning, and Davi was sound asleep in his arms. Quinn reached for his phone.

"Hello," he said quietly. "Hey, Luke, what's up?"

"Quinn, how was your flight?"

"Long. Davi's still sleeping."

"We need to meet. How about breakfast?"

"Let's do room service. I want to let Davi sleep as long as she can. Order breakfast for the three of us and have it sent here. I'll see you in twenty minutes. We're in the Compton Suite."

"See you then."

Quinn moved Davi carefully to her pillow then covered her up with the duvet. He headed for the bathroom and had a long hot shower. His muscles ached from the long hours flying. He could do with a workout now, but it wasn't possible. He'd stretch once he finished his shower. That would have to do.

His thoughts went to Davi as they always did. He thought about their lovemaking. He didn't need a photographic memory to remember everything about her. The way she tasted when they kissed and the way her scent filled his head. There was no doubt that he was head over heels in love with his wife.

Quinn thought about the *Olivia* show later that day. He thought of another actor's infamous crazy man performance when he talked about his newfound love on another talk show. Quinn would never do that. However, he knew he couldn't help but gush about Davi if asked about her. No matter how much he wanted to keep his life with her private, he knew that he couldn't if Olivia asked him. That damned stupid statement about Davi and kissing and telling. She was right. It was going to jump out and bite him on the ass.

Quinn turned off the shower and towelled off. He'd shave before he left for the studio. Quinn stretched for five minutes. He felt loose by the time he finished. When he walked into the bedroom, there was enough natural light coming through the drapes that he could make his way around the room without turning on a light and waking Davi. Quinn rummaged through his bag. He pulled out a pair of workout shorts then walked out to the living room, closing the door behind him. Last night, he'd sent some of their clothes out to be cleaned and pressed so that he and Davi would have something to wear to *Olivia*.

Looking out the hotel window, Quinn saw the chaos that had hit snow-covered Chicago. Traffic jams were at every intersection as cars moved slowly through the streets still covered in heavy snow. It bothered him, giving him a feeling of foreboding.

For some strange reason, Quinn ached to be back in Aruba. It wasn't the sun and sand or the honeymoon sex, but the feeling of being safe. Knowing that Guy Tremblant was locked up somewhere was somewhat comforting, but there was always the chance that there would be some other whacko wanting to harm Davi or him.

He'd been aware of the need for protection since he arrived in Hollywood. The studio provided security and the occasional leak to the paparazzi to get his picture in the news. He didn't mind it until there were one too many fans, men and women, getting through security and making it to his trailer or his hotel suite. That's when he brought in Jake to take charge of his safety. No one got by Jake or his men, except for Tremblant. Quinn felt the muscles in his neck and shoulders tighten. *Damn.* He didn't need this. He'd call Jake and have him increase the security, mainly where Davi was concerned.

He turned his head to the door when he heard a light rap against it. It was Luke.

Luke held out his hand to Quinn. "Hey, man, welcome back. You look great. You got a lot of sun. I thought you said you were busy all the time."

"Asshole," Quinn said, shaking the offered hand. "Get in here."

Luke chuckled as he followed Quinn into the suite. He tossed his overcoat onto an empty chair.

Quinn and Luke sat down in the living room.

"I don't need much time in the sun to get a tan, Luke. You're just jealous. Admit it."

"You're right. I am jealous. You have it all now—everything you ever wanted. I'm happy for you. How is Davi?"

"She's still sleeping. Flying all day knocked her out." Quinn's eyes lit up as he started to talk about her. "Davi's amazing. She thinks of things I'd never consider."

"Like what?"

"She bought every entertainment magazine she could find to read them on our flight here. She read them all in an hour, and when she finished, she told me what Olivia was going to ask me. Something stupid I said in my interview with *Vanity Fair,* and Davi thinks, no, she knows, it's going to be used to bite me on the ass today. Davi's been after me to be ready for it, but I've blown her off. But this morning, it hit me that she's right. I'm going to get destroyed."

"I read the article. It was great. What does Davi think you said that's going to bite you on the ass?"

"'When asked to compare my on-screen romance to that of my real one with Davi, what would I say? I said, 'I can't tell, but ask Davi. She'll kiss and tell.'"

"I liked it. I thought it was funny."

"What do you think I meant by it?"

"Nothing. It was a joke."

"But it wasn't a joke, and Davi knows it. It was something for her, and she got it, but she knows Olivia will get it and will want to know more about it. I'm screwed."

"You're making too much of this. It's not there. If I don't see it, I don't think anyone else will either. Relax."

There was a knock at the door, then a voice announcing room service. Quinn went to answer it. Room service had arrived with their breakfast and Quinn's laundry. He signed for the delivery then looked at the delivered spread with amazement.

"I didn't know what you wanted, so I ordered a bit of everything. Besides, I'm sure you've worked up quite the appetite after your honeymoon."

Quinn shook his head while he filled his plate with eggs, toast, and fruit slices. "I don't need a honeymoon with Davi to work up an appetite."

They ate in silence for a few moments.

"So, what are you wearing for the show?"

"I had our jeans and shirts laundered. I didn't take a suit with me to Aruba."

"That's okay. You'll look great. What's Davi wearing?"

"The same."

Luke's face froze as he heard Quinn's answer. "She's invited to be on the show with you. Both of you are guests."

"You didn't tell me that. You just said Olivia wants you to do the show. I thought the 'you' was me."

"It's both of you."

Quinn picked at his breakfast as he thought of telling Davi she would be on the *Olivia* show.

"Is there a problem?"

XO XO XO

Davi felt Quinn's warm kiss on her lips. "Is it breakfast in bed again?" She held out her arms for him.

"We don't have time today, love. You need to get up." Quinn's voice was quiet but urgent.

Davi opened her eyes immediately. "What's going on?"

Quinn searched her face for mercy. "I misunderstood Luke. Olivia wants both of us on her show. We've got to be there for noon."

"What time is it now?"

"Nine thirty—nine forty-five, somewhere in there."

"Oh. Okay. Did our clothes come back from the cleaners?"

"Yes."

"Did you order breakfast?"

"Yes. Luke's out in the living room eating. Come join us."

"Give me a minute."

Quinn stared at Davi, surprised at her reaction. She never reacted the way he expected her to.

Luke watched from the edge of his seat as Quinn exited the bedroom and shut the door behind him.

"She'll be out in a minute."

Quinn poured himself a cup of coffee then sat in an armchair, staring at the bedroom door.

"You don't know what she's going to do, do you?"

"Not a clue. I haven't been right yet." He took a sip of his coffee.

He had never known a woman like her. She was always calm and levelheaded. Perhaps that was the problem. Davi could talk her way out of anything. When Guy Tremblant made his move on her and tried to take her away from Quinn, she was relaxed and calm.

"Give me your best pickup line, Guy," she had told him. "If it's better than Quinn's, I'm yours."

Quinn couldn't believe her nerve—nothing fazed her. Guy walked away before Quinn could intervene. Davi had it all under control.

Then on their wedding day, when Guy tried to leave the reception with Davi—she still refused to call it an attempted abduction—she talked her way out of it with the help of Jake. Afterwards, she told Quinn, "Dance with me, husband. I won't let him ruin our party." Damn, she had her shit together. Would she lose it eventually? He hoped he'd never find out.

Davi opened the door wearing one of the hotel's plush guest robes. She looked adorable in the over-sized robe—the long sleeves rolled up to her wrists, and the collar turned up against her neck. She padded in barefoot with her red nails—a promise to Quinn to have them painted red always. Her long legs were visible from the robe's opening.

Quinn longed to take her in his arms and let the robe fall to the floor. He silently cursed Luke for being with them.

"Hey, Luke, it's great to see you." Davi kissed Luke as he hugged her.

"Davi, you look great."

"So I hear I'm a guest, too." Davi walked to the breakfast cart and began to fill her plate.

"Yep, I guess there was a miscommunication on my part. Quinn didn't know that I meant the two of you are the guests." Luke looked nervously at Davi.

"That's okay. Mistakes can happen. Quinn was busy. He may not have been giving you his full attention." Davi winked at Quinn.

"Quinn thinks you need to go shopping to find something to wear for the show."

"No, I don't, and Quinn would have told me that if he thought so. Quinn can speak for himself, Luke. He's not afraid of me yet." Davi smiled at her husband as she sat down in the armchair next to his. "What a delicious breakfast, husband. Thanks."

"Luke ordered breakfast."

"Thanks, Luke."

Luke looked pleadingly at Quinn.

"She's right, Luke. We flew back early from our honeymoon to make it for the show. We didn't take anything with us except for shorts and swimsuits. Davi and I will be fine with jeans and a clean shirt. It's okay."

"I have two 'It's better in Aruba' T-shirts if you'd like us to wear them," Davi offered sweetly.

"You two are killing me."

"This is who we are, Luke." She motioned to Quinn and herself. "This is what Quinn's fans and Olivia want to see—the real us." Davi smiled. "Today is going to be a great day. I can feel it."

They ate in silence for a few minutes, and then Davi put her plate down on the coffee table and pulled her legs up under her. Quinn handed her a cup of decaf coffee.

"Luke, Quinn said you had business to discuss. Have you done that already?"

"Oh, it's not much. We have *Lovestruck*, and I have to coordinate Quinn's schedule with *Second Harvest*. The studio is already starting to line up talk show interviews and press junkets. Then there are the premieres. I need to get Quinn on the same page as the studio."

"Do anything you have to do, Luke, but my weekends are mine. I'm going to be at home."

"Quinn, be fair. You know you can't do that. Every major city in every country wants to see you. You can't just do it for five days then fly home. It's not possible."

"It is possible. I'll work my ass off. Fly me anywhere. I'll put in twenty-hour days. Just get me home for the weekend. I promised Davi my weekends."

"Damn it, Quinn. You're not reasonable. You know it doesn't work that way. Just flying you to and from Europe takes two days, giving us three days for promotions. Then there's Australia and Japan. You can't do it without giving them your weekends."

Davi watched as the two men argued. She smiled and shook her head as they butted heads over something that shouldn't have been too difficult to solve.

"Luke," Davi said when she was able to get a word in between them. "I promised Quinn two weeks. See what you can arrange during that time. I'll tag along. I don't have to do interviews or attend premieres. I'll just stay in the background and be Quinn's bed buddy." She winked at Quinn. Only he saw it.

"Bed buddy! You aren't saying what I think you are, are you, Davi?"

"You know what she's saying, Luke. Arrange for Davi to come with me. That's the only way I'll agree to go on tour for two weeks straight."

"You're coming along just to sleep with Quinn?" Luke stammered.

"Oh, get over it, Luke." Davi laughed. "We're just having fun with you. I'm not coming just for the sex. You and I both know that Quinn won't settle and be at his best unless I'm with him. Maybe after this movie, he might be able to do it alone. He better because I don't think I'll be in any shape to fly in a few months."

"I can't go anywhere without my ball and chain. We're a team now, Luke. Get used to it."

"I know you're a team. I didn't know it meant joined at the hip."

Davi got up and put her plate and coffee cup on the food cart.

"We're joined at the hip and other places," Quinn said as he reached for Davi and pulled her onto his lap. Davi laughed with delight.

"Enough!" Luke said as he stood up. "I can't handle you two. The limo will be here at eleven-thirty. I'll see you in the lobby." Luke grabbed his overcoat then left the suite before Quinn or Davi could respond.

"I think you embarrassed him," Davi said as she kissed Quinn's chest.

"Good. Luke's wound a bit too tight sometimes. He needs to unwind."

"Speaking of unwinding," Davi teased as she untied her robe and straddled Quinn's lap. Her hands cupped his face as she leaned in to kiss him softly on the mouth. His breath had the bitterness of coffee. Davi's tongue pushed past Quinn's lips to explore his mouth. She moaned, enjoying his taste.

Quinn's fingertips dug into her buttocks and pulled her in closer to him. Davi rubbed against him, his gym shorts a thin barrier between them.

She sighed as she released Quinn from their kiss.

"You don't have to stop. We can make love here."

"I know, but then it wouldn't be breakfast in bed, husband. You know how much I love breakfast in bed."

"Well, I don't want you to go hungry, do I?" Quinn chuckled as he got to his feet, carrying Davi in his arms to the bedroom. He placed her on the rumpled bed. "Do you have anything in mind?"

Davi shook her head. "How about chef's surprise?"

Quinn stripped off his shorts and lay beside his wife. He touched her between her legs—she was ready for him. There was no denying this woman. Quinn moved on top of her, entering Davi slowly.

"Harder, stud," she begged him while reaching for his ears. She took hold of his lobes and tugged. "Harder."

Quinn groaned, hearing her demand. He slammed into her, sure she'd scream, but she smiled and kept her eyes closed. Davi's tongue ran over her lips, teasing Quinn for another kiss. He pressed his mouth against hers and kissed her hard.

Davi opened her eyes. "Is that all you've got, stud?"

"What more do you want?" he asked, breathless.

"Just love me."

"I love you. You know I love you, Davi."

"That's all I'll ever want."

Quinn moaned as he quickened his thrusts. Davi drove him wild. She could push every button then find one he didn't know he had. His climax came quickly and without warning. Quinn slumped onto Davi, thoroughly exhausted.

"I can't move," he said, his breath warm against her ear.

"Well, I have to move if I'm to be ready for Olivia. You can stay here and rest. It won't take you long to look your gorgeous self."

"And it won't take you long either. You know that."

Davi looked at the clock. They had plenty of time to get ready. They didn't need to rush, and Quinn could rest. Ten minutes was all that he needed to be Hollywood gorgeous.

Davi put the shower on cold and selected a floral-scented body wash. While she washed, her thoughts focused on their upcoming interview with Olivia. Luke had surprised her with the news that it would be both of them, but it was nothing Davi couldn't handle, and she had to admit she looked forward to meeting Olivia. She stepped out of the shower as Quinn entered the bathroom.

"You've worn me out. I think you'll have to fill in for me today." He winked at her as she towelled herself dry.

"I don't think Olivia would mind, but it's all the ladies in the audience who might object. You'll have to suck it up. What do you call it? Acting?"

Quinn grabbed Davi and hugged her. "You are naughty." Quinn inhaled her scent. "You smell delicious."

"No more. Sex is on hold until the end of the day." Davi pushed away from Quinn.

"Then don't tempt me."

"I promise not to tempt you anymore today. How is that?"

"No, it's not working. You're still tempting me." Quinn reached for Davi again.

"What will it take for you to let me go so that I can get dressed?"

"What are you offering?"

Davi thought for a few seconds. "After the show, I'll take you shopping for cowboy boots if there is somewhere in this snow-covered city that sells them."

Quinn's eyes lit up. "It's a deal."

"So you can be bought." Davi chuckled.

"But, you're the only one I'd sell to."

"You should have boots," Davi said as she applied body lotion to her legs. "Didn't you get a pair when you made *Coyote* or *The Engagement*?"

"I did have boots," Quinn said sheepishly. "They disappeared." Quinn started to shave.

Davi looked up at him. "How did they disappear?"

Quinn smiled in embarrassment but realized that Davi would appreciate the story. At least, he hoped she would. "You know the song about a guy, his boots and a bed?"

"Yes," she answered, already imagining the scenario.

"Well, my boots were under my bed when I had company, and they were gone when I woke up in the morning."

"Your company and your boots?" Davi laughed.

"Yes, ma'am." He finished shaving then wiped off his face.

"I guess your dates wanted a keepsake of spending the night with you. I'd never think about taking your boots."

"No. You only took my T-shirts."

"I borrowed them. Besides, I stayed for breakfast. Your dates didn't. Their loss." She smiled. "Is that why you didn't want to date me? You thought I'd steal your boots?"

Quinn turned to look at Davi and returned the smile. "No, that's not the reason. I've never considered you a date, Davi. We were meant to be together from the moment we met. You're the one who insisted on dating."

"Three dates. That's all you'd give me."

"That's all we had time for."

"But I did get something to remember you by." Davi put her hand on her abdomen. "And it's much better than any pair of cowboy boots."

four

"**Okay, so this is what we've got,**" Luke said, reading from his cell phone's screen as they walked into the studio's greenroom. "The clip from *Lovestruck* is your first-date scene. The studio is giving the audience free passes to the movie along with autographed photos. Try not to say too much about *Untitled*. You know what I mean. *Second Harvest* you can talk about even though you haven't done much with it yet. That's about it."

"Sounds like a plan," agreed Quinn.

Quinn walked over to the refreshment table prepared with drinks and snacks ready for them. He helped himself to a couple of bottles of water and offered one to Davi. Taking her free hand in his, Quinn led Davi to where his photo with Olivia was hanging on the wall. It was the first time he'd been on her show, and he had recently been named *People* magazine's heartthrob of the year. It was a wonderful picture of the two of them.

"This is why you aren't nervous about being here. You've done it before," commented Davi. "I should have known."

"Yes, but we're also friends. We do some charity work together. She won't feed us to the wolves if you are wondering, but she's smart. She'll get me with that *Vanity Fair* bit. You're right about that. Good thing my ass is hard."

Davi took a deep breath and closed her eyes.

"What is it?" Quinn asked with concern.

"It's finally hit me that I'm going to be on live television with Olivia and that millions of people are going to be watching the show. I don't know if I'm ready for this."

Quinn turned Davi around to face him. "Do you want to know what I do?"

"Act?" Davi joked weakly.

Quinn chuckled. "I tell myself I'm having coffee with Olivia. It's just the two of us, and I block out the audience."

"I know you can block out the audience. I've seen how you can tune out everyone around you."

"Everyone but you," Quinn corrected her. "Just don't think about the audience and don't even look at the cameras."

"Right . . . the cameras." Davi sighed heavily.

"You can't play to the cameras, Davi. Pretend they're invisible. That's what we actors have to do. I'm sure you can do it, too. You're great at pretending."

Davi's eyes opened wide. "What is that supposed to mean?"

Quinn's blue eyes sparkled with amusement. "You scared the hell out of me when you pretended to be in love with that asshole Tremblant. To hear you say that you were leaving me for him—I thought I'd die right then and there."

"I'm sorry."

"Don't be. Tremblant believed you, and that's all that matters. So don't worry about being on live television. You'll be fine."

"Kiss me, love, and take my mind off millions of people watching me."

Quinn took Davi into his arms and gave her her kiss. His hand pressed on her lower spine as he pulled her tight against his body. Davi's hands immediately went to his ears and held on to them as her thumbs caressed his earlobes.

Olivia stood in the doorway, watching the newlyweds kiss. She noticed how Quinn caressed Davi's back as he held her tight against his body. Olivia saw Davi's fingers playing with Quinn's ears and heard her soft moans. The television host tried to look away, but the kiss was so sensual, so arousing, that she couldn't take her eyes off them. When she heard Davi's soft moan of release, Olivia realized she had just witnessed Quinn Thomas make love to his wife with a single kiss.

Olivia stepped back from the door, counted to ten slowly, and then made her entrance again. She smiled as she headed for Quinn, offering him a hug and kiss.

She released him then looked at Quinn's head. "You are so lucky," she said softly. "We all prayed for you."

"Thank you." Quinn turned his attention to Davi and placed his hand on her waist as he introduced her to his friend. "Olivia, this is Davi, my wife. Davi, I'd like you to meet Olivia."

Without hesitating, Olivia hugged Davi. Davi could feel Olivia's strength and her warmth through her embrace.

"Davi, I have wanted to meet you since I first heard about you. I wanted to know who captured this man's heart. It is so nice to meet you finally."

"Thank you. I'm thrilled to be here. I thought I was going to be in the audience, but this is even better."

Olivia laughed. "You can always come to a show. Just let me know when you're coming to Chicago. We're on in ten minutes. I'll see you later." She then offered her hand to Luke, who managed to pull himself away from his cell phone. "Lucas." She smiled sweetly.

"Olivia, you're looking as beautiful as ever."

"Thank you. I have to run. I'll see you soon."

Olivia blew them all a kiss before she left the room.

Davi fell into the nearest sofa and sighed. "I met Olivia."

Quinn sat next to her. Together, they watched the large television screen. The crew worked on the audience, getting everyone excited for Olivia and her mystery guests. They'd be hysterical by the time Davi and Quinn appeared on the stage.

Quinn could feel Davi's tension build every time the audience screamed. He thought his kiss would help calm her, but it wasn't enough to keep her that way. Quinn stood up and then walked to the refreshment table and poured coffee into three mugs.

"Three minutes," sounded over the intercom.

Davi joined Quinn. "We don't have time for coffee."

"We're having coffee with Olivia, remember? Here," he said as he handed her a mug. "Careful. It's hot."

"Thank you. We don't have to do this."

"Yes, we do, and we are. It will be fun. You'll see—just you, me, and Olivia."

"Chatting over coffee."

"Exactly."

"So which one of us is the tagalong today?"

"I think you'll start as it, but once Olivia begins talking to you, I might as well go home. It will be you and Olivia."

"No. That would never happen. I'd never let you go home without me."

"Very funny." Quinn kissed her softly on the mouth then looked over towards Luke. "See you later, Luke."

"Have fun," Luke said, his attention once again focused on his cell phone screen.

An aide led the couple to the back of the stage. They could hear Olivia making her entrance and the cheers of the audience. When she told them who her guests were, their reaction was deafening. Davi watched a screen that showed what the audience was seeing. It was a short history of Quinn's movie career, and then it showed Davi and Quinn together. Quinn and Davi got the nod to walk on stage.

Much to Olivia's surprise, Quinn offered her a coffee mug. She took it happily and kissed him on the cheek. Then she greeted Davi with a kiss on the cheek.

"You brought me a coffee?" she asked Quinn when the audience's applause had quietened.

"I told Davi being on your show was like having coffee with a dear friend. It would be fun and relaxing."

Olivia offered Quinn the seat closest to her and Davi the seat next to him. Quinn took Davi's free hand and squeezed it gently. The women in the audience screamed for Quinn. He nodded to them and smiled, thanking them for their support.

"You get that a lot," Olivia observed.

"All the time. My fans are great."

"You weren't concerned you'd lose your fan base once you married?"

"I didn't even consider it. I just wanted to get married to Davi. I'm sorry, ladies, but you weren't on my mind."

"Has your fan base dropped?"

The women in the audience yelled, "No!"

"There's your answer," Quinn said happily.

"You two have great tans. You have recently returned from your honeymoon."

"Yes. We spent three weeks in Aruba."

"So let's run through how you two met. You were both on a flight to LA going to the same meeting but didn't know it. You sat beside each other, and during the flight, you fell in love with each other."

"I fell in love with her. She didn't fall in love with me. Davi made me work for her."

Davi laughed. "I'm not a romantic like he is. I needed to be convinced. I thought he was having fun with an older woman, you know, flirting with me to make my day. I didn't think he was serious."

"But he was serious."

"Oh, yes. Quinn called me that afternoon and reminded me that we still had a date for that night."

"So you went on that date . . ?"

"And we had a great time." Davi smiled. "Quinn cooked for me."

There was a collective sigh from the audience.

"So is Quinn as romantic as the characters he plays in his movies? My favourite is his character in *The Engagement*. He is so sexy and romantic in that movie. I got so hot watching him."

"Me, too," Davi agreed happily. "I made him watch it with me one night. It was torture for him."

Quinn got up and changed places with Davi. Olivia looked at him with surprise.

"I told her this show would be hers once you started talking with her. I'm the tagalong today. Go ahead. Keep talking."

"What's a tagalong?"

"A tagalong accompanies the star on the red carpet. He or she is the arm candy. I've been Davi's tagalong since the day I met her. Nothing's changed."

Davi turned to face him. "That's not true. You weren't the tagalong at our wedding."

"That was only with your sisters. That doesn't count."

There was more laughter from the audience.

"We'll have to take a commercial break now. We'll be right back with Quinn Thomas and Davina Stuart."

"Tagalong? That's a new one. Neither of you is a tagalong. You're both stars."

Quinn leaned towards Davi and whispered in her ear, "You're the star today, love. Have fun. You're doing great."

The audience cheered as the commercial break ended.

"Let's get back to the romantic side of Quinn."

A large television screen showed photographs of Quinn and Davi's wedding. Another collective sigh sounded from the audience.

"What would you like to know?" Davi asked.

"Kiss and tell, Davi. Kiss and tell."

Immediately, Quinn turned to Davi and gave her the biggest smile, his blue eyes sparkling. He kissed her hand and said aloud, "You were right."

Olivia looked at Quinn for an explanation.

"She is right all of the time, and I say that out of love and respect. I can't second-guess her. She knows everything. Davi read *Vanity Fair* on our flight here, and she found one sentence that stood out, and she said that you were going to get me. To be exact, she said, 'Olivia is going to bite you on the ass.'"

Olivia explained, "For those of you who don't know, Quinn said in the interview that he wouldn't compare his romantic skills on the silver screen with his real life skills. He answered that he doesn't kiss and tell, but his wife does."

The audience broke out into laughter.

"I said that for her. She was the only one supposed to get the meaning, but Davi said you would get it, too."

"Should I tell the audience what I think it means?"

"Go ahead."

"If I've interpreted this correctly, you're bragging about your wife bragging about you. You're—"

"A peacock," Davi said.

"Yes, a peacock. Although there's more to it than that, isn't there? Why did you say that?"

"On the surface, I'm saying, 'Hey, I'm so good my wife brags about me,' and that's the joke. I'm the one who is bragging about her. I want to show her off every chance I have. I want people to know that I'm wearing her ring, that she chose me. I'm the one who's kissing and telling. Davi's my muse, my lifesaver. Davi doesn't have to say anything about me to anyone. Her being with me is enough. Her love is all I want."

"Why do you love your wife so much? You were the one who pushed the relationship and the marriage. What is it about Davina Stuart that makes you want to be with her?"

Davi leaned back against the sofa so she could watch Quinn. She sipped her coffee slowly as she waited for him to answer.

"It was love at first sight. After we talked on the plane, I knew that I had to see her again. After our first date, I knew I had to make her mine. After she agreed to love me, I realized I was past that point. I had to marry her. Once she agreed, I knew I couldn't wait. I had to marry her before I did anything else with my life. I wanted it all with her— love, marriage, and a family."

"What about your age difference? Did you think about that at all?"

Davi and Quinn both smiled.

"I was waiting for her. As soon as I saw Davi, my heart said, 'Quinn, she's the one.' And why not her? She's a beautiful, smart, funny, and successful businesswoman. She's the one who has it all. The question should be, 'why me?' Why did she pick me?"

"Okay, Davi, why did you pick Quinn?"

"First of all, the age difference was a big concern of mine. For anyone who doesn't know, there's a fifteen-year age gap between us. I'd never considered dating a younger man before in my life. Then Quinn came along, and he said it didn't matter. His friends and family said it didn't matter, and my kids said it didn't matter. What mattered was our love. We got over that hurdle quickly.

"Second, I didn't pick Quinn. He picked me. I wasn't looking for romance. I was happy. I have a great life, a family, friends, and a thriving business. I wasn't looking for him. He found me. He wanted me, and he was impossible to resist."

"What is it about Quinn that's hard to resist? You haven't answered my question about what he's like."

Quinn set his coffee mug down on the end table then sat back on the sofa and gazed at Davi. His smile touched his eyes, making them sparkle. Davi tried to ignore him, but she could feel the heat from his touch.

Davi took a deep breath while she set her coffee mug on the end table. "Well, he's a gentleman. He's extremely polite. He's romantic."

"More, Davi, give us more."

"His blue bedroom eyes do sizzle. I can't resist them when he looks at me. I melt." Davi looked back at Quinn and smiled. "I love his shaggy hair. I miss it now, but he's still pretty gorgeous with this." Her hand touched his head. "Imagine what he does in his movies, then multiply it by ten. That's Quinn in real life. Quinn promised me I'd never get what he does on screen, and he's been true to his promise. I get more than that." Davi turned back to look at Olivia. "I love him. I don't know why he came into my life, but he did. And I am so thankful that he did."

"What about his kiss?" Olivia couldn't resist asking the question.

Davi smiled back at her without answering. The audience went wild.

Olivia leaned in towards Davi. "I saw the two of you kissing in the green room. It looked like just a normal kiss, but the way you reacted, it was as though—" Olivia searched for the appropriate words.

"It's orgasmic," Davi said without hesitation.

Davi had kissed and told on Quinn, and he was ecstatic. Quinn reached for Davi and pulled her into his arms. He kissed her. It was his movie kiss, and that was all he'd allow the audience to see since he had promised her that no one would know how he kissed her.

The audience applauded as the show cut to a commercial break.

"That wasn't it," Olivia said quietly to them, "and I understand why. I'd keep that a secret if I were you. Thanks for playing along."

The commercial break ended, and Olivia continued her interview.

"You have children from your first marriage."

"Yes, I have three children, all in their twenties. I was married for twenty-five years. My husband died from a brain aneurism two years ago. My kids are thrilled for us. They love Quinn. He's their new best friend."

"Not stepfather?"

"No. He's happy they accept him without question, and they are happy that I have someone."

"So when will you have time to be a family?"

Davi answered quickly, "We are a family. Separation won't change that."

Quinn squeezed her hand. "Davi's touring with me for the next two weeks. We're off to New York, then LA, and then Europe for *Lovestruck's* premiers. Afterwards, Davi is going to stay on the farm and look after her business and the rest of the family."

"Do you think you'll like living on the farm, Quinn? Are you going to be a farmer?"

"Living on a farm won't make me a farmer, Olivia. Living with the farmer is all I care about, although I'm sure I will learn about farming from her."

"Quinn, everyone's talking about *Untitled*, and it hasn't even been a month since you finished filming. They're saying there's a possible Oscar for you. What happened there? What made Guy Tremblant crack and attack you?"

"I don't know about an Oscar, Olivia,. It's too early to even think about that. I hope it does well when it's released. I'm sure people will enjoy it. As far as Guy Tremblant is concerned, I'm not a mind reader. I don't think the movie made him crack. He was obsessed with Davi. He wanted her the first time he met her, and he wouldn't give up."

"That would describe you too, wouldn't it?"

Davi didn't hesitate to answer for him. "The difference is that I loved Quinn back. When love is reciprocated, it's not an obsession. With Guy it was an obsession. He believed we had a relationship when there wasn't anything between us. It was all in his mind, his very sick mind."

"Do you remember anything about the attack, Quinn?"

"No."

"Davi, they say you didn't leave Quinn's side while he was in the hospital."

"Only when I had to, and it never worked out well for Quinn. He kept me by his side." Davi closed her eyes, forcing back the memory of the ordeal. Now was not the time to start crying.

Olivia took Davi's hand and squeezed it. "What happened? Will you tell us?"

"I'd rather not," Davi said softly.

Quinn still had hold of Davi's other hand.

"We're still a bit raw from the ordeal. I'm sure you understand."

"Of course. One last question though. Do you remember what it was like coming out of your coma?"

Quinn squeezed Davi's hand. "I haven't shared this with Davi. It was the strangest of dreams and yet I don't think it was a dream. It was more than that."

"Will you share it with us, Quinn?"

"I dreamt that I was walking in a park with Jack. Jack held my hand, and then he pulled on my hand and said, 'Daddy, wake up. Mommy needs you to wake up now.' Then that was it. I woke up, and Davi was asleep beside me in my hospital bed."

The audience went silent. Olivia's mouth dropped open, and again Davi closed her eyes, forcing the tears not to come.

"Who is Jack?"

"Jack's our baby. Davi's almost three months pregnant. I think of Jack as a gift. I'm thrilled to have the chance to be a dad. I thank Davi every day for giving me this gift."

"But, Davi, you have three children."

"I know. I'm excited about it, and we have the support of our family and friends. That means so much to us."

"You two don't waste any time, do you?"

"It looks that way, doesn't it?"

Olivia cut to another commercial.

"You two are full of surprises! Congratulations. So, when is the baby is due?"

"June," Quinn answered happily. "I'm going to be a dad in June."

The commercial break ended.

"So tell us about *Lovestruck*, Quinn. Its release is this week."

Quinn ran his hand over his head. His eyes sparkled with excitement. Davi saw that it was the Hollywood charm kicking in. She sat back and listened to Quinn talk about his movie. The man was selling the film, and everyone was buying.

"Here's a clip from that movie."

The three of them watched the clip on a screen off to the side. Davi smiled, watching Quinn trying to convince his costar to give him a chance at love. Quinn was right. What he did on the screen was not used on her. There was no Mr. Hollywood when he was with her.

"Davi, you smiled as you were watching that. Have you seen the movie?"

"No. I liked the clip. It was cute. Quinn's sexy, too, and that sure helps."

The women in the audience cheered in agreement.

"Did you think of this movie while you were trying to win Davi?" Olivia asked him once the audience settled.

"No. I knew that I had to be myself to win her heart. I couldn't use any Hollywood charm. She's immune to that."

"How did you know that?"

"I just did. Davi let me know right away on the plane that she wouldn't fall for any lines. She called me Mr. Thomas. She put me in my place right from the start."

"You called him Mr. Thomas?" Olivia asked, incredulous.

"It is his name," Davi answered sweetly, "and we had just met."

Olivia laughed and shook her head with disbelief. "Does anyone call you Mr. Thomas?"

"Yes, and I call her Mrs. Thomas."

Quinn brought Davi's hand to his lips and kissed it.

Olivia looked down at Davi's cowboy boots. "Your boots are green. Are they comfortable to wear?"

"Yes! I'd wear them with everything if I could. I've got four pairs, but these are my favourite."

"I have a belated wedding gift for the two of you," Olivia announced.

Two assistants came out with gift-wrapped boxes, one for Davi and one for Quinn. Quinn and Davi opened their boxes to find matching cowboy boots in black.

"We got your boot size from your manager, Quinn. Davi, one of your daughters helped us with this one. She told us the bootmaker and style you preferred."

Quinn pulled the boots out of the box and showed them to the audience. Then he took off his shoes and put on his boots. They were a perfect fit. He walked around on the stage to try them out.

"They're fantastic. Thank you, Olivia."

He leaned over and kissed her. The audience screamed.

Davi pulled off her boots and tried on her gift. The leather was elk; she could tell by its softness. They, too, fit perfectly.

"Thank you, Olivia. Your gift means so much to me. They're beautiful."

Music started to play in the background. Quinn recognized it instantly. It was the dance music from *The Engagement*.

"Mrs. Thomas, may I have this dance?" he asked as he took her hand.

"Of course, Mr. Thomas."

He took Davi in his arms and danced her around the stage.

Davi closed her eyes. The bright lights and Quinn's fast, fluid movements made her dizzy. She'd learned from their first dance that it was best to keep her eyes closed whenever they danced together.

"For our audience today, we have free passes to Quinn's movie, *Lovestruck*. And from Davi's publisher, everyone gets a free copy of *Second Harvest*. Quinn and Davi have volunteered to stay behind to sign autographs and have pictures taken with members of the audience."

The audience went wild again. Olivia had to talk above their noise as she thanked Quinn and Davi for being guests on her show.

XO XO XO

The ride to the airport was long, or at least it seemed that way to Davi. She wanted to be on an airplane headed for home. Although she had a wonderful honeymoon topped off with a great day on *Olivia*, she was ready to go home and sleep in her bed. How long had it been, two weeks or three? She had lost track of the days.

"We'll be married five weeks tomorrow," announced Quinn, as though he read her thoughts.

"I'd almost forgotten. Are we doing anything special?"

"Do you want to?"

"No. I just want to be at home with my family and have breakfast in bed." Davi's hand squeezed Quinn's thigh.

"That isn't asking for very much, Davi," Luke said. "You should expect more from Quinn."

"Have you ever been served breakfast in bed by Quinn?" Davi asked Luke innocently.

"No, I haven't. Is it any good?"

Quinn looked at Davi, watching her face for any clue as to what she would say next.

"Is it any good? Of course, Luke, it's delicious. He promised me breakfast in bed every weekend he's home. I'm planning on making him keep that promise."

"What does he make for you?"

"It's a secret recipe. If you haven't heard about it, I can't tell you. It's up to Quinn. Quinn? Do you think you'll ever share your recipe?" Davi winked at him.

"Never. I'm keeping that one close to the chest. Sorry, Luke."

"No problem. I don't like eating in bed anyway."

"Too bad," Davi murmured.

The limo pulled up to the departure area of the airport. Quinn helped Davi out of the limo while Luke got their bags out of the trunk. He was catching the next flight to LA. Quinn held Davi's hand as they walked to the check-in counter. The paparazzi had spotted them and kept close.

"Do you think they'll wait for us to check-in before they descend upon us?" Davi asked Quinn.

"We'll just have to wait and see. Word gets around, Davi. They'll let us through this time, so we'd better deliver."

Quinn and Davi smiled as they made their way to check-in. Once processed, Quinn led Davi to a suitable space. Fans and paparazzi followed them.

"Hey, guys, how are you? We haven't seen you in a long time." Quinn put on the Hollywood charm. Davi smiled with him.

"Congratulations on your pregnancy, Davi!" yelled out one of the fans.

"Thank you. News travels fast, doesn't it?"

"Do you know if it's a boy or girl?"

"No, it's too early to tell, and it doesn't matter."

"Quinn, what's the latest on *Second Harvest*?"

"Your guess is as good as mine."

Quinn and Davi gave fifteen minutes of their time to the crowd. They were both eager to sit down and have something to eat. It had been a long day.

"Okay, that's it, folks. Have a great day."

Quinn picked up his and Davi's bags and walked with Davi to the security gate. Luke had gone ahead of them. He had a table waiting for them at the restaurant.

"My office called. Every station has been calling to have you on their show. You two were a big hit."

"Olivia was nice. I enjoyed talking with her. I don't know if I could do another show. What would there be to discuss?"

Luke choked on his food. "Davi, everyone wants to know about you and Quinn. You two are hot right now. Your romance, your lifestyle, and your family. Anything you tell them, they'll eat up."

"Quinn's busy with the movie. There won't be time."

"Davi, love, there's always time. But if you don't want to do it, it's fine with me."

"Davi, they're asking for you. They'll take you, Quinn, or both of you. It doesn't matter."

"I'll leave it up to you and Quinn. I trust that you know what's best. Just don't have me flying all over the country. Make good use of my time, please."

"Your wish is my command, Davi. Thank you."

Davi devoured her meal. She didn't realize how hungry she was until she took the first bite of her grilled chicken. Quinn and Luke were busy discussing business and didn't notice her eating. It wasn't until she called the server over and asked for a dessert menu that Quinn saw that Davi's plate was empty.

His brow furrowed. "You're starved."

"I didn't realize it until I started to eat. It's been at least six hours since I ate last."

"I'm sorry. I won't let that happen again."

"It's not your fault. I'm an adult. I can look after myself."

"But it's my job now."

"Pardon me?" she asked, unamused. "It's your job?"

Quinn gave her his best bedroom eyes, trying to diffuse the situation. Davi held his gaze, not falling for the baby blues.

Quinn took her hand and gently squeezed it. "What I meant to say is that when we are travelling together, I need to pay special attention to you. I have to be mindful of you and Jack. Be the protector, hunter, whatever you need."

"You are what I need, and you are doing your job if that's what you call it. Now finish your meal, and I might share my dessert with you." Davi kissed Quinn's cheek.

"Davi, what did you do before Quinn came along?"

"I looked after everyone; I fed them, comforted them, and looked after their stuff. It's nice having Quinn look after me. It's nice getting pampered for a change."

Quinn leaned forward and kissed Davi. "I love you," he whispered.

"Me, too," she whispered back.

They heard the announcement for Luke's flight.

"That's me. I'll check in with you on Monday, Quinn, to see how things are going. At least you've got Monday's itinerary."

Quinn and Luke both stood up and shook hands good-bye.

Luke leaned down and kissed Davi. "I'll get back to you on some possible shows. You can say yes or no. No pressure, Davi."

"Bye, Luke." Davi smiled. "Have a safe flight."

"He'll look after you, Davi. Luke will make sure you get good press."

"Oh, I'm not worried about that. I don't know if I can do it all. We've been going nonstop since I met you. Our honeymoon was the only relaxing time I've had. I don't know if I can carry on the same pace while being pregnant. Jack takes priority here."

"I promise we'll take everything slow from here on."

Davi chuckled. "You can't promise me anything like that, Quinn Thomas. You haven't lied to me before, so don't start now. You don't know what slow is."

"Perhaps, but I'm willing to bet that you'll show me how to do slow."

"I may have forgotten how to do it, too. Maybe we can learn it together."

"I think we can do that."

Davi offered Quinn the remainder of her chocolate fudge cake. "Finish this if you want. I need to save some room for snacks on the plane."

"Do you have to?"

"Yes." Davi smiled. "I wonder what would have happened if I had been airsick when we first met?"

"I still would have asked you out, although we wouldn't have had our speed date. I would have looked after you, charmed you that way."

"Why would you have helped out an old woman who was being airsick?"

"First of all, I didn't see you as an old woman, and you aren't. Second, I knew who you were. Remember? You were and still are the woman of my dreams. I would have offered you my shoulder for comfort, and we would have talked then. That would have been our first date. So you see, it would have all worked out."

"You are always the gentleman."

"With you, I will always be the gentleman."

"Not always, though." Davi winked at Quinn. "You might need to practice."

"Practice?"

"You know. In case you accept that movie offer."

five

Guy Tremblant cursed at the tv as he shut it off with a well-aimed remote thrown through the screen. What a farce—Davina Stuart and Quinn Thomas pretending to be in love for the entire world to see. What kind of hold did that man have over her to make her pretend to everyone that she was happy? Could no one see the truth? Davina Stuart was miserable without Guy. She wanted him. She needed rescuing, and she needed it now.

He stumbled to his kitchen counter and poured himself a full glass of vodka.

Guy looked at his reflection in the microwave door's glass and raised his glass to toast it. "To our success," he slurred. "She'll be ours very soon."

Guy drained his glass quickly then smiled. Quinn Thomas had just announced that he and Davi would be coming back to New York. The fool was making it too easy for him.

It wouldn't take Guy long to finalize his plans. He already had his hideaway, a property he had purchased long ago under an alias, far away from the city, away from paparazzi and nosey neighbours. He had a car and fake identification. This time, he had a real gun. There would be no more playing with toys. If that security guard got in his way again, he'd pay with his life. Guy had shaved his head and started growing a beard. It wouldn't be long before no one recognized him—except for Davi. She would know him when she saw him. One look in his eyes and she would know her true love had returned.

six

The snowstorm that had almost crippled Chicago had died out before it crossed the border into Canada, bringing only a light dusting of snow to Toronto. Quinn and Davi were relieved to know they would be at the farm without delay.

"We're home," Quinn announced as the airport limousine stopped outside the farmhouse.

Davi opened her door without waiting for Quinn and inhaled the cool night air. Stepping out of the limo, Davi looked around her at the familiar surroundings. Instantly, she forgot about any foreboding she had once felt. Her home was where she should be. Davi was safe here.

"Home sweet home," Davi announced cheerfully.

Quinn paid the driver and gathered up their bags. The couple walked towards the house.

He sighed heavily as the fatigue from the long day caught up with him. "It feels good to be home finally."

Davi chuckled. "Don't say that yet. You don't know what you're walking into."

She opened the kitchen door, expecting to be pounced on by at least one of her daughters, but the house was quiet. Davi saw a note propped up against a fruit bowl on the kitchen table.

She picked it up and read it aloud, "Mom and Quinn—way to go on *Olivia!* You rocked it! We're at the Buck and Doe for Reid and Kelly. Join us at the town hall. We'll save you seats. Love, us."

Quinn put their bags down on the floor and closed the door behind him.

"What's a Buck and Doe?"

"It's a community shower for an engaged couple. There's dancing and lots of food and games to raise money for them." Davi put the note on the table and looked at Quinn. "We don't have to go. It's up to you."

XO XO XO

Davi held Quinn's hand as they entered the party room of the local town hall. A country and western band played a familiar tune on the stage. A group of young men gathered around the bar while a group of young women stood by, waiting to dance.

"Nothing ever changes, does it?" Quinn asked with amusement.

Davi nodded in agreement as she looked for her family. She was sure they'd be on the dance floor. None of her children ever passed up the opportunity to dance when the music was good.

"Mom! Quinn!"

Two sets of arms were immediately wrapped around Davi, pulling her in for a family hug. Davi kissed the cheeks of her daughters, Cat and Tigger.

"Hey, sweethearts, how are you?"

"Mom, did you have a wonderful honeymoon?"

The girls released Davi and turned their attention to Quinn before Davi could answer. She was used to their short attention span when Quinn was near.

"Girls," Quinn greeted them as they both hugged him.

"Big! How are you! Nice shirt." Big was the name the girls gave Quinn when he and Rich sang a Big and Rich duet at the wedding. It stuck.

"Thanks. I guess I have you to thank for this?" Quinn asked as he pointed to his new black western shirt with silver studs. The shirt and his Stetson had been left out on his and Davi's bed, making it clear that they attend the Buck and Doe.

"Since you got the boots, we figured we'd better buy you a shirt. You can't disappoint your fans," Cat teased as she pointed to the group of women hovering close by, watching them. "I bet they saw you on *Olivia* today. Way to go, Big."

"Great show, you two!" Tigger added.

Davi looked over at the group of women. She knew most of them from the PTA and her church. In the centre of the group was Lizzie Tanner. Davi could see her lips moving and the hatred burning in her eyes as she spoke. She knew the flames shot her way, but she didn't care. Lizzie Tanner was no threat to her, not anymore.

Quinn noticed the looks they were getting. "Let's dance. I think they're playing our song," he said as he took her hand and led her to the dance floor. "Anything I should know?" he asked as they moved away from the unfriendly stares.

"Later, if you don't mind. I'd rather not talk about it right now."

"Okay."

He wouldn't press her. He knew she'd tell him when she was ready. They had promised each other no more secrets after their last encounter with Guy Tremblant.

Quinn moved expertly over the dance floor, weaving around the other dancing couples as he held his wife close. Quinn inhaled the scent from Davi's hair. He hardened as her perfume filled his senses. No woman ever aroused him so quickly. He remembered he reacted the same way when he danced her into their wedding reception. It was the happiest time of his life. At least it was until Guy—

"Don't." Davi's voice interrupted his thoughts. "I know when you're thinking about him. Don't."

Davi could always tell. Quinn's body tensed, and she would swear he held his breath, too. He couldn't hide anything from her.

He chuckled. "Damn. My thoughts aren't private anymore."

Davi looked up at him with concern. "Not when you're thinking about him."

"He just popped in. I was thinking of our wedding reception and our entrance into the dining room. It was the first time we'd danced with each other."

"You were amazing,"

"We were amazing. It's the two of us. Don't ever forget that." Quinn leaned down and kissed her.

"So who is the lucky couple getting married?" he asked as he looked around the dance floor, tamping down any thought of Guy Tremblant.

"Right there," Davi said as she nodded her head towards a couple wearing matching western outfits.

Quinn smiled. "Introduce me to them?"

Quinn didn't wait for an answer as he guided Davi towards them. The couple noticed Quinn heading for them and stopped.

Davi made the introductions. "Reid and Kelly, Quinn wanted to meet you. Quinn, this is Reid and Kelly. Reid, Kelly, this is Quinn Thomas, my husband."

"Nice to meet you," Quinn said as he held out his hand to Reid. "Congratulations," he said as he smiled at Kelly. "May I have this dance?"

Davi smiled as she watched a blush heat Kelly's face. Kelly giggled as she let Quinn take her by the hand and dance away with her. Quinn held Kelly perfectly in his arms, not having her too close, with his hand placed correctly above Kelly's hip to guide her.

"Oh, man," Reid groaned. "I'm never gonna hear the end of this. She'll be talking about this for weeks."

"It's just a dance, Reid," Davi reminded him as she began to dance with Reid. "You'll always be her perfect partner."

"Why do you say that?"

"Because you're the one who will hold her tight and tell her that you love her and how beautiful she is when you dance with her."

Davi smiled sweetly up at Reid; he was as tall as Quinn although leaner. She had known him all of his life. He was a best friend to her son, Rich. Reid was one of the nicest young men Davi had ever known. When his parents divorced, and his father moved away, Reid spent his free time at the Stuart farm, hanging out with Rich and Ross, Davi's husband. Ross took Reid under his wing and taught him machinery maintenance and repairs. At that time, Davi was friends with Reid's mom, Lizzie Tanner. Then things changed. Davi didn't let it come between her and Reid since Reid had nothing to do with it.

When the song ended, Reid excused himself to go to the bar. Quinn escorted Kelly to her group of friends, where he stayed and chatted.

Davi made her way to the silent auction tables to look at the items for sale. Davi could smell Lizzie's cheap perfume as Lizzie came up behind her. Davi kept her attention on the bidding sheet in front of her.

"Well, isn't it Mrs. Quinn Frickin' Thomas," Lizzie sneered into Davi's ear.

Davi could smell the liquor on her breath.

"Hello, Lizzie. I had a dance with your son. How are the plans going for the wedding?" Davi asked as she turned around to face her.

"I would have been married by now if it weren't for you," she said bitterly, ignoring Davi's question.

"Really? To whom?"

"If you had let Ross go, we would have been married by now. But no, you had to keep your claws in him. You're a selfish bitch, Davina Stuart."

Davi sighed. She was tired of these confrontations. "Ross didn't want to go, Lizzie. He wanted to make our marriage work. I've told you this before."

"You lie. Just like your book was a pack of lies. You didn't love Ross. You didn't grieve for him when he died. I'm the one who grieved for him. I still do."

"I grieved for him, Lizzie. Ross was my husband, and I loved him."

"He loved me more."

Davi shook her head. "I don't think so."

"He was leaving you for me."

"He wasn't leaving, Lizzie. He never was. Ross just liked to have a different flavour now and again. He wasn't going to give up the kids and me for anyone."

"You lie!"

Quinn kept his eyes on Davi as he continued his visit with Kelly and her friends. He rarely let Davi out of his sight or out of his reach. Only Davi knew this and accepted his protectiveness. She knew the reason why—Guy Tremblant. Whenever Quinn left Davi's side, Guy Tremblant had his hands on her, trying to take her away. Although Guy was out of the picture now, Quinn couldn't relax when Davi was away from him, and he knew that it would take some time before he could relax again.

Quinn could see the conversation was getting heated. He excused himself from the group and made his way to Davi.

"Is there a problem here?" Quinn asked as he came up behind Davi and wrapped his arm protectively around her waist.

"Quinn, this is Lizzie Tanner. She's Reid's mom. She and Ross were friends."

Quinn knew what Davi meant. He took a hard look at the woman next to Davi. She was probably Davi's age, not as attractive, and her eyes made her look old. They were dull and lifeless, and it wasn't because of the alcohol. Quinn held out his hand to Lizzie, but she ignored it.

"She'll get tired of you, too, but she'll keep you around so no one else can make you happy. Don't say I didn't warn you."

Lizzie smiled bitterly, then turned and walked away.

"Are you all right?"

Davi sighed. "She does this every chance she gets."

"Ross cheated on you with her? What an insult." Quinn kissed the top of Davi's head.

Davi smiled appreciatively. "Thank you. I think so, too. He wasn't going to leave me for her. He had others he was bedding, only Lizzie doesn't know it."

"Are they here?" Quinn asked as his gaze took in the other women in the room.

"Does it matter?"

"I want to know if the man had any taste when he cheated. Show me, Davi."

Davi turned her gaze to where Lizzie now stood with her friends. "See the brunette standing beside Lizzie? She's Lizzie's best friend, Brenda. She slept with Ross the same time Lizzie was sleeping with him."

"Did Ross tell you that?"

"He didn't have to, Quinn. Their perfume gave them away. He reeked of White Diamonds—Lizzie, or Lavender—Brenda, when he'd been with them. Lizzie doesn't know that Brenda slept with Ross."

"Why haven't you told her? It might get her off your back."

"What's the point? She wouldn't believe me. Besides, Lizzie needs all the friends she can get. I wouldn't ruin their friendship over Ross. That would be cruel."

"So you let her think the worst of you?" Quinn turned Davi around to face him. "Why?"

"She can't hurt me, Quinn. Only people I care about can hurt me."

seven

"I can't believe you bid on all of this stuff!" Tigger laughed as the family made its way into the farmhouse kitchen well past one in the morning.

Quinn and Rich followed behind, carrying baskets and bags filled with items from the silent auction.

"Are you going to go into the junk business if acting doesn't work out for you?" Cat teased. "What are you going to do with all of this crap?"

"Girls," Davi said as she tried desperately to stifle a giggle, "be nice. Quinn got carried away. That's all. I'm sure we can use what he bought."

Quinn dropped his purchases on the kitchen table. He was laughing along with the rest of the family. He never thought that he'd be stuck with so much junk.

"To be fair, Momsie, Quinn was doing what we told him to do."

"That's right, Rich," Quinn agreed, happy to have some support. "You said to put good bids on the sheets so that the auction would bring in a sizeable amount for Reid and Kelly."

"Not by overbidding everyone by a hundred dollars!" Cat laughed, holding her aching sides from laughing too much. "Nothing was worth over fifty bucks."

"What about the bull semen?" Tigger asked. "It was worth about five hundred dollars, wasn't it?"

"Yes," Rich agreed, "but we get that semen a lot cheaper than what it sold for."

"We're keeping these," Quinn said as he picked out a set of coffee cups. "These are priceless."

"Coffee cups?" Davi asked, incredulous. "We have coffee cups."

"Yes, but do you have muumi mukis? You haven't had a real cup of coffee until you've drunk from one of these. Trust me."

Rich picked up one of the cups from the table. "What the hell is this on it?"

"They're Finnish ogres," Quinn explained as he ran his finger over the outline of the ugly creature. "There's a story to tell, but not now."

"Okay, so what do we do with the rest of the stuff?" asked Tigger.

"Leave it until tomorrow," Davi said as she took the mug from Quinn and put it on the table. "We'll go through it and see if there is anything we can use. If not, we'll give it all to the thrift shop."

"Well, I'm off to bed," Rich announced. "Someone has chores in the morning."

"We're off, too," the girls said together. "Good night, you two. It's good to have you home."

Davi and Quinn both said good night as Davi's children left for bed.

"Would you like a drink?" Davi asked as she plugged in the kettle. "I'm going to have a cup of green tea."

"No, thanks," he answered as he walked over to the liquor cabinet and took out a bottle of scotch. "Do you realize I only had one beer the whole evening?" he asked after he poured himself a drink.

"You were too busy bidding, Quinn."

"And I was dancing. Your daughters and my best friends had me dancing every line dance. Where do they get the energy?"

"You didn't look like you were having difficulty keeping up with them," Davi said as she poured boiling water into her cup. "You could have said no."

"And disappoint them? No way."

Quinn and Davi walked into the family room. Davi dimmed the lights then picked up the remote to start the gas fireplace. She took a seat on the oversized sofa. Quinn turned on the stereo and selected soft jazz music to play before turning his attention to the family room's contents. Family pictures set out on bookshelves, and various collectibles placed tastefully throughout the room. A glass vase with stones caught his interest.

"What's this?" he asked as he picked up the vase and examined its contents.

"It's our holiday jar," Davi answered thoughtfully. "Whenever Maggie and I go away together, we look for stones for our jar. Every once in a while, we take them out and reminisce about our family holidays."

Quinn put the vase down carefully in its place. He turned and faced Davi.

"What are you thinking?" she asked.

Quinn shrugged.

Davi patted the seat beside her. "Sit. Talk to me."

"I don't have anything like that," he said with regret. "With all the places I've been, you'd think I would have thought to collect something, to have a souvenir."

"Not everyone collects things, Quinn. What about your memories? You must have plenty with a photographic memory like yours."

"But they aren't anything I can share; they aren't out for display."

"No, but you can talk about them. What about your moomy—" Davi struggled with the words.

"Muumi muki," he corrected her.

"Right. You can share your story about that. I'm sure we'd all love to hear it."

"It's not about a place, love. It's about a friend. That's different."

A peaceful silence enveloped them as they sipped their drinks and watched the fire. Davi put her cup down on the table and snuggled into Quinn's chest.

"You and Ross made love in this room." His voice was soft, almost sad.

Davi didn't answer him.

"I can see why," he continued. "It has the perfect ambiance for romance. Fireplace, candles, a big sofa, a soft carpet, a great stereo—" He put his glass down beside her cup on the table. "Let's make love."

"Let me finish my tea, and then we can head upstairs."

"No. I want to do it here. Right now."

"Quinn," Davi said softly, "I'm tired. Let's go upstairs."

"Please." His voice was suddenly rough, urgent.

There was no blue bedroom sparkle in his eyes. Quinn reached for her and pulled her close. His mouth covered hers, pressing hard against her lips as he forced his tongue into her mouth. His hands found her head and fisted in her hair, keeping her head in place.

Davi tasted the scotch on his breath. It was intoxicating. Her hands instinctively found his ears and caressed them. They kissed for the longest time until Davi pushed away to catch her breath. Her lips were swollen and bruised from the sudden assault. Her gaze locked with his. Quinn's eyes were on fire. She knew that there was more to that fire than lust.

He didn't take his time with her. There were no gentle kisses. Nor were there soft caresses from hands that knew every inch of her body. His fingers found the buttons of her shirt and undid each one quickly.

"Take them off."

Davi obeyed, shrugging off her shirt and then reaching behind her to undo the clasp of her bra. She took off the bra and let it fall to the floor.

As she did so, Quinn's attention moved to her belt and then the button and fly to her jeans. Quinn's hands moved with deliberate speed as he pulled Davi's jeans and panties over her hips and past her knees and then dropped them onto the floor.

Davi could feel the heat course through her as her body responded to him. He'd never been like this with her. Yes, they'd had their five-minute quickies and their playful moments, but this was a side to Quinn she hadn't experienced before.

Quinn stood up beside the sofa. His gaze still focused on Davi. He undid his shirt's top buttons then pulled it over his head, tossing it to the floor. His hands went to his belt buckle, undoing it quickly. His pants joined his shirt in an instant.

He didn't give her time to gaze at his body or tease him with a smart remark as he returned to the sofa and pressed his body against hers. His mouth covered hers once again, before she felt the full force of him enter her, stretching her, filling her. Her hands went for his head. There would be no fondling of his earlobes this time. Instead, she rubbed against the short hair on his head, feeling the roughness against her palms.

Quinn's thrusts were hard and deliberate. He pounded into her, and she took all that he gave her. Davi wrapped her legs around his waist and held on tight. That's all she could do. It was all he'd let her do. She closed her eyes as she felt herself near orgasm. There was no standing at the edge of a cliff waiting to fall this time. No matter how hard she tried to fight it, Quinn was pushing her off it.

Davi was the first to moan her release. Quinn took it all from her then answered with a groan as he thrust into her twice more. For a moment, he remained still, then he released her from his kiss and rested his head on her breast.

Davi lay sprawled on the sofa with Quinn lying on top of her. It took her a few minutes to regain her senses as her hands caressed Quinn's back.

"I redecorated this room, you know," she said as a smile touched her lips.

"Huh?"

"I redecorated this room when I found out about Ross. You're the only man to have sex with me in this room since I had it redecorated."

Quinn's body tensed. Nothing escaped her.

"After I found out he had cheated on me, I couldn't bear to be in here and be reminded of where we had made love. The master bedroom I redecorated after he died. So, Quinn, you don't have to mark your territory. You are the one and only lover I've had in this room."

Quinn rolled off Davi and stood up. He reached for his jeans and dressed hurriedly. Davi pulled the throw blanket over her body as she watched him dress.

"I didn't do that," Quinn said as he avoided her gaze.

She stood up, wrapping the blanket around her. Davi cupped his cheek gently with one hand. She wouldn't let him look away from her.

"This house and this family are yours. I am yours."

"I know that."

"I saw you looking around this room. There's nothing of yours in here, but that will change. Give it time."

"Davi, I don't know what you're thinking, but you've got it all wrong."

"We'll put pictures of your parents in here and some of the gang. What about your awards?"

"They're in a cardboard box in Luke's office."

"We'll display them in my office. Would you like a desk, too? Maybe we can fit a big armchair in there, or we can renovate and make an office just for you."

"Davi, you're—"

"Making a home with you." She looked at him. There was no judgement in her eyes, only love and understanding.

Quinn reached for her and held her in his arms. "You amaze me."

"Give me twenty-five years, and then tell me if I still do."

XO XO XO

Davi stood in a field surrounded by beautiful women. She knew this field. It was where she had played flag football with Quinn's gang of friends. The women were past lovers and costars in his movies.

Rene Adams, Quinn's most recent costar and ex-lover, whispered in her ear, "You're not going anywhere near him. He's mine."

Davi looked across the field to where Quinn stood, looking Hollywood sexy in his tight jeans and a blue T-shirt. He was surrounded by more women, all reaching for him. He stood laughing, enjoying the attention. Quinn carried the ball and ran towards the goal. As Davi tried to run after him and pull the flag from his belt, familiar faces came between Quinn and her.

Sue, Jake's wife, screamed at her, "Keep your hands off him!"

Davi pushed by her, only to be stopped by Margaret, Quinn's mother.

"You're too old for my son," she shrieked as she pointed a bony finger at Davi.

Then Luke stood beside Davi and laughed. "He's signed the papers. He's letting you go."

"No," Davi shouted and pulled away from him, still trying to catch Quinn.

Then out of nowhere, Guy Tremblant appeared. Davi stopped as paralyzing fear coursed through her body.

"You are mine. All mine," Guy said with a sneer.

Davi tried to run away from him, but he caught her in his arms.

"You are mine, Davina. You can't escape me."

In one swift move, Guy Tremblant was on top of her, and blackness covered her.

"No," Davi cried out, terrified.

Davi awoke with her eyes opened wide. Her heart raced, and tears ran down her face. It felt so real. She hadn't had a nightmare in ages, not since Ross died. Davi turned to Quinn, who slept soundly beside her. She snuggled into his warm chest for protection from the dark. Automatically, Quinn's arms enfolded her and pulled her close.

"I've got you," he murmured in his sleep.

Davi wiped away her tears. *What the hell was that?*

eight

Quinn kissed Davi softly on her lips.

"What time is it?" she asked, keeping her eyes closed.

"It's just before eight."

"You don't sleep in, do you?"

"Not when I have a wife as beautiful as you holding on to me. Bad dream?"

"I needed my teddy bear."

"Care to tell me about it?"

"Just you and a hundred bimbos playing flag football," Davi drawled sleepily.

"And the bad part was?" Quinn asked playfully.

"You're awful!" Davi grumbled as she poked him in the chest.

"Are you hungry? I promised you breakfast in bed. Have you forgotten?"

"No. I'd never forget your breakfast in bed."

Quinn nestled into Davi's neck, giving her warm kisses. Then he touched her between her legs. She was wet and ready for him.

"How do you do that?" he whispered in her ear. "You're always ready for me."

"I wake up thinking of you. It only takes a second, and I'm ready." Davi responded as his fingers played with her.

"What do you think about?"

"Wouldn't you like to know," she teased as she gave him a mischievous smile.

"Tell me."

Davi replied slowly, giving one answer with every kiss, "Your kisses, your smell, your hair, your touch, and your body. The list goes on. Everything and anything about you get the juices flowing." Davi squirmed from the pleasure his kisses gave her.

"My hair?"

She opened her eyes and gazed back at his baby blues. "I love your hair. Even what you have now, I love. It tickles me, but I want your long hair back. It's mine."

"Just give it some time."

Quinn moved on top of Davi. His forearms framed her face as they supported his body above hers. He entered Davi, moving slowly, enjoying the feeling of being inside her. He wanted this moment to last as long as possible.

"Talk to me, love. Tell me what you love about me."

"I love that you love me. That's the biggest turn-on of all. I love that you want to spend your life with me. I love the way you look at me when you're trying to figure out what I'm thinking, and you can't. I love the way your eyes sparkle at me when you smile. Your smile tells me that life is perfect. I want Jack to have that smile."

Quinn closed his eyes as he thought of Jack. "Tell me more, love."

"I love your bum. It's small, and it's tight, and I can hold on to it anytime I want." Davi grabbed Quinn's buttocks and pulled him in closer. "I love your kisses. I love your taste, especially when there's a hint of scotch. But don't drink too much." Davi kissed Quinn lightly. "I love your smell." Davi breathed in his scent. "Don't do any cologne ads. You'd be doing everyone a disservice. I love the way you are comfortable about your body."

"It's just a body."

"That every woman and maybe some men want, too. You're gorgeous, Quinn. You are comfortable in your skin. It's great. It's sexy. You don't have any airs about you." Davi shifted her weight under Quinn as she tightened her legs around his waist. "And you've got a great package."

Quinn stopped and looked at her. "You love me because I've got a great package?"

Davi chuckled. "You have an unbelievably great package. I love your package. I don't love you because of it, but it sure is a nice benefit. Why else would I call you stud?"

"I thought it was because of what I did with it, not because of what I had."

"It's both. Keep going, stud. Breakfast is getting cold." Davi pulled Quinn to her mouth. She pressed her mouth hard against his as she devoured him with her kiss.

Quinn moaned as Davi's tongue worked inside his mouth. Her hips ground against his, her legs pulling him in. Quinn could feel himself get lost in her once again. Any thought of delaying his climax was gone. He was coming fast. A final thrust was all it took. Quinn kissed Davi one last time then lay down beside her.

"I'm going to see Maggie this morning," Davi announced.

"Do you want me to come with you?"

"No, not this time. Besides, aren't you helping Rich with chores today? You do remember telling him you wanted to learn how to be a farmer, don't you?"

XO XO XO

Davi parked her truck in front of Maggie's house and killed the engine. She stared at the front door for the longest time.

"Just ask her," she said aloud. "Don't be such a wuss."

Gathering her bag of presents for Maggie and her family, Davi got out of the truck and made her way to the front door. There was no knocking on the door or ringing the doorbell. Davi opened the front door and walked in.

"Hello," she called as she slipped off her boots and took off her jacket before making her way to the kitchen.

"Davi," Maggie cried out happily as she hugged her best friend. "I have missed you, girl. How are you?"

"I'm good," she answered as she kissed her best friend's cheek. "Here. I brought these for you." Davi smiled as she handed Maggie a gift bag.

"It's heavy," Maggie remarked as she tested the weight of it in her hand. "Two bottles?"

Davi laughed. "One's from me, and the other one is from Quinn. You'll know when you open it."

Maggie opened the bag and pulled out a bottle of Baileys Irish Cream. "Thank you," she said as she smiled at Davi. Maggie always had a bottle at the ready for heart-to-heart conversations over coffee. "Ooh," she crooned as she pulled out a bottle of single malt scotch.

"Quinn insisted on giving you a bottle of his favourite spirit for his heart-to-hearts, Maggie. He thought it was only fair."

"Does he have secrets to confess?" Maggie teased with her soft Irish accent.

"I don't know. Quinn wanted a liquor of his choice. That's all," Davi said as she sat down at the kitchen table. "I bought the girls some jewellery. You can give it to them when you see them. And there's something in there for Charlie." Davi looked around the room. "By the way, where is he?"

"He had some errands to run, and he thought that we should have some alone time to catch up on things," Maggie said as she sat beside Davi at the kitchen table.

"Smart man."

Davi helped herself to a muffin and poured them both a cup of coffee from the carafe.

"So?" Maggie asked as her eyes sparkled with excitement. "Out with it. How was the honeymoon sex?"

Davi chuckled as she shook her head. She had missed this—the no-holds-barred conversation that was a must with Maggie. Quinn had told Maggie before they left on their honeymoon not to expect any communication from his wife. She'd be too busy having honeymoon sex.

"I'm exhausted. Quinn wants to catch up on all the sex he's missed out on with me."

"How much sex is he talking about?"

"About ten years' worth. The man thinks we should have met earlier than we did."

"It wasn't in the cards for you. You wouldn't have strayed."

"I know."

Maggie nodded at Davi. "You look good, and you got some sun. So he did let you out of doors occasionally." Maggie took a sip of coffee.

"Yes. And we went dancing every night. I've never had so much attention from a man before. He's spoiling me."

"Care to tell me about it? Let me know how Mr. Hollywood does it," she teased.

"We had this amazing cottage on the beach. It was private, and we had our private patio with hot tub." Davi paused to take a sip of her coffee. "The ocean was just outside of the cottage. We could hear the crash of the waves from the patio."

"Sounds nice, but what did you do?"

"We took lots of walks on the beach every day. They had an amazing restaurant that overlooked the ocean. We would sit out on the patio and have a romantic dinner for two. Quinn would hold my hand, and we would talk about everything. Then afterwards, we went to this piano bar. It was quiet, and not too many people went to it. We danced—all slow dances. Maggie, I don't know when I danced so much. He'd hold me in his arms, and it was like we were the only people in the room."

Maggie sighed. She was happy for her friend. It was good to see her happy and in love with a man who truly loved her. She only hoped it was enough to get them through what was about to happen.

Davi reached into her purse and pulled out her old leather-bound book. She handed it to Maggie.

"I also wrote this when Quinn gave me some alone time."

Maggie took the book and opened it. She scanned the first few pages then looked up at Davi with amazement.

"I remember another book just like this one. It was about your life with Ross. You called it *Second Harvest*. What's this one about?"

"They are stories for Quinn," Davi explained. "With everything we've been through, he feels as though he's let me down. He wasn't the one to save me from you know who."

"Men and their egos," Maggie teased.

"It's not his ego. He made a promise to keep me safe. Quinn's not a man to break his word. Anyway, my stories are about a knight and his fair lady. The knight fights dragons and wizards, and other unsavoury characters to keep his lady safe. Quinn's the knight."

"Obviously," Maggie deadpanned. "Why are you showing me this? Isn't it private?"

"Maggie, when have I ever kept anything from you? I have a favour to ask. I need you to copy this for me and keep it safe. I don't have notes or anything. I wrote everything in this book. If something were to happen to it, I don't know what I would do."

"Can't you do it?"

"I don't have the time to copy it. We're off to New York tomorrow, and we'll be away for two weeks. I'd feel better knowing that you had it and made a copy of it. Please, Maggie."

"May I read it? Or is it for his eyes only?" Maggie asked as she closed the leather book and placed it on the table.

"Of course, you can read it. Nothing is embarrassing, nothing that would come as a shock to you."

"As long as you don't describe Hollywood's private parts," Maggie teased. "I don't need to know what he has, although I'm sure it's pretty good."

Davi and Maggie laughed together. Davi had missed Maggie and their naughty banter.

She reached for Maggie's hand and squeezed it. "Read my cards."

Maggie resisted the urge to look away. She couldn't lie to her best friend, but neither could she tell her the truth. "I can't."

Davi pulled back in surprise. "What do you mean you can't? I want you to, Maggie. I'm serious."

In the past, Davi tried not to take Maggie's ability in reading the tarot cards too seriously. She humoured her friend when Maggie told her what the cards said about her future. They told her that her book would be successful and that she would find love. Davi wanted her book, *Second Harvest*, to be successful, but she had no faith in finding love. Then she met Quinn, proving the cards right.

"I know, Davi," Maggie said softly, trying to keep her expression even, keeping the fear from showing in her eyes. "Believe me, I would if I could, but I can't see anything right now. Everything is black for me. I can't read anyone."

"What do you mean everything's gone black?" Davi asked with concern. "What does that mean? Have you lost your gift?"

"No!" Maggie said quickly, waving away the words as though it were that easy to make things right. "Don't say that. It's just gone temporarily. That's all. I'm sure I'll get it back soon."

"You're not worried about it disappearing?"

"No. It will come back when I need it. I have faith, Davi." Maggie gazed at her friend. Could it be that Davi knew something was coming for her? "Why the sudden interest in having your cards read? I usually have to force a reading on you."

"I've been having nightmares." Davi picked at the last of her muffin. "They're becoming more frequent."

"Can you remember them?"

Davi sighed. "They're always the same. At first, I thought it was just my subconscious telling me that I'm too old for Quinn, but now I'm not so sure."

"Go on," Maggie prodded her when Davi didn't continue.

"We're playing this silly game of flag football. Quinn's there, and his team is all of these beautiful blonde bimbos, all of his ex-lovers and ex-costars. I seem to be the only one on my team." Davi took a deep breath as she tucked a stray strand of hair behind her ear. "I'm trying to grab Quinn's flag, and every one of them stops me and warns me that he's not mine and that he's moved on. And then—"

"What?"

"Guy Tremblant appears and tells me that I'm his, and then everything just goes black. I scream, and then I wake up in a sweat, and my heart is racing. I know it's just a dream, but it scares the hell out of me. What does it mean? Can you tell me?"

"Davi, you and Quinn went through a terrible ordeal because of that man. He tried to abduct you, and when that didn't work, he tried to kill Quinn. I think it's fairly obvious that your brain is beginning to deal with it now. You suppressed a lot, as you always do. It's just coming out now."

"I want it to end. I don't think about Guy. It's Quinn who can't seem to forget about him."

"Well, maybe he's rubbing off on you, and you are dreaming about it instead of talking about it. The dreams will stop, Davi. That's all I can tell you."

"If you knew something, would you tell me?"

Maggie felt the knot in the pit of her stomach. She'd never lied to Davi before. "If I could tell you anything, I would. Believe me."

nine

Davi returned to a quiet and empty house. Quinn was with her kids learning how to be a farmer. She smiled as she thought of it. The man was keen. She hoped he knew what he was doing.

She loved the sound of quiet. She headed to her office to see what awaited her after being away for three weeks. She turned on her computer and sorted through her mail while waiting for the computer programs to open. Most of the mail was for the farm.

Davi's e-mails popped up. Over one hundred waited in the in-box. She sighed as she quickly scanned them, sorting them into important and can-wait categories. Luke had sent her an e-mail. Davi opened it immediately. It read,

> *Davi, I'm sending an attachment with the magazines that have requested interviews. I've put them in order of importance (in my opinion). Let me know which ones appeal to you, and I'll make the arrangements. Tv interviews will follow shortly.*
> *—Luke*

Davi opened the attachment. There were five listed. She was familiar with all of them. She was happy to see two Canadian publications listed. She would agree to an interview with them. Two of the magazines she didn't recognize. The last was a celebrity gossip magazine. She'd pass on that. Perhaps she was superstitious, but every time a newlywed couple promoted their marriage in this magazine, they usually wound up divorced within the year.

By the time Davi finished with her e-mails, an hour had passed. She spent another hour in the office, paying bills. It felt good to get her desk cleared. She was ready for a break. Looking at the clock, she knew that her family would be in for lunch soon. She wondered how Quinn's first lesson in farming went.

Davi entered the kitchen as her family returned from outside. One look at Quinn was all it took to know the results. He was covered in cow manure and sporting the beginning of a black eye.

"I know. I look like shit," he said as a boyish smile crossed his face.

"What happened?" Davi asked as she moved towards him to get a better look at his injury.

"One of the heifers got affectionate with Big, Mom. She wouldn't take no for an answer," Cat offered.

"So she swatted him with her head," Tigger finished for her sister. "You should have seen him fly. He went right over her shoulders and into the shit."

"Are you okay?" Davi asked as she touched his battered face. "Did you hit your head?" Her hands moved to the back of his head for a closer inspection.

Quinn smiled, appreciating his wife's concern. "I'm fine. It's nothing that a hot shower and an ice pack won't cure."

"I warned him, Mom"—Rich laughed—"but you know these macho Hollywood types. They think they can do everything and don't need a stunt double."

"I use stunt doubles," Quinn said in his defence. "I just didn't think I needed one for the farm."

"Cat, get him an ice pack, please."

Cat walked to the refrigerator and took out an ice pack from the freezer compartment. She handed it to Quinn.

"The way you flew through the air—" Cat marvelled.

"We should have caught it on film," Tigger said.

"No, thanks. That's something no one needs to see."

"Go get cleaned up, Quinn. I'll have lunch ready by the time you come downstairs."

Davi watched as Quinn made his way to the staircase, then she turned to admonish her kids.

"What were you thinking, letting him work around the heifers? You know how crazy they can be!"

"Momsie," Rich answered soothingly to calm his mother, "he was fine around the heifers. This one just took him by surprise. She would have done it to anyone of us. It didn't faze him at all. He said he'd done tougher stunts in his movies."

"Did you consider for one moment that he's recovering from a fractured skull and brain surgery? The doctors told him to be careful and not to hit his head." Davi's eyes filled with tears as she remembered Quinn's ordeal in the hospital. "I can't go through that again. I just can't."

Rich reached for his mother and hugged her tight. "I'm sorry, Mom, we forgot about that. Quinn's such a natural around the animals. He fit right in. We'll be more careful. I promise."

"Just look out for him, okay? I don't want anything to happen to him."

XO XO XO

Davi and her family sat around the kitchen table, enjoying their lunch of grilled cheese and tomato sandwiches with homemade vegetable soup. She marvelled at the relaxed atmosphere as her three children, all of whom were in their twenties, accepted Quinn, who was old enough to be their big brother, as their mother's husband. The conversation was friendly and familiar, relaxed and full of humour. They were her family.

"How is Maggie?" Quinn asked, pulling her back into the conversation.

"She's good, and she thanks you for her present. She's wondering why you think you may have to have a heart-to-heart with her."

All eyes were on Quinn as they waited for him to swallow his food before he answered. Instantly, Quinn realized that he didn't mind millions of people watching him on the silver screen, but having four sets of Stuart eyes on him made him feel naked and exposed.

"You never know," Quinn said, trying to appear casual. "Maybe I'll need some advice on a movie offer, and Maggie will advise me. Just think of it as part of my business plan. Has she read anything exciting in her cards?"

Davi knew he hadn't given them the full answer. Quinn didn't lie, but she could tell when he held back, especially when answering questions from the paparazzi. She'd get the answer later when they were alone.

"She can't read her cards right now. It's strange. I've never heard of her gift disappearing, but that's what she says has happened."

"What?" the girls asked together in their uncanny fashion.

"She says her gift has left her, but she's confident it will come back. She doesn't seem to be upset about it."

"That's odd," Quinn said with concern.

"I know, but I wasn't going to push her and upset her. She seems okay with it."

"I'd be upset if I lost a gift like that," Quinn said. "Are you sure she's okay?"

"Quinn, Maggie will be touched by your concern. But believe me, she's okay."

XO XO XO

Maggie sat at her kitchen table, rubbing her hand over the old leather-bound book Davi had left with her. Sometimes, visions would come to her when she touched a personal item of someone whose future she was trying to see. Nothing came to her. It was still black.

Charlie brought her a hot cup of tea then sat beside her. He waited for her to speak.

"She knows something's coming."

"What? How?"

"She wrote these stories for Quinn, but she's leaving them with me for safekeeping. She is having nightmares about the darkness, Charlie. Davi knows it's coming for her."

"What did you tell her?"

"I told a white lie. I said it was from the stress she's been suppressing. It all has to do with that lunatic, Guy Tremblant. I said it would end. It would just take time."

"She believed you?"

"Why wouldn't she? I've never lied to her before, and I don't consider this a lie. I honestly don't know what or who it is coming for her, Charlie, but it is coming, and it's coming soon."

ten

Quinn and Davi spent the afternoon in their new office. It wasn't new; it was Davi's. With the addition of an old leather armchair reclaimed from the attic, Quinn now had his own space. The tan-coloured leather was soft and hid its age well, except for the scrapes along the legs from years of being hit with the vacuum cleaner or the toy tractors of Davi's children when they were toddlers.

Quinn liked his armchair and its place in Davi's office. It faced Davi's desk, giving him an unobstructed view of his beautiful businesswoman wife. It was also close enough to her that he could prop his feet up on the edge of her desk and stretch out and relax as one hand held an ice pack to his black eye and the other dealt with various e-mails and text messages on his cell phone.

Davi didn't mind his feet on her desk. She found him incredibly sexy as he sat across from her in bare feet, wearing his tight faded jeans and a black T-shirt. Even his darkening black eye looked sexy. She was never attracted to the tough-guy look, but Quinn pulled it off perfectly. Davi smiled as she turned her gaze to the black and white framed photograph of a younger Quinn that she had bought at the *Vanity Fair* charity fundraiser —the one that had cost her twenty-five thousand dollars and almost Quinn's life. It was for her eyes only, something to go on her desk to gaze at when her husband was away working on some remote movie shoot. Now she had the real deal sitting in their office, for her eyes only.

"A penny for your thoughts." Quinn's voice pulled her back to him.

Davi looked over to him and smiled. "I am thinking about my incredible luck. Who else is surrounded by their family and everyone who means the world to them?"

Quinn looked around him, then turned his gaze back to Davi. "I know you don't mean just me, but I'm the only one here at the moment."

"Look. I have you in the flesh and your picture right here facing me. I have my family facing me from there." She pointed to the dark panelled wall where various family photographs and pictures of Maggie and her family hung. "As long as I have all of you surrounding me, I'll want nothing more."

"You make it sound so simple."

"It is, for me anyway. As long as I have the love and support of the people who matter most to me, I can get through anything."

Quinn got up from his chair and walked around the desk to Davi. He offered his hand to her, which she readily accepted.

Pulling her up to him, he hugged her and rested his chin on the top of her head. "I don't want anything else to happen to us. We've been through enough to last a lifetime."

She felt his sculpted chest through his shirt and the strength in his arms. Every fibre of Davi's body tingled when he touched her, whether it was the soft touch of his hand, the light brush of his lips in her hair, or the strong arms that wrapped around her body. She couldn't bear to lose this. Not ever.

"I've been having nightmares about losing you," Davi confessed into Quinn's chest. "Maggie says it's the stress finally coming to the surface. She says it will pass."

"I hope that's all it is. I'm feeling it, too, as though I could lose you in a heartbeat. I'm adding more security for you when we're back in the States. I'm not going to risk anything happening to you."

"I hate what he's done to us. I hate the anxiety and the fear."

"So do I, love. So do I."

The rich aroma of beef stew cooking in a slow cooker wafted into the office. Quinn and Davi held hands as they walked into the kitchen, following their noses to the mouthwatering food.

"We were wondering when you two were going to leave your office," Cat remarked as the couple entered the room. She poured a glass of nonalcoholic wine for her mother and a beer for Quinn. "Supper's almost ready."

"What can I do to help?" Quinn asked as he offered a chair to Davi.

"You can cut the bread if you'd like," Tigger suggested as she handed him the bread knife.

Quinn shifted right into helper mode. Davi watched as the girls gave Quinn directions, and he followed them happily. Davi sipped her wine. It didn't taste as good as the real stuff, but she would not complain.

Rich entered the house through the kitchen door.

"It smells good in here. How long before we eat?"

"Ten minutes."

"Good. I have time to shower. See you in ten." Rich was gone before Davi could respond.

Davi continued to watch her family. Quinn and the girls worked effortlessly together. If a stranger had walked into the room, he would have thought this was a family, one that had been together for ages, not a few days. They laughed and kidded each other as they tried not to get in each other's way.

Davi stared at Quinn's bum. He was gorgeous from behind. The thought of that ass belonging to her caused her to sigh loudly. Quinn heard her and turned to give her a wink. She tingled as though he knew what she was thinking.

"Later," he mouthed to her.

Davi blew Quinn a kiss.

"Need any help?" She felt obliged to offer although she liked watching them work.

"No, Mom, we have it all under control. Do you want a refill?"

"Please." Davi handed her glass to Tigger. "It's pretty good without the buzz." Tigger handed her back a full glass. "But I miss the buzz," she joked.

Rich walked back into the kitchen, dressed in jeans and a T-shirt, with his hair still wet from his shower. Davi marvelled at her son. He was gorgeous, too. The last couple of years had been tough on Rich. He had taken over the farm management, switching from worker to boss, and put in more hours than he was used to. His eyes looked older, and he had lost a few pounds, which enhanced his muscular frame. He was a slightly younger version of Quinn. Their hair was even the same length right now. Rich liked to keep his hair short. Quinn's hair would be grown out before long. Davi looked forward to the two men in her life not looking so much alike.

Davi noticed Quinn was looking at Rich, too. Was he thinking the same thing? That they looked too much alike? Did he feel uncomfortable?

"Rich, you look so much like me right now. You could be my double. No one would notice."

Davi sighed. *Men.*

Everyone sat down at the table. Rich sat at the head of the table, the girls sat on one side, and Quinn and Davi sat across from them. Quinn liked to have Davi close to him, and Davi didn't mind.

Rich said the grace, "Thank you, God, for the food on our table and our family, friends, and health. Amen. The Leafs are playing tonight. The game's on in thirty minutes."

"How are they doing?" Quinn asked, genuinely interested.

"Great, but then again, they're always great for the first part of the season, and then they tank. They need to get better goalies."

"And defence," added Cat.

"And forwards who can score," Davi said knowingly.

"I take it that this is a Maple Leafs' house."

"Got a problem with it?" Davi teased.

"Who are they playing tonight?"

"Boston."

"Ten on Boston to win. Any takers?" Quinn asked.

Rich laughed. "They're on a winning streak, Big. I don't mind taking your money."

"I'm in," Cat said excitedly.

"Not me. I don't care about hockey," Tigger added.

"I won't bet either," Davi said, shaking her head. "The three of you go for it."

Quinn's phone rang. He pulled it out of his pocket. "Excuse me. It's Luke. I'd better take it."

Quinn walked out to the family room. His voice became louder as he spoke to Luke, making it easy to overhear his conversation.

"Luke, I'm sorry, man, but no way am I flying out tonight. It feels like I just got here. It's family time, and I'm not going to skip out on my family now because a studio asshole wants me to." There was a long silence. "Luke, technically, I'm still on my honeymoon. The studio gave me until Monday morning, and that's how it stays. There's no changing my plans this late in the game." There was another long silence. "Can you deal with it or not?" A shorter silence followed. "I'm hanging up, Luke. Good night."

Quinn returned to the kitchen and noticed all eyes focused on him. "The studio wants me back for tomorrow. I said no, and Luke's got to deal with it." Quinn took his seat beside Davi. "Don't worry. It's not a big deal. It's his job."

"Why do they want you back?" Tigger asked.

"I didn't ask. It's nothing that can't wait until Monday. I've stopped running back to them every time they call. It's never as important as they claim." Quinn clapped his hands together. "So—what's for dessert?"

"Mind if we head out to the family room? The game's about to start," Rich asked.

"Go ahead. We'll join you in a few minutes."

Davi got up and started to clear the table. She was lost in thought while she stacked the dishes in the dishwasher in silence.

"Anything you'd care to share with me?" Quinn asked as he made a pot of coffee.

"Are you sure it's nothing to worry about?"

"I'm positive. Davi, this happens all the time. Someone gets an idea, and immediately, they call an emergency meeting to discuss it. It's nothing that can't wait until Monday." Quinn placed his hand on her shoulder. "Are you thinking about the last time I raced back to the studio?"

"Aren't you?"

Quinn shrugged. "It crossed my mind, but I know there's no crazed costar trying to break us up. Rene has a new man in her life now, remember? One of those celebrity magazines you bought at the airport reported it. No, it's just that I'm not as eager to run back to the studio like I used to. I have more important things to do at home."

"That's nice to know. Care to tell me what's of great importance at this moment?"

"Watching my Boston Bruins kick your Toronto Maple Leafs' ass."

XO XO XO

On Sunday morning, Quinn, Davi, and the family went to church. It was an old red brick building situated in the farm community's hub, surrounded by open fields. The sanctuary walls had large stained-glass windows dedicated in memory of loved ones lost many years ago. The morning sun shone brightly through them, creating a beautiful sparkling of colour. Quinn hadn't noticed the windows the last time he was here. His full attention had been on Davi as she walked down the aisle on their wedding day.

They took their seat in their favourite pew. Quinn liked the feeling he got as members of the church stopped to offer a good morning greeting.

"Everyone's very welcoming," he remarked.

"We're United," Cat whispered in his ear. "We welcome everybody."

After church, the family went out to lunch and toured the countryside. Quinn wanted to get to know his new neighbourhood. He marvelled at the rolling hills, the pristine estates, and the farms where horses or exotic cattle grazed behind expensive fences. Davi sat in the backseat with the girls, while Rich drove and Quinn sat shotgun.

"There's Austin Allan's farm." Davi pointed out to him.

"I know," Quinn said casually. "I was there."

"When?"

"The week of the Toronto Film Festival, he invited a hundred people or so to a bbq. I didn't realize you lived so close to each other."

"Maybe you and Mom crossed paths that week and didn't know it, Quinn," Cat suggested dreamily.

"But couldn't meet because it was your destiny to meet on the plane," finished Tigger with a romantic sigh.

"Oh, give it a break, you two," grumbled Rich.

Quinn laughed. "You never know."

Davi pointed to another estate. "That mansion up in the hills is supposed to belong to Marcus, the singer."

"We'll have to have him and his family over to dinner."

"What? Are you kidding?" the girls shrieked. "You know Marcus?"

"You don't? You're practically neighbours," Quinn said as he looked out at the gated mansion.

Davi knew he was playing with the girls, and they believed every lie he fed them. She stared out the window, not risking giving anything away.

"Mom, did you hear that? He's inviting Marcus and his family over for dinner!"

"Yes, I heard. Quinn's doing the cooking, though."

"When?"

"When what?" Quinn asked.

"When are you inviting them over?"

"I don't know. Marcus is probably very busy. I'm busy, too, you know."

"Yes, but you're not that busy. Do you know his number? Can you call him right now?"

"Now?"

"Yes. Call Marcus. Maybe we can drop by and see his place."

"Oh, I never thought about that. He could be in Europe or the States, you know."

"Call him."

Quinn took his cell phone from his pocket and punched in a number.

"You're calling him?"

"How else do I talk to him?"

Davi forced herself not to look at the girls. Quinn was sucking them deeper into his prank. They were going to kill him when they found out. Rich kept his eyes on the road. He wasn't being fooled by this either.

"Hello, Marcus? Hi, it's Quinn Thomas. How are you?" Quinn was silent for a moment. "That's great! I'd love to help you with that. Could you send me the details? Look, Marcus, I'm out driving in the countryside here north of Toronto, and my family thinks you have a place out here."

Davi listened intently. *Who the hell is he talking to?*

"What road are we on, Davi?"

"Hillside at Ten."

"Hillside at Ten, whatever that means. There's this huge gated mansion looking down on all of us mortals. Is that yours?" There was a long silence. "He has to check," he whispered to the girls. "He doesn't know the address." Quinn nodded. "Are you home?"

The girls had their hands over their mouths, trying to hold in their screams.

Davi shook her head. What an actor.

"Okay, another time then. You'll have to come out to our place— see what real country living is all about." Quinn laughed. "Thanks. She is amazing. I can't wait for you to meet her. We'll see you soon. Bye."

"What did he say?"

"That's his house, but he's not at home. He's in California right now. He sends his congratulations on our marriage, Davi, and he'll call us next time he's up this way."

The girls screamed.

"Oh, give it a rest," Rich moaned. "I'm trying to drive here."

The girls wouldn't settle.

Davi touched Quinn on the shoulder. He turned his head to listen to her.

"Good one," she whispered. "You got them. Now they need to be told that it was a prank."

Quinn turned to look at Davi. His eyes sparkled. "What prank, Davi? That was Marcus, and he is coming for a visit next time he's here. Don't worry. I'll do the cooking. I know what he likes."

eleven

Guy Tremblant turned off his laptop and snapped it closed. The paparazzi were useless, so he thought until he needed someone to keep an eye on Quinn Thomas. He checked two websites before he found what he needed. Quinn Thomas was back in town with Davina Stuart. There was no mention of where they were staying. It didn't matter. Guy knew the hotel. He'd met with Quinn in his penthouse suite a few times when they were discussing the script for *Untitled*. Quinn gave Guy a tour. Guy knew every square inch of that suite.

The couple would only be in New York for two days before leaving for Los Angeles for the premiere of *Lovestruck*. Then they would return to New York before flying to Europe for a week to promote the movie. Guy had hoped they would stay longer in New York, but it didn't matter. He knew how to work under a deadline. He'd be ready for Davina when they returned.

Guy got up from his desk and headed outside to complete the final inspection of his home—one last look to check on the bolted-down shuttered windows.

twelve

Davi awoke with a start and had no idea where she was. She was in total darkness, and she was afraid. Fear coursed through her as she reached out in the king-sized bed and felt nothing. It was empty where Quinn should have been. She found his pillow, clutched it, pulled it to her face, and then breathed in deeply. His scent filled her. She exhaled slowly and felt the slightest bit of relief. He was here. Somewhere.

Davi reached clumsily for the bedside lamp. "No switch," she muttered. *Think, Davi. Wall switch.*

Her hand felt for the panel above the bedside table and found the switch. Immediately, a bright light blinded her. She closed her eyes and fell back into bed.

"Quinn?" she called out.

Ready to try again, Davi opened her eyes and looked around the room to see a king-sized bed, designer furniture, and no personal items she could identify. She knew this room. It was Quinn's hotel penthouse suite, but which one? She scrambled out of bed and fell towards the window. She pulled back the heavy drapery and looked outside. They were in New York City.

Davi rested her forehead against the cold glass and sighed. "Get a grip," she admonished herself. "You're losing it."

The aroma of freshly brewed coffee wafted into the room. How could she forget? They were back to their routine where Quinn woke up early and went to the hotel gym to work out, but not before setting the automatic timer on the coffeemaker to start at eight o'clock. Davi walked to the bathroom and started the shower. She stepped in without checking the water's temperature.

It bothered her, the feeling of something not being quite right. It followed her from her honeymoon and stayed with her. Last night, leaving her children behind on the farm had been difficult for her. They laughed at how she cried. Davi never cried when she said good-bye. "Hormones," they teased as they blamed it on her pregnancy. She let them, not acknowledging the real reason.

"Mind if I join you?"

Davi startled. Strong arms reached for her and pulled her in tight.

"Hey, it's me. What's wrong? Damn, Davi, this water's freezing." Quinn reached for the dial and turned the water to warm. He held her and waited for her to relax in his arms. "Talk to me."

"You closed the drapes."

"I didn't want the light to disturb you. We had such a late night I thought you could use the extra sleep."

"It was so dark." Davi shuddered.

"Davi?"

"Quinn, what's wrong with me? I was afraid of the dark. I've never been afraid of the dark before."

"Come with me to my meeting," Quinn said to Davi as they drank their morning coffee. His voice was soft and soothing.

Davi appreciated his sensitivity. It had taken several minutes for him to calm her enough for her to finish her shower.

"I'm okay. I don't know why I'm feeling this way."

"You don't think it's your hormones?"

Davi shot him a glance that squashed that suggestion immediately. "Unless you make superhuman babies that can screw with a woman's hormones, I don't think this has anything to do with that. I've been pregnant before, and not once was I terrified of the dark."

"So you think it may be post-traumatic stress?"

"I hope not, but if it is, then that's what it is. Don't worry. I'll deal with it."

"No, Davi. We'll deal with it. We'll make an appointment to visit your doctor. Let's see if we can stop this thing before it goes too far."

"Just leave it for now. If I get worse, I'll see someone. But for now, just let me deal with it. I'll be fine."

Quinn knew well enough not to argue with her. For now, he would keep an eye on her. If she needed help, he knew she would ask for it.

"Come with me to my meeting. We'll have lunch afterwards." His voice changed to low and lusty. "Or we can come back here and do what newlyweds do. We're still on our honeymoon."

Davi smiled. "Do a crossword together?"

"Oh, love, is that a challenge?"

"You'll have to wait and see."

XO XO XO

Looking very prim and proper, two older women stood waiting at the penthouse elevator as Quinn and Davi arrived.

Quinn gave them his best Hollywood smile. "Good morning, ladies. How are you this morning?"

"Good morning, Mr. Thomas," they said as they both nodded to him.

The elevator doors opened, and Quinn and Davi followed them into the car. The two women stood in the back, keeping a polite distance from the couple. Quinn placed his hand on Davi's waist.

"They are that couple we saw on *Olivia*, Marge. I told you they stayed in this hotel," one of the ladies whispered loudly to her friend.

"They're cute, aren't they? She said he's one hundred times better in the sack in real life than what he does in his movies."

"I wouldn't mind putting him to the test."

"I bet you'd show him a trick or two."

"You know I would. There's lots of life still left in this old girl."

The elevator stopped at the lobby, and the doors opened. Davi exited first, then Quinn.

"Ladies," he said as he held the doors back for the two women.

Quinn caught Davi by the waist and walked her to the front doors. "You know, if you ever leave me, I think I've got someone who'll take me. She can even show me a trick or two."

"I heard that. And she thinks you're a hundred times better in the sack in real life. I think you'd kill her if that were the case."

"Then you have to stay with me, Davi, if only for her sake."

Jake waited for them at the entrance, looking somewhat sheepish as he kept his hand on the handle of the limo door.

"Before I open this, please remember that she's one of your biggest fans and that I had to let her come if I ever wanted to have sex with her again."

Jake opened the door, and Quinn peered in first. Squeals of excitement pierced the air. It was Sue, Jake's wife. Quinn stood back and let Davi get in ahead of him. Sue was on top of Davi, hugging her before she could sit down.

"Oh, I've missed you," she cried. "Jake had to bring me along. I had to see you, both of you. I couldn't wait to see you tonight."

"How are you, Sue? It's been ages. You look great!" Davi kissed Sue on the cheek.

"I've been lonely. There's been no excitement since you two went on your honeymoon. Jake had nothing to do and no stories to tell. You can't leave me for that long ever again."

"She's been moping around the house for days," Jake piped in as he got into the front passenger's seat.

The limo headed out into traffic.

"I'm with Quinn for two weeks before I head home." Davi saw the disappointment in Sue's face. "I promise we'll spend as much time together as we can, okay?"

"Oh, thank you, thank you, thank you." Sue sighed with relief as she hugged Davi again. "So tell me all about the honeymoon. Was it romantic?"

Quinn sat back and let Davi do all of the talking. He enjoyed watching two of the most important women in his life have fun together.

"It was wonderful, Sue. I can't even begin to describe it. Quinn had his fan club there, men and women. But they gave us our space, so it was nice."

"And how was Quinn? Was he romantic? Did he do honeymoon stuff for you?"

Quinn leaned forward. "What's honeymoon stuff?"

Davi and Sue looked at him and laughed. "No!" they said in unison.

"Jake!" Quinn called up to him. "What's honeymoon stuff?"

"If you have to ask, man, then you didn't do it. And you're supposed to be the romantic heartthrob. I'm so disappointed in you." Jake shook his head in disapproval.

Quinn furrowed his brow as he stared at Sue. "What's honeymoon stuff? I want to know."

"Did you make your bedroom a love den? Did you sprinkle rose petals on the bed? Did you have champagne waiting for her and candles burning? Did you take her for long walks on the beach, make love to her in a secluded cove, did you take her skinny dipping in the sea?"

"She can't drink, Sue. Davi only drank sparkling water or ginger ale."

"You could have improvised."

"It was a public beach, Sue, and in case you didn't see the pictures, the paparazzi took a lot of photos of us. So no to the nudity and what we did on the beach, well —"

"I know you, Quinn Thomas. You would have found a way. You have a reputation to uphold!"

Quinn laughed heartily. "Is that you or my publicist speaking?"

Sue ignored him and looked directly at Davi. "So what did the two of you do?"

Davi gazed at Quinn and smiled. "We did crossword puzzles, lazed in the sun, worked out in the gym, swam in the sea, had long romantic dinners, and danced every night. And when we weren't doing that, we were having incredible, mind-blowing sex."

"All the time," Quinn added. "We had mind-blowing sex all of the time. That's what honeymoon stuff is. Isn't it, Davi?" He winked at her.

"That's everyday life, Quinn." Davi winked back at him. Sue laughed with delight, and Jake groaned.

"I knew it! I'll get details later, Davi." Sue turned her attention back to Quinn. Her tone was now serious. "What happened to your eye?"

"One of Davi's heifers got a bit frisky with me, and the next thing I know, I'm on my ass covered in shit."

"You realize the press is going to have a field day with this."

"All because he got a black eye from a cow?" Davi asked, surprised.

"They'll think he was fighting off another man, Davi. Let's face it, you have a track record."

Davi would have dismissed Sue's opinion immediately if it weren't for Sue's reputation as a gifted publicist—a career she managed along with being a mother of two and the wife of Quinn's head of security.

"She doesn't have a track record. It was one crazed man. He was obsessed with Davi without any encouragement from her."

"Quinn, it doesn't matter. It's how the public sees it. That's why Davi has to go on this tour with you. You two started hot and heavy from the moment you met. Your fans loved the fantasy romance. But—and this is a big but—this crap with Guy Tremblant has set you up. You two will be the couple that has the happy ever after, or you'll be plagued by bad karma—all because of Davi."

"You don't seriously mean that?" Davi asked, horrified, as her hand reached for Quinn's. "No one's going to think that I brought this on, are they?"

"You're talking about millions of fans who have fantasized about being Quinn's lover, Davi. It won't take much for them to think you're bad news for him. Fans can be a fierce and heartless bunch. Appearing on the *Olivia* show together was a great first step. Now you've got to keep it going."

"For how long?" Davi asked as she imagined her two weeks away from her family stretched out into months.

"Don't worry, Davi." Sue smiled cheerfully. "You'll be home for Christmas."

The limo stopped.

"We're here," Jake announced.

Jake got out of the limo and opened the door for them.

"We'll see you tonight," Davi said to Sue as she accepted Quinn's hand to exit the limo.

Sue blew a kiss to Jake. "Keep them safe."

"I will. I'll see you later," Jake said before he closed the door and joined Quinn and Davi.

"It looks like the honeymoon is over," she grumbled once they stepped away from the limo. She couldn't hide her disappointment.

"Don't worry about what she said, love. You know what a romantic Sue is, especially where we're concerned, but it's her job to let us know how everyone else sees us."

"It sucks," she muttered. "I'm beginning to hate this Hollywood crap."

Luke waited for them in the lobby of Apex Studio's New York office. He stood up as soon as they came through the entranceway. His gaze went immediately to Quinn's black eye and then to Jake.

"Farm accident," Quinn answered before Luke said a word. "What's this meeting all about?"

Luke kissed Davi's cheek and whispered in her ear, "Tell me about it later." He nodded toward Jake. "Hey, man."

"Luke," Jake replied.

"The studio heads are keeping the reason for the meeting to themselves. They're waiting to spring whatever it is on you first."

Quinn's hand moved to Davi's waist as they walked to the elevator.

"How do you want to play this?" Quinn asked as he pushed the call button for the elevator. "They're up to something since they didn't want us to talk about this beforehand."

Davi watched Luke as he stood by the elevator door. When they first met, she remembered his youthful Californian appearance—short dirty blonde hair on a permanently tanned boyish face with a surfer's lean body. He and Quinn had met at Harvard. The two young men hit it off instantly and became the best of friends. When Quinn made it to Hollywood, he asked Luke to be his manager and his lawyer. He trusted no one else with his career.

"Let them do the talking, Quinn. We'll just listen."

"What about me?" Davi asked as they entered the elevator car.

"Be yourself, Davi. You'll be fine."

"And Jake?"

"They won't notice I'm there," Jake answered.

His answer made Davi smile. "I can't see that happening. You're the backup plan, aren't you?" Davi imagined Jake grabbing two studio executives by their necks and bashing their heads together.

"Jake's here for your protection, Davi. Nothing more."

"What?"

"I told you that I'd be adding more security."

"But I'm with you. We're going to a meeting. What could happen to me?"

XO XO XO

They weren't ten minutes into the meeting before Quinn was livid. Davi knew Quinn had a temper. She didn't realize how quickly it would ignite once the executives announced their plans.

"There's no way in hell I will agree to this!" he argued as Davi squeezed his hand to give him support as well as herself. "Are you out of your minds? What makes you think I'd agree to this?"

The studio heads thought it was a win-win situation. Quinn had initially signed on to play Davi's son in *Second Harvest*. That was before he met her, married her, and got her pregnant in real life. Numerous polls showed that Quinn's fans wouldn't accept him in that role. He had to play the lover she met at the end of the story. They wanted the movie to continue where the book had left off, with the Davina Stuart and Quinn Thomas romance with crazy Guy Tremblant thrown in. They wanted it all.

"Quinn, if it's about your contract—"

"This has nothing to do with the damned contract. It has to do with privacy and self-respect, and doing what is right. Our relationship is not for sale."

One of the executives appealed to Davi, "Davina, you signed over all rights to your book. We can write the script however we choose. We're not changing your story; we're only adding to it. What is wrong with adding more of the truth to it?"

"The truth? Do you know the truth, or are you just adding what the tabloids have published as the truth? What I sold you was my story up to a certain point in time. You gave me your word that you would respect my work. I see no respect in what you are offering."

"Don't you see how advantageous this would be to all of us if you gave us your support?"

"We won't support this. We won't be involved in this vulgar self-promotion," Quinn retorted as he stood up from the table. "Let's go, Davi. We've got nothing more to discuss."

"We thought you'd see it as great publicity," one executive stammered.

Davi stood up beside Quinn and looked at the men sitting at the table. "Gentlemen, I have never been a fan of reality television. I hate seeing what people will do to make a buck to promote themselves. My husband is justified in being upset with you. Regardless of your intention, you have insulted our marriage and our dignity."

"I'll catch up with you later," Luke said, remaining in his seat. "These gentlemen and I have more business to discuss."

Jake, Quinn and Davi left the office in silence. Jake pressed the call button for the elevator. He kept his gaze locked on the floor indicator.

"What's Luke going to discuss with them?" Davi asked softly.

Quinn didn't answer.

"Quinn?" she asked, moving to stand in front of him to get his attention.

"I'm sorry, Davi, but it's the only solution."

A knot formed in her stomach as the heavy silence hung over them. The elevator door opened, and then Quinn guided her into the car. Jake followed, then pushed the button for the lobby and waited for the doors to close.

"Quinn?"

"I'm sorry, love, but Luke's going to kill *Second Harvest*."

thirteen

She didn't cry or say one word to him on the way back to their hotel suite. Davi let her husband hold her in his arms and kiss the top of her head. Quinn didn't say anything to her. He knew that words of love would sound trivial, and explanations as to why he had to do it would meet deaf ears. Davi's labour of love, *Second Harvest*, was now being put to death. Quinn couldn't imagine what was going through her mind. He hadn't figured out how she thought and could never presume her reactions. He waited.

Once inside their suite, Davi headed to the bathroom and started the water running in the Jacuzzi. She stripped off her clothes and let them fall to the floor. As the water filled the tub, Davi turned on the bathroom stereo and selected a compilation of her favourite sad love songs.

Quinn heard the music from the other side of the door. In one hand, he held a glass of scotch, and the other had a glass of chocolate milk—Davi's comfort drink. The bathroom door wasn't shut completely. With one push of his foot, he opened the door. Quinn sat on the edge of the tub with both drinks in hand. Again, he watched and waited.

Her eyes were closed as her head rested against the back of the tub. She knew he was there, waiting for her to say something. She knew that he loved her and that what he did was the right thing. It just hurt so damned much.

Davi thought back to how *Second Harvest* came to be. She'd never planned to write it. It was all because of Maggie.

"Open it," Maggie said as she pushed a gift bag towards Davi at a coffee shop.

"What is it?" Davi asked. "It's not my birthday, and I know it's not our anniversary for being friends. So . . ."

"Just open the damned bag."

"All right," Davi groaned. "Don't get your knickers in a twist."

She opened the bag and pulled out a leather journal and an engraved ballpoint pen. There was no inscription on the journal. Everything about it was understated, but the warm brown leather's look and feel made her love it instantly.

"What's this for?"

"Writing," she answered.

"Writing what, though?"

"I don't care. Write about your dreams, what you like on television, or what you hate or love. Write something that will help you get out of this funk of yours."

"I'm not in a funk, Maggie. I'm grieving. My husband died."

"Three months ago, and you haven't grieved. Not the way you should—you're holding a lot inside you, Davi, and it's not good for you. You won't talk to me, and you won't see a shrink, so the next best option is for you to tell it to this journal."

"I'm not a writer."

"You don't have to be, even though you know you can write. Just put it all down here so that you get it out of your system."

"And then what?"

"Burn it or bury it or put it on your bookshelf. I don't care. Just get whatever you're feeling dealt with, then move on. It's time, Davi."

"I didn't know you were a grief expert."

"Maybe I'm not, but I know you too well to let you continue like this. Your family will fall apart if you don't get rid of this damned grief. The kids need you, and you're not showing them how to move on."

"Do you think I haven't tried? I don't know how to move on. He was my life, and now he's gone. I feel so lost without him here, Maggie, so utterly and completely lost. How do I help the kids when I can't even help myself?"

"Write about it. Maybe you'll find the answer in your writing. I remember when you wrote all of the time. The church newsletters, the stories you wrote the kids for their birthdays. You can write, Davina Stuart. You've just been too lazy to do it."

"I'm not lazy."

"Prove it."

"Do I have to show you what I've written?"

"Only if you want to. It's more important that you write. You have to get out of this funk. Get over your grief. Life goes on."

"It's easy for you to say."

"It is when I know I'm right."

Davi sighed heavily then opened her eyes. She took the offered glass of chocolate milk from Quinn and took a sip.

"Thank you."

"I'm sorry."

She shook her head. "Don't be. You've done nothing wrong." She finished her drink then handed the empty glass to Quinn. "*Second Harvest* is my tribute to Ross and my family. To change the story would be wrong. We don't need this bullshit."

"You're honestly okay with it?" Quinn asked cautiously.

"It hurts like hell, but I'm okay with it. I'm disappointed that I won't see my story on the silver screen, and I'm pissed that my gorgeous husband won't be in the movie. But, the changes they wanted to make"— she sighed—"I don't even want to think about it."

"I'll make other movies."

"But not something of mine." She couldn't hide the disappointment in her voice.

"Then write something for me, Davi. Write me a story." Quinn reached for her hands and brought them to his lips, kissing every finger. "Your fingers have the magic touch. You can do it."

"You make it sound so easy."

"Well, isn't it?" he teased.

"No. It isn't like acting. Writing is hard work."

"You don't think what I do is hard?" Quinn asked as his eyebrow arched perfectly over his right eye.

She loved how he could do that. It brought a smile to her face. "It's not hard for you. You do it for fun."

"I do it for fun?"

"That and you get to work with luscious babes, and you get lots of hot sex."

"Right. Hot sex. How could I forget about that? I'd better sign on for a new movie right away." Quinn stood up from the tub and pulled out his cell phone from his pants pocket.

"What are you doing?"

"I'm texting Luke to tell him to sign me up with the first movie that offers hot sex."

"Don't you dare!" Davi laughed as she splashed him.

"Who's going to give me hot sex then?" Quinn asked as he leaned over the tub and gazed into her eyes.

"I will, stud, but we have a bit of a problem. I'm in this tub, and you're out there."

"Quickly remedied," Quinn lustily replied as he scooped one arm under her knees and the other under her arms and picked her up from the tub.

Davi shrieked as he lifted her. Quinn's clothes were soaked, and he dripped a trail of water as he carried her to the bed.

"You're not going to dry me off?" Davi asked as he laid her across the bed.

"I know you can do it wet, and so can I."

Quinn peeled off his wet clothes then pounced on his wife. Davi laughed as his body pressed hers against the mattress. Instinctively, her legs wrapped around his waist, pulling him in tight.

"You're the only luscious babe for me. You know that." Hot kisses trailed down her neck to her collarbone.

"I know." She sighed, feeling the tingle flow through her body.

"And you're the only one who makes the sex hot," he said as his mouth found her left nipple and suckled it. He kissed a hot trail to her right nipple. "No one else gets this." His tongue circled the tip before he took it in his mouth.

"Give me what's mine. Please."

Quinn moaned as he brought his face to hers. He pressed his forehead against hers. "You are everything to me. Everything I give you is for you only."

"Then show me, Quinn. Give me what is mine now."

Davi hugged his neck and pulled him in for a kiss. She needed this—to forget the loss of her movie and forget the darkness that haunted her. She needed Quinn's love, something that was only hers and that no one would ever take away from her.

Quinn's tongue pushed past her lips and mated with her tongue. Davi loved the taste of scotch on his tongue. She sucked it hungrily, wanting more of the bitter taste. Davi inhaled his scent as though needing it to stay alive. She filled her lungs hungrily and moaned as she felt the air escape when his mouth left hers to kiss a trail down her body.

Instinctively, her hips rose, and her legs opened in anticipation of his hot mouth. She felt the vibration of his chuckle against her skin as he acknowledged her eagerness for him. She was always ready for him, wanting him. Quinn had never known a woman who was as responsive to him, with a sexual appetite as insatiable as his own. They fed off each other, giving and taking, knowing what each other needed, finding that sexual button that only they could push.

Davi's hands reached for his head. There was not enough hair for her to pull or run her fingers through, so she scraped her nails across his scalp. Quinn shuddered as sensitive nerves responded to her touch. His hardened cock jerked, and his balls ached with need. He groaned, letting her know she'd pushed another button.

His mouth covered her sex, his tongue licking her hungrily. Davi jerked suddenly as his tongue found a tender spot. Quinn reached for her buttocks and held her tight against his mouth. He held her captive as he devoured her, tasting the sweet juices that were made for him, swallowing hungrily yet never sated.

"Quinn," she moaned as she felt the beginning of her orgasm.

His tongue plunged into her, eager to taste her as she came. She ground her pussy into him, wanting more, needing more. "Yes, just like that. Yes, oh yes." Davi bucked against him as her orgasm tore through her. She writhed against the bed, her head tossing back and forth as the intense explosion of her climax coursed through her body. She prayed that he would stop for just one second so that she could breathe, and then she prayed that he would never stop.

She hungered for his kiss, his taste And then Quinn's mouth covered hers. His hands cupped her face, holding her tight to him. She cried out when he penetrated her with one thrust. He withdrew slowly then thrust again.

Quinn breathed in Davi's scent. It always made him crazy. His cock hardened, and he swore it thickened with every breath he took. She flowed through him. He ached with a need so intense that all he could do was bury himself deep within her. Yet, he still needed her touch, and then her hands were on his back, her nails digging into him, making her mark on him. He ached to feel her body underneath him, and then her legs wrapped around his waist, pulling him in tight against her. He felt the softness of her breasts, the hard nipples against his chest, and her arms around his neck. Quinn heard her soft moan and felt her grip tighten, pulling him in. Quinn gritted his teeth. He wasn't ready to let this go—he had to hold on to this moment, to shut out the world around them. He wanted.

"Davi," he moaned as she pulled him over the cliff with her.

She held him tight against her as his orgasm raced through him, sending shudders throughout his body until he quietened.

"I love you," she whispered in his ear. "I hate Hollywood, but I will always love you."

fourteen

There would be no discussion of the results from Luke's meeting with the studio executives. Nor would there be any mention of the death of *Second Harvest*. Quinn's small group of friends knew the drill. Keep the conversation light and the alcohol flowing when it was party night. No business talk on party night. Ever.

"You've got that glow about you, Davi," Sarah remarked. "I don't know what you use, but it works. You look incredible."

Sarah, Quinn's longtime friend and studio mom, was close to Davi in age, beautiful and always well dressed. She looked after Quinn's wardrobe and makeup. Quinn trusted her with all of his secrets. Besides Davi, she was the only woman who could answer the question, "boxers, briefs, or commando?"

"It's Cupid's arrow," Sue offered. "It's love pure and simple." She reached for Jake's hand and squeezed it.

"I thought it was the mind-blowing sex," Quinn teased as he kissed Davi on the cheek.

"I'm waiting for that arrow to hit me full-on, just like it hit the two of you," Luke said with a hint of longing.

"Good luck with that," Davi teased. "I think Cupid might have used all of his ammo on me to get me to fall for Quinn. He may not be back in action for a while."

Quinn laughed. "I wasn't that hard to fall in love with, Davi. I don't recall you putting up much of a struggle, especially on our first date. You were very agreeable to sleeping with me."

"That's because I thought you were a one-night stand. I didn't have anything to lose. You were going to be history by the morning."

"Ouch! I don't remember it that way, but then love has a way of softening the memory."

Luke joined the conversation. "You are such a liar, Davi. You were in love with him by the next day. Both of you were crazy about each other. There's no way you were treating Quinn as a one-night stand. No way. You aren't that kind of person anyway." Luke took another sip from his beer.

Davi laughed. "I'm glad you think so highly of me, Luke. But really, Quinn started as a one-night stand. Think about it. Hollywood heart-throb hits on an older woman on a plane. She thinks he's bored and is just amusing himself. What does either one of them have to lose by hooking up? If Quinn hadn't asked me out that night, my life would have gone on. It was no big deal to me."

"But he did ask you out."

"And we had a fantastic time."

"Were you planning to have sex with him? Davi, you wouldn't!" Sue teased.

"Only if he initiated it," Davi said, smiling back at her friend. "I wouldn't have been so bold."

Quinn chuckled.

"What's so funny?"

"I have such a different recollection of that night. It was romantic. We talked about everything."

"Especially sex."

"With some sex. You always bring sex into the conversation, but you came onto me. I remember it quite well, Davina Stuart Thomas. You seduced me. You talked about sex, you tasted me, you smelled me, and then you squeezed my package to make sure I had what you wanted. I initiated nothing. It was all your doing."

Davi leaned back against the back of her seat. She smiled mischievously at Quinn.

"You grabbed his package?" Sue and Luke asked together.

Jake laughed, enjoying his wife's keen interest in his friends' love life.

"I wasn't going to waste my time if he didn't have what I wanted," she answered lightly.

Everyone looked at Quinn.

"It's true. Davi made it quite clear. If she didn't get great sex, she was moving on."

Luke groaned. "Talk about pressure."

"There was never any pressure, man. I knew I had what she wanted."

"You two are unbelievable," Sarah said, wagging her finger at the two of them. "You talk as though your relationship is all sex. There's more to it than that!"

"Of course, there's more to us than sex," Quinn said. His tone now filled with emotion. "The sex is just the fun part. You know that I can't settle unless I know where Davi is. I can't go to sleep at night unless her voice is the last thing I hear. I can barely leave her side. That's why I had to marry her. I couldn't go on with my life until she was a permanent part of it."

"But you went over the top. I don't know of anyone who fell so hard for a woman so fast before," Luke said.

"Blame it on Cupid's arrow. It has pretty strong stuff on it."

"I don't know if anyone would get the same jolt as you. You two are one of a kind."

"You'll get the jolt, Luke. Wait and see."

XO XO XO

Davi and Quinn returned to their hotel suite in high spirits. It was good to see their friends and laugh again.

Quinn went to the kitchen and poured himself a scotch. Davi walked over to Quinn's music collection and looked through the compact discs until she found what she was looking for. She popped the disc into the player and turned the volume up. It was a compilation of love songs, all slow dances.

Davi held out her hand to Quinn. "Dance with me." She smiled sweetly at him.

"Are you trying to seduce me?" he asked as he took her in his arms and started to dance with her.

"No, I'm not. I just wanted to dance with you. We get very few opportunities to dance, and I thought now would be perfect. We've come back from a nice evening out, and neither one of us is tired. Or maybe you are tired."

"I'm never too tired for you." Quinn pulled her in closer.

Davi could hear him inhale her scent. Immediately, she could feel his arousal push against her.

"I was only asking you to dance with me."

"You always make me hard, love. I have no control over that. I thought you'd be used to it by now."

"And I thought you'd be so used to me by now that that wouldn't happen."

Quinn's hand touched her chin and tilted her face up so that he could gaze into her eyes. "I hope I never get used to you. Your scent and the feel of you next to me drive me crazy. I only have to be in the same room as you, and I want you."

"We can't do anything without sex getting involved, can we? You say I always talk about it, and you're always thinking about it."

"That's why we're so good together. We're always up for it, any way you look at it."

Davi snuggled into Quinn's chest. She loved the feel of him. The way he held her tight when he danced with her. He made it all too easy, loving him. They could joke about it all they wanted, but there was nothing more important to them than each other.

It was getting late, but neither one minded as they held each other close and moved to the music. The songs blended into each other. Quinn sang along with each melody as though they were his love songs to Davi.

"You have a beautiful singing voice. I could listen to you forever."

"I only sing for you. I think your ears are biased, love."

"No, they aren't. You could make it as a singer. You really could."

Before Quinn could answer, his phone rang. Quinn looked at the call display. His tone immediately changed for business. "Luke."

Davi listened to the silence as Luke did the talking, and Quinn answered with the occasional "yes."

"No. I agree. That's the best way to deal with it. What figures did they give you?" Quinn laughed. "Assholes." He kissed the top of Davi's head. "She's Davi, truly amazing. She's fine. Yes, I know." There was silence for a moment. "They want me, huh? Tell them thanks but no thanks. I've given it some thought, and it's not the right fit for me. We'll talk about it later. I'll see you and Jake at eight. 'Night."

Quinn held Davi close and continued to dance. Davi waited as long as she could, but the silence pricked at her. Finally, she stopped dancing, making Quinn stop with her.

"What?" he asked, as though he had no idea what she wanted.

"Out with it. Nothing was mentioned about the meeting all evening. Now Luke calls you, and you act as though nothing's happened. What's going on, Quinn Thomas?"

"You're a millionaire, Davina Thomas."

"I know that. I was one before I met you."

Quinn smiled. "Now you've got more millions."

"How? I gave up all rights to the book. The studio doesn't owe me anything."

"So they led you to believe, but Luke found a loophole. You'll have five million in your bank account by the end of the week, and *Second Harvest* will happen if they stay true to the book."

Her knees buckled as the image of five million dollars flashed in front of her eyes. If she hadn't been in Quinn's arms, she would have been on the floor by now.

"I don't believe it," she stammered. "Why would they . . . Why would you do this?"

"I didn't do anything. I told you. It was all Luke."

"But, he works for you. Why, Quinn?"

Quinn gazed down at her with serious eyes. "No one messes with my wife and gets away with it. That was your story, yours and Ross's and your kids'. They had no right to change it and make it about us. What we have is ours, not to be shared with anyone."

"You had your heart set on that movie."

"You'll write something else for me. I know you will." Quinn kissed Davi softly on the lips.

"What else? You left something out."

"Oh, that. I turned down the part for that sex movie—you know which one."

"Why? I thought you wanted to do it?"

Quinn shook his head. "I thought about it and realized that there is only one woman who gets to see all of me, and I'm married to her."

"It's supposed to be a blockbuster."

"Maybe, but it's not for me. Another actor can show his ass to the world."

Davi hugged Quinn. "Thank you."

"You don't have to thank me. However, if you want to show your gratitude, there's something I would like to try with you."

"Fluffy handcuffs?"

"Something better."

fifteen

Davi loved waking up to the smell of freshly brewed coffee. She stretched then ran her hands over her belly, feeling for her baby bump—it was there.

"Good morning, Jack," she whispered.

She got out of bed and headed to the bathroom. Steam from the shower filled the room. Davi smiled as she thought of Quinn enjoying his simple pleasure of hot showers. Davi wiped the mirror so she could see herself. Other than bedhead after a night of lovemaking, she didn't look too bad. Was it the sex, the baby, being in love, or a bit of everything? Whatever it was, Davi felt younger, maybe even looked it, too. Davi made use of the bathroom while Quinn showered.

Davi slid the shower door open. "Do you want company?"

"I've been waiting for you."

Quinn pulled Davi into the shower. The water was warm. Quinn had turned it down just for her. He greeted her with a kiss and an erection.

"Been waiting long?"

"Long enough to wonder if I'd have to look after this if you didn't hurry up."

"You poor man, what did you ever do before I came along?"

"Suffered."

Quinn picked up Davi as she wrapped her arms around his neck. Quinn guided himself into her.

"Did you sleep well?" Davi asked.

"I always do when you're with me. I got up early and went for a workout. No one was in the gym. It was great." Quinn moved slowly inside Davi. He would take his time this morning. "It's going to be a busy weekend. I may not get the chance again."

"And you want to look buff for Kimmy," Davi teased.

"She's married, you realize."

"Married women lust after you too, husband. You're a forbidden fruit now. You're irresistible to all women, single or married."

"As long as I'm irresistible to you, the rest don't matter." Quinn nuzzled Davi's neck and kissed it.

Davi sighed as she tingled from where Quinn's lips touched her. She moved her face to meet his. "Kiss me."

Quinn kissed Davi softly, but she kissed back hungrily. She wanted more from him.

Quinn pulled back to gaze at Davi. "Are you in a hurry?"

"Suddenly, I find you irresistible. Maybe it's because I'm married." She smiled playfully at him. "Just do it. You know what I want."

Quinn laughed. Davi's readiness for him always amazed him. Quinn braced Davi's back against the shower stall wall as he held her tighter. His thrusts increased as Davi kissed him hard, devouring him. Her moans vibrated through him as her legs gripped him harder around the waist.

Quinn broke free from her kiss. "Damn. I can't stop."

They clung to each other as they climaxed together. Silence enveloped them as the shower's warm water ran over them. Quinn was the first to move as he released her.

Davi sighed. "I don't want to let you go. I like it here."

"Me, too, but we're going to look like prunes if we don't get out of this shower." Quinn kissed the top of Davi's head. "Hurry up, love. We don't have much time until the troops arrive."

Quinn opened the shower door and stepped out while Davi finished her shower. She enjoyed hearing Quinn humming while he shaved. Davi realized that there was no fear when she awoke this morning. She had forgotten the darkness.

Quinn walked into the bedroom to get dressed, while Davi went to the kitchen to get them both a coffee. When she returned, he was wearing black jeans, a form-fitting black turtleneck sweater, and a leather jacket.

"Very nice," she said as she passed him his coffee. "Kimmy will fawn over you this morning."

Quinn laughed. "You are so wrong on this. I've been on her show before. She didn't fawn over me. She was very polite."

"She will fawn over you, and she will lament the fact that you got married, and then she'll want to know what possessed you to marry finally. She won't be able to help herself. I will be watching you. I can't wait to see what happens."

"Would you care to bet on this?"

"I don't have to bet on this. I know I'm right."

"Ten bucks, Canadian or American, I don't care."

"No."

"Come on. I know you've got the money," he teased.

Davi shook her head and smiled. She couldn't resist those baby blue eyes gazing at her. "It's a deal. Kimmy fawns over you and bemoans you getting married."

"And I bet that she's full of congratulations and best wishes. There will be no fawning. No bemoaning."

Davi kissed him to seal the pact. "You're going to lose. It's like taking candy from a baby."

Davi dressed while Quinn made them breakfast. Sarah arrived in time to join the couple for coffee.

"David Paul should be here any minute. He is excited about this. Your wedding photos were great promotion for him. Everyone's knocking at his door, wanting his designs. What you wear these next couple of weeks will be the icing on the cake."

David Paul was an up-and-coming designer whose menswear Quinn admired. When Quinn asked David Paul to design Davi's wedding gown, David Paul jumped at the opportunity. He also designed Davi's bridesmaids' dresses along with the men's tuxedos.

"What about your shiner?" Sarah asked casually. "Are you showing it off or covering it up for Kimmy?"

"What did Sue say?" Quinn asked knowingly. Sue would have made sure Sarah would know what to do.

"No to the cover-up. Everyone's already seen it. Tell Kimmy Davi hit you."

"What?" Davi choked on her coffee. "She wouldn't say that!"

Quinn laughed. "She's joking, love."

"Sometimes, she's one sick girl."

Quinn's phone rang. He looked at the display. "Jake's here. It's time to go. Have fun this morning, ladies."

Quinn pulled Davi in tight and kissed her good-bye. He could hear Sarah sighing behind him.

He released Davi and turned to his friend. "Would you like a kiss, too?"

"You won't give me what she's getting, so what's the point? Just hug me and let me dream."

Sarah held out her arms to Quinn. He hugged her then kissed her lightly on the lips.

"Bye, ladies."

"Bye, sweetie. Have fun with Kimmy," Davi said as she waved good-bye. "Quinn and I have a bet going. We'll have to watch the show," Davi told Sarah once Quinn closed the door.

"Tell me more."

"I said Kimmy would lament the fact that he's married. He says it won't happen. That's about it in a nutshell."

"What's the bet?"

"Ten bucks."

"You two! You couldn't think of anything better?"

"It was his idea, and besides, I don't need or want anything that he doesn't already give me." Davi smiled at Sarah.

"Give me a break," Sarah groaned.

There was a knock at the door. David Paul and his assistants had arrived. Davi opened the door, only to be immediately hugged and kissed by her favourite designer.

"Davina Stuart, you are more beautiful than the last time I saw you, if that could be possible." He stood back and examined Davi. "Bare feet? They look good on you. Nice shade of red."

David Paul moved to the side while his assistants entered, pushing a clothing rack between them. They stopped in the middle of the living room then pulled off the protective cover.

"They're beautiful," Davi remarked when she saw the magnificent gowns and dresses hanging on the rack.

"Of course they are, but we have to find the perfect match for you. What underwear do you have on?"

"Strapless bra and thong. I thought that is what you would want. No straps and no panty lines."

David Paul laughed. "Why do you know what to wear when others more famous show up for a fitting without wearing the proper underwear or no underwear at all? I don't understand women of today."

"I don't know if I'm a woman of today, David Paul."

"Nonsense, you are my woman of today. Now undress."

David Paul clapped his hands and waited for the assistants to hand him the first dress from the garment bag. "I think you'll look great in short dresses, Davi, but you'll have to wear a few gowns. We'll get them over with first."

David Paul looked at Davi's tummy and stared. Davi noticed his stare. Could he see her bump? Quinn hadn't noticed, and nothing ever escaped him.

"I'm pregnant. There isn't much of a bump showing. I hope it doesn't change things for you."

David Paul smiled. "Maternity wear? I've never thought of that. You are opening so many doors for me. I am thrilled. You'll have to keep me up-to-date on how big your bump is getting. I'll have to make adjustments along the way. Sarah, you can send me her measurements."

Davi kissed him on the cheek. "You are a sweetheart."

Davi stepped into the first dress.

"Very nice," commented Sarah. "Not too flashy."

"We don't want flashy for Davi. We want style. Anyone can have flash, but not everyone can have style. Davi has a definite style." David Paul had Davi turn around. "It's good, but not great. I'm glad we started with this one. Now I know which ones are for you." David Paul went to the rack and brought Davi the next dress. "This is the style for you."

Davi looked at her watch. She had fifteen minutes before Kimmy started. Sarah, noticing this, turned on the television, set it to the right channel, and then muted the volume not to disturb David Paul. He didn't miss a thing.

"What are you doing?"

"Quinn's on Kimmy in fifteen minutes, and Davi promised to watch him. I hope you don't mind. I'll keep the volume down until he comes on."

"Is he going to be talking about you, Davi?" he teased.

"I have no idea what Quinn will say. I'm more interested in what Kimmy has to say. I have a bet with Quinn. I know I'm going to win."

"I won't ask what it is. We'll watch it together, shall we? In the meantime, put this on."

Davi slipped into the dress. It was an off-the-shoulder gown that accentuated Davi's long neck and cleavage. It flowed gracefully over her curves down to the floor. It was off-white but in no way resembled a wedding gown. Davi looked like royalty.

Sarah smiled her approval. "It's simply breathtaking. Davi, have a look."

Davi walked over to the floor-length mirror in the foyer. "Oh my, David Paul, I love it!"

David Paul circled Davi this time. She watched his expression reflected in the mirror. He was smiling proudly.

"I remembered your body perfectly. Not one alteration is needed. Keep your jewellery simple. Sarah, you know what we need?"

"Yes, I think I brought the right pieces with me." Sarah opened her large tote bag and pulled out a velvet-covered box. Inside were sparkling sapphire earrings and a pendant necklace. "They match both your eyes and Quinn's. I think they'll be a staple for a while," Sarah said as she put the jewellery on Davi.

David Paul looked at Davi. "What do you think?"

"I love it, but you have the final say. It's your dress I'm wearing."

"Is she always this agreeable?"

"I think so," Sarah said as she removed the jewels from Davi then put them back in the case. "I'll turn up the volume. It's coming up to nine."

The assistants helped Davi take off the dress while David Paul waited with the next one. "This one is for fun. It's short, but not too short. Your derriere is covered. I wouldn't want to embarrass you."

"What can I wear this to?" Davi asked, admiring the sparkling cherry red dress she now wore.

"Anything. It suits you perfectly. You'll wear a long dress in LA, but the other appearances won't be as stuffy. You can wear whatever you like. Sarah will help you decide."

The Kimmy show started. Kimmy opened with her usual banter with the audience. She wouldn't get to Quinn for ten minutes. Davi had time to try on more dresses. They timed it perfectly, adding the last dress to Davi's wardrobe by the time Quinn's interview with Kimmy began.

Davi dressed then sat on the sofa between Sarah and David Paul. His assistants hovered around them, trying to look busy.

"Quinn Thomas is here." The audience cheered wildly. "I heard he was in town, and I had to have him drop by before he starts his tour, promoting his latest movie *Lovestruck*. So please welcome Quinn Thomas."

Quinn walked onto the stage, looking his usual heartthrob handsome self. Davi smiled as she heard the two assistants and David Paul sigh.

"I see he washed with his usual gorgeous soap this morning," Sarah said, amused.

"He had a very long shower this morning."

"That explains that smile then. Good going there, Davi."

David Paul admonished them. "Ladies, please."

Quinn hugged Kimmy.

"Now, before we start to talk about your movie, I have a bone to pick with you, Quinn Thomas," Kimmy said once they took their seats on the sofa.

Quinn took her hand and gazed into her eyes. A collective sigh escaped from the audience.

Quinn's voice was low and lusty. His Hollywood charm in full gear. "Did I do something wrong?"

"Three months ago, you were on this show, and you said you weren't dating anyone and that you were going to stay a bachelor for a very long time. I was devastated the day I heard you were engaged. And then, just like that, you're married, and you and your wife are expecting a child."

A flicker of surprise crossed his face. "But you're married," Quinn said slowly. Then he smiled at Kimmy playfully. "You fantasize about me, don't you?"

Kimmy blushed. "How do you know that?"

"Davi told me. She says women will want me more than ever now. I guess being married makes me more attractive." Quinn took Kimmy's hand in his. "I'm so sorry, but I had to get married. I found the love of my life, and I couldn't lose her. I had to marry her right away." Quinn gazed into Kimmy's eyes. "I won't mind if you still fantasize about me. You can have fun with me. Do anything you want."

Davi could see Kimmy melting under Quinn's gaze. His baby blues had her right where he wanted her. The audience went wild. Kimmy didn't move.

"Do you think she's going to talk about the movie, or is she going to stare into his eyes for fifteen minutes?" Sarah asked.

At that moment, Quinn's gaze moved from Kimmy to the television camera. He winked.

Sarah laughed aloud. "What the hell was the bet?"

"No fawning or bemoaning. Just congratulations. Kimmy didn't think of him that way."

"Does he not know anything about women?"

"Nothing."

David Paul silenced them again.

"Tell us about your movie, Quinn."

Quinn gave the usual spiel but made it sound genuine. He enjoyed making this movie. They showed the same clip from the film that premiered on *Olivia* four days ago.

Once it was over, Kimmy continued her interview. "So you're married."

"Very happily married."

"To a famous writer, Davina Stuart. Where is she right now? Does she ever leave the farm?"

"Davi's in New York with me. She's watching the show right now. She would have come with me, but she had an appointment."

"She's watching the show?"

"I'm sure of it. She's probably laughing at me as we speak."

"Why would she be laughing at you? That doesn't seem very nice."

"Oh, she has every right to laugh at me. I can never get things right where she's concerned. No, I take that back. It's not where she's concerned. It's where women are concerned. I know nothing about the female sex."

"Did you ever know anything about women?" Kimmy asked with interest.

"I thought I did. I thought I knew everything, and then Davi came along and wiped the slate clean. I know nothing."

"Is that why you have a black eye?"

Quinn laughed. "This is what you get when you rebuff an enamoured cow. I said no, and she tossed me over her back. I kid you not. One of Davi's cows did this to me. There is no spousal abuse."

"Did you get hurt?"

"Only my pride."

"I want to talk to Davina. Can we phone her?"

"Oh, oh," Sarah moaned. "You're about to get a phone call, and I wonder what she wants to say to you."

"Will you phone her, Quinn?" Kelly handed Quinn a studio telephone. Quinn smiled and dialled Davi's number.

Davi picked up after the first ring. "Hello, Davi Thomas speaking."

"Hello, Davi, this is Kimmy."

"Hi, Kimmy. Hi, Quinn. What's up?"

Quinn smiled warmly into the camera. "Hey, Davi, Kimmy wants to talk to you, and I think you know why."

"I'm sorry I couldn't make it to your show this morning. I had a morning appointment for dress fittings. We just finished so that we could watch your show."

"Who is your designer, Davi?"

"David Paul. I love his dresses. He's watching your show with me." David Paul kissed Davi's cheek for saying his name on live television. "Did you have a question for me, Kimmy?"

"Did you hear what your husband said to me earlier—that I should continue to fantasize about him?" Kimmy asked, feigning indignation.

"Yes, I did. Quinn's a cheeky devil, isn't he? But that's why we all have a big crush on him. Go ahead, Kimmy, he's all yours."

"How can you say that? What kind of woman wants other women to fantasize about her husband? What kind of woman lets her husband tell other women to go ahead and fantasize about him?"

"If fantasizing about him makes you happy, gives a boost to your love life, puts that little bit extra in your step, go for it. It's harmless, and it's normal. Fantasies are private. I don't need to know what your fantasy is or what any woman's fantasy is when it concerns Quinn."

"Do you have fantasies?"

"I used to, but they've been put on hold indefinitely."

"What's that supposed to mean?"

"I've got Quinn. He's all I need right now."

"Was he your fantasy?"

"He was a fun fantasy. Nothing I ever expected to become real."

"I want to have you on this show, Davi Thomas. I want to talk to you about how you got this man and find out your secrets."

Davi laughed. "I have no secrets. I didn't get Quinn. He wasn't a prize to be won. He chose me. You can ask him why. He's the better storyteller."

"Aren't you the writer?"

"Yes, but when it comes to us, Quinn tells the story best. He's the romantic. He makes you believe everything he says."

"You mean it's not the truth?"

"No, that's not what I'm saying. Quinn makes you believe that the impossible can become possible. That's why he's such a great actor. You should be talking with him."

Kimmy got the signal to cut to a commercial.

"Davi, when you come back to New York, you and I are going to talk, okay?"

"I'd love to. It's been great talking with you."

"My producer is telling me I've gone way over the time limit, but I don't care. I think the ladies wanted to hear you. I know I did. We'll finish up with Quinn, so he doesn't feel bad."

"Thanks. I appreciate it. Give Quinn a hug and a kiss for me?" Davi hung up the phone. Sarah and David Paul stared at her. "What?"

"You took that interview away from Quinn. Kimmy ignored him."

"That wasn't my fault. Let's wait and see what happens after the commercial."

The show came back on.

"Davi had to go," Kimmy explained to her audience. "Our producer was getting upset that she was getting too much airtime." The camera showed the audience booing. "Don't worry. She said she'd visit us when she comes back to New York. Do we invite Quinn, too, or is it just his wife?" Kimmy listened to the voice coming from her earpiece then answered her question, "It's just his wife."

Kimmy took hold of Quinn's hand. "Do you have the same effect on her as you do on the rest of us?"

"Yes and no. We're just two people who fell in love. Does her heart skip a beat when she sees me or hears my voice? You'll have to ask her. But I can tell you that she's my life. There's no one else for me. She's it."

"So what's next for you in terms of your work?"

"The usual press junkets, movie premiers, and television appearances. However, what I'm most looking forward to next is Jack. It's a Davina Stuart and Quinn Thomas production."

The audience cheered as Quinn beamed proudly.

"Jack? What a great name. So you're having a boy."

"We have no idea, but we call the baby Jack."

Kimmy thanked Quinn for being on the show. She hugged Quinn and kissed him on the lips. Quinn pulled her in close, then smiled when he released her. Kimmy blushed. The show cut to a commercial.

"Thanks so much for coming on the show, Quinn. I know it wasn't the interview you were expecting."

"It was a great interview and fun. Thanks for inviting me and calling Davi. I know she was thrilled."

"I did mean it when I said I want her back here for an interview."

"Oh, I know it. She'll be here."

Quinn waved to the audience then walked off the stage. Luke waited for him in the limo.

"What the hell happened in there?" Luke said excitedly. "No guest stays on for that length of time. You were supposed to be in and out. Ten minutes tops."

"It's Davi. Everyone wants to talk to her. Kimmy wouldn't let it go. I'm the tagalong, Luke, and it feels great."

XO XO XO

Sarah turned off the television. "What is it with you two, Davi? I've never seen a show like that before."

"I don't understand it, Sarah. They're crazy for us, and I don't know why."

David Paul patted Davi's hand. "You're too close to it to see it. They see your love, and they want it, too. You make them believe in true love. It's as simple as that."

"But I wasn't even on the show!" Davi rose from the sofa to get herself a drink of water.

"It doesn't matter. The audience heard your voice and saw Quinn's reaction to you. It was there. They want to know how you do what you do to him. They want the magic."

Davi sighed. "There is no magic. Everyone says there is, but there isn't. It's just us."

"That's the magic of it, Davi. You are the magic."

Davi's phone rang. "Hey, Quinn, nice show."

"It was all you. You're the star."

"So I've been told."

"We're running late. Do you mind getting our gear together and meeting us at the limo? Jake says we'll be there in fifteen minutes at the latest."

"Okay. See you then." Davi turned to her company. "We have fifteen minutes before he'll be waiting for us downstairs."

David Paul's assistants already had Davi's dresses and Quinn's tuxedos packed in travel garment bags.

"We'll let you get ready. Have fun in California," David Paul said before he kissed Davi good-bye, then trailed after his assistants and the clothing rack, exiting the suite.

Sarah went into the kitchen, turned the coffeemaker off, and started to clean up. "Get yourself ready, Davi, do whatever you have to do. Just bring Quinn's travel bag with you."

Quinn had it made. He only needed his travel bag filled with a few toiletries, scripts for reading, and earphones. He had two identical hotel suites, one in New York and the other in LA, and now the farmhouse, all fully stocked with his clothing.

"Are you sure he has everything?"

"Yes, but I keep a set of his clothes and shoes with me, so I don't have to stress about it. The last thing I need to think about is whether he has the right shoes or a pair of black socks to wear with his tux."

"He gets the royal treatment, doesn't he?"

"He pays for it, but he's worth it. There aren't too many stars as easygoing, Davi. He loves to get dressed up, but it's not who he is. He picks his designer then lets me look after everything else. He trusts me to look after him and do my job. The same goes for you. He trusts me to make sure you're taken care of."

"So, do you carry around clothes for me, too?" Davi asked, intrigued.

"I will, starting tonight. Pantyhose, underwear, shoes—whatever you may need in an emergency, I'll have it waiting for you."

"I can do that myself."

"I know you can, but you'll be with Quinn, so I have to be in the background looking after you. Now, get ready. You've got five minutes."

Davi ran into the bedroom. She changed out of the thong underwear. Socks and boots were next, and then she changed from a T-shirt to a turtleneck sweater to wear under her leather jacket.

"I'm ready," Davi announced when she came out of the bedroom with her luggage and Quinn's travel bag.

"You are fast. You and Quinn make a good team."

Sarah and Davi made their way down to the hotel lobby to find Quinn waiting for them. His eyes sparkled as he gave Davi a broad smile.

"Hey, lover, did you have fun with Kimmy?"

"I had an excellent morning. It cost me ten bucks, but it was worth it." Quinn handed Davi a ten-dollar bill then kissed her. "I don't know what I was thinking doubting you."

"You weren't thinking. That was the problem. You'll know better next time." Davi tucked the money into her pocket.

"There won't be a next time. No more bets."

Sarah snorted. "Chicken."

"I'm not a chicken if I know when to quit while I'm ahead. My wife knows everything, Sarah. She's on a roll. No more going against her."

"Chicken," Sarah called out as she exited through the lobby doors, heading towards their waiting limo.

XO XO XO

Guy Tremblant watched from across the street, parked in a black Ford SUV. Through his camera lens, he noticed that Quinn Thomas had extra security. Guards were stationed at the hotel's entrance and around the limo. He recognized the face of the man who opened the door for the passengers. He was the one who had tricked Guy, the one who dropped him with a left hook. Guy wouldn't get fooled again. His right hand felt the inner pocket of his jacket. Next time, he'd get the drop on him.

Once again, Guy Tremblant found out Quinn's schedule from a fan's website. Quinn's itinerary for the week was posted online before getting deleted after fifteen minutes. Guy laughed when that happened. Someone's head was going to roll for that gaff in security.

Guy followed Quinn's limo from the television studio to the hotel and timed it. Quinn would be using this route when he returned to New York in two days. The added security guards would be a bit of a problem, but Guy could see around it. He always saw a way around problems.

XO XO XO

Maggie watched the Kimmy show and laughed for the first time in weeks. Seeing Quinn's face on television, his happiness, and his love for Davi in his eyes made her a bigger fan of his. To hear Davi's voice so happy and confident—Maggie prayed the darkness would stay away.

sixteen

When they arrived at the airport, Jake got out of the limo first and checked out the crowd.

Luke whistled through his teeth as he peered through his window. "Look at the size of the crowd. Did Sue plan this?"

"No. Of course not." Sarah said, shocked that Luke would even think it.

Police were everywhere, trying to hold the crowd back. Fans were desperate to get close to the limousine and get a glimpse of the famous couple.

Quinn pulled Davi in close. "Don't wave or acknowledge them. Not yet. Wait until we're secure, or else all hell will break loose."

A black security van pulled up beside their limo. Davi watched as eight burly men got out of the vehicle and then took their positions around the limo.

Jake opened the door and poked his head inside. "Don't even think about stopping and shaking hands or signing autographs. We are getting you checked in and getting you past security as quickly and as safely as possible. Everyone understand?"

"Yes," the foursome chorused before he allowed them to exit.

"This is another one of the things about Hollywood I don't like," Davi whispered in Quinn's ear as he hooked a protective arm around her waist and walked with her, holding her tight against his body. "Two weeks, then I'm home."

Quinn didn't answer her. She was right. For the first time, he truly feared for their safety.

A wide roped-off passageway waited for them. Police and airport security lined both sides, holding people back. The crowd yelled to get their attention. Davi didn't know where to look. Signs of "We love you Quinn and Davi" were everywhere. Davi saw one "I'm *Lovestruck* for Quinn Thomas." Davi pointed to it and smiled. "Me, too!" she mouthed.

In an instant, a man pushed past the security guards and scrambled towards Davi and Quinn. His hands outstretched towards them with something shiny reflected in his right hand. Quinn saw him coming. Instinctively, he pushed Davi behind him to shield her from the attack. At the same time, Jake and two of his security guards moved to tackle the man.

"Quinn," Davi screamed as memories of Guy's attack on Quinn hit her hard and fast. Her legs weakened, and her heart pounded as fear coursed through her body. She fainted as the darkness took her down.

"I've got you," Luke said as he caught her in his arms. "Quinn's fine."

"Get us the hell out of here," Quinn yelled as he snatched Davi from Luke and cradled her limp body in his arms. "Jake, get us the fuck out of here now!"

XO XO XO

She heard the murmuring of voices and felt the warmth of a familiar hand and a soft kiss on her forehead. Davi knew the kiss—Quinn was safe.

"Davi, can you hear me? Davi, please open your eyes, love."

"I'm okay," she said as her eyes slowly flickered open. "What happened?"

"Some idiot tried to get your autograph." Quinn's voice was soft, but she could still hear the anger he tried to hide.

"Did he have a copy of my book with him?"

"What? No, he had a pen."

"He should have known I only sign my autograph if it's in a copy of my book." She smiled up at Quinn.

"Don't joke about this. Something bad could have happened to you. I'm so sorry." He kissed her softly on the lips.

"I'm the one who's sorry. I don't faint, Quinn," she said as she struggled to sit up. "I don't know what's going on with me."

Quinn opened his mouth to speak.

"Don't you dare say it's my hormones," she warned him.

He swallowed the words as he tucked a stray strand of hair behind her ear.

"Where are we?"

"In a private lounge. There's a doctor here to check on you."

"I'm fine. I don't need—" Davi stopped when she saw the concern in his eyes.

"We can't board the plane unless he gives you the go-ahead."

"I need my junk, Quinn. You know I can't travel without my junk."

Quinn smiled. "It's right here." He held up a bag from the airport magazine shop. "How could I forget?"

XO XO XO

"So what happened after I passed out?" Davi asked Quinn once their plane was in the air.

"It's all a blur to me. I don't know."

"Quinn, you have a photographic memory. Whether you want to tell me about it or not, you remember every detail."

"I was terrified, Davi. I thought that you were having a miscarriage. I didn't let go of you until the doctor came to check you out. You scared the hell out of me."

"I was terrified something was going to happen to you. All I could think was that Guy—"

Quinn squeezed her hand. "Don't think of him. He can't hurt us. It was just an idiot trying to get an autograph."

"This time," Davi said softly.

"Tell me about this morning with David Paul," he asked, eager to change the subject. "What are your dresses like?"

Davi's eyes lit up. "We had fun this morning. He remembered my measurements perfectly. He's excited about the baby, and he's looking forward to designing maternity clothes for me. He's such a sweetheart. Anyway, the dresses are fabulous. One is a gown, and the rest are short dresses. David Paul said I needed a long dress for tonight, and then I could wear whatever I wanted. I have the legs for them."

"I could have told you that." Quinn stroked Davi's thigh. "Tell me about them."

"No, I'll surprise you. You deserve a good surprise today."

Quinn wouldn't argue with her. Jake warned him that today's occurrence at the airport was only the beginning. New York was the easy airport for managing security. They'd have more guards waiting for them in LA, but there was no telling what waited for them there. LA was known for its craziness in many ways.

"Nice move with Kimmy this morning, telling her it was okay to keep fantasizing about you doing whatever she wanted."

"I thought you'd like that. I know she did."

"You were so smooth, so Hollywood."

"But, she didn't know that. That's all that matters. You're the only one who can tell the difference between Hollywood Quinn and regular Quinn."

"There's nothing regular about you." Davi smiled then kissed him softly on the lips. "I prefer to think of you as being Hollywood Quinn or my Quinn. That's where the difference lies. My Quinn gives me what no one else gets. You."

"Only you."

Quinn cupped her face in his hands. His blue bedroom eyes sizzled as he gazed into her eyes. "There's something that I'd like to give you now if you want it."

"I was just going to ask you for it," Davi replied with a voice low and sexy.

"I've never done this before."

"Really? I'm the first?" She licked her lips teasingly.

He was hard for her, and seeing the tip of her tongue as it slid across her lips made his cock jerk in anticipation. "Yes."

She placed her hand on his thigh and caressed it. "I can see you're excited."

"Oh, I am."

"I'm surprised you lasted this long. You don't like to wait."

"For you, I'd wait a lifetime."

She licked her lips once again, taking her time as she ran the tip of her tongue over the bottom lip. "It's been torture waiting for you to give it to me, husband. What took you so long?"

"We've only been in the air for thirty minutes," he said as he caressed her cheek. "I thought we would wait. We have the entire flight to have sex."

"Sex? Who's talking about sex? I thought we were talking about my junk. I need my licorice, Quinn, and I need it now." Her luscious lips formed a naughty smile.

Their eyes locked for the longest moment. Davi had done it to Quinn again, sucked him into her sexual fantasy, then left him high and dry.

He chuckled and shook his head. "You are wicked, love."

"And you are always thinking about sex." She kissed him on the lips then promised, "Later."

Quinn reached for his carry-on bag and pulled out a plastic bag filled with Davi's junk. "Here you go. Sarah got it for you."

Davi smiled and opened the bag with excitement. Quinn couldn't help but think how the little things gave her so much pleasure—a good cup of coffee, a cold shower, and junk food. If these were all she ever needed, he'd be a happy man.

XO XO XO

As Quinn slept beside her, Davi finished reading her celebrity magazines while enjoying her red licorice. She spent ten minutes on the crossword on one of the magazines' back pages and chuckled when Quinn's name was one of the answers. *He's made it. My man's finally made it big.*

Davi put the magazine away. She had the feeling of déjà vu. She turned off her music, slowly took her earplugs out then turned to look at Quinn. He was staring at her and smiling.

"You caught me," he said. "I hope I didn't disturb you, but I was enjoying watching you work. You're very sexy when you're reading."

Quinn recited the first sentence he used to romance her when they met on a plane nearly three months ago.

Davi's heart skipped a beat. It was the same reaction she had the first time she heard him say those words.

She smiled and said, "I've heard that line before. Some Hollywood stud tried it on me a few months ago."

"Really? Well, he stole it from me, the bastard." Quinn winked at Davi. "Did it work? Did he get you?"

"I don't know what you mean by getting me, but I have his ring." Davi waved her ring finger in front of Quinn's face and smiled.

"Good for him."

"Yes, I'm very good for him. I'm quite the catch."

"I know you are." Quinn laughed and pulled Davi into him. "I love waking up and watching you. I do it every morning I'm with you."

"What do I do when I'm sleeping? Snore, drool, talk?"

"A bit of everything, but when you talk, you say my name. That's the best part of all."

"I'm glad it's not the snoring or drooling that you prefer. Did you have a good sleep?"

"Yes, and I dreamed of you. I saw you in various dresses, each one shorter than the first until you were eventually naked. You wore heels, too. Five-inch heels."

"Was I naked in public?"

"No, at least I don't think so. That's not the point."

"What is the point?"

"You were giving me later."

"Oh. Was it good?"

"It still is."

Davi looked down at his bulging crotch. "No. Change the channel, stud. It's not happening."

"Please, don't make me beg."

"When have you ever had to beg?"

"There's always a first time."

"Kiss me then. Give me my kiss, and let's see if it works on you like it does for me."

"Ah," Quinn sighed as he leaned closer towards Davi. "If only it would."

"Think about me in that dress and those shoes. Let me do the rest, stud."

She moved into his embrace, tilting her chin to meet his kiss. His mouth covered hers. His tongue pushed past her lips, allowing their tongues to touch in a soft mating.

Davi moaned as his right hand rested on her lower back and pressed against it. She didn't know why his touch in that particular spot sent intense shivers of pleasure through her body. She didn't care. Davi's hand reached instinctively for Quinn's hair. Her fingers ran through the short strands, tugging at his scalp. Quinn tensed as his scalp tingled, sending a shudder down his spine. His balls ached. She was doing it to him. Her scent filled him, her taste made him want to swallow her whole, and now her touch was pulling at him. She touched his head, and his cock responded. Her nails scraped across his scalp, causing sharp tingles to course through his body. He felt himself harden more, the ache for release tearing at him. He was close to orgasm. It couldn't be, but he'd be damned if he stopped kissing her now. Davi shifted in her seat, her body pressed against his. He could feel her tense, then quietly moan her release into his mouth.

Quinn cursed quietly against her lips.

He thought of Davi in a short red dress and black stilettos. The garment barely covered her ass. Those long legs, the ones he loved to caress, the ones he loved to have wrapped around his waist, pulling him in deeper. He was nearing his climax, and she still wasn't touching his cock. Quinn Thomas, Hollywood heartthrob, was about to come in his pants, and he didn't care. He hadn't done this since he was a teenager. Hell, he'd do it every day if it felt like this. Ecstasy and torture—Davi gave him what she had promised him in his fantasies and what she promised him now.

"Damn." He tensed, unable to stop his release. He cleared his throat in an attempt to block out the sound of his orgasm.

Their foreheads touched as they separated from their kiss. "Davi," he whispered. "What did you do?"

"I kissed you. Sorry it took me so long to learn how."

"You realize I've just jizzed in my pants."

"And?"

Quinn sat back in his seat and looked down at his crotch. "Excuse me," he said as he got up and headed for the lavatory.

"What's Quinn up to?" Luke asked, keenly interested as he stood by Davi's seat.

"Washroom," Davi answered as she reapplied her lipstick.

"Mind if I take his seat? I need to speak with him."

"He's all yours," Davi said happily as she got up and moved to sit in Luke's vacant seat. "Hey, Sarah, how's it going?"

Sarah smiled at Davi. "Good now that you're here. Luke never stops working. I don't know if I had a real conversation with him. Not once did he take his eyes off that damned laptop."

"Sometimes, I think he's married to it. They can do that in California now. Marry their electronic devices. I'm sure I read it somewhere in one of my magazines. It was the article right after how to lose thirty pounds in a month. I'm keeping that one for after Jack arrives."

"You won't need that."

"After the fourth baby? I'm sure of it. I gained forty with my third. I kept the weight off until the end of the second trimester then it all packed on. It took a year to lose it. I don't want to even think about what's going to happen with this one."

"Every pregnancy is different. You'll be fine."

"I know. I just want Jack to be healthy. I don't care about my weight gain or anything else."

Sarah squeezed Davi's hand. "He will be, or she will be. It's hard not to think of Jack as anything but a boy. You two are messing with us."

"Blame it on Quinn. He came up with the name, and it stuck."

"How are you? You scared us at the airport. Quinn was beside himself with worry. He thought you were having a miscarriage."

"When I saw that man come towards us, I thought of Guy Tremblant, and it must have overwhelmed me. I passed out."

"He put you through the wringer, that's for sure. Quinn mentioned the possibility that you might need help. You should think about it, Davi. Both of you should."

Davi knew that Quinn didn't keep secrets from his friends. They were his gang of seven who supported him, the ones who knew him as a regular guy first.

"We will after we get through the next two weeks. If I don't get any better, I promise I will see my doctor right away. I don't like being afraid, Sarah. I don't like fear having control over me."

"Promise?"

"I promise. Now tell me about Quinn. What was he like before I met him?"

"I'm sure he's told you everything."

"I want your version, Sarah."

"Which version would you like, the Hollywood or the truth?"

"The truth, please, and all of it."

Sarah waited while the flight attendant served them drinks. Davi didn't take her eyes off her while she waited to hear Sarah's version.

Sarah took a sip of her drink then exhaled audibly. "Okay. Here it goes. Quinn and I met during his first film. They usually gave me the newbies, so I could watch over them and let the studio know when I thought there might be problems."

"Like drugs?"

"Like drugs or alcohol, or they were just feeling a bit overwhelmed by it all. Not everyone has an easy time of it, Davi, and not everyone has someone to watch over them when they land their first movie role. I was like the studio mom. I watched over them and tried to give them advice and show them the ropes.

"Anyway, one morning, in walks Quinn Thomas. It's six in the morning, and he's the happiest young man I had ever met. He was young, charming, and gorgeous. My first thought was, 'Oh no, they're going to eat him up alive.' We talked, and he wanted to know about makeup and my job and my whole life story. He just asked questions, and I did most of the talking. I felt like I had found my new best friend. I had to hang around him most of the day for touch-ups and wardrobe changes, and he kept the conversation going. He didn't forget a thing. I kept asking him if he needed to look over his lines, and he'd say he knew them. And he did. He'd get called in for a shot. Walk on, do his part amazingly well, then come back and sit with me while he waited for them to call him back."

"That's Quinn."

"Yes, that's Quinn. He told me later that he had a photographic memory and knew his lines instantly. The first day was rather slow for Quinn, so we had lots of time together. He didn't tell me much about himself, though. He said there wasn't much to tell. He was an only child, didn't have many friends, and chose acting over medicine. I could tell right away that he was smart, but he didn't advertise it. He didn't show anything of what was underneath the looks. He had to let you get close to him to see that part of him. The girls hovered around him. Anyone could see that he had that heartthrob look, and after the first movie, we all knew he was a star. The man could act."

"He didn't get eaten alive then?"

"No. Not even close. Quinn's smart—he can read people. He knew right away who to trust and who to avoid. He kept the same friends from way back. It's our gang. We keep him grounded, and he wants that."

"How did you get to stay on with Quinn? I thought you worked with the newbies?"

"Quinn and I got along great, and I think he wanted me to be around him. Not like a studio mom, but as a friend. He felt comfortable with me and trusted my opinions. So when his next film came up, he asked for a customized trailer and me. He got his trailer and joked that I came with it. We were a package deal, and we've been together ever since."

Sarah took Davi's hand. "I'm not going to lie. He had plenty of women. In a way, it was expected of him, and he couldn't ignore them. But he wasn't happy. He was always looking for that one true love. So almost a year ago, or is it more than that? Anyway, one morning, he walked into his trailer and said he had finished with dating. No more starlets or women he met in bars. From now on, Quinn would wait for the woman of his dreams, his true love. At first, I laughed at him. We all did. No way would Quinn Thomas give up sex, that was impossible, but he did."

"How do you know that? Did he tell you everything about his sex life?"

"Davi, I knew everything. I was his confidant. It's hard to keep secrets from someone who sees you naked every day. He'd tell me about his dates and give me details when they ended up badly, and that was most of the time."

"Why did they end up badly?"

"He must have told you this. You knew he'd been celibate for over a year. He told me he told you that."

"I want to hear your version."

"He wanted someone who loved him and not his name. He hadn't found her until he met you."

Davi closed her eyes and put her head back against her headrest. It was challenging to imagine Quinn waiting for her. She pictured him, all six foot, three inches of him, built like a Greek god, oozing sex and yet choosing celibacy over meaningless sex.

"Was he that miserable?" she asked, turning to face Sarah again.

"Yes and no. In front of the camera—no. Off-camera—yes. Quinn stuck to himself. He did the celebrity promos, but he wasn't into it, and having to have a starlet on his arm just ate at him. But he put on his Hollywood face, and no one was the wiser."

"I could tell. Quinn looks uncomfortable in all of his photos. He didn't like having anyone in his personal space."

"You saw that?"

"Yes, before I ever met him. He looked like he wanted to be left alone. You couldn't see it?"

"I thought I was the only one. Being alone was hard on Quinn. We all made a point of being with him. Jake was great. He was around Quinn almost every minute of the day and had him over to his place all the time. We started our weekly nights out, spent as much time as we could with him to keep him happy, but he wasn't." Sarah stopped and smiled.

"He's behind me, isn't he?" Davi turned and looked up. "Would you like something?"

"You are a much better flying companion than Luke. He only talks business. He needs a life. Maybe I should fire him so he can go find one."

"I heard that," Luke said from behind Quinn. "Davi, we can trade places anytime. I know when I'm not wanted."

"Thanks for the chat, Sarah, even though it was short." Davi got up out of her seat. Both men stood back to let her through.

Quinn sat in his seat and turned to smile at Davi.

"What's gotten into you?"

"I can't help it. I'm excited. I have you with me. We're doing the Hollywood thing, and I'm looking forward to it for the first time. It's going to be great, Davi. I promise you. We're going to have so much fun. It will be a night to remember."

seventeen

The foursome made their way through the arrivals gate with their luggage. Sarah had a firm hold on Davi's garment bag. Nothing was going to happen to David Paul's designs.

"Remember. No stopping. Security wants us out of here," Luke reminded them as the doors opened and the waiting mob started to scream.

Quinn's security team met them immediately, forming a cocoon around the foursome. Davi did her best to smile, but this morning's episode put a damper on her spirits. Quinn gave them his best Hollywood Quinn, but underneath, he wanted out of there fast. The crowd was the largest Davi had ever seen, perhaps twenty people deep on both sides of the security tape lined up out the doors of the airport. Airport security and police kept the crowd a safe distance from the foursome.

"Incredible," Davi said to no one in particular.

"Remember the good old days, Quinn, when you were free to come and go as you pleased? I think those days are over." Luke chuckled, impressed by the attention his friend was getting.

The foursome made it to their waiting limo.

"Hey, Ben," Luke said excitedly, acknowledging Quinn's head of LA security.

"What the hell have you been up to, Quinn?" Ben asked as he ushered the foursome into the limousine.

"It's Davi," Quinn answered as he put his arm around her shoulder. "Everyone wants her."

"Lucky you, Davi."

"Thanks," she deadpanned.

Luke looked at his watch. "We'll be cutting it close. You'll have maybe twenty minutes to get ready before Quinn's press interviews and Davi's magazine interview. Quinn, you'll be in Ballroom A. Davi, the interview will be in your suite. I'll stay with Davi, and Sarah will go with Quinn."

"How long does an interview take?"

"However long you want to give them. This one we've allotted thirty minutes, but you can go longer if you want. It all depends on your comfort level. If you want to quit, just give me the signal. Don't worry, Davi. I'll be there to guide you."

"Davi will be fine." Quinn squeezed her hand. "She can think on her feet. I wish I could be there with you for your first interview. I'd like to see how you interview with the press because you do so well with television." Quinn's eyes were sparkling. Davi could tell he was genuinely excited for her.

"Now you're making me nervous. How much longer before we're at the hotel?"

"Five minutes."

"Do you think I could get out and walk for a bit?"

"No," Ben answered with authority.

"Thinking of escaping?" Quinn asked her.

"No."

"What is it then?"

"Personal space. I need a few minutes."

"Without me?"

"Without anyone." Davi looked out the window. She needed five minutes without anyone to talk to her, no distractions and no Quinn.

The limo pulled up to the hotel. Security had cleared an entrance for them. Quinn and Davi's fans lined the sidewalk and driveway. Quickly, they exited the car and made their way into the hotel. Luke and Sarah headed for the elevator. Davi headed for the stairs. Quinn caught up with her and grabbed her by the arm.

"Davi, this isn't a good idea."

"I'll be in the stairway. Do you think someone's lurking in there ready to attack me?"

"Anything's possible. Why are you making this difficult?"

"Please, Quinn, I need some quiet time."

"Will you let someone go with you then?"

Davi wanted to refuse, but she knew he'd feel better if she knew she had security with her.

"Fine. But, tell them to keep their distance. I want to be alone."

"What's the plan?" Ben asked when he came up to them.

"Davi wants to take the stairs without me. Will someone go with her?"

"Thirty floors?" Ben asked in disbelief. "You won't do that in twenty minutes, Davi."

"Give me ten minutes. Then we'll take the elevator up the rest of the way. I need some time to walk, Ben. That's all I'm asking for."

Ben signalled to one of the security men standing nearby. "There's no way I can take the stairs, but Curtis can. Curtis," Ben said to the man when he reached them, "follow Mrs. Thomas up the stairs. She has ten minutes and then takes the elevator up the rest of the way."

"Take my purse," Davi said as she handed it to Quinn. "See you at the top."

"I'll be waiting," Quinn said, smiling as he opened the door to the stairway for her.

Davi started to climb the stairs. She concentrated on each footstep and her breathing, blocking thoughts of anything or anyone else. She listened to the sounds of her footsteps and her breathing, ignoring the markings of the floor numbers. She didn't look back at the security guard following her. She knew she had ten minutes of uninterrupted walking.

Quiet, it's so quiet. I miss the quiet of home. Davi kept climbing. Her legs were starting to feel fatigued. *Good. Keep going.* Davi glanced at the door on the landing. She was on the twenty-fifth floor already. She picked up her pace, counting down each floor as she passed it. *Five, four, three, two, one.* Davi looked up to see Quinn sitting at the top of the stairs, waiting for her. The security guard stopped, staying a few stairs down from them.

"Davi, you're fast and in great shape. I knew you'd make it in time."

"Thanks for your confidence in me."

"How was your walk?"

"Quiet." She sat down beside him on the landing.

"Did I upset you?"

"No. I needed quiet, and I don't get that around you."

"I can be quiet."

"It's your energy, Quinn. It's everyone around us. I needed my time for me. I haven't had that in quite a while."

"You will soon. I promise."

Davi chuckled. "There you go again, making promises. How much time do we have?"

"Five minutes. We'd better hurry. Let's go."

Davi took his hand and walked with him to their suite to find Luke pacing the floor and Sarah waiting for them in their bedroom.

"The shower's on. Be fast. Quinn, your clothes are on the bed. Davi, I hope you don't mind, but I picked something out for you to wear. It's on the bed, too. You have five minutes. How are you going to do this?"

"Watch us." Quinn led Davi to the bathroom, where they undressed quickly. Quinn showered first, turning the water temperature down. Quinn yelled once the cold became too much for him. "It's all yours."

Davi stepped into the shower as Quinn walked out. Thirty seconds and she finished. Quinn had a towel waiting for her when she stepped out of the shower.

"I'll get dressed. The bathroom is all yours."

Davi knew Sarah would do her makeup, so she brushed her teeth then stepped out into the bedroom to find Quinn dressed and Sarah struggling to do something with his hair.

"Leave it, Sarah. It will look fine once it dries."

"What about your black eye?"

"Leave it, too. It'll give me something to talk about."

Davi dropped her towel and dressed in black slacks and a baby blue cashmere sweater. She shook out her ponytail and then ran her hands through her hair.

"Wow."

Davi turned around to find Quinn and Sarah staring at her. "What?"

"You're fast."

"I'm a mother. We learn to dress quickly. You told me five minutes. How much time do I have left?"

"Thirty seconds."

"Davi, we need to do your face. Sit down, please."

Davi sat on the edge of the bed, and Sarah began to work on her face.

"We'll just touch you up a bit. There. All done."

"She doesn't need anything, Sarah. I told you that."

There was a loud rap at the door. "Let's go!"

Sarah led the way out of the bedroom, with Quinn and Davi following.

"See you later, Davi."

"Have fun."

Sarah and Quinn left the suite.

Luke offered a seat to Davi. "Are you ready?"

"As ready as I can be."

"I've made decaf coffee. Let me know if you want anything. I'm here to look after you."

There was a firm knock at the door.

"Perfect timing. Your interviewer is here." Luke walked to the door and opened it. "Hi. Come on in."

Davi stood behind Luke.

"Hi. I'm Davi Thomas," she said to her as she held out her hand to greet the young girl.

"Hi. It's great to meet you. I'm Courtney." Courtney grabbed Davi's hand and shook it excitedly.

"Luke made decaf coffee. Would you like a cup?"

"No, thanks. But you go ahead."

Luke walked into the kitchen and returned with a mug of coffee for Davi.

"Where would you like to sit, Courtney?"

"Oh, right here is fine," she said, pointing to one of the armchairs. "I'll get out my notes, and we can begin." Courtney sat and pulled out a folder from her bag. Loose papers fell out over the floor. "Oh, shit. Oh, sorry," she stammered, flustered. "I had these all in order." She tried putting them back together.

Davi could see this would take a while and saw the interviewer becoming more upset.

"Here, let me help you." Davi took the papers away from Courtney and put them on the table. "I have a confession to make. You are the first person to interview me. I'm kind of nervous myself."

"Really? This is my first interview, too. I recently got hired by this website, and no one else was available to come here, so I got the job."

"Oh."

"Oh. I didn't mean it that way. We're a small independent website, but we're getting tons of great reviews because of our reporting. There is only one reporter, but she's down with the flu, so they had to send me."

"And what is your job?" Luke asked, irritated.

"I help run the website. I'm responsible for updating our file on Quinn and you right now, but I'd love to do some reporting. I did some for my college paper."

"So, were you going to write anything down?"

"Oh, I have a recorder. I planned on asking you questions and recording them."

"Can you remember your questions?" Davi asked.

"No. Not really."

"Okay. Why don't we do this? Press record, I'll start talking, and if anything comes to mind where you want to ask me a question, ask me. Later, you can read through your notes, and if there's something we missed, e-mail me, and I will send you my response." Davi took a sip of her coffee.

"Really? You'll do that?"

"Let's start." Davi began by giving a brief history of herself. "I was born and raised in the city of Toronto. I studied English and history at the University of Guelph, where I met my first husband. We married after graduation and ran the family farm together. We have three children, all in their twenties. I wrote *Second Harvest* shortly after my husband died from a brain aneurism. That's me in a nutshell."

"How old are you?"

"Forty-five."

"But you don't look forty-five. You're older than my mom, and yet you look years younger. Why do you think that is?"

"I don't know. Good genes? A healthy lifestyle? I don't know why. I'm just glad I do."

"What do you think of today's music? Do you listen to any of it?"

"Of course I do. I'll listen to anything once. I need a melody and lyrics that I can understand. I try to listen to what's new, but I've found that much of what's coming out are remixes of old tunes. Some of the remixes are good. The others are terrible."

"Do you have a favourite group or singer?"

"No one that comes to mind, but I'll let you in on a secret. Quinn's got an amazing singing voice. He sang to me at our wedding, and it was incredible. He sings to me at home, and I just melt. If he ever quits Hollywood, I would encourage him to try singing, maybe even Broadway."

"What about Quinn's movies?"

"I've seen them all but his last two, *Lovestruck* and *Untitled*. Tonight will be the first time for me at the premiere."

"Are you excited?"

"Yes, I am. I don't know what happens at premieres, so I'm looking forward to it. Quinn doesn't like to watch himself on the screen."

"Why is that?"

"It makes him uncomfortable. I think it's like watching himself show off and make a fool of himself at the same time. It's embarrassing. Although he isn't showing off, he's acting. And he doesn't look like a fool."

"Do you have a preference for what type of movie Quinn does? Romance? Action?"

"Good question. No, I don't have a preference. Quinn's very versatile, obviously because of *Smashed* and *Untitled*. I think Quinn can act in anything. It doesn't have to be the lead either. It just has to be a role with substance."

"You're doing some PR work for him?"

"It sounds like it, doesn't it?" Davi smiled thoughtfully. "Maybe I am."

"She'd be good at it, too," Luke offered.

"Are you his biggest fan?"

"If it's Quinn Thomas, movie actor, the answer is no. I know many out there would put me to shame with everything they know about him and his work. If it's Quinn Thomas, the man, the answer is a definite yes."

"Will you share any secrets or insider information on Quinn Thomas, the man?"

"I can't tell you secrets, but I'm sure there is plenty you don't know."

"Tell her about breakfast in bed. Quinn makes it for her every weekend," Luke piped in.

Davi looked at Luke and smiled. "It's true. Quinn makes an amazing breakfast. I can't tell you about it. It's a secret recipe. I don't want to tell on Quinn." Davi turned back to Courtney. "Quinn's amazing at crossword puzzles. I got him interested in them, and now he's always doing them. We work together on them now. Sometimes, he throws in a wrong word just to throw me off, but I've caught on to him."

"Does he cheat?"

"No, he's mischievous. He wouldn't cheat to win. He's just having fun."

"Do you have much time for fun? If Quinn's working most of the time and you're back on the farm, it doesn't seem like you get much chance."

"We have fun when we're together. We're always joking and laughing. There's always something to make us smile."

"What do you think of all of your press in the celebrity magazines? Sometimes, it's been quite cruel."

"They started cruel, didn't they, when they called me a cougar. I must admit that I used to read magazines and believe everything I read. Now I know that so much of what is published isn't true. That is why I've decided to make myself accessible to the press. I'd rather be interviewed and show myself as I am, warts and all than have someone make up something about my family and me."

"You said warts and all. Isn't that a bit naïve?"

"Maybe it is, but I like my warts. They're what make me me. We have to like being in our skin if we expect to be liked by others."

"Does Quinn have warts?"

"Yes, but they are the nicest you'd ever want to see."

"Can you describe them to me?"

"They're only for me." Davi drained her coffee cup. "I'd like a refill. Luke, would you mind?" She handed her cup to him. "Courtney? Would you like a drink?"

"No. I'm fine, thanks." Courtney looked at her watch. "The time went by quickly. It seems like we just sat down."

"That happens when you're relaxed and just talking, doesn't it? Do you think you have everything you need?"

"Oh, I know I do. Thank you."

"You didn't ask many questions about Quinn. Did you get enough information on him?"

"We wanted you. You haven't given an interview yet, and we wanted to be the first. I know our readers will love reading about you." Courtney stood and packed up her papers and recorder. She held out her hand to Davi. "Thanks so much. I enjoyed speaking with you."

"E-mail me if you ever want to talk with me. Good luck with your new job."

Courtney left, and Luke shut the door behind her.

"That was excellent, Davi. You did great in your first interview. How did it feel?"

"Great. I think I came across well."

"You did. I was impressed."

"We need to talk about Quinn's breakfast in bed. I don't think you should be mentioning it."

"Why, because it's a secret recipe? Will he be upset?"

"No, I don't think he'll be upset. Knowing Quinn, he'll think it's quite funny."

"So what's the problem then?"

"Quinn's breakfast in bed isn't food."

"It's not sex, is it?"

Davi smiled at him.

"You two are rabbits."

eighteen

Jocelyn Love, Quinn's costar, looked utterly bored as she sat and played with the charms on her Pandora bracelet. After the second question asked of her was answered with a blank stare, Quinn realized that his talented but troubled costar was once again high. Sometime during the short walk from Ballroom A to Ballroom B, Jocelyn took a hit of her latest drug of choice.

Quinn, always the gentleman, came to her rescue and answered the question. "I think it's fair to say that it's not as easy to date today as it was a generation ago. We don't have the large groups of friends, the town dances, and the opportunities that were so prevalent then. Today we rely more on social media and online dating to help us meet people."

The press, realizing that one of the two stars on the stage was unable to put two words together, politely ignored her and focused on the one who could answer their questions. The questions were the standard questions that anyone could answer.

"Yes, I think this movie applies to relationships of today. No, I don't think that the characters are unbelievable. If that were the case, I wouldn't have made the movie. Yes, it was a fun movie to make."

Then Quinn's face lit up, and everyone in the room took notice. They turned their attention to see what had brought on the change. Davi and Luke stood in the doorway, watching him.

She'd changed her clothing and now wore one of David Paul's designs. Quinn knew his style. The dress was short, safely covering her ass—just, and form-fitting, showing off every soft curve of her hot body. It was blue to match the sparkle in her eyes, her sinfully sexy eyes. Quinn worked his gaze down her long legs to her toes. Red toenails poked through black open-toed shoes with five-inch heels.

In an instant, his cock went painfully hard. His balls ached with the need to take her. Quinn didn't care about the others in the room. Davina Stuart Thomas was asking to get—

"Quinn?" Davi's voice called him back. "I'm sorry. I didn't mean to interrupt your interview. Please continue."

One young reporter looked up to the stage and asked, "Do you mind if we ask Davina some questions?"

"Not at all," the studio rep answered. "As long as they are related to the movie."

The rep waved Davi up to the stage. Quinn had barely recovered to stand to greet his wife. Davi walked up to him, kissed him softly on his lips, and then took the offered chair.

"Mrs. Thomas," he murmured in her ear, "it's so nice of you to drop by. You changed your outfit."

"Thank you, Mr. Thomas. I'm glad you noticed."

Quinn sat beside her, then took Davi's hand.

"Ask away," said the rep.

"Davina, what do you think of *Lovestruck*? Is it realistic?"

"To be honest, I haven't seen it yet. I've only seen one trailer."

"Why is that?"

"Quinn asked me to wait. The premiere will be our first movie date. I'm looking forward to it."

"Which trailer did you see?"

"The one where they are at the restaurant and Quinn's character is trying to persuade the woman to love him."

"What did you think of that? Is it realistic?"

Davi turned to look at Quinn then shook her head. "Yes and no. It is realistic because people are desperate to find love and try to find it quickly because they're afraid it won't come their way again. Quinn's character is desperate for this woman to love him, and he's trying everything to win her over. I don't know how the movie ends, but it seems to me like he's trying too hard. If you have to try that hard, maybe the person you want isn't worth it."

Quinn laughed. "That's the ending, Davi."

"Oh. Did I ruin it for anyone?"

"What's not realistic about it?"

"Oh, just that it didn't pertain to us. There was no trying. It just happened when neither one of us was expecting it. That's the way falling in love should be. You shouldn't have to work at it so hard, but I know people do."

"Would you say you have a storybook romance?"

"Oh, no, far from it!"

"What? Am I not your knight in shining armour?" His eyes were sparkling.

Members of the press laughed.

"I didn't need rescuing, there was no dragon or wicked witch, and I wasn't dreaming of you. You weren't in my story."

Davi heard the women gasp.

"It's true," Quinn said, coming to her defence. "Davi didn't need me. She wasn't looking for me. I was the one in need of saving. She's my lady in shining armour."

"Not many men would admit to that, Quinn," one of the female reporters commented.

"True, but they should. We need to admit when we need saving. Machismo won't get you very far if you're miserable inside and lonely."

"Was that you?"

"Most definitely."

"You hid it well."

"I'm an actor."

"You said you were miserable and lonely. Did you ever turn to drugs or alcohol? If you did, you kept it well hidden."

"And you think I'd admit to having a problem now?" Quinn chuckled. "No, sometimes I may have drunk too much, but never did I turn to drugs. That's no way to deal with problems." Quinn looked at his costar, who was still staring at her bracelet. "Davi's my drug of choice. She's all I need."

"We need to wrap this up, folks. Any more questions for Quinn or Davi?"

"Davi, now that you're married to Quinn, do you think the way you see him in movies will change or stay the same?"

"I honestly don't know. I enjoy watching Quinn's movies. I don't feel jealous when I watch the love scenes because I know that what we have is different and special."

"What about his latest movies? Will you be as open-minded?"

"We'll have to wait and see. If I do find it to be a problem, I'll have to deal with it."

"How?"

"These are all what-ifs. If I can't watch my husband on the silver screen anymore, I'll find another actor to watch. It won't be a reflection on our personal life, only our Hollywood life."

"I know who that will be," Quinn said under his breath.

"Okay, that's it, folks. Thanks so much," the studio rep announced, eager to bring the interview to a close.

Quinn stood up and put his hand on Jocelyn's shoulder. "Jocelyn, it's time to go. Where's your manager? Is there someone here to look after you?"

"No. I sent her away. She was getting on my nerves."

"Wonderful. Let's get you to your room. Do you have a key?"

"It's in my bag. Room 222."

"Good. Let me help you up." Quinn helped Jocelyn to her feet. "We have a detour before we head back to our suite," he said to Davi.

"I see that. What can I do to help you?"

"Take her purse. And I'll try to get her to walk with me." Quinn waited for Luke to reach them. "Care to offer an arm?"

Both Luke and Quinn helped Jocelyn walk to the elevator, where Sarah waited for them. Not one word was said as they entered the elevator car then travelled up to the second floor. The elevator door opened, and Sarah led the four to Jocelyn's room. One swipe of the key and they were inside. Luke and Quinn deposited Jocelyn on the bed, and then Davi took off Jocelyn's shoes and covered her with a blanket. Quinn dropped the key on the bedside table.

"Let's go."

They exited the room as silently as they had entered it.

Davi couldn't stay quiet another minute longer as they waited for the elevator to arrive. "Why wasn't anyone with her? Doesn't she have a handler or something?"

Quinn bristled at her comment. "She's not an animal, Davi."

"You know what I mean. You have Luke and Sarah with you. She has no one."

"She does have people, but she sent them away. If they were smart and doing their job, they would have been hanging around to get her back to her room. But they're pissed at her, so they've left her on her own. She won't remember how she got back to her room. Her group will take the credit for it, and they'll keep their jobs. That's how it always works with her."

"That's sad."

Their elevator arrived, and the topic on Jocelyn finished as the doors opened for them.

"How was your interview? I couldn't stop thinking of you," Quinn asked as he held the doors for the women to enter the elevator car.

"I think it went well. It was the first time for both of us. The interviewer was filling in for their journalist who was sick."

"It was amazing," Luke joined in. "Davi was relaxed. She put both of us at ease. The two of you make it seem effortless for an interview. You talk. Good job back there with the press, by the way. You're reeling them in. They love you."

"Next time, make sure we've got a cast for the press to interview. It makes it tough if it's just me. I didn't make the movie on my own, and we can't have Davi coming to the rescue. We're going to burn her out in no time."

"I didn't mind."

Quinn placed his hand on her waist. "Thank you." Quinn looked at his watch. "How much time do we have?"

"Three hours. You have time to take a break, get something to eat, and then get ready."

"Sarah, give us an hour, then we'll have something to eat. Will you look after it?"

"Sure. I'll order the usual."

"Luke, go do whatever you do. Pick up your girlfriend, and we'll see you in the limo. I'm going to spend some time with my wife." The elevator doors opened, and Quinn whisked Davi out before Luke had time to answer.

"That was rude," Davi said with embarrassment as Quinn pulled her into their suite.

"No. It was the truth. We'll see Luke in three hours. Sarah will be at the spa for an hour. She always does that. Come with me, love. I have plans for us." Quinn locked the bedroom door behind them.

"What brought this on?" Davi asked, feigning surprise as Quinn started to kiss her.

"You did when you walked into the ballroom wearing this. I got an immediate hard-on. It was torture making it go away." His mouth left a hot trail of kisses down her neck to her shoulder.

Davi shuddered. "It's one of David Paul's. Do you like it?"

"I dreamt about this dress. It was the last dress you wore before you were naked."

"So I picked the right one then," she said, smiling. Her eyes closed as she enjoyed the attention. "How did you get rid of your hard-on?"

"I can't remember," he said as his hands found the zipper to her dress.

"Liar. You don't forget anything." Her breath hitched as he nipped her left nipple.

"It's a trade secret then. I can't tell you, or else I'd have to kill you." He traced a path to her right breast with his tongue.

"You're killing me now, stud," she gasped as his fingers touched her between her legs.

He'd done it again. Davi stood naked before him, wondering how he'd managed to get every article of clothing off her without her feeling it. Quinn went down on his knees. His hands gripped Davi's hips as he continued to kiss a trail down to her belly.

"Close your eyes and your ears, Jack. Daddy's going to make love to Mommy."

"I don't think he can hear you. And why would he have to close his eyes?"

"You never know what we might get up to."

Quinn's mouth moved to Davi's sex. He kissed her softly then used his tongue to play with her. Davi moaned. Her hands took hold of his shoulders and held on tight.

"I love it when you're wearing heels," he said, his breath a soft caress. "Your legs go on forever."

"I only wear them for you, stud. You know how much I love my boots."

She lost her train of thought as his hot kisses and expert tongue made her mindless from pleasure. His fingers, oh, those fingers. Davi arched her back as she felt them enter her. His fingers stretched her, played with her, and tormented her. Davi writhed against the intensity.

"That's it, Davi, come for me."

She shuddered as her orgasm coursed through her. Her nails dug into Quinn's muscled shoulders as she stood on her toes in a feeble attempt to move away from him. He didn't let her go. His mouth worked hungrily, tasting all of her.

"Quinn," Davi cried out.

Quinn stood up in one fluid motion and took Davi in his arms, carrying her to their bed. She watched him with heavy-lidded eyes as he stripped quickly. She reached out to him. He fell into her arms, pressing her body against the mattress. Davi didn't mind his weight on her as she wrapped her legs around him, pulling him tight against her.

"Hurry."

Quinn winced as Davi's five-inch heels dug into him. He pushed back, supporting his weight on his forearms. "I'm not one of your bulls, love. I'm not going to go faster if you dig your spurs into me."

"I don't have bulls on the farm. You're my only stud, and you will go faster if I want you to." She dug her heels in one more time.

"Damn it, Davi!"

Davi kissed Quin hard. She found his ears, grabbing onto his lobes and held tight.

Quinn groaned as her nails dug into the fleshy part of his ears. Her scent filled his head and her taste. She was doing it to him again, pulling him in, making him love her the way she wanted. And he would because he belonged to her, heart and soul.

Davi's heels dug in one more time as she cried out. Quinn bucked against her as they climaxed together, fast and explosive.

Quinn collapsed onto Davi, thoroughly spent. "I'm going to have scars," he complained as Davi caressed his back.

"Then don't take me to bed with heels on, stud."

"I like the heels."

"So do I."

Quinn rolled over, pulling Davi with him. She cuddled into his chest and was soon fast asleep. Quinn closed his eyes but didn't sleep. He fantasized about his life with Davi and their baby. He smiled as he imagined them as a family. His heart longed for the day it became real. He couldn't wait. *Hurry up and get here, Jack. Daddy wants you here.*

"Food's here. Come on, you two!" Sarah called out to them as she knocked on their bedroom door.

Quinn kissed the top of Davi's head as she slept in his arms. "We have to get up. Wake up, rodeo queen."

Davi stretched then laughed as she realized she still had her shoes on. "I died. I must have been tired to crash like that."

"Bull riding's a tiring sport, even for the bull."

"Did you sleep at all?"

"No. Jack and I just daydreamed."

"What did you two do?"

"We dreamed of our life with mommy. We played at the park."

"I'm jealous."

"Don't be. You can daydream with us next time."

Sarah banged on the door. "I'm coming in there if you two don't get out of bed, and I mean it."

"Sarah has things to do, and so do we. Let's not keep her waiting," Davi said as she wiggled out of Quinn's arms. "Coming," she shouted back to Sarah.

Quinn and Davi walked out to the kitchen, wearing their bathrobes. "Everything's ready. We don't have much time."

"Quinn said you went to the spa. How was it?"

"One hour of heaven. A forty-five-minute massage with aroma-therapy and then a scalp massage. It de-stresses me before I have to get Quinn ready. I love it."

"So you do it every time?"

"For about five years now. I started this after Quinn forgot to bring his clothes with him. Now I look after everything, and he repays me by giving me an hour of spa time before every outing."

"Only an hour?"

"That's all I can afford, Davi. The woman is very expensive to keep on the payroll." He winked at her.

Sarah laughed. "You get off so easy, Quinn. You don't know how lucky you are to have me."

"He knows, Sarah. And I do, too." Davi took a bite of her salad. "This is delicious. How did you know what to order?"

"Tradition. You'll know it all soon enough. We can't have the tummy too full before going out. Otherwise, the bathroom breaks become a nightmare. Don't nibble the designer-style finger food, and stay away from all seafood. Cheese and crackers or something veggie is always good. The alcohol will be flowing. You won't have a problem with that, but Quinn will. Keep his hands occupied, so he's not drunk before the movie starts."

"That won't be happening this time. I have Davi with me. I don't need to drink."

"You'd get drunk? How bad?"

"Not bad, but Sarah objected to my wandering hand."

"I didn't mind the wandering hand, Quinn. It gave me a thrill. It was the ladies you hooked up with afterwards that I objected to."

"Don't tell me. I don't want to hear it."

"And we're not going to talk about it, are we, Sarah?"

"No. Because we know it won't be happening ever again." Sarah looked at her watch. "Davi, your hair is fine. Just get a shower, and we'll get you ready. Quinn, I forgot your ugly soap, so you'll have to make do. Your clothes are in your closet. Davi's dress is in the other bedroom. Davi, come out here once you've showered."

"She's a drill sergeant, but I love her." Quinn got up and kissed the top of Sarah's head. "Mrs. Thomas, your shower awaits you." Quinn pulled back Davi's chair and offered her his hand.

"Does he do this at home?"

"Yes. The gentleman never turns off. I love it."

"Go. I'll be waiting for you."

"You first," Quinn offered as he turned on the shower. "Do whatever you have to do. I'll want to stay in longer."

Davi put her hair back into a ponytail. She rummaged through her toiletry bag until she found a razor, just in case she found some errant hairs and her perfumed soap.

"You shave?" asked Quinn.

"The chest, remember? Once I started drinking scotch, I haven't been able to keep the hair from coming back."

"Right. I forgot about that. Need any help?"

"No, thank you." Davi stepped into the cold water. Quickly, she inspected her body for stray hairs. She soaped her body, rinsed, then stepped out of the shower.

"Amazing," remarked Quinn. "No hair, I take it?"

"None. It's all yours. Enjoy." Davi wrapped her robe around her wet body.

Quinn grabbed Davi and pulled her in close. "There's something else I would rather enjoy."

He kissed Davi longingly. Davi kissed him back. Her hands instinctively went for his ears, pulling him in closer.

"I knew you two would be at it if I didn't come in here. Quinn, let your wife go. We have to get her ready."

Quinn released Davi from the kiss. "You did notice that she had hold of my ears. It wasn't all me."

Davi laughed. "Get in the shower, Quinn, before she kills you. I don't want to be a widow again."

Quinn dropped his robe and stepped into the shower without checking the water. He howled as the cold water attacked his skin.

"Sorry!" Davi called out to him, smiling at her forgetfulness. "Just let me brush my teeth, Sarah. I didn't make it to the sink."

Davi raced to the sink and started to brush her teeth.

Sarah stood in the doorway, watching her. "Have a quick pee, too. I don't know when you'll get the chance again."

Sarah left Davi and waited in the bedroom for her.

"All done," Davi announced as she walked into the bedroom. "What's next?"

"Follow me, madam." Sarah led Davi to her bedroom. She had her makeup and hairstyling equipment set out and ready to go. "Sit," she commanded Davi as she pointed to a salon chair.

"Very professional," commented Davi.

"That's me. Now let's get that hair done."

With quick hands, Sarah brushed out Davi's hair and had it into an instant updo. Davi watched with fascination as Sarah's expert hands moved quickly, pinning every hair into place.

"So what did you two get up to this afternoon, or should I even ask?"

"I slept. I was exhausted. I find I need more sleep now that I'm pregnant. As soon as my head hits the pillow, I'm out."

"I don't think it's that fast," Sarah teased.

Davi smiled at Sarah. "After that, my head touches the pillow, and I'm fast asleep."

Sarah stood back from Davi.

"Wow."

"Not bad for someone who came with the trailer, huh?" Sarah chuckled.

"You have an amazing talent, Sarah."

"I do, don't I? Makeup time. Close your eyes."

Davi sat humming to herself while Sarah worked on her face.

"I know that tune," Sarah said. "Quinn sang it to you at your wedding. I cried like a baby."

"So did I."

"Mouth closed, please."

Davi felt the brushes on her face and Sarah's cool breath as she blew specks off the skin.

"Open, please. How do you like that?"

Davi looked at herself in the mirror. "How did you do that so quickly?"

"You have your magic, and I have mine. You're not hard to do. You're beautiful all on your own. Show me your nails." Davi raised her hands. "Good, they're still perfect. Are you ready for your dress?"

"Yes. I'm excited."

"Me, too. Quinn's going to love this. Everyone is going to love you in it."

Sarah walked to the closet and took out the dress while Davi put on the underwear laid out for her. Davi stepped into the dress as Sarah helped her with the zipper.

"Oh, my," Davi said, seeing her reflection in the mirror.

The dress was more beautiful than she remembered, and she had only tried it on a few hours ago. The long dress hugged her curves, flowing gracefully to the floor.

"Put these on. I don't want you tripping on the hem." Sarah handed Davi her shoes.

"These aren't mine."

"They are now. Put them on."

The shoes matched the dress perfectly. "Do I ask where you found these?"

"They are the same style as the shoes you wore for your wedding. I knew they'd fit you, and they are comfy. They aren't donated, so you don't have to mention anyone's name. Just remember that the dress is by David Paul, and your jewellery is your own."

Sarah opened a velvet-covered jewelry box and removed two sapphire and diamond drop earrings. She handed them to Davi.

"These aren't mine." Davi hadn't seen these exquisite pieces before now. "I have sapphires. Not like these, though."

"These are yours, as is the necklace." Sarah moved behind Davi to help her with the necklace while Davi put on the earrings. "They're a present from your husband. They match your eyes and his perfectly."

"These are from Quinn?" Davi's hand went to her throat and touched the necklace.

"He doesn't know it yet, but he won't mind."

"Sarah!"

"Trust me." Sarah made sure she had everything for Davi before she let her leave the bedroom. "Here's your evening bag. It has everything you need in it, which isn't much—tissue, mints, lipstick, a bit of cash, and your phone. It's turned off right now. Have I forgotten anything?"

"I don't think so."

"Good. Go out and check on Mr. Gorgeous while I get myself dressed. I'll be ten minutes at the most. Don't let him mess with your hair or your dress. You are off-limits until you come back here for the night. I won't put up with any fooling around."

"Got it. Thanks, Sarah."

"You're welcome. Now let me get ready."

Davi opened the bedroom door and walked out to find Quinn sitting in an armchair, sipping a scotch. He was Hollywood gorgeous, and he was looking right at her.

"Davi, you look amazing," Quinn said as he stood to greet her.

"So do you."

Davi offered her hand to Quinn. He turned her around so that he could take in all of her.

"Very nice. I love the dress and the hair. Nice sapphires."

"Thank you. They're a gift."

"Oh? From anyone I know?"

"I'm told they're from you."

Quinn smiled. "She likes to spend my money. You'd think we were the ones who were married. Sarah does know my taste. I don't think I could have chosen better for you. They make your eyes sparkle."

"And yours, just by looking at them."

"It's not the sapphires. It's the woman wearing them."

"Will you kiss me?"

"Am I allowed? What did the drill sergeant say?"

"Don't mess with the dress or the hair. Sarah didn't mention my lips."

"Good."

Quinn held Davi gently and kissed her. Davi couldn't resist running her hands through his damp hair. Quinn's hand pressed on Davi's lower spine. Davi melted into Quinn as he gave her her kiss. She loved the taste of the scotch on his lips and his breath. Davi moaned as the pleasure ran through her body. Quinn pulled her in tighter. His arousal pressed against her.

"Ahem," Sarah said briskly to interrupt them politely.

Davi loosened her grip on Quinn's hair. Quinn responded by pulling her in closer. He wasn't going to let her go. He was enjoying this too much.

"Quinn!"

Quinn groaned instantly and released Davi. "I'm allowed to kiss my wife."

"But not like that, not now. Everyone is waiting for us downstairs." Sarah held out Quinn's tuxedo jacket to him.

Quinn shrugged on his jacket, adjusted his perfectly tied bow tie and then offered his arm to Davi. "Let's go, beautiful."

Luke and his date were inside the limo, waiting for them. Sarah got in first, followed by Davi and Quinn.

Luke made the introductions. "Everyone, this is Beth. Beth, this is Davi, Quinn, and Sarah."

"It's nice to meet you, Beth." Davi offered her hand. "Luke's been very secretive about you."

Beth shook Davi's hand. "Thank you. It's a thrill to meet you, all of you."

Quinn reached over and shook Beth's hand. "Beth, it's nice to meet you." He held back on his Hollywood charm, keeping his tone sincere.

Davi asked, "What time does the movie start? Is there a lot that goes on beforehand? No one's told me how this works."

"Well, normally, I arrive with a beautiful starlet on my arm. We walk the red carpet, wave to the crowd, answer dumb questions asked by the press, and quickly and quietly get drunk while everyone and anyone tries to get their picture taken with us. Then we go in and watch the movie for the millionth time, or we sneak out and start the party early."

"How nice," Davi drawled. "I could have stayed home."

"But tonight is the new normal, so it's even better. You'll be glad that you didn't stay home. You and I will walk along the red carpet, and we will answer dumb questions from the press. We will smile and wave to the crowd, and we will have our picture taken a hundred times, if not more. Then you and I will go inside, and everyone will want to talk to us so that they can go home and tell their friends that they got to see and talk to the real Davina Stuart Thomas in person. They won't even mention my name."

"That's not true. They'll mention you in passing," Davi teased. "Like, oh yes, her husband was there, too."

Quinn laughed as he pulled her in close. "Then we will go in and watch the movie, and for the first time, I will truly enjoy sitting through one of my films because I will have my wife with me. Tonight is our first movie date, you know."

"Although we have watched two and a half of your movies since we met."

"But they weren't dates. The first was torture, the second was foreplay, and the third—"

"Enough. Will you two promise not to talk about sex while I'm with you? Give it a rest," Luke said.

Sarah laughed. "Quinn, everything you do with Davi is foreplay. I can see you working on her. You never stop."

"That's because she's an iceberg, Sarah, cold and hard. It takes all day of foreplay just to get her to give in to me at night but by then, I'm exhausted, so nothing happens. We still haven't consummated our marriage. I could have it annulled anytime."

"Oh, give me a break." Luke groaned. "Don't listen to anything he says, Beth. These two are rabbits. They never stop. Davi won't have one baby—she's going to be giving birth to a whole batch of bunnies."

"Rabbits have litters, Luke. She'd be having a litter," Beth informed him.

"Does that mean we'll have to call the baby Jack Rabbit?" Davi laughed.

"Jack Rabbit Thomas. It has a bit of a ring to it. I like it. Thanks, Luke and Beth. You've helped us with Jack's middle name. It's a good thing Rabbit can fit a girl or a boy."

"Jack Rabbit is a boy's name, but Jack Bunny Thomas might work for a girl, then you could call her Bunny." Beth offered, enjoying the conversation.

"Don't encourage them, Beth. They don't need any help."

"Bunny? It fits with Tigger and Cat. It's something to think about," Sarah said happily.

"Cats and bunnies can coexist, too. My aunt had cats and bunnies on her farm. They were so cute," Beth said eagerly.

The limo stopped.

"We're here," announced Quinn, unable to hide his excitement. "Our first movie date, Davi."

nineteen

"Let me have one last look at you, Davi," Sarah said as she checked Davi's makeup. "Perfect." Then she turned her attention to Quinn. "No kissing your wife until you enter the theatre, got it? And don't pull her into your side. People want to see the dress and her body. If you pull her in, they'll think you're trying to hide something."

"Like what?"

"I don't know. Just don't do it, okay?"

"You haven't given me orders like this before," complained Quinn.

"You haven't been with Davi before."

"How do we do this?" Davi asked as she tried to hide her excitement.

"Here's how it works," Luke answered her, his voice steady and reassuring. "You and Quinn take the lead. Your groupies, that's us, hover behind you. Stop for photos at the marks on the carpet. You can't miss them. You can hold hands, wave, and smile. Talk to the reporters when they ask you a question. Quinn knows the drill. You'll be fine." The limo door opened. "Let's go, folks!" Luke waved them out the door.

Quinn got out first, then offered his hand to Davi. They stood beside each other and smiled at the cameras. The cheers from the crowd were deafening.

Quinn instantly put his arm around Davi's waist, and then he whispered into her ear, "I'll put my arm around my wife whenever I damn well please. David Paul won't care."

Davi relaxed, feeling secure in his arm.

"Lead on, Mr. Movie Star, I'm your tagalong now."

Quinn chuckled. "Sweetheart, you have no idea how much you're a part of this, do you?"

"Tonight is your night. I want it to be all about you. Let me be your tagalong tonight."

The couple stopped at the first mark and smiled at the photographers and cameras.

A reporter from one of the entertainment shows approached them first. "Davina and Quinn, how does it feel to see so many of your fans out here tonight?"

"It feels great," Quinn answered. "We appreciate their support."

Davi looked around her. She could only see blurred faces in the crowds that surrounded them on both sides of the red carpet.

"How many people are out there? Do they know?"

"Lots." Quinn chuckled. "You can read about the number tomorrow."

"Davi, over here!"

Davi looked to her left. The young woman who had interviewed her that afternoon stood with other members of the press.

Davi waved to her. "Hi, Courtney!"

"Quinn, are you excited about tonight?"

"Of course I am. It's my first movie date with my wife."

"What designers are you and Davi wearing tonight?"

"We're both wearing David Paul. He's our man in New York."

"And her jewellery? Those sapphires are dazzling."

"They're hers."

Quinn guided Davi down the carpet towards the theatre. They stopped for more photographs and questions as Quinn kept Davi by his side, never letting go of her.

A reporter stepped towards the couple. "Davina Stuart," he asked her, "when do you know you've found true love?"

Davi smiled. "When you see the love in his eyes—it's the eyes that tell us everything we need to know about a person."

"You mean Quinn's bedroom eyes?"

Quinn gazed down at Davi and smiled. His blue eyes were sizzling.

"It's more than that. But yes, I could see it in his eyes."

Quinn leaned down and kissed her. "I knew it the moment I saw you."

"I know you did."

The cast and director waited patiently for Quinn to make it to them for a group photograph.

"Where's Jocelyn?" Quinn asked, noticing her absence.

"No idea," one of them grumbled. "She's probably off stoned somewhere, as per usual."

"Crazy bitch," Tom Braden said as they readied themselves for the photographer.

Davi stood back and watched as the Hollywood smiles instantly appeared on their faces. She could see past Quinn's smile. It was in his eyes. She saw that look before when he helped Jocelyn back to her room. It was only natural for him to be concerned about his costar. Quinn wasn't as callous and thoughtless as his castmates.

"You're worried about her," Davi said to him once Quinn joined her.

"Yes, but she's done this before. No one thinks twice about her absences now. They expect it."

Quinn motioned to Luke, who stood close by. "Call the hotel and have someone check on Jocelyn. I'll feel better knowing she's okay."

"Sure."

Eventually, they made it through to the lobby. It was full of celebrities, movie stars, and entertainment executives, all out to support the movie and Quinn and perhaps get the chance to have their picture taken with Quinn and Davi. Davi saw a partitioned section filled with people waiting for admittance.

"Who are they?" she asked as she pointed to the group.

"They're fans who've won free tickets to the premiere. Radio stations and my website give away tickets throughout the month. It's my way of saying thanks for their support."

"We should go over and talk to them and thank them in person."

"Of course." Quinn guided Davi over to them.

The group went wild, screaming both of their names.

"Hey there! How are you tonight? Are you excited?"

The crowd responded with louder cheers. Quinn and Davi shook hands with whomever they could reach. They posed for pictures and signed autographs.

Luke approached them and whispered in Quinn's ear, "It's time to move on. It would help if you mingled elsewhere. Important people are waiting to meet you."

"No one is more important than the fans, Luke. Without them, you and I wouldn't be here." Quinn turned back to the crowd. "We have to go. Enjoy the movie. Let me know what you think of it. I check the website every day for your messages."

The crowd cheered as Quinn and Davi walked away.

"When do you have time to check your website?" Davi asked him, surprised that he had time for something like that.

"There's always time, Davi."

Quinn, Davi, and Luke stopped at a group of studio executives, the same group who had tried to rewrite Second Harvest.

"Gentlemen," Davi said, offering her hand.

"Davina," they answered, each one shaking her hand. "Quinn, Luke," they said as they nodded to the two men.

"Gentlemen," Luke and Quinn chorused.

"Our lawyers feel that we'll have this matter settled by the end of the week. There'll be no announcement until then."

"That's fine with us," Luke replied. "Quinn will act as though the movie's still a go."

"If you care to reconsider, you can always contact us."

"Thanks, but I don't think so," Davi answered for them.

An event photographer approached them and asked to take their picture. Instantly, smiles appeared as though the group was the best of friends. As soon as the photographer walked away, the smiles disappeared.

"If you'll excuse us," Quinn said as he gave them a thin smile and walked away with his arm around Davi's waist.

They arrived at another group. The photographer approached them and took more pictures with the couple giving their best Hollywood smiles. Then they moved on to the next group.

"Do we have to do this every time?"

"Yes." Quinn stopped a passing waiter with a tray of full drinks and took two glasses from the tray. "Here, Davi, hold this in your right hand so you won't have to shake any more hands, and I'll hold on to your left hand. There, we're covered."

"You are smart," Davi teased.

"No, just selfish. I will not share you with anyone else tonight. Come on, let's join the ladies."

Quinn led Davi to where Sarah and Beth were standing, drinking champagne and ogling the various male celebrities in the room.

"So, how are you making out?" Sarah asked knowingly.

"Everyone wants a piece of her. I'm not sharing Davi anymore tonight."

"You used to love the attention, Quinn," Sarah teased.

"Very funny."

"Did you know that Beth's an entertainment lawyer here in LA?"

"Is that how you and Luke met? Over business?" asked Davi.

"Yes. It's been good dating someone familiar with the business— the long hours, the craziness, and the Hollywood mentality."

"Why entertainment law?" asked Quinn.

"I was born and raised here. My parents were in the business. I wanted to practice law and be a part of this crazy world. I've always wanted to work here."

"The money's good, too."

"I'd do it for free some days. Sometimes, it's meeting the stars or the directors that gives me that warm and fuzzy feeling. I don't always get that with a paycheque."

"I like that," Davi agreed. "You've got the right attitude."

"Thank you."

The theatre bell started to chime.

"It's time to go in," announced Quinn. Davi could feel his grip tighten on her hand.

"Getting nervous?"

"No. I'm excited. I want to see this movie with you. It's the last one I made before I met you. It marks the end of that chapter in my life."

Davi looked up at Quinn. "No second thoughts?"

"None."

They entered the theatre. An usher led them to their seats.

"What happens now?" she asked once they were seated.

"Wait and see. Afterwards, we party."

Davi shared Quinn's excitement. Quinn hadn't told her anything about the movie. What she did know, she had learned from press interviews with Quinn. Today, she had guessed the ending, but she didn't know what happened to get there, so she was looking forward to watching it. Sarah sat on Quinn's left, and Beth was on Davi's right side.

"I miss the popcorn and the drink," she whispered to Quinn. "I like to keep my hands busy during a movie. Any suggestions?" she teased.

Without hesitation, Quinn took Davi's hand and put it on his crotch. "How's this?"

"Behave, please. I'll just hold your hand if you don't mind." Davi moved their hands away from Quinn's crotch and rested them on his lap. "Here, will do nicely."

Davi listened intently as the director of *Lovestruck* walked onto the stage and introduced the actors in the film. Quinn stood up and waved at the announcement of his name. Jocelyn Love was said to be under the weather and unable to attend. The director then moved on to the supporting cast, all of whom were on hand to take their bows. Without more fanfare, the director thanked everyone for attending and hoped that they enjoyed the movie.

The lights dimmed. Davi squeezed Quinn's hand. As the opening credits started, Davi gave her full attention to the movie, unwilling to miss one detail. She smiled as she recognized the movie's soundtrack. Quinn had put the songs on her cell phone. He knew more about the finished version of the film than he had let on. Quinn was full of surprises. As soon as Quinn appeared on the screen, there were cheers in the audience that were quickly hushed. Davi tingled from excitement. For the first time, she was watching her husband on screen. He was his usual Hollywood gorgeous with his thick shaggy mane of dark brown hair framing his chiselled face and famous baby blues. Davi's gaze moved down his body. There was no attempt to conceal the full pecs under his snug shirt nor the well-muscled legs covered by the tight faded jeans. *Lovestruck* would be another classic Quinn Thomas movie. Davi sighed, happy knowing he was hers. Her heart burst with pride.

Davi felt Quinn's hand tighten around hers. "Relax," she whispered.

As the movie progressed, there were a few scenes where out of the corner of her eye, Davi saw Quinn put his hand to his face, covering his eyes. She could tell he was embarrassed for his character. Davi was, too. His character put himself out there for romancing his love interest.

Jocelyn Love was phenomenal. They both were. Davi could see the connection between the two characters growing. It was so realistic that Davi thought it was happening. Maybe it did.

"You may want to close your eyes for the next scene," Quinn whispered to her in an urgent tone.

Davi chuckled, wondering why he would say that. It didn't take long to find out the reason. It was Quinn's love scene with Jocelyn. Davi heard Sarah groan.

What could be wrong with this? It's a romantic comedy, for goodness' sake.

Quinn's grip tightened on Davi, almost to the point of being painful. Davi kept her eyes riveted on the screen. She watched Quinn as he and Jocelyn made love. She saw how Quinn touched Jocelyn and kissed her. Then it hit her. It was Quinn's kiss for Davi. She watched as Jocelyn responded to Quinn. The camera showed Quinn's eyes, the bedroom eyes that sparkled, but they more than sparkled. They were Quinn's eyes for Davi. Those eyes were only for her. He had promised.

Davi held her breath as the scene went on for what seemed like hours. Her stomach knotted. She closed her eyes as she fought off the wave of nausea, forcing the bile back down her throat. She let go of Quinn's hand and wrapped her arms around her stomach.

Quinn leaned over to her and whispered, "Davi, I—"

"Don't say anything, not one word. I'll get through this," she said through clenched teeth.

She didn't see anything else. The movie passed by in a blur as memories from her past filled her head. The headaches and nausea she endured, knowing that Ross was in someone else's bed. All of the lies and fake smiles from so-called friends who wouldn't tell her what was going on. Lizzie Tanner's face—smirking at Davi, knowing what Ross was like in bed and enjoying the knowledge that she knew firsthand.

She remembered the night Quinn showed her the difference between his on-screen kiss and his kiss for her. *That kiss is for you and no one else. Whatever you see me do on the screen with the women, I guarantee you'll not get from me.* He lied.

It was painful to see Quinn with Jocelyn. Davi recalled his other movies where he played the Hollywood lover. There was no hint of the Quinn that belonged to her, but this movie was not like the rest. Quinn and Jocelyn had been lovers. Davi knew the truth, and it hurt like hell.

The movie ended, the lights brightened, and the audience gave a standing ovation. Davi stood with the rest of them but did not smile.

She turned to Beth and said, "I need to pee. Care to come with me?"

Beth followed Davi across the aisle and down to the washrooms. Davi didn't want the company, but she knew it would look better than to race off alone. Sarah followed them. She stood outside Davi's stall and listened while Davi emptied the contents of her stomach into the toilet.

"You can't stay in there all night, Davi. Please come out."

"I'm throwing up, Sarah, or can you not hear it from out there? I don't feel well."

"I know you don't. I saw the same thing as you, Davi. I don't know what to say, except that it ended before it began. Honest."

Davi flushed the toilet then came out of the stall. She washed and dried her hands.

"You don't have to explain it to me. I figured it out for myself. Quinn lied to me, Sarah, and that's one thing he promised he'd never do." Davi saw Beth's reflection in the mirror. She looked confused. "Quinn had an affair with Jocelyn. You can see it on the screen. If you know Quinn, you can tell he wasn't acting up there. It was real."

"They didn't have an affair. It was one-sided. Quinn fell for Jocelyn, but she didn't feel the same way. He thought that if—"

"Don't make excuses for him, Sarah. He can tell me for himself."

Davi examined her reflection in the mirror and groaned. "I look like crap."

"Let's fix you up, hon. You do look a bit pale." Sarah reached into her bag and freshened up Davi's makeup. "Luckily, you didn't mess up your dress. Take a breath mint."

A loud knock rapped against the door, startling Davi.

"I locked it. You needed privacy. Beth, you can unlock the door now, please. Remember, Davi—it's all in the past. He made a stupid mistake, and he knew it as soon as he did it."

Sarah hugged Davi then led the three of them out to the lobby. Quinn paced, waiting for the women to exit the ladies' room. His worried eyes locked on Davi.

"Later," Davi said to Quinn as he took her by the hand.

"Great movie, Quinn. I felt so sorry for your character. You sure got it rough."

Davi didn't recognize the man who addressed Quinn. A woman stood beside him, expecting an introduction.

Quinn forced the Hollywood charm. "You haven't introduced me to your lovely lady."

"Quinn Thomas, this is my wife, Lacey. Lacey, this is Quinn and his beautiful wife, Davina."

Davi held out her hand. "Hello, Lacey."

"Your husband was amazing, Davina. I'm sure every woman got hot and bothered watching him. I know I did. You are one lucky woman to have him all to yourself."

"Excuse us, will you?" Quinn said without letting Davi answer. "We need to talk," he said under his breath as he led her away.

Davi stopped. "No, not here. I can't."

"I've hurt you."

Davi closed her eyes and forced the tears back. "You and Jocelyn were lovers. It's obvious to anyone who knows you. You should have told me, Quinn. Why the hell didn't you tell me?"

"Quinn, old buddy!" Tom Braden greeted Quinn as he put his arm around his shoulder. Davi could smell the liquor on his breath as his face came between Quinn and Davi. "Great movie, man. Another one where you get the women all wet with fantasies about you. How do you do that?"

"Excuse me," Davi said as she extricated herself from Quinn's grip. "I'll let Quinn tell you his secrets. I'm sure he doesn't mind."

"Davi!"

Quinn called out to her, but she ignored him. She wanted to escape, needing quiet and time to think.

Sarah was immediately by her side and hooked her arm through hers. "Everyone's watching you, Davi. You've got to keep yourself together."

"I need to leave, Sarah. I can't think with all of these people around. Get me out of here, please."

"We'll go to the limo. It's time to head to the party now anyways."

"No. No party. I can't."

"You have to make an appearance, at least."

"And listen to people talk about how great my husband's acting was and how he made all the women wet? No, thank you. I think I've been humiliated enough."

Quinn caught up to them with Luke and Beth in tow. Beth didn't have the chance to fill Luke in on what had happened.

Once inside the limo and on their way to the post-premiere party, Luke couldn't contain his excitement. "Oh, man, what a movie! You'll get an Oscar for this, Quinn. Did you hear the crowd? They loved it. You and Jocelyn! What chemistry. It's too bad she missed out on tonight."

Beth jabbed him in the ribs.

"Ow! What was that for?" Luke noticed Sarah and Beth glaring at him. "What's going on?"

He looked over at Quinn, staring out the passenger window. Davi sat apart from Quinn, looking down as she stared at the beading on her purse.

"Will someone tell me what's going on? We've done a complete one-eighty from three hours ago. What have I missed?"

"Leave it alone, Luke," Quinn grumbled as he continued to stare out the window.

"I'm not going to leave it alone. Something happened between you two. Out with it."

Davi looked up at Luke with teary eyes. "I didn't like the movie. It was too real for me."

"What do you mean it was too real for you? Davi, it was just acting. Quinn's a great actor, and so is Jocelyn. You can't be mad at him for making it look real. You, of all people, should be able to tell the difference. If you believe it, it means the movie's going to be a hit."

It was Sarah's turn to jab Luke in the ribs.

"Ow! Why did you do that?"

Quinn turned his attention to Luke. "Davi's right, you moron. Everything I did with Jocelyn was the real deal, and Davi had to sit through that movie and watch it all."

"What do you mean the real deal? You and Jocelyn? But that was before you met Davi. Way before Davi came into the picture," Luke stammered.

"We both know that, Luke, but I promised Davi she'd never see me on the screen the way I was with Jocelyn. I conveniently forgot to tell her there was one exception to the promise. I didn't know that movie would look the way it did."

"But, you knew what you were doing when you filmed that movie, especially that scene," Davi said quietly.

"Yes. I fell for Jocelyn. I wanted it to be real, so I didn't hold back. I should have, but I didn't. I'm sorry."

"Don't be sorry for that. I don't want your apologies for what happened in the past."

"Then what do you want?"

"I deserved a heads-up on that movie. Something like, 'Davi, Jocelyn and I had a thing going during the making of the movie, and you might see me getting personal with her. Everything I do with you, I did with her, even though I promised you I never did that with any of my co-stars.'"

"Davi—"

"You never once mentioned Jocelyn's name. All the women you slept with, but hers never came up in conversation. Why was that?"

"There wasn't anything to tell you," Quinn said softly.

Davi looked at him with disbelief and shook her head. Another lie. "This is not the time or the place, Quinn. Please don't say another word."

"We're going to talk about this now."

"You may like to put it all out there in front of an audience, but I don't." Her steely gaze silenced him.

"We're here," Luke announced, relieved that the limo had stopped.

"Go." Quinn nodded towards the door. "Davi and I need to have a talk."

"Quinn, the press—they're waiting for you. You can't stay in here."

"I can do whatever the hell I want," Quinn yelled. "Luke, get out, now."

Luke stared at his friend for a brief moment then opened the door. "Ladies," he grumbled as he held out his hand to Beth. "Don't be long, Quinn. I can't hold them off forever." Luke slammed the door.

"Drive," Quinn ordered the driver.

Quinn raised the divider, then turned to face Davi. He reached out for her, but she cringed from his touch.

"Davi, it was just that one scene."

"Liar! I could see it in your eyes, Quinn. The way you looked at her. You were falling in love with her right from the very beginning."

"I was lonely. I was tired of waiting for you."

Davi laughed bitterly. "So this is my fault?"

"No. Let me finish. I was lonely. I hated not having anyone in my life. Jocelyn and I had the chemistry on screen, so I thought it meant we'd have it off-screen, too."

"You thought?"

"I wanted it so bad. I put it all out there for Jocelyn to notice me. Sarah said I was a fool, but I didn't listen."

"Did you sleep with her?"

"Does it matter?"

Davi stared at him, incredulous that he would ask her.

"Yes," he answered.

"You still care for her. I could see it in your eyes this afternoon."

"Only as a friend. I can't stand the way she abuses herself, but I'm helpless. I've offered to help her, but she won't take it. So the best I can do is look after her when there's no one for her, like today."

"You asked Luke to call the hotel—"

"She's okay. The hotel manager checked on her."

"I'll ask you again. Why didn't you tell me about Jocelyn? Don't tell me that it slipped your mind, Mr. Photographic Memory."

"I don't know why."

"Liar."

Quinn winced. He cursed himself for wondering what Davi was like when she was mad. She was holding in her fury, but her barbs stung.

"She's more to you than you'll admit, you bastard. I've been such a fool. You made me feel like I was the only one. I'm not, am I?"

"You're jealous?" he asked in disbelief.

"Jealous? I could handle being jealous, but this is a reality check." Davi tried not to burst into tears. "There will be others. I can see that now. You won't be with me for long."

"What the hell's got into you? I love you. Forever, remember?"

Davi shook her head and looked out the window. "I think we have different definitions of forever, Quinn. I think yours is the Hollywood version. It won't last for long." Davi knocked on the barrier separating them from the driver. "Pull over, please."

"What are you doing?"

"I'm getting out. I can't stand spending another minute in here with you."

"Are you crazy? You aren't leaving. We're going to talk this out."

Davi felt the limo stop. She looked out the window and recognized where she was.

"I have money and my cell phone. I can look after myself, Quinn. I did just fine before I met you, and I will continue to do so. Now let me out of this limo."

Quinn took hold of her arm. "I'm not letting you leave."

"Like hell, you aren't." Davi's voice was icy as she stared at his hand. "Let go of me now."

Quinn released her. "You've got this all wrong." His voice was rough as anger blazed in his eyes.

"You don't get it, do you? Your promises mean nothing, and I was naïve to think that I could expect you to keep them. I can't do this, Quinn. I can't wonder how many other women you've forgotten to mention. I won't tolerate cheating."

"I didn't cheat on you! Damn it, Davi, this is just a stupid movie! I made a stupid mistake. I fucked up big-time. It's got nothing to do with us."

"I sat back and watched one husband cheat on me, and I vowed I would never let that happen again."

"It won't, I promise!"

"No more promises."

Davi opened the door and scrambled out onto the sidewalk. Quinn followed her.

"It's not safe out here, Davi. Get back in the limo."

"Go back to your party, Quinn. Celebrate your Oscar-worthy movie with people who loved it. Your fans are waiting on you, especially the wet ones."

Davi hailed an approaching cab and got in without taking another look at Quinn. She'd be damned if she let him see her cry.

twenty

Davi told the cab driver to drive. She didn't care where to as long it was far away from Quinn. She needed time to think and to cry. She hadn't wept like this before. She wouldn't allow herself to, but for some reason, she couldn't help herself from doing so now. She hurt, and as much as she wanted to forget about the movie, she couldn't. Images of Jocelyn and Quinn flashed before her eyes, then Ross and Lizzie joined them. She cried until no tears remained.

When she arrived back at their hotel suite, Davi was numb. She didn't wonder why no one was waiting for her. She didn't care. Davi walked to the bathroom and turned on the Jacuzzi. She kicked her shoes off and then undressed, taking special care of her gown. She tossed the sapphires on the dresser drawers.

Davi turned on the bathroom stereo, selecting classical music because she couldn't bear to hear anyone's voice. She winced as she stepped into the hot water. She should have checked the temperature first.

She closed her eyes and was powerless to stop the replay of the evening's events. She had mishandled the entire situation. In hindsight, she should have handled it better as a Hollywood wife would have. She should have sat through the movie, congratulated Quinn on a job well done, kissed him on the cheek, and then smiled as women revelled in knowing Quinn's lovemaking secrets. Although it hurt that he was himself in that movie, it wasn't the reason behind her fury. Quinn had lied. He hadn't told her about Jocelyn, and there was more to the story than he was letting on. Saying nothing was lying by omission. Davi couldn't let it go.

Davi stayed in the tub until the water got cold. She stepped out of the tub, dried herself then pulled the pins out of her hair. She cursed Sarah as she found more and more pins hidden beneath her hair. It felt good to free her hair and take the weight off her head.

The bed called to her. It was cold and empty. Davi crawled onto her side of the bed and turned off the light. She pulled Quinn's pillow to her face and inhaled his scent, then waited for sleep to come. It took its time.

When she awoke, Davi turned to reach for Quinn to find his side of the bed untouched and cold. He hadn't slept with her. Had he come home? Davi got out of bed and went to the bathroom. Quinn hadn't been in here either. Davi brushed her teeth, then put on her robe before heading to the kitchen.

She could smell freshly brewed coffee. There was a note beside the coffee maker.

I've gone for the day.
—Sarah

Davi poured herself a cup of coffee then turned to face the living room. Quinn sat in an armchair, watching her. He looked incredibly sexy with his morning stubble, his pouting kissable lips, and his blue eyes gazing at her.

"Good morning," she said softly.

"Is it?" he replied gruffly, exhaustion filled his voice.

"I hope it is. I'd like it to be." Davi poured another cup for Quinn then sat down across from him. She handed him his coffee. "You didn't come to bed last night."

"I just got in."

"Oh?"

"I went looking for you. Sarah had the good sense to figure out you'd come back here. She phoned me to tell me you were sleeping. She stayed in the other bedroom."

"What did you do?"

"I did what you told me to do. I stayed out and partied. It was my premiere, you know. I'm a shoo-in for an Oscar. Everyone thinks so. Even my wet fans think so."

She ignored his barb. "It's a great movie, Quinn."

Quinn laughed bitterly. "Who's the liar now?"

"I'm not lying. It is a great movie. It's funny, the story is wonderful, and it's because of you and Jocelyn."

Quinn gazed at Davi with tired eyes. He ached to reach out and touch her, but the memory of her cringing from his touch the previous night still hurt him.

"How was the party?"

"Fantastic," he drawled. "I had all of these women trying to hook up with me—beautiful, large breasted, plastic women. They all wanted to have sex with me. They'd have blown me right there at the table if I'd asked them."

Davi didn't flinch at his words. She knew he spoke the truth.

"I could have gone home with any one of them last night, but I didn't. Do you know why?"

"Tell me."

"It's because every square inch of my body and my heart belongs to you. I don't give anything to anyone but you, especially my package."

"Thank you for coming home to me."

"I took my time."

"I know. But you came home when you were ready."

"I was furious at you, Davi. Would you like to know why?"

"Yes."

"You don't play by the rules."

"What rules?"

"You don't get mad when you should, so I have no idea what reaction to expect from you. Since I met you, I haven't seen you lose your cool once—not with that bastard Tremblant, not with surprising you with being on Olivia's show, not even when I told you about *Second Harvest*. You're a rock. I didn't think anything could upset you."

"I guess the rose-coloured glasses are off now. The honeymoon is over."

"Don't joke about this, please."

"I'm not joking."

"You sat through the filming of that damned rape scene with Rene. You watched while I took another woman, and afterwards, you said it was great acting. What am I supposed to think when you say something like that?"

Davi opened her mouth to speak, but Quinn stopped her.

"I knew the sex scene with Jocelyn was going to be a shock, but I convinced myself that you'd be the same as with the rape scene. You would say it was great acting and then forget about it. Then as I watched the movie, I saw the look on my face and the way I kissed her, and I saw myself doing everything I promised would be for you only. I knew that you would see that. I knew that you'd be hurt. I'm sorry."

"You were so real, you and Jocelyn. It was as though I was watching you cheat on me. I couldn't get the images out of my head, and then I saw Ross and Lizzie. It was too much for me, Quinn."

"I'd never cheat on you. I promise you that."

Davi sighed. "No more promises."

"I fell for Jocelyn and thought she had fallen for me, too, but it was just the acting. She played her part twenty-four seven, and I couldn't see it. Sarah warned me, but I didn't listen. That love scene was my last chance to put it all out there for her. It was me loving Jocelyn." Quinn ran his hands over his head and took a deep breath. "That night, after we wrapped up for the night, I went to her trailer. I knocked on the door. She didn't answer, so I let myself in. I found her with Tom Braden." He winced at the memory. "God, I was such a fool."

"I told you about Ross. Why didn't you tell me about Jocelyn?"

"I don't know, and that's the truth. Maybe I was embarrassed. Maybe it was male pride, and I didn't want to admit that I was a fool."

"Maybe it's because she's the only one you cared about. You don't kiss and tell, remember?" Davi's voice was soft and filled with understanding. "You're a gentleman, Quinn. You only talked about the women who didn't get to your heart. You never talked about the women who did."

"I don't love her. You have to believe me."

"I do."

"I'm sorry that I didn't give you a heads-up."

"Me, too. Maybe I wouldn't have reacted so terribly."

"You're not mad that I gave up our secrets?"

"The jury is still out on that one, stud. You do realize that you have your work cut out for you."

"What kind of work?"

"I told the world you were ten times better in real life than what you were on the silver screen. You've got to come up with something that's only for me, that's never been seen before."

"Is that a challenge?"

"It's a demand. No negotiating."

"How much time do I have to come up with something new?"

"You don't. I want it now. I had a very lonely night."

Davi stood up and walked over to Quinn. She took his coffee cup from him, placed it on the table before sitting on his lap.

Quinn smiled. "Does this mean our fight is over?"

"Did we fight? I thought it was a simple misunderstanding," Davi teased as she pulled on Quinn's bowtie.

She was doing it again—working her magic on him, making him hard. Quinn groaned at the thought of stopping her, but he had to.

"I have to have a shower. I smell of other women's perfume, and my mouth feels like the bottom of my shoe. And since I've still got this tux on, my night hasn't officially ended yet, so making love to you will be the highlight to a very long and exhausting day."

"Do you want company?"

"Oh, Davi, you know I do, but not this time. I need to shower by myself."

"Isn't that my line?"

"Just proves I listen to you. Now, if you don't mind, let me have my shower."

Davi stood up and took Quinn's hand as they walked into the bedroom. She helped Quinn off with his clothes. Quinn was right— he did stink of bad perfume. Davi threw his clothes into the closet.

"I won't be long," Quinn said as he walked off to the bathroom.

Davi thought of slipping on one of her nighties and dabbing on some perfume, but she didn't feel romantic or sexy. She needed to reconnect with Quinn, and dolling herself up wouldn't help the situation. Naked, Davi got into bed and waited for him.

Quinn finished his shower, shaved, and then made his way to their bed. He sat down beside Davi. Leaning down towards her, he gazed into her eyes and smiled. Davi smiled back. She couldn't resist his blue bedroom sparkle.

His hand cupped her face. "You are my life, Davina Stuart Thomas. I am so sorry for the pain I caused you. Please forgive me. I love you more than you will ever know. There is no one else on this planet for me, and there never will be."

"You're supposed to say in this universe."

"Why?"

"Because you're a star, stud."

Quinn kissed her on her forehead. "I'm only a star if you are my universe. I can't exist without you. You scared the hell out of me last night. I thought you were leaving me."

"Never." Her voice was quiet and soothing. "It will take a lot more than a hot and steamy sex scene to separate us." She gave him a soft kiss on his lips. "Speaking of which, aren't I supposed to be getting some of my own hot and steamy?"

"Oh, woman," he moaned as he took her in his arms and kissed her.

His tongue pushed into her mouth and played with her tongue. Davi sighed, enjoying the tingle from something as simple as his kiss. Without breaking their kiss, Quinn rolled over onto his back, bringing Davi with him. His hands caressed her back, stopping at the soft round globes of her ass. He massaged them tenderly, loving the feel of her soft flesh in his hands.

Davi moved against Quinn's hard body. She wanted to climb into him and let his heat warm her. Her body ached for him. One night separated from him, and now her body let her know what she had missed—the strong muscled arms that held her close, the comfort of his heartbeat as she used his chest as her pillow, and his body heat that warmed her to her soul.

"I missed you. I don't sleep well without my teddy bear," she said against his lips.

"Neither do I."

Quinn rolled over onto his side, taking Davi with him. Their lips still touched without kissing as they gazed into each other's eyes.

"You are so beautiful," he said softly as his fingers traced the curves of Davi's body. His fingers lingered at her breasts and played with her nipples. Davi moaned, enjoying the attention.

Quinn pulled Davi's leg over his hip and pulled her in close. Davi shifted so that he could enter her.

"This is the way it should be. Face to face, our eyes gazing into each other's." Quinn placed his hand over Davi's heart and hers over his. "I feel your heartbeat, Davi. It gives me such a rush." He kissed her. "I missed your kisses tonight. All I wanted was for you to kiss me and tell me everything was fine, that we'd be okay. But you weren't there. No one has your lips. No one." Quinn pulled her in again and kissed her fiercely.

Davi held on tight to Quinn's hand, feeling the tingle that flowed between them. She pulled him tight with her leg, holding him close to her. She needed his warmth, and she needed to feel his heartbeat as he made love to her. They devoured each other with their kisses, hungry for each other. A low moan escaped from deep down in Quinn. Davi shuddered as she felt it vibrate through her. She held on tight as his thrusts increased, pushing her to the edge, and then they climaxed together.

Davi nestled into Quinn's chest and listened to his heartbeat. She loved the sound of it, steady and even. She loved the comfort that she found in his arms, surrounded by a gentle strength that kept her warm and safe.

"I've changed my mind," she said into his chest.

"About what?" Quinn asked cautiously.

"You don't have to love me any differently. I want what I'm getting."

"What about everyone knowing our secrets?"

"They may know our secrets, but I'm the only one who gets to enjoy them with you. You are mine, Quinn Thomas, and that is all that matters."

twenty-one

He was singing in the shower. Quinn never sang in the shower, or at least, Davi had never heard him sing there. She loved his voice and wished he would sing more. Davi stretched out in their bed and let the sound of his voice flow over her. She knew that song. He sang it to her at their wedding.

Davi got out of bed and made her way to the bathroom. Her body ached. *Quinn.* She looked at herself in the mirror and groaned. She was too old for this. Her hair was a mass of tangles. Her eyes were blackened from mascara, giving her ghoulish raccoon eyes. *I thought I washed that off.* Her lips were swollen and red. *Quinn.* He wouldn't stop kissing her, and she wouldn't let him.

"Good morning, love," Quinn greeted her cheerfully as he stepped out of the shower.

"It's afternoon. And thank you very much, by the way."

Quinn winked at her as he towelled himself dry.

Davi couldn't take her eyes off him. "I can barely walk, Quinn, and look at this!" She pointed at her face. "I look like something from a horror movie."

Quinn reached for her and took her in his arms. "You wanted something different, and I gave it to you."

"I changed my mind, remember? I said it didn't matter to me anymore."

"Didn't you like what I gave you? I didn't hear you complain. I remember you kept calling out my name."

Davi blushed as she remembered their lovemaking. "That's beside the point."

"No, it's not. We made love this morning like we'd been separated for years instead of hours. We couldn't get enough of each other. It was both of us, not just me. We're insatiable when it comes to loving each other. So don't be mad about it, be proud about it."

"True words said by the peacock."

"Who loves his peahen more than she'll ever know."

Davi sighed. "I have to shower. Then feed me, Mr. Peacock. I'm starving."

XO XO XO

Within fifteen minutes, Davi and Quinn were dressed and heading out in Quinn's Porsche.

"I have someplace special I want to take you," he told her. "It's my favourite restaurant in all of LA. The owners are like family, and I want you to meet them."

"I'd love to," Davi said eagerly. "Maybe I'll get to learn some secrets about you."

"I'm sure Rosa will have something to say about me. She always liked to mother me. Her daughter Bella should be at the restaurant. She's a sweetheart."

Quinn pulled up in front of the restaurant. Davi read the sizeable wooden sign situated over the entranceway, Rosa's. A smaller sign on the front door read Closed.

"Are we out of luck?" Davi asked as Quinn opened the car door for her.

"No. It's closed to the public at this time of day, but friends and family are always welcome. Rosa makes the best pasta. I hope you like Italian food."

"I love it."

Quinn pulled open the restaurant door and let Davi walk in ahead of him.

"Hello! Anyone here?"

Immediately, a small woman hurried out of the kitchen, wiping her hands on her white apron. "Quinn! Oh my, Quinn, it's so good to see you."

Quinn picked the woman up in his arms and kissed her. "Did you miss me? Are you losing weight, Rosa? You feel as light as a feather."

"Put me down." She laughed giddily. "I'm too old to be picked up like a doll. You of all people should know that." Rosa turned to Davi once her feet touched the floor. "You must be his wife, Davina. We were hoping he'd bring you around so we could meet you." Rosa hugged Davi and kissed her on both cheeks. "You're beautiful. You could do with a pound or two."

Davi laughed. "Don't worry. It will be coming on soon enough." Davi saw the confusion in Rosa's face. "We're going to have a baby, Rosa."

"This calls for a celebration. Have you eaten? Of course not. You never come here on a full stomach. Let's go to the kitchen. I have fresh pasta, and the sauce is almost ready. Tony is out for the day. It's too bad he's not here to meet you." Rosa took Davi by the hand and led her into the kitchen. "Bella will be so excited to meet you, Davi. She was heartbroken, of course, when she heard that Quinn was married, but she knows that Quinn will always be her boyfriend." Rosa called into the huge kitchen, "Bella! Come see who is here!"

A girl's face popped around the corner, cautiously looking before she entered the room.

"Quinn," she shrieked when he saw him, then went running to him.

"How's my Bella?" Quinn asked excited as he picked her up and swung her around.

"I'm fine. I missed you." She gazed into Quinn's eyes then kissed him quickly on the cheek.

"I missed you, too. I brought someone to meet you. Her name is Davi. She's my wife." Quinn put Bella down.

Slowly, Bella turned to look at Davi. Bella was compact. Her long brunette hair framed her round face with chocolate brown eyes perfectly. Bella had Down syndrome.

Davi smiled at Bella. "Hi, Bella, it's so nice to meet you. I hear Quinn's your boyfriend. I hope you don't mind sharing him with me. That's what friends do. I'd like us to be friends, Bella."

"What do you say, Bella, will you be friends with Davi? I'd really like that."

"Okay," she said casually. "Your hair is short." She pointed at Quinn's hair.

"I know. But I'm growing it back to the way it was. Davi likes it long. You do, too, don't you?"

"Yep."

As Rosa busied herself getting the meal together, Quinn went to the shelf and took out some plates while Bella brought out the cutlery.

"Sit," Rosa said to Davi. "Quinn, get your wife a drink. Open a bottle of wine, will you? You'll find soda and juice in the bar. You know where it is."

Quinn kissed Rosa on the top of her head. "Why is it all the women in my life boss me around?"

"It's because you need it. Handsome men don't have brains. You need to be told what to do, and you like it." Rosa looked over at Davi. "I'm right, aren't I? Quinn likes to be told what to do."

"I don't know about that. Although, he does say that I am always right."

"Same thing. We know where Quinn's brains are, don't we, Davi? And you can't complain." Rosa winked at her.

"I heard that," Quinn yelled from the bar. When he returned to the kitchen, he asked, "Why do women think they can talk about my package and not offend me? If I spoke the same way about you, you'd kill me."

"But you wouldn't because you're a gentleman." Rosa reached up to his cheek and pinched it. "Just keep your wife happy, Quinn. Don't share that package with anyone but her."

Davi laughed as she listened to their conversation. Rosa admonished Quinn as a mother would her son, and Quinn's eyes sparkled with mischief as he responded to her.

"What if I'm too tired for her, Rosa? What do I do then?"

"You're never too tired to make love to your wife," Rosa warned him as she pointed a spoon at him. "My Tony always has time for his Rosa. Besides, you're still young. You have no excuse."

"Hear that, Davi? No excuses."

"She can say no, but you can't. She'll be looking after your bambinos. She will be tired once in a while."

Quinn helped Rosa fill the plates with steaming pasta then delivered them to the table. Bella was already seated, waiting patiently for Quinn to sit beside her. Quinn offered Rosa the chair beside Davi then sat down beside Bella.

"I always sit beside Bella. It's a tradition," Quinn explained as he reached for the bottle of wine and poured a glass for both Rosa and himself.

"How did you meet Rosa?" Davi asked before she took a bite of her pasta.

"I found this place a few years ago. I loved Rosa's cooking and asked her to teach me how to cook Italian food. She had already fallen madly in love with me, so she couldn't say no. Whenever I have the chance, I pop in and hang out in the kitchen. Rosa's is my sanctuary. Just like when I'm on the farm with you."

"Do you have children, Davi?"

Davi finished chewing her food before she answered, "I have three. They're at home. This pasta is delicious."

Rosa ignored the compliment, focusing on Davi's children. "Who is looking after them?"

"They're old enough to be left on their own, Rosa. The youngest is twenty, and the oldest is twenty-five. Davi's children aren't babies." Quinn answered.

"My, you must have started young. You don't look like you have adult children. Quinn said you were older, but I never thought by how much."

"I'm fifteen years older."

"Did Quinn tell you that he came here to tell me about you the day he met you?" Rosa didn't wait for Davi to respond. "He came rushing into this very kitchen, and he said to me, 'Rosa, I have found the love of my life.' I thought he'd been dating someone and finally got the feeling that she was the one. So when I asked him how long he'd known you, I was shocked when he said he had only known you for a few hours. He sat me down here, poured me a glass of wine, and told me all about you. Everything that ran through his mind about you, he told me. He didn't stop talking until I knew the whole story. We were on our second bottle of wine by then."

"No, we weren't."

"Hush. This is my story. So when he finished, I asked him if you had any faults. Everyone has faults of some sort. Quinn's smart. He would have noticed something about you. Do you know what he said to me? He said, 'She doesn't have any faults, but I know she will never need me the way I need her. She already has a life and a family. Davina isn't looking for love, and she doesn't need anything I can offer her. I have to make her want me. That's the only chance I have to win her love.'"

Davi's mouth dropped open. She could feel a blush come to her face. "Quinn said that just after meeting me?"

"Yes. Was he right?"

"Yes, I think I would have been perfectly content to have never met him. Of course, I wouldn't have known what I was missing, but I would have been happy without him. It may sound cold, and I don't mean it that way."

"You have to tell Davi what you told me, Rosa. It's only fair."

"Have some more pasta first. You're still hungry." Rosa took Quinn's plate and refilled it, then handed it back to him. "So I told Quinn, 'You can make her want you. That won't be a problem for you. She'll want you and love you more than you deserve, but because she doesn't need you, you will not be her life. Do you think you can live with that if you are not her life?' Then Quinn looked me in the eye and said, 'Rosa, I only know that I cannot live without her, so I will gladly take anything Davina gives me.'"

"Why would you say that?"

"That's what I felt. That's what I still feel. I tell you every day that you are my life."

"I know that. But, how could you know that after spending five hours with me on a plane? We talked. It was a speed date."

"Yes, but I fell in love with you immediately. That's what you did to me in that short time. I was yours. Forever."

Davi sighed. "Why did you bring this up, Rosa? I find it somewhat depressing."

"Depressing? Why on earth do you feel depressed when you hear that your husband wanted you in his life the moment he met you?"

"Because I didn't feel that way, and perhaps the real love of his life was waiting for him on his return flight. Maybe I'm his second choice, and his true love is waiting for him around the corner."

"Do you believe that?"

Davi closed her eyes. What was she thinking? It still haunted her, the image of Quinn and Jocelyn making love on the silver screen. It didn't matter how much Quinn loved her now. Davi couldn't shake the feeling that he would lose his heart to someone else.

"Davi?" Quinn's voice was urgent, demanding an answer.

"Yes. In the back of my mind, I see you walk around the corner, and someone is there waiting for you."

"Davi, I—"

"Let's be real. I'm so much older than you. I'd be a fool to think that it couldn't happen."

"That doesn't say much about me," he retorted.

Davi turned to Rosa. "I'm sorry. I'm not a very good guest. Thank you for the delicious meal." Davi stood up. "Bella, it was so nice to meet you. I hope we get to see each other soon. Quinn, I'll wait for you outside. You can take your time."

Davi walked out of the restaurant. She wanted to continue walking but knew it would make things worse for Quinn to find her gone. Davi leaned against the hood of the Porsche and stared down the street. The bright sun hurt her eyes, so she put on her sunglasses.

She could feel the tears starting. Her emotions were taking control of her. It was so unlike her. Davi was never rude to people, never getting emotional over nothing.

"Fuck!"

"I don't think I'll ever get used to hearing that word uttered from your beautiful kissable mouth." Quinn stood in front of Davi. He gently removed her sunglasses and wiped away her tears. "I'm sorry."

"For what? I'm the one who was rude and walked out."

"Yes, but Rosa and I put you in a tough position. It takes Rosa a while to get to the point. If we had let her get there, maybe you wouldn't be here outside, crying."

"What was her point other than I am your life, but I will never need you, and my love for you doesn't compare to what you feel for me? I didn't see it going anywhere else."

"Rosa was going to say that she wouldn't have believed it until she saw us together—that she could see our love for each other. She wanted to give us her blessing. And even if you don't feel that you need me, there will come a time when you will, and I will be there for you. Always."

"She could see that, too, that you will always be there for me? Don't tell me that she tells fortunes on the side."

"You can't be the only one to have a fortune teller. I need one, too." Quinn winked at her. "Rosa knows me. I promised you forever, and that is what I will give you. Not one day less."

Davi started to cry. Quinn pulled her into his chest. "What's wrong now?"

"I don't know."

"You're sure it's not—"

"Don't you dare say hormones, or I will drop you where you stand."

Quinn chuckled. "I was going to say that you had a long day yesterday, and it was rough on both of us. We're both smarting from that damned movie."

"Oh."

"I love you. Nothing will ever change that."

"I do need you, you know," she sniffled.

"I know you do. Come on, let's get you back to the hotel. You can rest before we head out again." Quinn walked Davi to her side of the car and opened the door for her.

"I should say good-bye to Rosa."

"No. She understands. We'll be back again, and we'll steer away from all conversation regarding my crotch and our relationship. It will be completely boring, and you'll love it." Quinn closed the door and got in on his side. "I can't believe Rosa gave me advice on my sex life." He shook his head and chuckled.

"She likes your package. I wonder what she thinks you've got there."

"I don't even want to think about it. Rosa's like a mother to me."

Davi laughed. "Your mother talks about your sex life all the time!" Quinn laughed with her. "You're right."

Quinn pulled out into traffic.

"I wonder how she'd react if I told her you're hung like a horse." His eyes fixed on Davi. "A horse?"

Horns blared when he swerved into the next lane, then back into his lane.

"Well, your nickname is Big, isn't it?" Davi put her hand on his crotch and squeezed it. Davi felt him harden. "Care to make use of that, stud?"

"Give me five minutes. We're almost home."

"What if I can't wait? What if I want you now?"

Davi squeezed him again. She felt the Porsche accelerate, the force pushing her into the back of her seat. Davi closed her eyes as the scenery sped past them. The car made a sharp turn into the underground parking lot, causing the tires to skid along the pavement. A few quick turns and the squealing of brakes, and then the car stopped.

In one quick motion, Quinn undid his seat belt and then Davi's. With a flick of his hand, the passenger seat went back enough to give him some room to manoeuvre his six foot three inch frame onto Davi. He kissed her hard as his hands worked on her jeans. With two strong pulls, Davi's jeans and panties were down to her ankles. Davi reached for Quinn's zipper and belt buckle. She struggled with the prong until Quinn took over and undid it himself.

With one move, he was inside her. Davi cried out, her back arching against his invasion. There was no touching. Quinn's hands braced his body for support on top of Davi as he thrust into her. She felt his power, and it excited her. It was fast and intense. Davi moaned her release, and Quinn came with her with a loud groan. He crumpled onto her, and Davi hugged him close.

"Wow."

"Wow," he said, breathless. "I just had fast and furious with my wife."

"What made you do it?"

"Honestly?"

"Of course, honestly."

"I haven't done anything like that before."

Davi laughed in disbelief.

"Don't laugh. It's true. At least I've never used my beloved Porsche for anything like that before. These cars aren't designed for big guys like me doing this kind of thing. Do you think I'd risk putting my back out for anyone? It's the limo that's seen action, and you already knew that."

Quinn pushed away from Davi and fumbled with his pants. It was a struggle for him to get back into the driver's seat, banging his leg against the gearshift as he did so.

"Damn it!"

"There must have been a reason, though," Davi said while pulling her pants up and fastening them. She pulled down the car's visor and looked at herself in the mirror. "I'm a mess." Groaning, Davi reached for her purse that had slipped under the seat. She retrieved her hairbrush and lipstick and made the necessary repairs to her appearance. She turned to look at Quinn, whose gaze never left her.

"That was the reason. I needed to give you something that I haven't done before and that I knew you would know was just for you."

"Thank you." She leaned into him and kissed him.

"Let's go before I have to drop my pants again."

Quinn opened his door and got out. Davi waited for him to open her door. He expected her to.

"So what's the plan now?"

"We have time to ourselves until we have to get ready for tonight. Sarah will be waiting for a call to let her know we've made up."

"She'll know we did. Why wouldn't we?"

"Both of us were crazy last night, and we didn't know what we were doing, nor did our friends. Not hearing from us today would keep them guessing, too."

"But surely, one of them would have called you. Your phone hasn't rung all day."

Quinn pulled his phone out of his pocket and showed it to Davi. "I never turn it off unless it's serious time with you." Quinn turned his phone on. Immediately, it flashed with voice mail alerts and texts. "See? They've been worried." Quinn scanned through the messages quickly. Quinn laughed after he listened to a voice message.

"What is it?"

"It's Jake. He heard about what happened last night. He's reminding me that my balls are in jeopardy. If you haven't forgiven me, he's warning me to steer clear of New York."

"Good old Jake. He's my protector, you know."

"He has a crush on you. If he weren't married, he'd be after you in a flash."

"Got you worried, huh?"

"Every day, love. Every day."

twenty-two

Davi looked out the limousine's window and gazed at the hospital. Of all the places to have a charity event for a hospital, why didn't she think of it? She could feel the knot form in her stomach. It wasn't too long ago that Quinn was in a hospital fighting for his life. Davi remembered praying that she wouldn't be back in one for a long time.

Davi didn't understand the difference between an informal and formal red carpet event. Everyone still dressed in formal attire. They walked the red carpet while having their pictures taken by the press, and fans crowded outside, waiting for a glimpse of their favourite celebrities. This time, those in attendance would see *Lovestruck* in a lecture hall instead of a movie theatre. Davi was impressed by the interest the press showed in the charity and Quinn's involvement with it. There were no questions about whose dress she was wearing or who did her hair.

Quinn held Davi's hand the entire evening. Davi could feel the tingle and tried her best to tone it down. Quinn was in overdrive, trying to compensate for last night's fiasco. Davi tried to assure him it was unnecessary, but Quinn wasn't going to take any chances.

As the various celebrities and attendees mingled in the theatre's foyer, Quinn and Davi made their way to where some hospital patients entered the lecture hall. The charity event supported the hospital's cancer ward, and most, if not all, of the patients attending were from that ward. All were in wheelchairs, accompanied by family members or hospital staff. Davi and Quinn did their best to visit with every one of them.

Sarah stood by, watching as Quinn and Davi talked with the patients and their escorts. Quinn was charming, but it wasn't his usual Hollywood charm. He was kind and genuinely interested in every person he met. He hugged and kissed them or just held their hand, looking thoroughly at ease. Davi knelt gracefully beside every wheelchair so that she could be eye to eye with those with whom she spoke. She gave hugs and kisses, too. Sarah watched as Davi would wipe away a tear, and then her smile would come back before she moved on to the next patient.

It wasn't until the last patient was wheeled into the lecture hall that Quinn and Davi were ready to follow. Sarah offered to escort Davi to the ladies' room before the movie began, but Davi declined.

"Only if you think I need a touch-up, Sarah. Otherwise, I'm fine. Thank you."

"It's time, Davi. It's not too late. You can fake a headache or something," Quinn whispered in her ear.

"I'm sorry. I can't fake a headache, but an orgasm, yes." Davi smiled. "I'll be okay. It's just a movie, remember?"

"You fake your orgasms?"

"Later, Quinn, we have a movie to watch." Davi hooked her arm through Quinn's as he escorted her into the lecture hall. Davi smiled, knowing that Quinn would be thinking of her orgasms, every single one of them, while he tried to watch the movie.

Davi hated *Lovestruck*. It had a great storyline, and Quinn and Jocelyn were terrific in their roles. She could see one of them winning an Oscar, but it hurt to watch Quinn with Jocelyn.

Quinn leaned over and whispered in her ear, "Was it our first night together? You weren't expecting much."

She smiled and shook her head no.

Quinn sat back in his seat, and Davi waited.

His warm lips brushed against her ear. "The shower? Sometimes it's hard getting the friction right."

Again, she shook her head no. Davi liked this game.

"The morning my parents came to visit? We were both tired, and you were stressed." He forgot to whisper this time.

She put her finger over her lips to warn him to keep his voice down as she shook her head no. Davi noticed Quinn shifting in his seat. Her plan was working.

"Today?" His voice was lower but more demanding.

She turned and looked at him. She leaned towards him and whispered, "When today?"

Quinn flinched. "This morning."

"When this morning?"

"The last time. I was tired."

"No."

Quinn groaned then faced the screen.

Davi waited, but he didn't ask her again. She wondered if she had gone too far. Davi looked up at the screen to find she'd missed the love scene. Mission accomplished. Now she could watch the movie knowing there would be no more sex scenes, and she didn't mind the way Quinn kissed Jocelyn. It didn't look like it gave her an orgasm. *Tough luck, Jocelyn.*

The movie credits started to roll on the screen as the audience cheered and applauded. Quinn stood up and waved to the audience, then looked down at Davi and smiled. She looked back at him, wondering what he was thinking.

Quinn extended his hand to her. "Mrs. Thomas, care to join me?"

Davi took his hand. "Certainly, Mr. Thomas, I would love to join you."

Quinn, Davi, and Sarah walked out into the foyer. Davi smiled her best as many of the attendees made their way to the couple and congratulated Quinn on a movie well done. Quinn helped himself to an offered cocktail as he settled into his Hollywood mode. It was Davi's turn to be the tagalong tonight as she stood by his side. This time, Davi would celebrate Quinn's movie with him because he deserved it, and she had ruined last night's celebration. Then when they returned to their hotel suite, she would tell him she would never watch *Lovestruck* again.

After every guest had been spoken to and had their picture taken with Quinn and Davi, the couple said their good-byes and headed back to their hotel suite.

"So photo shoot for tomorrow. You won't need me. Do you mind if I pack up and head out early? I wouldn't mind getting home to Pete."

"No. Go ahead. Thanks for coming out, Sarah. You did great. Take a few days off. You deserve it."

"Gee, thanks, boss. I don't think the studio will like that. I've got a movie to get ready for, remember?"

Davi looked at Quinn, realizing that he hadn't told Sarah about *Second Harvest*. She squeezed his hand.

"Sarah, there's something you need to know." His voice was soft and low.

Sarah looked at both of them then swore. "I'm not working with you, am I?"

"No one's working with me, Sarah Bear. *Second Harvest*'s dead. The studio wanted to rewrite it into the Davi and Quinn love story. I had Luke stop them."

"No! That was Davi's movie. How could you do that to her? You should have fought for her."

Davi put her hand on Sarah's lap. "It's okay, Sarah. I'm okay with it. It's the right thing to do."

"When did this happen?"

"Monday."

"Monday? And you didn't tell us? Why the hell not?"

"We haven't signed the papers. No one can know about this until then."

"That's no excuse." Sarah stared at Quinn, her eyes reflecting her pain. "We're family, Quinn. Davi needed us, and you didn't tell us. No wonder she had a meltdown last night."

"I didn't have a meltdown."

"Davi, think about it. Quinn gets his head bashed in and almost dies, and then you find out your book isn't going to be made into a movie, then you pass out at the airport, thinking someone's going to kill Quinn, and then you sit through that damned movie and watch your husband make love to another woman. It's been too much for you."

"I don't think—"

"That's right, Quinn. You don't think. You need to look after your wife. She's too important for you to take for granted."

"I—"

"She's given up her life for you, and you don't seem to care."

"Sarah!" Davi snapped, shocked at Sarah's accusations. "I haven't given up my life for Quinn."

"Your family lives in Canada, Davi. When was the last time you stayed at home for more than a week?"

"Enough, Sarah." Quinn did not attempt to hide the threat behind it. "What we do or don't do is none of your business. Stay out of it."

The limo stopped.

"I'll pack up my gear in the morning. Leave the tux and dress on a chair. I'll find them. Good night." Sarah opened her door and got out of the limousine, slamming the door behind her.

Quinn waited, giving Sarah plenty of time to get ahead of them. Davi sat in silence, wondering what had just happened.

"She's right, you know."

"No, she's not. I'm an adult, Quinn. I make my own decisions."

"Do you? You didn't want to come out here, but I made you. You're terrified of the dark now, afraid something's going to happen to you, and I keep putting you in these stressful situations. What am I thinking? I'm an idiot. I'm sorry."

"Don't," Davi said as she put her finger over his lips. "I knew what I was getting into when I married you. I'm a big girl, Quinn. I'll admit that I'm still terrified at the thought of what Guy could have done to you, but I'm dealing with it. Last night, I saw my husband try to win the heart of another woman before he met me. Last night, I didn't handle it well because I thought you would cheat on me as Ross did. I was wrong, and it wasn't your fault."

"She's right about one thing. I should have fought harder for *Second Harvest*. It was yours, and I had Luke kill it instead of fighting for you."

Davi sighed, unable to answer him. Part of her wished he had put up a fight for her. She didn't want five million dollars. She wanted her movie, and now it was too late.

Quinn could see the truth in her eyes. He'd let her down again. He'd never be her hero, not when he let others step in and do the hard work. Jake. Luke. They were Davi's heroes. He only signed their paycheques.

"Let's go."

"Wait," Davi said quickly. "This ends here, tonight. We won't take it inside with us."

"What?"

"Don't let anyone tell you how to be my husband. Don't follow anyone's version of who you are supposed to be with me. Be yourself."

"I am myself."

"Then don't doubt what you are doing. Ever. I trust you to do the right thing. Hollywood isn't my world. It's yours. If the only way to handle the studio was to have them pay, I trust that you and Luke did what was best. Where I come from, a handshake is all that's ever needed. You and Luke know your way around a contract. You did the right thing."

"What about Guy? I let Jake take control."

"He knew what to do. We both trusted him to do the right thing. You did nothing wrong." Davi searched his face for understanding. "Follow your script, husband. Yours is the only one for me."

Quinn sighed heavily. "I'm tired of this shit."

"Me, too. Let it go. It's exhausting."

Quinn leaned over and kissed her. "Come on. It's getting late."

Quinn opened the door then held his hand out to Davi. She took it and stepped out of the limo. Quinn put his hand on the small of her back as they walked to the elevator in silence. Davi didn't mind the silence. They both needed it.

When they entered their suite, Davi said, "I need a bath. Would you like to join me?"

"Yes."

Quinn stood in the doorway as he watched Davi lean over the tub to start the water. Davi gathered her hair up and clipped it to the top of her head to keep it dry. She washed her face and brushed her teeth.

"I have to use the toilet, Quinn. Are you going to watch me do that, too?"

"No. I'll get us a drink. Call me when you're finished. I want to watch that dress come off."

Quinn left and closed the door behind him. By the time Davi finished, the bath was ready for them. She opened the door to find Quinn standing naked, waiting for her. He held a glass of chocolate milk in one hand and his scotch in the other.

"Thank you," he said as he walked into the bathroom.

"I need your help. I can't reach the zipper." Davi turned her back to him.

With slow deliberateness, he pulled the zipper down. Quinn kissed the exposed skin of Davi's back. She shuddered from the heat of his touch. Davi slipped the dress off and bent over slowly to pick the dress up off the floor, allowing Quinn to take in the view. She still wore her lingerie and heels. Davi hung the dress up on the door hook and then turned and faced Quinn. Reaching for the back of her neck, she undid the necklace and placed it on the counter. Her earrings remained untouched. She kicked her shoes off towards the wall while her hands reached to her back and undid her bra, letting it fall to her feet. When her hands went to her panties Quinn stopped her.

"Allow me," he said as he bent down, kissed her belly, then slowly slid the panties down her legs and let her step out of them. Quinn stood up and took Davi into his arms. He inhaled her scent and moaned.

"Bath."

"Later," he replied.

"No later. Bath now. I'm tired."

Davi stepped into the tub. She turned on the Jacuzzi and then the stereo. Quinn joined her, facing her. Davi stretched out her legs and rubbed her feet against Quinn's inner thighs.

Quinn's eyes sparkled.

"What?" she asked. "Tell me what you're thinking."

"You know what I am thinking. Why did you say what you did? You know it wasn't true."

Davi smiled. "What I said was true, but you didn't listen to what I said. I said I could fake an orgasm. I didn't say that I did. And I most assuredly did not say that I faked it with you, but you didn't hear that, did you?"

"No."

"So you watched that entire movie, trying to figure out when I faked it with you, and you couldn't come up with one time, could you?"

"No."

"It either comes, or it doesn't, Quinn. I wouldn't fake it with you. You should know that."

"I do now." Quinn leaned forward and reached for Davi, pulling her towards him. "You wanted me to think of us through the entire movie. You took my mind off Jocelyn and me and made me think of you and me. You are smart."

"You think I did that on purpose?"

"I know you did, and I thank you." Quinn kissed Davi tenderly. "You are the only woman I want to think about ever."

Davi turned around and leaned back into Quinn. Quinn kissed the top of her head as he held her close. "There's no one else in this universe for me, Davi, no one waiting around the corner, no one waiting to sit beside me on the airplane. It's you. It has always been you and always will be. If it takes my whole life to convince you of that, then that is what I'll do."

XO XO XO

Quinn left for the photo shoot under protest. He wanted to cancel the day's booking when Davi was too exhausted to accompany him. A restless night and her first day of morning sickness gave her the perfect excuse to stay in their hotel suite.

"Go. I'll be fine," Davi assured Quinn. "Go do your Hollywood heartthrob thing, and I'll stay here and do my barefoot and pregnant thing."

"Aren't you supposed to be chained to the kitchen stove or something?" he asked her as he hugged her.

"Just try that, stud, and see what happens."

Davi sat in the dark in the living room wearing one of Quinn's hooded jackets. She gazed out the window as lightning flashed and thunder rumbled. The storm was a perfect mirror to last night's nightmare as she remembered it. Once again, countless women separated Quinn from Davi in a never-ending game of flag football. Once again, Luke waved papers in her face, screaming, "He's signed the papers." Then Guy stood over her, claiming that she was his, followed by flashes of light, a loud bang, and then darkness. Davi recalled jumping out of bed as fear raced through her. She tore open the bedroom curtains, only to be disappointed to find no comfort in the dark morning sky.

She reached for her cell phone and called Maggie.

Maggie answered on the first ring. "This is a surprise," she chirped.

"Tell me you can see again," Davi blurted out, unable to hide her fear.

"Davi, what's wrong?"

"These damned nightmares won't stop. They're getting worse."

"The darkness?"

"It's suffocating me. I'm afraid of the dark now. This is insane."

"What's going on? What's happening out there?"

Davi pulled Quinn's jacket tight around her. "Quinn's movie, I hate it."

"Care to explain?"

"He and his costar were hot and heavy when they filmed it. It's up there for everyone to see."

"Everyone or just you?"

"Does it matter? It's Ross and Lizzie all over again, Maggie. I can't watch it." Davi closed her eyes and sighed.

"Quinn knows?"

"Quinn and his posse know. Nothing's a secret in Hollywood. I hate it here."

"Is there anything else going on?"

"They've killed *Second Harvest*. It's not getting made."

"In heaven's name, why not?"

"The studio wanted to make it into the Quinn and Davi story and forget about the rest. They wouldn't back down, so Quinn killed it."

"He can do that?"

"He can, or at least Luke can. It's not official yet, so don't tell anyone. I haven't told the kids."

"Oh, Davi, no wonder you hate it there."

"Do you think the nightmares are related? I started having them before I came out here. Were they trying to tell me about this?"

Maggie bit her lip, thankful that Davi couldn't see her face. "Most likely. Our dreams have a way of telling us what we can sense but can't see."

"That explains Luke waving those damned papers in my face. I thought they were divorce papers when I first dreamt about them."

"Divorce papers? Never."

"I told you it was a nightmare."

"How is Mr. Hollywood? Is he still gorgeous and crazy about you?"

"Yes. He's a shoo-in for an Oscar, Maggie. At least that's the buzz going around here. He's amazing in this movie."

"The one you hate."

"Yes."

"What are you going to do about it?"

"Tell him the truth. I won't sit through another screening, not even if my life depended on it."

twenty-three

The New York horizon seemed the perfect fall sunrise with its orange-red stripes. Quinn and Davi had taken the late-night flight back to New York. Quinn preferred late-night flights for the quiet and the chance to sleep or catch up on his reading. He hoped Davi would like flying at night, too. She slept most of the night away once she finished reading her magazines and eating her snacks.

"You're going to get huge," he had teased her as she nibbled on her licorice.

"Don't make me fly with you, and I won't eat. It's your choice," Davi countered as she waved a licorice stick at him.

Quinn gazed out the window. Two more weeks of this, then Davi would be at home and staying there. She wanted her time to prepare for Christmas. He didn't want to think about being away from her. Quinn sighed, then turned to gaze upon his sleeping wife. She was beautiful and sexy. He could watch her sleep forever. Quinn reached out to Davi and tucked a stray hair behind her ear.

Davi smiled but kept her eyes closed.

"Are you awake?" he asked her quietly.

"No."

"Dreaming?"

"Yes."

"Am I in your dream?"

"Always."

"What am I doing?"

"Well, you're not talking. That's for sure." Davi chuckled and opened her eyes. "Good morning. Are we landing?"

"Soon. I love watching you sleep."

"And I love watching your old movies."

Quinn smiled, remembering their conversation from yesterday. Davi did most of the talking, and he listened. "I love your movies, but not this one. It's just too painful to watch you and Jocelyn without thinking of Ross and Lizzie. Blame it on Jack, tell them I'm not well, but I will not sit through one more premiere of this movie with you."

"You did all right last night."

"I can't make it into a game every time I have to sit through it with you. It's torture, Quinn."

"What am I supposed to do without you?"

"Whatever you did before I came along. You can duck out early or tap into your memory bank and watch old memories in your head. It's up to you."

Davi sat up in her seat. "I still have today off, right? You and Luke haven't made plans for me?"

"You have today off. I'm doing the morning show tours. You could always come with me."

"And be hoodwinked into being on the show? No, thank you. You and Jocelyn are the stars. You two can do the Hollywood thing together." Davi saw him wince when she said Jocelyn's name.

"But the movie—we're going to talk about it. The love scene—"

"Quinn, it's my problem, not yours. You and Jocelyn are terrific in the film. Talk about whatever you want to. Enjoy it. Please."

"I'll never understand you, Davina Stuart Thomas."

"Yes, you will. The first twenty-five years are the hardest. Then it's smooth sailing."

XO XO XO

Jake met Quinn and Davi at the arrivals gate. The airport was busy for six in the morning. The paparazzi were in full force to get the latest pictures of Hollywood's most famous couple.

Jake hugged Davi as soon as she reached him. "Lovely lady, it's good to see you."

"Hey, Jake, I've missed you."

"Don't I get a hello?" Quinn asked, joking.

"You're lucky I don't hit you." Jake glared at Quinn in response.

Davi put her hand on Jake's arm. "Jake, we're good. Thank you for offering to hit him for me. That's sweet of you."

"Sweet?" Quinn choked. "My best friend wants to hit me, and you think it's sweet?" Quinn held out his hand to Jake. "Jake, we're fine. Honest. And thanks for offering to defend Davi for me."

Jake ignored the offered hand. "Sue will be relieved to know I didn't hit you in the face. I'd have been in the doghouse for months if you got another bruise. Come on, let's get out of here."

The trio walked to the waiting limo. Jake put the bags in the trunk.

"Sit with us?" Davi asked sweetly. "Let's talk."

The three got into the limo with Jake sitting across from them. His eyes looked worried and tired.

"What's Sue up to today? Will she be free for coffee?"

"She's waiting on your call. Her mom has the kids today."

"I will call her. We've got lots to talk about."

The men stared at each other. Quinn's face was calm, while Jake's started to look like a volcano about to erupt. Davi had to say something.

"Jake, look at me. Quinn did nothing wrong. He made the movie before he met me. I overreacted when I saw it. I felt betrayed. We fought, and I walked away. The next morning, we made up. We're better than ever. Honest. It's my problem with the movie, not Quinn's. Don't make it yours either."

"It's not the movie. Your husband didn't go after you."

"We've dealt with it, Jake. As far as I'm concerned, it's over. You have to let it go. Don't be mad at Quinn."

"Anything could have happened to you. You just don't let your wife walk away from you in LA at night. He was reckless."

"That was my fault. I took off in a taxi."

"Still, he didn't know where you were going."

"No, but it's over. I'm sorry that we had an audience for our misunderstanding. It happened. And, I'm sorry that you got dragged into it. No one should have said anything. If I'm not mad at Quinn, you can't be. Save it for when he really screws up."

"You're expecting me to screw up?"

"No, but if you do, Jake's got my back. I'll be counting on it. Do we have a deal, Jake? Get over being mad at Quinn. You can be mad when I need you to be mad."

"Which will never happen," Quinn added.

"We're coming with you tonight. I won't let you out of my sight."

They rode the rest of the trip in silence. Davi closed her eyes, still tired from their flight. Quinn gazed out his window while Jake glared at him.

The limo stopped.

"You have fifteen minutes before we have to leave for the studio. I'll wait here for you."

Quinn took their bags out of the trunk. It was a quiet ride up the elevator and then down the hallway to their suite. Quinn opened the door and headed to the shower, with Davi following close behind.

"You're unusually quiet," she remarked as she sat on the edge of the Jacuzzi. "Care to share your thoughts?"

Quinn finished his shower and reached for a towel.

"Jake's in love with you. I knew he had a crush on you, but he's passed that now. He won't go after you, but he's made it clear he'll be watching out for you."

"He must know that I would never do anything."

"Oh, he knows. And he won't do anything either."

"I should talk to him."

"No. I'll talk to him. You were good with him in the limo, but he needs to hear it from me now. We'll talk on our way to the studio."

"What do I tell Sue?"

Quinn smiled knowingly. "Don't worry about it."

"Why are you so calm about this? You're usually jealous and very possessive."

"I am jealous, and I am possessive, but Jake is my best friend. He loves you, and he's looking out for you. I can't fault him for that, but I can make sure that he knows the rules and doesn't cross the line no matter what I do."

"What makes you think he'll listen?"

"Because Jake gave me the same talk when he married Sue."

Davi chuckled. "You were bad?"

"No, but I had it bad for Sue. They were newlyweds, and I liked the idea of being married, too, except that I was giving too much attention to Sue. Jake made it clear that it had to stop. His friendship meant more to me than anything. It wasn't hard to comply."

Quinn walked into the bedroom and got dressed. Davi sat on the edge of the bed and watched him.

"Why is there always drama? We're still on our honeymoon. We should be carefree and enjoying ourselves."

"Stay with me, and I'll give you a honeymoon every night."

"Tempting, stud, but not good enough. I want my bed in my own home, and I want you there with me."

Quinn held out his hand to Davi and pulled her into his arms. "Me, too."

"You have to go. Let me know when you're coming back here, and I'll make sure that I'm here for you."

"I will call you and give you twenty minutes warning."

"Have fun this morning."

Quinn released Davi. "Call Sue. She needs some excitement."

Quinn opened the door to the backseat of the limo and sat down across from Jake. Both men stared at each other, expressionless.

"She's my wife, not yours. I don't have to tell you hands-off and don't cross the line."

"I think I said it better with fewer words when the shoe was on the other foot."

"Yes, 'fuck off' worked, but I wanted to be a gentleman with you."

"Message received, but don't you mess it up with her or else nothing will stop me from punching you out."

"If I mess up with her, you have my permission to punch me out." Quinn held his hand out to Jake, and they shook hands.

XO XO XO

Davi and Sue met for coffee in the hotel's restaurant. Davi wanted to get out of the confines of the suite, but she didn't want to be too far away for when Quinn called. She had things to do once she had her twenty-minute warning.

"Here," Sue chirped as she offered Davi a white box with a blue ribbon on it. "It's for you."

"What is it?"

"You have to open it to find out. That's why it's called a present."

Davi smiled at Sue then opened the box. She pulled out a silver bracelet engraved with the words mother-to-be and small crescents. "It's beautiful. Where did you find this?"

"It's secondhand. I hope you don't mind. I saw it at the market, and I thought of you. The crescents are to bring good luck to the mother and the baby."

"I love it. Thank you." Davi put the bracelet on then kissed Sue on the cheek.

"So have the boys sorted things out?" Sue asked casually.

"What things?" Davi asked as she examined the detailing on the bracelet.

"Has Quinn told Jake to mind his business and look after his own wife instead of jumping in to save you?"

Davi laughed. "He was going to have the talk with him on the way to the studio. How did you know?"

"When Jake got the call about you and Quinn having that fight, it was all I could do to make him stay in New York. I told him the two of you would have made up by the time he got there, and he would have looked like quite the fool. Jake loves you, Davi. I know that, but it's this fantasy he has of you—he feels that he's your protector. It's his job, but it's more than that, too."

"Sue, it's not—"

"Oh, I know nothing is going on! I'm not crazy. It's like puppy love. I know Jake loves me, and he'd never cross the line. He knows it, too, but right now, he's not thinking straight. Quinn will straighten him out, though. It's his turn."

"I heard, but I didn't get the details."

Sue smiled as she recalled the incident. "Quinn had a crush on me when Jake and I got married. He was always hanging around, bringing me gifts. I thought it was sweet. Finally, Jake had had enough. One day, Quinn arrived on our doorstep, and Jake told me to stay in the kitchen while he answered the door. You know me. I couldn't stay put. I had to hear what was going on, so I stood in the hallway. Anyway, Jake opens the door and very calmly says, 'She's mine, now fuck off,' and then closes the door. The next day, everything was back to normal. No more crush."

"Were you heartbroken?" Davi teased.

"Of course! My husband had just told this gorgeous movie star to leave me alone. I got over it, and now Jake lets me know every day how much he loves and adores me, and Quinn and I are best friends, the way we should be."

"Jake wanted to hit Quinn. I told him he could have a rain check for when Quinn deserved it."

"He won't forget, you know. He will hit him if something happens."

"Oh, I know, but the plan is for it not to happen."

"So tell me about this movie! I know we're seeing it tonight, but tell me the dirt, girl!"

"It's a fantastic movie, Sue. Both Quinn and Jocelyn are so believable, Quinn especially. But—"

"But, what?"

"To watch it is like watching him cheat on me right in front of my very eyes. It made me sick. I didn't handle it well."

"Obviously, or why else would my husband want to go rescue you. What's the story?"

"He fell for her during the making of the film. He put it all on the line to get her, and it didn't work out. I know he made the movie before he met me, but it's just too real for me. It's torture to watch it." Davi took a sip of her coffee. "My first husband cheated on me. All of the bad memories, the doubt, and the anger overwhelmed me. It's not Quinn's fault, but I can't go through that again, not even when it's acting."

"What are you going to do? You've got a two-week tour ahead of you."

"I'm working on it."

"How?"

"I told Quinn I couldn't sit through another premiere. He promised me that I wouldn't have to. I can always lie and say I'm not feeling well and blame it on the pregnancy."

"His movie is that bad?"

"No. It's that good. Everything you possibly imagined about Quinn is there right before your eyes."

"Wow."

"I don't know if it's being married to him, it's hormonal, or just that movie, but I cannot stand to watch it. It's two hours of torture."

"I don't know if I want to see it now."

"You have to." Davi reached for Sue's hand and squeezed it. "It's fantastic, and he's great in it, really great. I'm so proud of him."

"That's just weird, Davi. You're proud of something you hate."

Davi's phone vibrated. Davi looked at the message. "I have to go. Quinn's on his way back."

Sue hugged Davi. "You know that I think the world of you and Quinn, but I don't envy you this part about being married to him. I honestly don't."

"Thank you for my bracelet. I won't take it off until Jack is born."

"You're welcome. I'll see you later. Or will I?"

"We'll see what the cards have planned. If I bow out, sit between Jake and Quinn. You can be the rose between two huge thorns."

twenty-four

Davi stopped at the newsstand and looked at the magazines. She wanted something to read for tonight when she came down with something and had to miss Quinn's New York premiere. One news magazine caught her attention, "French ambassador called back to France. Shocking sex scandal." Davi picked up the magazine and browsed through it, stopping at the featured article. "Jean Luc Fournier, the brother-in-law to movie director, Guy Tremblant, has been recalled to France while under investigation in a sensational sex scandal." Davi started to put the magazine back in the rack but then changed her mind and made the purchase.

Davi made her way to the elevator. She pressed the call button and waited. Her mind wandered as she thought about Quinn and their lovemaking. She pictured the negligee she had placed on their bed. She hadn't worn lingerie to bed in days. Quinn had her naked before she had the chance to dress for bed. She imagined him running his large hands over her body as his hot mouth made a trail of hot kisses down her neck to her breasts. Davi closed her eyes and shuddered in anticipation of what was to come.

"Just like a teenager," she said softly.

"No, you're a beautiful woman."

A familiar voice broke through her thoughts. Davi's body tensed, and her stomach knotted. She opened her eyes and turned around.

"Guy."

He had tried to change his appearance by growing a beard and shaving his head, but there was no disguising his grey skin and dark, lifeless eyes peering at her from under his cap's brim. She shuddered at the sight of him.

"Davina, I've been waiting for you. You're never alone. He has such tight security on you, but not today. Bad for him. Good for me."

"I thought you were —"

"Locked away in some insane asylum or rotting in jail?" His black eyes stared intently at her, making Davi turn away.

"Yes."

Guy laughed. "Maybe I should be, but when you have connections—"

"Such as your brother-in-law?"

Guy nodded. "You're smart. Yes, like my brother-in-law."

"What do you want, Guy? You tried to kill Quinn. Are you after me now?"

"I'm after you, my dearest Davina, but not in that way."

He lifted his hand to her face and brushed his knuckles against her cheek. Davi pulled her head away in disgust.

"I've come for you. My car is waiting." Guy took hold of Davi's arm.

Davi resisted. "I'm not going anywhere with you, Guy."

"You are coming with me, Davina, my love, one way or another." Guy opened his jacket to expose a gun tucked into his pants. "I came prepared this time. It's real. No security guard or husband is going to stop me from taking what should be mine."

"You're going to kill me."

"No, I would never do that. However, I will kill whoever tries to stop us. I'm not letting go of you this time. Come, let's go."

Guy snatched Davi's purse from her and tossed it into a nearby planter. He wouldn't risk being tracked by Davi's cell phone signal.

Then he took hold of her arm and led her through the lobby. Davi cringed. The thought of him touching her repulsed her. She wanted to cry out, but she knew that Guy would use the gun, and then a sudden calmness flowed through her.

They walked out through the hotel lobby doors. Davi saw Sue out on the sidewalk, talking on her cell phone. Sue looked at Davi and was about to call out. Davi nodded no with the slightest movement of her head. As they walked past Sue to a waiting car, Davi dropped her magazine.

Sue followed behind them and picked up the magazine. She called Jake as she kept her eyes focused on Davi and the strange little man. She knew the drill. Jake had taught her well.

Jake and Quinn were heading back from the studio, with Jake now the driver. The tension between the two men was now long gone as Jake gave Quinn an update on his two children, Rachel and Connor.

"Man, they're growing like weeds. Some nights I get home, and I swear one of them has grown an inch. Sue's constantly buying new clothes for one of them. And the food—I don't know where they put it all."

"They run it off, Jake. It's what kids do."

"I don't know how Sue manages. They're on the go constantly."

"I want to be home with Davi when she has Jack. I'm thinking of taking the year off."

"A year? You'll go crazy. They're great to come home to, but you'll need a break, both you and Davi. Trust me."

Quinn laughed. "I don't care. There's nothing I want more than to stay at home with my wife and family. It's been my dream since forever."

"Since Davi, you mean."

"Same thing."

Jake's phone rang. He pressed the button for hands-free, then spoke, "Hey, baby, I've got the phone on speaker, so watch what you say." Jake winked at Quinn in the rearview mirror.

"Jake, listen. A man took Davi. They're getting into a car. The license number is BERC789. It's a black Ford SUV. I don't recognize him, but he's little, and he looks creepy. He's wearing a black baseball cap, black leather jacket and jeans. Davi gave me the signal not to talk to her then she dropped her magazine. He's put her in the backseat. Hold on. They're heading towards Forty-Eighth Street. Now he's turned left there. Jake, you have to save her. Save her, Jake."

Jake held his hand out to keep Quinn silent before speaking to Sue in a calm voice, "You did great, baby, now look at the magazine. What does it say?"

Sue looked at the front cover. "French ambassador called to France. Shocking sex scandal."

"Tremblant," Quinn yelled. "That son of a bitch!"

"Sue?" Jake continued, "Call the police, then tell them they can reach me on my radio frequency 502. Got that?"

"Got it."

"Okay. I'm going to hang up now."

"Get her back, Jake."

"I will. I promise. I love you. Now hang up and call the cops."

Jake cut the call then flipped on his radio. "Head to Seventh Avenue and go south. Davi's been abducted. I repeat. Davi's been abducted. We're only a couple of blocks away. Maybe we can catch up to them. Look for a black Ford SUV licence number BERC789."

"Jake!" Quinn roared. "What the hell are we going to do?"

Jake slammed on the brakes. "Get in the front. I need your eyes."

Quinn moved to the front seat in seconds. His hands gripped the dashboard as he stared out the window.

"You heard Sue. Look for a black SUV with the licence number BERC789."

"Dammit. Every car's a black SUV or a yellow taxi!"

"Look!" Jake's voice was strong, commanding Quinn to pay attention. His mind was reeling. Guy took Davi. The bastard didn't let up. For a month, his name hadn't crossed Jake's mind, and now the man was back in their lives. He held out his hand, demanding Quinn's phone.

He punched in a number quickly. "Bob, it's Jake Goodman. We believe Guy Tremblant has abducted Davina Thomas." Jake listened for a few seconds. "Yes. We're heading south on Seventh Avenue. He's probably heading for the tunnel. What can you do for us?"

Quinn stared out the window, reading every licence plate he could find. "Come on," he said with angry impatience. "You've got to be here somewhere, you bastard."

"I thought he was locked up," Jake said as he looked for Guy Tremblant's car. "Well, put someone on it and find out why. Heads are going to roll, man. If anything happens—just do it!"

Jake clicked on his radio. "Anyone see anything?"

"Negative."

Jake knew they'd need a lot of luck to spot the right vehicle. The rage boiled silently inside him. He should have taken that man out when he had the chance. He'd never killed a man before, but if he had the opportunity this time, he would. Three strikes and Guy was out. He wasn't going to mess with Quinn and Davi anymore.

"Get whoever's available onto Fourteenth and have them work their way towards us. We should see something soon. Do it now."

"Can't we go any faster?" Quinn barked.

"Traffic's slow, which is good. Tremblant's not going very far or very fast. This is the only route for him if he's heading for the tunnel."

"What makes you think he's heading for that?"

"He's got no other choice. Think about it. Tremblant has to get her out of the city and fast. As far as he knows, we don't know he has her, so it makes sense for him to take the most direct route out of here. Once he's on the other side of the river—" Jake couldn't finish the thought.

"Damn this traffic," Quinn groaned as it slowed to a crawl.

"No, it's good. If we're stuck in it, so is he. We're coming at him from both ends. We'll catch him, Quinn."

Jake was confident he knew where Guy was heading. He had to be. There was too much at stake to be wrong. He ignored the honks of the other cars as he pushed his way forward in the limousine.

"There he is," Jake said. "There's the son of a bitch." He pointed straight ahead of him.

"What now?"

"We stay on his ass."

"The windows are too dark. Dammit. I can't see anyone inside." Quinn hit the dashboard in frustration.

Jake flipped on his radio. "We're right behind him. Traffic's slow. We'll get him at Twenty-Third. We don't know if he's armed. Just box him in and wait for the police. No firing of weapons. I repeat. No firing of weapons. I don't want anyone getting shot."

XO XO XO

The SUV's blackened rear windows kept Davina hidden. Guy tied her hands behind her back, and then he went too far. When he covered her eyes with a blindfold, Davi screamed, terrified of the darkness that enfolded her. Unable to silence her, Guy slapped her hard.

Davi sat upright in the backseat of the car, crying silently. Her cheek smarted, and she wanted desperately to rub it.

"Don't make me hurt you again, Davina," Guy warned her as he looked at her from the rearview mirror.

"I'm terrified of the dark, Guy. Please take off the blindfold."

"You're safe. Nothing is going to happen to you, my precious. The blindfold stays on."

"Where are we going?"

"I'm taking you home where you belong."

"Where is home?"

"Just wait and see."

Davi concentrated on what she could hear and feel. She listened to the blaring of horns in city traffic and sensed that the car wasn't moving quickly. A traffic jam would give them time to find her. She was confident that Sue had phoned Jake. He would know what to do. He had to.

"I've been waiting for you for a long time, Davina. But that's okay. Everything is ready for you."

Davi's skin crawled at the sound of his voice. His intimidating self-confidence always bothered her. He was a condescending misogynist. She remembered when he had called her Quinn's latest acquisition. She'd bristled at the comment.

Nothing about Guy's appearance appealed to her. He may have been considered good-looking at one time, but something had changed him. His skin was grey, and his eyes were dark and lifeless. She remembered his hair as being thin and greasy, but he had shaved his head. She wondered why. Davi couldn't help it as the thought crossed her mind. He reminded her of Gollum, the little creature from *Lord of the Rings*—the one obsessed with the ring, his precious. Davi shuddered as she realized that she was Guy's precious.

"Where have you been, Guy?"

"I've been in New York waiting for you. I haven't worked since *Untitled*. You're the only thing I've been able to think about, you and my plans for us."

Davi swallowed the urge to scream. "What are your plans for me?"

Guy stared back at Davi and smiled. "Wait and see. Now be quiet. I have to think."

She recalled her wedding day after Jake and his men had stopped Guy from leaving with her. She had tried to explain him to Quinn.

"Guy is sick. He's obsessed with me, and no matter what I tried, he wouldn't leave me alone. He thought if I could love you, I could love him."

"You're my obsession. I didn't give up on you either."

"I guess that's the weird and wonderful part about love at first sight. If the person you fall in love with loves you back, it's a blessing. But if the person doesn't love you back—"

"You become Guy Tremblant."

"Merde," Guy cursed in French, bringing Davi out of her thoughts. "We're being followed. Who could have seen you?" He didn't give her time to respond. "That woman on the sidewalk—you dropped the magazine."

"Who is it?" she asked, fighting to keep from sounding hopeful.

"It doesn't matter. They'll be dead if they try anything. I'm not playing with toys this time."

"Don't kill anyone, Guy. Please don't kill anyone."

"I will if I have to. I'm not letting you go this time, Davina. Not for anything."

Davi prayed. *Please, God, keep everyone safe. Please.*

The traffic light turned red. Guy would have run the red light if it weren't for the vehicles blocking the intersection. He cursed again as the limo trailing him moved closer. Without time to react, Guy watched as a van pushed its way through the intersection, stopping in front of him. Then the limo following him rammed him from behind, pushing his SUV into the van blocking him. Guy was trapped.

Guy cursed himself for being so careless. He should have seen this coming. He had planned everything down to the smallest detail. Quinn didn't have security at the hotel, relying on the hotel's staff to keep him safe. He only used security for public appearances. It was that damned woman on the sidewalk. He should have shot her.

"Tell them that you're going with me, that you want to be with me, Davina. Tell them, or I'll shoot."

"Guy, they won't believe me. It doesn't matter what I tell them. They won't let you take me."

"They'd risk your life?" Guy laughed bitterly. "I promised you the world, Davina. I promised you wealth beyond your imagination. I promised you fame. I promised you my love. Why won't you accept what I promised you?"

"I promised my love to Quinn, Guy. I don't break my promises."

"I will keep my promises to you. Quinn won't. He's too young for you. He'll leave you. I know his kind."

Davi kept her voice even. "It doesn't matter if he keeps one promise to me, Guy, but I expect me to keep all of mine."

The blaring of police sirens filled the air. Davi wished she could see what was happening outside of the SUV. Once again, fear chilled her to the bone.

"Guy Tremblant! This is the New York City Police. Come out of the car with your hands up!"

Guy pulled out his gun, lowered his driver's window, and then shot three times at the nearest car. He raised his window and then waited.

Davi fell over onto her side, desperate to protect herself. "Guy, don't shoot, please," she begged him.

Guy cursed in French—condemning the police, his wife, and Quinn. Davi heard the sound of the automatic window, and then shots fired. She rolled onto the floor, lying flat on her stomach, desperate to protect herself and Jack.

"Be safe, Jack. Please be safe."

XO XO XO

Quinn and Jake took cover in their limo.

"Jake!" Quinn yelled as the sound of gunfire echoed around them.

"We can't do anything from here, man. The police will get him. Look over there. There's a sharpshooter. He'll get Guy."

"What about Davi? For God's sakes, man, Davi's in there!"

XO XO XO

Davi heard Guy reload his gun. Who was his target? Was it Quinn and Jake? Were they shot? Her stomach knotted at the thought. *Stay calm, Davi. Jack. Keep Jack safe. That's all you can do. Keep him safe.*

"We could have had a beautiful life together, my love. You would have loved me. I know it. Please forgive me."

Davi's world went to black. She didn't hear the shot or feel the impact of the bullet. She didn't see Guy's head explode as the sharpshooter's bullet penetrated the windshield and hit him in the back of the head. Davi didn't hear the silence that filled the SUV, or the terrifying roar from Quinn as Jake held him back from running to her.

XO XO XO

Maggie stood at her kitchen sink, washing up after a quiet afternoon of baking.

She sang an Irish Blessing that had stayed with her all morning, "When the storms of life are strong. When you're wounded, when you don't belong, when you no longer hear my song, my blessing goes with you."

A chill ran through Maggie's body as pain pierced her temple. She held on to the edge of the sink as the sudden impact forced her to her knees.

"Davi," she cried out, her voice no louder than a whisper.

twenty-five

Quinn stood leaning against the wall, facing the emergency trauma room. He stared at the door with fear blazing in his eyes. Only minutes ago, he yelled at the doctors and nurses, demanding to be allowed with his wife as he tried to push his way past them. He needed to touch her and feel the tingle from her hand. Then he'd know she would be all right. That's all he wanted.

It took all of Jake's strength to hold him back. "Calm down, Quinn. You're not helping her by getting in the doctors' way. Let them look after her."

"Why did he have to shoot her? What kind of man does that?" Quinn asked as he stopped pushing against Jake. "She's my life, Jake. She's everything to me."

Quinn looked down at his left hand and touched his wedding band. He wore her ring. He belonged to her. She couldn't leave him.

Jake nodded to one of his men to stay with Quinn while Jake took a moment to call Sue.

"Sue."

"Jake! What happened?"

Jake tried to get the words out but choked on them. "She's been shot. I don't know anything else, but it's serious. Call Maggie. Let her tell the kids. They shouldn't be alone. Get them out here right away and—" He couldn't finish his thought.

"I'll make the call, Jake. I know what to do. You look after Quinn."

"Thanks. I have to go. I love you."

"I love you."

The line went dead. Jake looked over at Quinn. The man didn't move as he stared at the door. Jake joined Quinn and stood beside him.

"Quinn—"

"There's nothing to say, Jake. The only one to blame here is Guy, and he's dead."

A hospital security guard approached them. "Excuse me, but you're causing a distraction. Would you mind moving to the waiting area?"

"My wife's in there," Quinn replied angrily. "I don't care if I'm a distraction. I'll stand outside her door as long as I damn well please."

Jake looked around him. People were gathering in the hallway, gawking at Quinn.

"You're security, aren't you?" he asked the burly security guard. "Do your damn job and get these people out of here. If they're not here for treatment or with a patient, they have no right to be here. If you can't do the job, I'll bring in my security team to do it."

Jake stared the man down until he turned around and made the crowd disperse.

"They'll be back," Jake said with disgust. "I'll get my men in here." He put a hand on Quinn's shoulder. "You'll be okay for a few minutes?"

"Go, Jake. Fix this."

What am I supposed to fix? Jake wondered. *Was it the security, or did Quinn ask me to fix Davi?* Jake walked away quickly before he lost it altogether.

Jake phoned his men and arranged extra security for the hospital. Next, he called Luke. Luke was already heading to the airport. Jake contacted Sue again. Sue had reached Maggie, and Maggie would look after Davi's family. She'd phone once they made it to the airport.

"Any news?" he asked when he returned to Quinn.

"None. I feel so helpless. There's nothing I can do except stand here. It's torture, Jake."

"I know."

"You went through this with Davi when I was the one in there." Quinn nodded towards the trauma room. "I don't know how she did this."

"She was positive that you'd be okay. You have to be the same. Stay positive."

"I don't have a plan B. She has to come through this. I have nothing without her."

A nurse exited the trauma room and then approached Quinn and Jake. "Let's go in here," she said as she motioned to a private lounge. She looked directly at Quinn. "Your wife has sustained a bullet wound to the head. We're trying to stabilize her so that we can run a scan on her brain so the doctors can assess how serious it is right now."

"Isn't a bullet wound to the head serious?"

"Yes, but your wife may be one of the lucky ones. It all depends on what part of the brain was injured and where the bullet stopped. The scan will give the doctors that information."

"What about the baby? She's in her third month."

"We saw the bracelet. We'll run an ultrasound as well."

"Bracelet? What bracelet?"

The nurse handed Quinn the silver bracelet. "She was wearing this."

"Sue gave it to her today," Jake said as he put his hand on Quinn's shoulder.

"Mother-to-be," Quinn read aloud. He closed his fist around it and held on to it.

"Here are her rings, too. She wasn't wearing any other jewellery. I'm sorry that I can't tell you much more."

Quinn put the rings in his pocket. "Is she conscious?"

"No."

"So we just wait?"

"Please. Wait here. I'll come to get you as soon as there is any word on your wife."

"Thank you," Quinn said softly.

XO XO XO

Quinn sat in a chair facing the door. His large hands played carefully with the silver bracelet as he thought of Davi. The coffee Jake had brought him half an hour ago sat untouched on the coffee table in front of him.

Jake stood staring out the window. He watched as down below in the parking lot, television news stations parked their broadcast trucks, and reporters scrambled to interview anyone who might have something to say about Quinn and Davi. He hated this part of the business—the way the press pounced on any bad news or embarrassing situation, hungry for a story, and the fans, those who gathered on the grass outside, standing in silent vigil as they waited for news. Were they there for Davi or the camera? Jake turned away in disgust.

Quinn stood up quickly when two doctors entered the room. Quinn tried to read their faces but couldn't. They introduced themselves, but Quinn didn't register their names.

The first doctor spoke, "I know you've had a long wait, but we had to make sure we did a complete examination of your wife. The bullet entered the side of the skull and stopped at the base of the brain. We want to operate and remove the bullet. To be honest, 80 percent of gunshot victims don't survive. Your wife is fortunate."

"What about brain damage?" Quinn asked quietly.

"Surgery is always a risk, but without it, your wife will not survive. She may end up with some brain damage. The bullet can make a mess of the brain, but don't think about that now. We won't know for sure."

Jake asked, "What about the baby?"

"I performed an ultrasound on Mrs. Thomas," the other doctor answered. "Did you know she's carrying twins?"

"What?" Quinn asked in shock. "No."

"Well, she's carrying twins, and the pregnancy is strong. I'm telling you this so that you can give it a lot of thought. There may come the time when you will have to decide if you want to continue with the pregnancy."

"Excuse me?"

"How important is this pregnancy to you and your wife, Mr. Thomas?"

"It's extremely important."

"If your wife survives the operation but is severely brain-damaged, we can keep her on life support until the twins can survive outside of the womb. Or you may decide to let all of them go."

"You have time to think about it," the other doctor advised. "But please think about it carefully."

"I don't want to think about that now. I want to see my wife. Please let me see my wife."

Quinn and Jake returned to the trauma room. Jake froze in the doorway when he saw the blood-soaked pads on the floor, the tubes and wires flowing from Davi, and heard the whir of the machines keeping Davi alive. Quinn didn't hesitate, walking steadily to Davi's side and taking her free hand in his. He kissed it and held it to his cheek. He closed his eyes and thought of his love for Davi and Jack and his twin.

"Come back to me, Davi. Please come back. I love you so much." Quinn opened his eyes and looked at her. Her face was pale and bloodied. Gauze covered the bullet wound on the side of her head. He closed his eyes and concentrated. "Come back to me, wife. There's no plan B, so you have to come back. Do you hear me?" Quinn squeezed her hand tight, willing Davi to feel him, to feel the tingle.

"Mr. Thomas, we have to take her to the OR now. You'll have to let go of her hand."

"Not yet," he said softly. "Give me a moment." Quinn thought of his love for her. His heart ached for her. "Hear me, Davi. Feel me, please."

Quinn felt the tingle. It was weak, but it was there. He opened his eyes and kissed Davi on the cheek. "Come back to me, Davi. I'm here waiting for you. I promise you that I'll be here."

Jake put his hand on Quinn's shoulder. "Quinn, let her go. They have to take her now."

Quinn placed Davi's hand on her abdomen. "Come back for them, Davi. Jack's got company."

twenty-six

Jake stayed with Quinn while they waited in the surgical waiting lounge.

"Did the doctors say how long the surgery would take? I don't remember."

"Brain surgery is delicate, Quinn. It will take a few hours. Try to relax."

"What do I tell the kids?"

"That Davi's been shot in the head. That the odds aren't in her favour, but we need to be hopeful. Don't mention the twins until she comes out of surgery. They don't need another heartbreak if Davi doesn't make it." Jake faltered on the last few words.

"She's going to make it, Jake. I felt her. She's going to be all right."

"Quinn—"

"No plan B, Jake. She's going to make it." Quinn played with the bracelet. He remembered Davi's wedding rings in his pocket and pulled them out and ran the bracelet through the rings. He thought of Davi as he did so. "You're not leaving me, Davina Stuart Thomas. You promised me forever, and I'm going to keep you to that promise."

XO XO XO

The door to the lounge burst open. Tigger was the first through, closely followed by Cat and Rich. Sue and Maggie were a few steps behind them. Both girls ran to Quinn as he got to his feet.

Quinn pulled them against his chest and hugged them. "She's still in surgery. There's been no word." He looked over to Maggie. "Thanks for coming with them."

"I had to come. I had to see our Davi. I have to know." She put a hand on his shoulder.

Quinn resisted the urge to ask her what the cards said. He could tell by the way that she looked at him that she knew something.

"Sue told us what happened to Mom. I'm glad that maniac's dead," Rich said angrily.

"Let's not talk about him. He doesn't deserve any of our thoughts. Send your thoughts and prayers to your mother. She needs you." Maggie motioned for Rich to sit down.

The girls pulled Quinn to the sofa and sat down with him.

"Mom's going to come out of this, Quinn. She has too much to live for. She's a fighter."

"A rock," Tigger added.

"What did the doctor say, Quinn? Can you tell us?" Maggie wanted Davi's family prepared. They should know the truth.

"Without the surgery, she would die. She has about a 10 percent chance of making it. The bullet lodged at the base of her brain, and it may have caused a lot of damage. Even if they get it out, the doctors said that she may not make it."

Maggie could feel the dark cloud descending over Quinn. She could see what Davi had seen when he let his thoughts wander, when he thought about not having Davi in his life, the sense of hopelessness and despair. Then as quickly as she saw the black cloud descend on him, she saw it disappear.

"I felt her tingle," he said, his voice now filled with hope. "I held her hand, and I sent her everything I had. I felt it in her hand. It was weak, but it was there."

"We're scared, but we know she's going to come out of this okay. We have faith." Cat hugged him.

"Got some to spare?"

"You have it, too. You just don't know it yet."

"I can't believe we're going through this again," Jake mumbled.

"Tell us about Mom and Quinn and what happened the last time. They haven't told us anything."

"You know, it wasn't a good time for me. I'd rather not talk about it."

"Everything worked out okay, though. Quinn woke up, and he's pretty well back to normal. What happened that freaked you out?"

"It's the helplessness. It's holding someone's smashed head in your hands and not being able to make it better. It's knowing that your best friend could die and you can't do anything for him, except look after his wife. Taking care of your mom became the priority. She wouldn't leave Quinn's side. The way she fought for him scared me. I'd go home at night and just lie in bed, wondering how she did it. She kept telling Quinn to come back to her. It was as though she was at one end of a long dark tunnel, and he was trying to find his way to her. She kept talking to him to help him find his way." Jake went quiet with his thoughts.

"And then he did," the girls finished for him.

"And then I did," Quinn answered. "I don't know if I can do the same for her. I want to. I have to. I only hope that I can."

"Whatever she needs, you'll be able to give it to her. You haven't let her down yet, Big."

Quinn excused himself from the girls and motioned for Maggie to join him out in the hallway.

"They're terrified, Quinn. Don't let them fool you," she said as she walked with him. "They are just like their mother. They'll keep it together until it's safe to let go."

"You knew this was going to happen to her, didn't you, Maggie?"

"No."

Quinn grabbed her arm and stared down at her. "You knew something was going to happen to her. Why wouldn't you say anything?"

Maggie held his gaze. "Saying nothing was the only thing I could do that would help her."

"What?"

"After you were married, my gift changed. It didn't matter whose cards I read. Davi's future was all that I could see. I didn't see this happening to her. I had no idea what was in store for her, only that it was darkness."

"You could have warned her."

"What good would that have done? She was already afraid of the dark. Did you want her to be afraid of the daylight, too?"

"We would have been prepared."

"For what? My gift isn't an exact science, Quinn. I saw Davi get pulled into the darkness, and I saw the twins."

"You saw them?"

"Yes. I've known for quite some time."

"Will they be all right? What about Davi?"

Maggie turned her gaze away from Quinn. Say nothing, a voice inside her head warned her.

"Maggie!"

"It's your decision, Quinn. It's always been up to you."

XO XO XO

Hours went by as they waited for news of Davi's surgery. Maggie and Sue went to the cafeteria to bring back food for everyone, while Rich and Jake made the rounds checking security. Quinn and Cat sat on opposite ends of a sofa, while Tigger slept soundly between them, her feet on Quinn's lap and her head on Cat's.

"You're so much like your mother. You can change the mood in a room in an instant. You're such a positive influence."

"I'm her clone. Tigger is Dad's, and Rich is the combination of both parents. It's funny how it works out."

"Your mannerisms are even like Davi's. You play with your hair and your rings. Your mom does that when she's thinking. What are you thinking about, or do I even have to ask?"

"I'm not thinking of Mom. I've prayed for her. I know she'll be okay. It's called having faith." Cat smiled at Quinn. "She loves you the most, you know. More than she did Dad. And that's okay."

"Cat, you can't say that. Davi would never say that."

"Oh, but she does all the time with her eyes. I watch her when she's with you or when she's talking about you. She didn't have that with Dad."

"You were young. You wouldn't be looking for that."

"It was just over two years ago, Quinn. I know that look, and she didn't have it for my dad. At least she didn't have it for him then."

"Cat, this isn't the time."

"Yes, I think it is. I know about my dad. I know what he did to Mom, how he broke her heart. He told me. He said it was the biggest regret of his life, and if he could have undone it, he would have in a heartbeat."

"Why would he tell you?"

"He wanted to stop me from taking back a boyfriend who had cheated on me. He wanted me to know that if a man could cheat once, he could do it again. Dad didn't want me to settle for someone who could easily disrespect our relationship and me. It was a real eye-opener."

"I'm sure it was."

"Dad knew that he'd lost Mom's love. He said he saw it in her eyes every morning, the sadness. He said they were working on their marriage, but he knew he'd hurt Mom too much. He didn't think they'd ever be the same."

"What about your dad? Did he say he still loved Davi?"

"Yes, but he knew it wasn't the love she deserved. I always thought that was strange. I didn't know there were different types of romantic love. Now I know there are."

"I love your mother more each day, and I don't know how that is. But every morning, I find something new to love about her."

"It's the honeymoon phase."

"What do you know about the honeymoon phase? You've never been married."

"Mom told me you promised to always be in the honeymoon phase for her."

"Did she call me an idiot?"

"No. She called you the love of her life."

twenty-seven

Luke stood in the doorway to Davi's room with the distinct feeling of déjà vu. He'd been here just over a month ago. The room and the medical equipment looked the same, except this time, it was Davi fighting for her life and not Quinn. He watched Quinn caress Davi's hand and kiss it. He listened to Quinn speak to her in a clear voice as though she were awake and talking with him. Davi had done the same thing with Quinn.

Quinn looked up and noticed him. "Luke," he said, smiling, as though Luke had dropped by for a casual visit, "have a seat."

"How is she?" Luke asked, trying to show his best calm lawyer's face but failing miserably.

"She made it through surgery. Now we have to wait it out. She's in a drug-induced coma. It has to do with the swelling of the brain and healing."

"How long will she be in a coma?"

"I don't know."

"Quinn . . ."

Quinn looked up at Luke. He could see the torment in his eyes.

"I'm sorry."

"For what? Tremblant's the one to blame and no one else."

"I should have kept on top of things and made sure he was still locked up."

"France took custody of Tremblant and didn't notify our government that he escaped. There's no way you would have known he wasn't in jail unless you tried to visit him or the French admitted they'd lost him."

"But still . . ."

"A very wise woman told me that if I gave any thought to Guy Tremblant, I was giving him power over me. He's dead, Luke, and I won't ever give him power over me again."

"She's a wise woman," Luke agreed as he gazed at Davi.

"Yes, she is."

"What do you need me to do?" Luke asked as he sat down beside Quinn.

"I hear you're the man for getting hospital suites."

XO XO XO

Davi could feel the sharp pain bursting through her head, like fireworks going off in her head, and then it was over. Blackness enveloped her.

"It's okay, sweetheart, I'm here for you. Relax, Davi, you're okay."

Jake knocked lightly on the door then entered. He shook his head when he saw Quinn's large body lying beside Davi in a hospital bed not made for two.

"You're going to fall off that bed and take her with you. Your ass is hanging over the edge." Jake looked at the tangled mass of wires and intravenous lines. "What have you done?"

"I haven't disconnected anything. I need to hold my wife and let her know I'm here for her."

"They have larger beds, you know. Davi had one for you."

"We'll get it, but not until she's off the respirator. They don't want me messing with that."

"You already are."

"I promised to keep her warm, Jake. She gets cold if I don't hold her."

Noise filtered through Davi's ears. Voices buzzed, but she couldn't make out the words. She felt warm. For so long, she had felt cold, and now the warmth spread through her. The blackness pulled her down again.

XO XO XO

"I have something for you," Maggie said to Quinn once he released Davi's best friend from his hug. "Call it an early Christmas present from Davi." She smiled at him as she handed him the wrapped present.

Quinn looked at Maggie with confusion. "Where did you get this?"

Maggie leaned over Davi and kissed her forehead. She tucked a strand of hair behind her ear and touched her cheek lovingly before taking a seat.

Quinn sat down across from Maggie on the other side of the bed. He took Davi's hand in his and kissed it. Then his gaze locked with Maggie's. He waited for her to answer him.

"Open it first, then I'll tell you."

Quinn tore open the white tissue paper then examined the old brown leather book Maggie had given him.

"She wrote this for you when you were on your honeymoon. They are stories for you and about you. Davi gave the book to me to copy in case the original ever got lost. I think—" Maggie shivered, still feeling the cold from the darkness.

"Maggie?"

"I think she knew something was going to happen to her. And, she wanted to make sure you would get this."

Quinn opened the book and read the dedication aloud, "I dedicate this book to my knight in shining armour, my one true love, Quinn. Forever yours, Davina." Quinn closed his eyes, trying to stop the tears from flowing. "I haven't let myself cry for her. I thought that if I did, it would mean that I've given up hope."

"It only means you love her, that's all," Maggie said gently. "We've all cried for her, Quinn."

Quinn wiped away his tears then took in a deep breath. "Her doctors checked on her this morning. They say she's coming along well. The twins are good, too."

"Did they say when they'd wake her up?"

"No. Only that Davi's not ready. It's been three weeks. She's taking her time healing."

"She likes to do things in her own time," Maggie said knowingly. "Even with you, she took her time."

"She was so stubborn. I knew she fell for me just like I fell for her, but she insisted on making me date her."

"Quinn, you dated over a weekend. I don't think that was asking too much of you."

"She tells everyone she only wanted me for a one-night stand."

"She did." Maggie chuckled.

"She's not that kind of woman."

"She wanted a fantasy. No one would have ever known."

"She would have told you, though. She tells you everything."

"We have no secrets." Maggie reached for Davi's hand and squeezed it.

"She was terrified of the dark. Could she tell something was coming for her? Does she have your gift?"

"We all have a gift, Quinn. It's just whether we choose to accept it. She knew the darkness was coming for her. She didn't know why, but she could feel it. You have it, too, you know—the tingle you both feel when you touch each other. Davi calms you with the touch of her hand, and you excite her with the touch of yours. It's your gift for each other."

"I thought our tingle was sexual," he teased.

"That, too."

"I have to touch her. It's torture when she's away from me. Does that make any sense?"

"Yes. That's why it's so important for you to stay with her. Talk to her and touch her. Let her know you're here for her just like she did for you."

twenty-eight

Quinn looked forward to the evening when the hospital ward quietened, and the lights dimmed. There'd be no more interruptions from nurses checking on Davi's vitals or from those wanting one last look at the Hollywood heartthrob camped out on the third floor.

He enjoyed this time of night when he could slip into bed beside his comatose wife and hold her tight. He'd been with her every night. Leaving Davi was not an option for him. For days on end, he sat next to her bed, holding her hand and talking to her. He lived on Davi's favourite beverages, coffee and chocolate milk, and hospital food. Sue stopped bringing him home-cooked meals. He didn't have the appetite to eat the good stuff while Davi received her nourishment intravenously.

Quinn stretched out beside Davi in her hospital bed. He held her and cradled her head against his chest, then kissed the top of her head and breathed in her scent. He swore he could feel her relax in his arms, but she was still in a coma. That wasn't supposed to happen.

"Let's read my story," Quinn said softly to her as he opened the book at the first chapter. "Once upon a time, in a land far away, there lived a knight and his fair lady."

Quinn read slowly and steadily, trying to hold back the tears as he read to her. Davi had captured him perfectly from the top of his

294 Forever Love

six foot three inch muscled frame down to the tips of his toenails on his size 10 feet. "He stood before her, tall and broad-shouldered. His muscled chest rose with every breath he took, stretching his bloodied shirt tight across it. She looked down at his large hand still holding the severed head of the slaughtered dragon, its blood dripping onto his black leather boots." She described his voice, low and lusty when Davi drove him mad with desire. "You're my one true love, my lady. You own my heart and my soul. I would gladly face one hundred of these brutes than dare face a day without your love." She wrote about his blue eyes that sparkled with love and mischief. "He gazed at her from across the table. She could feel the heat from her blush as she felt him undress her with his eyes." She wrote of how she ached to be in his arms, constantly feeling cold until his body wrapped around hers. She wrote about his lips and his endless hot kisses. She wrote about their lovemaking, sizzling and passionate. "His lips were hot against her skin as he left a trail of soft kisses down her neck to her breast. She quivered under his touch, wanting more, needing more. His large hands cupped her buttocks as he lifted her onto him, entering her with one hard thrust. The rough wall dug into her back as he pressed her against it. She cried out his name."

Quinn chuckled, then gazed down at Davi. "You are clever, Davina Stuart Thomas—unwritten rule, my ass."

XO XO XO

Davi had a dream about Quinn and her walking along the beach. He was talking to her, but she couldn't make out what he was saying. A massive wave approached them, and Davi reached for Quinn but couldn't grab hold of his hand. Davi called out to Quinn. He smiled at her. The wave crashed over her, pulling her down into the darkness.

Quinn squeezed Davi's hand, and she felt the tingle flow through her. Keep holding on, she begged, don't let go. Quinn let go. Davi felt herself falling further into the darkness.

XO XO XO

"Shouldn't she be waking up soon?" Cat asked as she stood at the end of Davi's bed.

"Every coma patient is different," Sue answered her. "At least, that's what the doctors told Quinn." Sue put her arm around Cat's shoulders. "Thanks for getting him to leave the room. He listens to you."

"He looks like shit, Sue. He hasn't left the hospital in weeks. Mom will kill him when she finds out he let himself go."

"He still looks pretty damned hot."

"At least his hair is getting long. Mom will love seeing that."

"What about the beard?"

"Bet it's gone when he comes back. Mom doesn't like beards." Cat could feel Sue's arm tense around her shoulder. *Here it comes.*

"May I ask you something?" Sue asked haltingly.

Cat turned and faced her. "No. Never. Not once did I have the hots for him or wonder why he chose my mom."

Sue chuckled at Cat's answer. "You've been asked that before?"

"Whenever someone starts a question like that, I know what they want to know. Sure, we're closer in age, but that doesn't mean anything. Quinn's my best friend. Period. He loves my mother, Sue. You can see it in his eyes. Anyone who tries to take Quinn from Mom will be very disappointed."

XO XO XO

"You clean up well, Big," Cat said to Quinn as he sat down beside Davi's bed and took her hand in his.

"Thanks. How is she?"

"The nurse checked on her and said everything looks good. I think that's the only phrase she knows." Cat rubbed her mother's abdomen with care. "Mom's belly is showing."

"It's beautiful, isn't it?"

"I wonder how she's going to take the news that she's having twins."

"I have no idea. I have yet to be right when it comes to knowing how she'll react."

Davi felt the tingle again. Quinn was back. Davi dreamt of a park she and Quinn had visited in New York. Jack pulled at Davi's hand. Davi asked him where they were going. Jack smiled and pointed to Quinn, who was holding a little girl's hand. Davi looked at the little girl. She looked like Davi. She smiled at her then ran to her. Hugging Davi's legs, she looked up to her and said, "Mommy." Davi felt a warmth flow through her body before the dream faded to black.

XO XO XO

Davi heard voices. One of them sang to her in a familiar voice—warm and soothing. When the singing stopped, Davi wanted more. Davi felt the warmth of another's hand and the tingle. She held on as tightly as she could. Davi heard her name. She fought to open her eyes, but she couldn't. She held on tight and listened to the voice. It was calling to her, telling her to come back. Back from where? Davi could feel the darkness come. She tried to fight it off. Davi's world went to black.

Davi felt his presence and listened to his soothing voice. She couldn't make out the words. They didn't matter. He was with her, and she was safe.

"Mommy, it's time," Jack said to Davi as he led her to the barn.

A cow was giving birth, and Jack wanted to watch. They stood on the gate, watching as the calf came into the world. Jack smiled as the cow licked its newborn calf clean.

"Let's name the calf," Jack said excitedly.

"What will we call her?" Davi asked.

"Stevie, after my sister."

"You don't have a sister named Stevie, Jack."

Jack looked at Davi and smiled. "Yes, I do, Mommy, don't be silly."

XO XO XO

Davi opened her eyes. She could hear the buzz of machines around her. She felt the weight and warmth of Quinn, who slept soundly beside her. Davi couldn't move. Various tubes and wires connected her to the machines that kept her alive. Davi felt the weight of Quinn's hand on her belly. She reached for his hand, her arm heavy and aching as she tried to move it. Davi placed her hand over his.

"I'm back," she said, her voice no louder than a whisper.

Quinn stirred and opened his eyes. He felt the tingle from Davi's hand.

"I'm dreaming," he said softly.

"If you're dreaming, then so am I. I like this dream. Mind if I join you?"

Quinn sat up and instantly leaned in to kiss Davi. "I've missed you. Welcome back, love."

"Hello, gorgeous," Davi rasped. Her throat felt dry and sore.

"We've done this before, but the other way around."

"What happened?"

"Do you remember anything?"

Davi closed her eyes and tried to recall the last thing she remembered. She took her time as she tried to recall past events. "No. My brain
feels fuzzy."

"That's okay. It may take a while."

"I ache, and I feel stiff."

"You've been in bed for a long time."

"For how long?"

"Davi . . ." Quinn didn't know if he should tell her.

"How long, Quinn?"

"Three months. You've been in a coma for three months."

"Three months? Then it's—"

"Valentine's Day, love. Happy Valentine's Day."

Davi closed her eyes, and the blackness took her down again.

XO XO XO

Davi had a dream. Quinn was her knight in shining armour, and she
was his lady. They lived in their castle, their lives filled with love, music,
and laughter. One day, Quinn went out to fight a dragon that was
terrorizing the local village. Davi stayed in the castle and watched
through the window as she waited for Quinn's return. Dark clouds
descended upon the court. Suddenly, there appeared a bright flash of
light in her room. The dragon's mate had found her. Flames shot out
of the dragon's mouth towards Davi. She ran for cover, but there was
none. Davi cowered in a corner and screamed as she saw the face of
the dragon descend upon her.

"Davi, love, wake up. You're having a nightmare. Davi, it's okay.
I'm here, love. Open your eyes. Open your eyes, Davi."

Davi opened her eyes slowly. "It got me," she whispered, terrified.

"What got you?"

"The dragon."

"There is no dragon, Davi. It's just a story."

"It did get me." Slowly, Davi raised her hand to the side of her head and felt the scar. "See? I can feel it. The dragon bit me here." Davi's eyes closed. She could hear Quinn calling to her, but the darkness pulled her back. She was powerless to fight it.

Davi heard voices arguing. The loudest and angriest voice belonged to Quinn. She heard Cat's voice and recognized the calm tone of her persistence. Davi concentrated on the words.

"Quinn, you're going. Mom won't forgive herself if she finds out you passed on the Oscars. You have to go."

"I'm not leaving her. She'll be conscious any day now. The doctors say she's bound to come out of it soon. She's staying with us longer. I can't be away when she does."

"I'll be here with Tigger. Hell, we'll have everyone here watching you on television. Maybe when we yell out and cheer for you, Mom will wake up for good. Wouldn't that be a great wake-up present for her to watch you win an Oscar?"

"I can stay here and watch it. It doesn't matter to me."

"Liar."

"I'm not lying."

"Then you're a chicken. You're afraid to leave her."

"Being afraid to leave her does not make me a chicken."

"No?"

"No," Davi whispered, "he's not a chicken. He just has separation issues. You're going to the Oscars, Quinn. No discussion."

"Mom!" Cat ran to her mom and hugged her. "Stay awake this time. Okay?"

Davi smiled weakly. "I'll try."

"There is no try, Davi. Stay with us." Quinn came up to her on the other side of the bed. He kissed her forehead.

"I remember that line. You acted out a scene from Star Wars—the X-rated version."

"You remember?"

"I hope I never forget it. It was great sex. It always is."

Quinn laughed. "Cat's here, Davi."

"I know. She knows about great sex, too. I'm not telling her anything new." Davi took Quinn's hand. "You're going. No argument. I want to watch you at the Academy Awards. I think that's one show I can watch with you in it."

"You remember."

"If I've forgotten something, I don't know it. Not yet anyway." She tried to smile.

"I love you, Mom. We've missed you."

"How long?"

"You've been in a coma for three months and in and out for two weeks. Do you remember being awake at all?"

Davi felt the side of her head. "The dragon got me. I remember that."

"Dragon? There was no dragon, Mom," Cat said with concern.

"Yes, there was a dragon," Quinn answered Davi. "And it's gone."

"You killed it and its mate?"

"Yes. They're both dead."

"Happily ever after?"

"Yes. Happily ever after."

Cat asked Quinn, "What the hell's the dragon? What is she talking about?"

"It's all right, Cat. Davi's remembering a story she wrote for me."

"But she said it got her where she got . . . you know."

"Dragon bite or bullet wound. I think they'd feel the same, don't you?"

Cat nodded her head in agreement. Davi closed her eyes.

"She's going again. This is crazy."

"I'm here. I'm thinking," Davi said.

"Do you have to close your eyes, Mom? Every time you do, you're out for a few days."

"Not on purpose."

"I know, but—"

"Talk to us, Davi. Tell us what you're thinking."

"I remember my dreams."

"About the dragon?" Cat asked her.

"No. I remember the park in New York. The one where we watched the children play. Do you remember it, Quinn?"

"Yes, I do."

"Was it the same park in your dream when you saw Jack?"

"Yes, it was. What happened in the park?"

"We played there a lot of times on the swings, the slides, and the monkey bars. We had so much fun. You and I were there. Jack was there. I met Stevie."

"Stevie? Who's Stevie, Mom?"

Quinn squeezed Davi's hand. "You met Stevie?"

Davi brought her free hand down to her belly and caressed it. "They're beautiful, Quinn. I can't wait until they're born. Stevie has your eyes." She opened her eyes and smiled at him.

"Are you sure her name is Stevie? Couldn't it be Steffy like Stephanie?"

"Quinn, it's Stevie like Stevie Nicks. Jack made it very clear that her name is Stevie."

Cat chuckled, shaking her head in amazement. "I don't believe it! How do you two do it? You get a whack to the head and come out knowing everything! It's fricking unbelievable."

Quinn kissed Davi. "We're having twins, love, a boy and a girl, just like you dreamed."

"And they are both healthy?"

"Yes."

"How do you know?"

"The doctors ran an amniocentesis. We thought it was for the best."

"For the best?"

"In case I had to make a decision, I had to know."

"Why would you have to make a decision?"

Quinn gazed at Davi with teary eyes.

"Was I that bad? Tell me."

"You beat the odds, love. Welcome back."

twenty-nine

Davi woke up in the warm embrace of Quinn's arms. It felt good to be warm again. The nurse walked in, more surprised to see Davi awake than to see Quinn in bed with her.

"Good afternoon," she whispered. "How are you feeling?"

"Like someone who's been in bed for three months—achy."

"Have you been awake long?"

"I've just woken up. I was awake for a few hours this morning. I must have fallen asleep. I found this hunk of gorgeous sleeping beside me. Any idea who he is? If he doesn't belong to anyone, I'll take him." Davi winked at the nurse.

The nurse took Davi's vitals. She nodded towards Quinn. "He's been with you constantly. We just can't seem to get rid of him. He's had offers to go home with some of the nurses, even a doctor or two. But for some reason, he likes it here best. I think you're stuck with him."

"That's what I thought. Quinn hasn't been here for the entire time, has he?"

"Yes. If he leaves, it's not for long. There's always someone here with you."

"He has separation issues, silly man."

"I heard that," he mumbled into her hair. Only Davi heard him.

"Well, you're fortunate. All of us thought it was very romantic. Your husband made sure you had fresh flowers every day, and he read to you all of the time."

"He did?"

"Yes. You know, I thought *The Engagement* was the most romantic movie I've ever seen. But I have to admit, watching your husband with you every day for these past months has been the most romantic and incredible experience I have ever had. He truly loves you."

"And I love him. Thank you."

"Your doctor's making his rounds. I'll let him know you're awake. May I get you anything?"

"No, thank you."

The nurse smiled at Davi then left the room.

"I heard you. I don't know what you read to me, but I recognized your voice. Thank you."

"You're welcome."

"Go back to sleep if you want. I'm okay."

"I was just napping. I can sleep later when you come home."

"When will that be?"

"Your doctor said you'll need physiotherapy, and he'll have to assess you to see if you have any brain damage."

"I think my brain is fine. I remember you and my family, and I know my name."

"That's good."

"Tell me about the kids. Cat looks great."

"We're a family now, Davi, stronger and closer than I ever imagined possible. Rich took it the hardest. Maggie said it's the mother-son bond. Tigger's been great, coordinating everyone's visits, and Cat's been my rock."

"She kept you in line?"

"No, I didn't need that. I needed her advice. She's so much like you. You two think alike."

"About what?"

"Not now. Later, okay?"

Davi let it drop. "What have you been doing all of this time? Tell me you didn't just hang out here."

"Where else would I be? I promised you I'd stay with you. I keep my promises."

"What did you do?"

"I read my stories to you. Thank you for my book."

"You're welcome. I'm glad Maggie gave it to you."

"Now I know why we had that silly rule about different positions and locales within twenty-four hours. I didn't know I was giving you writing material."

"Every day, husband," Davi said as she caressed his arm.

"I read scripts and other books to you. I held your hand and told you to come back to me. That is all I did."

"Three months." Davi groaned. "I've been in a coma longer than I've been with you. We've missed out on so much."

"Shh," Quinn said softly, then kissed her forehead. "We've missed out on being with each other, but I've learned so much about you. Your sisters had a lot to tell me about you, and so did Maggie. It didn't take much for them to open up to me."

"I won't even ask you what you know. I don't care."

"It's all good, even the embarrassing parts. They love you. You scared the hell out of them, out of everyone."

"How's Jake? I can't even imagine what he went through. I hope he knows it wasn't his fault. It wasn't anyone's."

"You remember? All of it?"

"I remember it. The man was insane. He said he had a place for us. That's where he was taking me. I'm so glad Sue saw us. If she hadn't, I don't know if you would have ever found me."

Quinn held Davi tight. He didn't want to think about the possibilities.

"Once I knew she saw me, I knew that you and Jake would find me. I remember thinking of Jack and that I had to keep him safe."

"Why we ever thought we were safe from Tremblant, I don't know. I'm so sorry. He won't be bothering us again, ever."

"Is he dead?"

"Yes."

Davi shivered. "No more about Guy. He's taken so much time away from us. Let's not give him any more."

"Agreed. What would you like to talk about then?"

"No more talking. I want you to kiss me, husband."

Quinn kissed the top of her head.

"My head doesn't need to be kissed."

Quinn brought his lips to her cheek and kissed her.

"That's nice," she said, "but not there, stud."

"If I kiss you on the mouth, I won't be able to stop. It's been more than three months since we've made love."

"I don't think we can do much here. It's just a kiss," she teased.

"It is never just a kiss with you."

"Please, Quinn. Kiss me."

Davi turned her face to him. Her mouth slightly opened as she ran the tip of her tongue over her lips.

"Davi," he cautioned her.

Davi reached for Quinn's hair and ran her fingers through it. "Lover," she cooed.

He couldn't resist her, not when he first laid eyes on her on the flight to Los Angeles, not when she begged him to watch one of his movies with her, and not now. Quinn pulled Davi into his arms and kissed her softly. Davi kissed him back hungrily. Suddenly, Quinn broke their connection.

"It's me, isn't it?"

"Of course it's you! Davi, have you not noticed that you're attached to all of these machines? Everything about you is monitored. You even have a catheter. You want more than what I can give you."

"Does my breath stink?"

"No. You're fine." Quinn smiled as he got the hint. "You want your kiss."

"Give me my kiss. Please." Her eyes searched his face, pleading with him.

"Tell me if I'm hurting you."

"I will, but you won't hurt me."

Quinn took Davi in his arms once again. He brought his mouth to hers and kissed her. Davi's fingers wove through his long dark brown mass of hair. Slowly and carefully, he slipped his hand down her back and pressed against her lower spine. Davi sighed as the tingle flowed through her.

Davi didn't hear the alarms on the monitors. She didn't hear the door open as two nurses came running in to revive her. Davi didn't notice them stop and sigh as they watched the two lovers kiss. Davi only heard the beating of her heart and felt Quinn's heartbeat against her breast. She felt the tingle grow as it coursed through her body. Davi pulled harder on Quinn's hair, feeling her release shudder through her body. She loosened her grip on him but kept kissing him. Slowly, she became aware that they had an audience.

"We have company," she whispered as she released Quinn.

Quinn turned around to smile at their audience. "Hello, ladies. We were just trying something out to see how sensitive the monitors are. See, Davi? They pick up anything." He turned and winked at her.

"They're very sensitive," Davi agreed.

Both nurses laughed as they attended to the machines and reset them.

XO XO XO

Davi sat up in her bed. Earlier, she had been tended to by the nurses, bathed, and given Quinn's fresh T-shirt to wear. She almost cried when they informed her that Quinn had insisted she wear one of his T-shirts from the beginning. What once hung loosely on her now clung to her belly.

She looked at her reflection in a hand mirror. She never thought about her hair. Her head had been shaved for surgery, just as Quinn's had been. She rather liked how it had grown back, short and spikey. She turned her head slightly and noticed a line of silver hair covering her surgical scar. Davi rather liked the marking. Not everyone survived the bite of the dragon.

"You look beautiful," Quinn commented as he walked into the room.

"You like my new look?"

"It's very sexy."

"Even my touch of silver?" Davi showed him the marking.

"Yes." Quinn sat on the edge of the bed and held her hand. "How are you feeling?"

"I'm tired. The nurses say that's normal after waking up from a coma."

"Go to sleep then. I'll be here."

"No. I'm going to wait if I can. The doctors should be here anytime."

"I can wake you when they arrive."

"No, but thank you."

They gazed at each other for the longest time, as though their eyes could say more than words could ever convey. Davi cupped Quinn's face in her hand.

Quinn's eyes became teary. "It was hard."

"I know."

"You were kept in a coma. The doctors said it was the best thing for you and the babies. It would allow your brain to heal, and it would take the stress off your pregnancy. Then you wouldn't wake up. No one could figure out why. Maggie said you liked to do things in your own time. I had to agree with her."

"Is that when you decided to have the amniocentesis done?"

"No. Right from the beginning, I had to know who to save—you or the twins. I needed to make an informed decision. I hated having to do it, Davi. You don't know how much I did. The doctors said it was necessary."

"It's okay."

"I feel like such a hypocrite. I was so resistant to you having an amniocentesis test. Then when you got shot, I couldn't wait to have the test run. I'm sorry for what I put you through. I didn't know I could be so utterly and thoroughly selfish."

"Why do you think you are selfish?"

"Because, when the test results came back that the twins were fine, I decided to make your survival the priority. Having children didn't matter to me anymore. I only knew that I'd waited so long to find you, and now that I had you, I couldn't risk losing you. I was willing to lose our babies because I wanted you more. What kind of father will I make when I could give them up so easily?"

"You didn't give them up. You made a decision—one you hoped you'd never have to carry out. It wasn't right or wrong. It was just the one you could live with."

"But it eats away at me. I love you more than I love anyone in this world. I want children with you. I practically forced this pregnancy on you, and then I was so ready to end it to keep you alive. It doesn't make sense to me."

"Listen to me, Quinn. It doesn't matter. It's all in the past. I understand what you did and why."

"Don't try to make me feel better."

"Did you run your decision by Cat?"

"She fought me on this. She said you'd gladly give up your life for your children. She said that you would never forgive me if you survived and the twins died because of my decision. She said I had no idea what being a parent was all about and that I'd better be a better parent to the twins when they were born. She didn't talk to me for days."

"She's very headstrong."

"Like her mother."

"Yes, like her mother. It doesn't matter now. We're all fine."

"Don't brush it off like it was deciding to paint the nursery blue or pink."

"Then don't ask me to beat you up over what you did. I'm sure you've had plenty of time to do that."

"More than enough time. Cat was right, wasn't she? Did I make the wrong choice?"

"It worked out, Quinn."

"Tell me."

"No. You'll figure it out for yourself someday. Let's not talk about this."

"I have to talk about this. I want to get this all out in the open."

"What else happened that has you so upset?"

"You're going to call me an idiot, but I know I did the right thing. It was the right thing for me."

"What did you do? Is it public knowledge? Was it in the papers?"

"No. It's personal. I'm sure the gang knows about it by now. The kids do, but no one else."

"Did Cat fight you on this, too?"

"I didn't tell her until afterwards. She called me an idiot."

Davi laughed. She searched Quinn's face for a clue. "You want me to guess? Did you get a tattoo, something like 'Davi' on your chest? It better be on your chest and not your ass, Quinn."

"It's not a tattoo. I know you don't like them."

"They're okay on other people, just not on you." Davi smiled at him. "What did you do?"

Quinn squeezed Davi's hand. "I didn't get a tattoo, although it's something that can be just as permanent though not visible to anyone." Quinn took a deep breath. "I got snipped."

"You what?"

"I got snipped, had a vasectomy. I'm not putting us through this again. No more kids, Davi."

Davi gazed lovingly at Quinn's face, seeing the lines around his eyes, the stress and the fatigue. The man had been through hell the past three months.

"You think a vasectomy will make life easier?"

Quinn didn't answer her.

"You are an idiot," she said, shaking her head. "But you are my idiot. I can't believe you did that after everything we've talked about."

"It was my choice. No more kids with you, not for a while anyway." He winked at her.

"You've got a backup plan?"

"The doctor insisted I store a few vials of my soldiers just in case. I have a whole army waiting if ever I need them. I thought you'd approve."

"Plan B."

"No. No plan B. I'm not going anywhere. It's in case you decide to have more. That's all. I promised you forever. I'm in this for the long haul."

"You don't think two is enough?"

"I never know with you. You could always change your mind."

"Let me deliver these two first."

"I love you."

"I love you, too." Davi glanced at her left hand. "Where are my rings?" Quinn pulled down the neck of his T-shirt, exposing Davi's rings hanging on a silver chain around his neck. "I have them and your bracelet."

"It's a different look for you," Davi teased. "You're not a necklace kind of guy."

"It's my ball and chain. It reminds me of you every day, and it keeps you where you will always be—close to my heart." Quinn put the bracelet on Davi's free wrist. "I think you can have this back now."

"I'm so sorry. This ordeal has been tough on you."

"Just get better soon. I want to take you home."

thirty

Davi didn't spend much time with the doctors, at least not as much time as she thought would be needed to assess her. A quick check of her vitals, a routine check of her reflexes, and a short memory test to assure her she made a remarkable recovery. Physiotherapy would start the next day to improve her muscle tone and mobility. She would also undergo a more thorough test of her mental abilities. Davi would be released when she could prove that she could walk unassisted and use her arms fully.

"The babies," she asked the obstetrician, "they're fine?"

"They are developing according to schedule. There's nothing to worry about."

"What about sex?"

"I thought you knew. You're having a boy and a girl."

"No, not that," Davi said, smiling. "When can I resume my sex life?"

The doctor smiled back at Davi and Quinn. "Resume your sex life anytime you feel up to it. You'll be the one to judge when it's not comfortable anymore, Davi."

Quinn laughed once the doctor left the room. "You had to ask, didn't you?"

"I knew you'd want to know but didn't want to come across as the sex-starved husband. I thought I should ask for you."

"You weren't asking for yourself?"

"No. I don't need a doctor to tell me when I can have sex. We are having sex when we get home, Quinn. Be prepared. I have expectations."

XO XO XO

Quinn left Davi's room once the girls arrived to see their mother. He appreciated that they needed time to be alone to reconnect.

After numerous hugs and kisses and many tears, the girls sat on Davi's bed and told her about the public's response to the shooting.

"The flowers, Mom, you won't believe all of the cards and flowers you received. We took pictures of them and saved the cards. They're in a big scrapbook for you."

"A scrapbook?"

"Two, actually," Cat corrected Tigger. "We had to start a second one."

"I think everyone sent you a get-well card. You're famous!"

"Olivia, Kimmy, friends and family, and tons of fans all sent you stuff."

"We organized them by friends, family, fans, famous people, and fiction."

"Fiction?"

"The press. We had to keep the Fs going, Mom."

"Smart and very creative."

"Thanks. We thought you'd like it. Everything's at home waiting for you. What did the doctors say?"

"Once I can move around and use my arms properly, I can come home. I start physiotherapy tomorrow, and I'll have another assessment of my brain." Davi stopped and put her hand to her mouth. "Oh no," she moaned. "I've missed it all, haven't I? All of the holidays—Thanksgiving, Christmas, and New Year's!"

Tigger laughed. "It's okay, Mom. We had a great time with you. You didn't miss a thing!"

"What does that mean?"

"Big wouldn't leave you, Mom, but he wanted to have all the family stuff, too. I don't know how he does it. Does the man ever sleep?" Tigger asked.

"Anyway," Cat continued for her sister, "he had everyone come here. You have this amazing party room. Luke got it for you, but that's another story."

Tigger continued, "Sue and Jake brought all the food. All of your New York pals came, and we celebrated their Thanksgiving with them right here. Quinn's folks flew in, too. They were great."

"So let me get this straight. I'm out cold in this bed, and there's a party going on in the same room? That's sick."

"It wasn't a party, Mom. We know how much family means to you. We shared a meal, and we thanked God for our blessings. We thanked Him for not taking you away from us. We—" Cat started to cry.

Davi held her arms out to her. "Come here, sweetheart."

Cat fell into her mother's arms. "You can have your job back. I don't want it anymore."

"My job?"

"I don't want to be the rock of the family. It's all yours," she sniffed. "I don't know how you do it. Quinn—he got stronger every day. He'd sit here and hold your hand, and he'd just start feeling better. You could just see him getting his strength from you."

"I could feel him. I thought he was giving me my strength. He said you two were amazing. You kept him going, Cat, and Tigger got everyone organized. He said you all became a family through this."

Cat wiped her eyes then pulled away from Davi. "Rich took it really hard, Mom. He could only visit you a few times. When he did come to see you, he'd sit right here, hold your hand, and talk to you. He'd make sure everyone was out of the room. It was as though he were confessing to you. He didn't let anyone hear what he was saying."

"How is he now?"

"Cautious. He's going to wait a day or two to make sure you're going to stay with us. Doesn't that sound like him? He sends his love, though."

"How are things on the farm?"

"Good. Rich did great, Mom. You'll be proud of him."

"Christmas," Davi said slowly. "What about Christmas?"

Cat and Tigger laughed. "It was the best. We had Christmas here."

"Of course, you had it here."

"Everyone came, Mom. Quinn put everyone up at the hotel. Maggie and Charlie and the girls came, too."

Davi felt her eyes tear. "Don't get me crying," she warned. "Everyone came?"

"Not all at once, but they flew in through the week. We got to see everyone, and they all got to visit with you."

"Did Santa come?"

"Of course, Santa came! Why wouldn't he?"

After all of these years, Davi still played Santa with her kids, filling their stockings every Christmas Eve. They knew it was her, but no one ever talked about it. They all played along with the game.

"What did Santa give you?"

"Santa must have had a good year," Tigger teased. "He's never filled our stockings like that before."

"What did he give you?" Davi asked her.

"He gave us tickets to Paris."

"Paris?"

"Yes! Quinn says he knows of a few chateaus we can stay at and a few of his friends we can visit."

"Friends? What friends?" Davi didn't remember Quinn ever saying he had friends in France.

"Movie stars and rock stars, Mom. Especially you know who."

"You know who?"

"Marcus! He's given us an open invitation."

Davi closed her eyes. She wondered how she would ever top this for next Christmas.

"You're not mad?"

"About what?"

"We told Quinn about Santa. We never thought he'd do anything, and then he ends up doing this. He had stockings made up for us with the tickets and other goodies inside. Mom, we couldn't give them back."

"No. You were right to accept the tickets. When are you going?"

"Once Tigs is finished school, and I'm on summer break, Rich will work it out with you about leaving the farm."

"That's fine. I don't think I'll ask about New Year's."

"It was great. We had dinner here with you, then Quinn stayed here while the rest of us went out and partied. We were in Times Square for midnight."

"I've always wanted to know what it's like to celebrate New Year's in Times Square."

"You and Quinn can do it next year. Tigger and I will babysit for you."

XO XO XO

A few hours later, Quinn walked into the room, bearing gifts.

"What's this?" Davi asked in surprise.

"It's a great day. You're fully conscious, and you're healthy. I think that it's worth celebrating."

"It looks more like Christmas. What are you up to?"

The girls laughed. "Way to go, Big. Go big or go home, right?" They jumped off the bed to help him with the bags. "Are you trying to tell Mom something?"

Cat poked her nose in the most expensive-looking bag. "What's in here?"

"It's not for you," Quinn said as he pulled the bag away from her. "It's for your mom. If she wants you to see it, she can show you. Later."

Davi gazed at Quinn. His baby blues sparkled with mischief, but he still looked tired.

"I thought you were going to go to the hotel and sleep."

"I sleep here with you, Davi, and nowhere else. I had things to do, but I did get a shower, and I changed my clothes."

"And go shopping."

"I love shopping. I get great service."

"You always get great service, Quinn. It's part of being a super-star," Cat drawled.

"I'm ignoring that comment. Anyway, I bought you some things."

"Looks more like a lot of some things," Tigger remarked. "Can we stay and watch, or is this private stuff?"

"Do you mind if I keep it private for now? Davi can show you later if she wants."

"We're getting the boot," Cat said. "Mom's awake, and Big wants her all to himself."

Cat and Tigger turned and kissed their mother good-bye. "We'll see you tomorrow. Call us if you need anything."

Davi kissed them back. "Bye, girls. I'll see you tomorrow."

Davi waited for the girls to leave before she spoke to Quinn. "So what have you been planning? Is it a seduction?"

Quinn smiled as he arranged the vase of multicoloured roses on Davi's bedside table. "If you want to seduce me later, it's totally up to you. Seduction is not in the plan, but my plans are always flexible."

"Usually, your presents lead to great sex."

"Do they? I haven't noticed."

"I take it back. Everything you do leads to great sex."

Quinn kissed Davi softly on the lips. "Do you want to keep talking about sex, or do you want to open your gifts?"

"I think I can do both, but I'd like my gifts, please."

"There's a story that goes with the gifts. Do you want to hear it?"

"Is it a true story or a fairy tale?"

"Both."

"Then tell me, please."

Quinn sat down on the edge of the bed and took Davi's hand in his. He gazed into her eyes. Davi could feel him pulling her in, and she let him.

"Once upon a time, there was a knight in shining armour who won the heart of the love of his life. They lived in a beautiful castle."

"You're telling me our story."

Quinn reached into his coat pocket and pulled out the brown leather notebook. "This goes everywhere with me, Davi. It's my connection to you when I have to leave your side. However, tonight, I'm going to tell you my version of our story. May I continue?"

Davi felt movement in her belly. One or both of the twins were kicking her. She put her hand on her abdomen, enjoying the feeling of life inside her.

"Life was perfect. The knight would go out and slay dragons by day, while his fair lady looked after the castle and kept everything running smoothly."

"Can he just kill the bad guys like the black knight? I think dragons got an undeserved bad rap."

Quinn smiled at her. "Do I tell you how to write your stories?"

"I thought you liked my stories."

"I do."

"I was just helping, but if you want it to be dragons, go ahead."

"I thought you didn't like dragons. Didn't one bite you?"

Davi touched her scar. "Yes, but it was a very sick dragon. Usually, they are quite nice, but go ahead and kill them in this story. After all, it is your story."

"Thank you. One day, the knight went out and slew one of the largest, fiercest dragons of them all. He returned to his castle wanting to celebrate, but there would be no celebration. While he was out fighting the dragon, another dragon, the dragon's mate, attacked the castle and attacked the fair lady. The lady did not die but fell into a deep sleep from the dragon's venom, one from which she could not rouse."

Davi inhaled sharply. "What is it?"

Davi took Quinn's hand and put it on her belly.

"When you talk, I get kicked. I think the twins recognize your voice."

"I don't feel anything."

"Keep talking. Does the fair lady have dragon scars all over her body?"

"No. Just her head, but she was still stunning, and the healers said the scars would fade with time."

"Okay."

"For days on end, the knight would sit by his lady's bedside and think about their life together. He thought of the short time they had spent together and the love they had shared. The knight dreamt of their future and everything he wanted to do with his lady—raise a family, travel the world, and live very happily ever after." Quinn smiled. "I felt that. I really felt that."

"Amazing. I think they react to you."

"Why do you think that is?"

Another kick pushed against Quinn's hand. "You talked to me every day and read to me."

"I didn't know if you'd remember us, and I wanted to tell you about us every day. I told you I was worried."

"The twins know you, Quinn. They're letting you know they hear you. Talk to them, Daddy."

Quinn went quiet as he became lost in his thoughts. Davi could see tears forming.

"How would they travel the world? By horseback? That would take forever."

"What?"

"How would the knight and his lady travel the world? By horseback?"

"No, by ship. They lived close to the sea."

"Keep talking."

"Anyway, the knight began to feel sorry for himself because he thought of all the time he missed spending with his lady love while he was out slaying dragons."

"He had a tough job. Someone had to do it."

"I thought you didn't like dragons getting slain?"

"I don't. But if the knight had to do it, he'd be the one to get the job done, right?"

"Right."

"That's my knight," she said proudly.

"But the knight didn't see it that way. He thought he should have been at home with her."

"They probably had an agreement. The knight's lady love let him leave the castle as long as he didn't futter the wenches. She was very understanding."

"Futter?"

"Yes, it's a word I came across in a historical romance novel. When the men had sex with the barmaid, milkmaid, or servant girl, it was called futtering."

"He would never futter anyone. His love was true. Please don't say words like that in front of the children. May I go on?"

"Please do. When does a present come into this?"

"When I stop getting interrupted." Quinn's eyes sparkled at Davi. He was having fun with this as much as she was.

The babies were still kicking.

"Okay."

"Anyway, the knight thought about the time he'd missed with his wife, and he vowed to spend more time with her when she awoke. He would make her his top priority and place her above slaying dragons."

"That's a big sacrifice." Quinn gave Davi a look. "Oops, sorry."

"He thought of their future, and he fretted that there may not be as much time for them as he had hoped."

"Why? Was she going to die, or was she a lot older than he?"

"No. He just worried. He didn't think about her age or his."

"Does he always worry?"

"When it comes to his lady love and her health, yes, he worries. She was his life, and he couldn't imagine going on without her."

"That's very sad but very romantic."

"It was, and he was helpless to do anything. You can't imagine how it played with his fears." Quinn's hand ran over Davi's belly, gently caressing it.

"But if he's a knight, he shouldn't be afraid of anything. He's tough and strong and handsome and always knows what to do. He's supposed to get over it and move on. That's what makes a hero."

"What if the hero can't be like that? What if he finds himself truly and utterly lost?"

"On the inside maybe, but everyone looks upon him as the one who knows what to do. From that, he would get his strength to carry on, to do the right thing, and then he wouldn't be afraid anymore. Everything works out in fairy tales. You know that. What happened to his lady love?"

"A healer arrived from the nearest village and gave the lady a special potion. It didn't take long for her to awaken and have a full recovery. When she did awaken, the knight decided to shower her with gifts to show her how much he loved her and how much she meant to him."

"He didn't think a card and flowers would do it?"

"No. The knight wanted to make up for everything he had missed with his lady love, and he wanted to show her his undying love."

"She probably thought he over did it, but she didn't say anything to hurt his feelings."

"Are you telling this story, or am I?"

Davi made the motion to zip her lips closed.

"So the knight gave his lady love many roses to show his love for her." Quinn reached for the vase and then showed it to Davi. "Lavender represents love at first sight. Yellow stands for remembrance and for welcoming her back. Red is for love and courage. Their perfume was heavenly and reminded him of her."

Davi inhaled their perfume.

"The blooms were beautiful, as was she." Quinn put the vase back then reached for a bag. "Then he gave her this as a reminder of their passion."

Davi opened the small gift bag and reached inside. She pulled out a small box of chocolate-covered raspberries.

"Where did you find these? I didn't know they made these. Chocolate-covered strawberries, yes, but raspberries?"

"I have connections."

"Thank you. Should I eat one now or wait for when we want some passion?"

"Taste one and tell me if you like it."

Davi opened the box and took two raspberries out—one for her and one for Quinn. She popped hers in her mouth and put the other in his.

"Mmm, delicious," she said. "Just like making love with you. Thank you."

"You're not going to forget about the sex, are you?"

"No, and neither did you when you woke up from your coma. Blame it on the head injury. What's next? What else did the fair lady get from her knight?"

"The knight gave her a bag full of everything she needed for travel because he wanted to travel the world with her, remember?"

Quinn handed Davi another bag.

She looked inside then chuckled. "Airplane travel? You said they would travel by ship on the sea."

"Poetic license."

"False advertising, more like it," Davi muttered.

She pulled the items out of the bag. They were her must-haves for travelling: red licorice, gum, candies, chocolate bars, and bottled water. There were also celebrity magazines, the ones she loved to read for entertainment.

"Where exactly are we going?"

"Home. When you leave here, we're going to spend at least a month at home. We won't go anywhere. We'll stay at home and spend quality time with each other. I want that. I owe it to you."

"You don't need to feel guilty about anything. We both knew what we were getting into."

"Did we? Davi, I've been so selfish and self-centred when it came to you. You did everything I asked, came running when I needed you. I didn't do the same for you. I couldn't give you the time you needed to be with me. I see that so clearly now. Things will change. I want to go home to stay."

"What? You don't mean that. Please tell me you're not quitting the business."

"Would that be so bad? I don't have to act. I can do something else, something that keeps me home and close to you and these two."

"Take a month off if you need to. I'd love that, but you're not quitting acting. I need you to be who you are, Quinn. You're not giving anything up for me. Promise me that you won't quit."

"I will quit eventually. I can't do this forever. You know that."

"No. I don't know that, and neither do you. I'll be on Hollywood's hit list if you give up acting. I'm not going to let you do that. You have commitments."

"They don't matter."

"They do. Everything matters. You are not abandoning your career. Got it?"

"You said you hated Hollywood. Why would it matter to you?"

"I may hate Hollywood, Quinn, but I love what you do. That will never change."

"I'll find work closer to home then. Toronto's quite the hot spot for making movies now."

"Fine. Work close to home then, but you are not quitting." Davi nodded towards the other bags. "What else did you get me?"

"You'll like these. I promise. In all honesty, these gifts are for me and purely selfish. I think you'd call them a typical valentine's gift from the husband." Quinn handed Davi another bag.

She recognized the logo. "Lingerie? You have to be kidding." Davi pulled out a black negligee. It was sheer and very feminine. "It's gorgeous."

"The saleswoman assured me that it would fit and that you'd love it. It even comes with panties. I didn't care about that part of it, but she assured me they'd fit, too." Quinn watched Davi as she examined the negligee. "You told me you wanted sex. I thought this would be appropriate. When you put it on, I'll know you want me."

Davi looked up at Quinn. "No more saying, 'Quinn, now'?"

"That works, too."

"What else do you have?"

"Getting impatient? You like getting presents," he teased.

"I have to pee, and I don't want to interrupt the story."

Quinn handed her the last bag that contained a jeweller's box.

Davi opened the lid slowly. "A charm bracelet?"

"You need something for our shared memories. I thought I'd start it for you."

Davi examined the charms. "An airplane, a movie reel—our first date?"

"Yes."

"The sun?"

"Our honeymoon."

"A heart?"

"Our love. I know you don't have to remember it, but I want you to know that my love is always with you."

"Thank you." Davi's hand went to her belly. "They're still kicking. You haven't ended the story."

"The lady loved her gifts and thought they were the best gifts she had ever received in her life. She showered her knight with kisses, and they made sweet love. Later, the lady discovered that she was with child, and the knight was very excited and happy. His lady love was, too, so they decided not to travel the world but stayed in their castle and waited for their child to be born. Time passed by quickly, and one summer day, the lady gave birth to twins, a boy and a girl. The girl looked just like her mother, and the boy looked like his father. The knight named the children, as was his right as being lord of the castle. The boy he named Jack because it was a good, honest, and strong name. The girl he named Stevie because he knew that this girl would be full of mischief but kind and loving and Stevie would suit her. The end."

"Are you sure about your rights?"

"Most definitely. If a knight doesn't have control over his castle, where does he have control?"

"The lady has no say in the matter?"

"Of course she does, as long as she agrees with the knight. That's how it works, from the beginning of time and on into forever." Quinn winked at her.

"Fine."

"What? You're not going to disagree with me?"

"Not now, Sir Quinn. If you remember, I have to pee. Not wetting the bed is a higher priority than arguing over who is the king of the castle."

"That's knight. But if you want to look upon me as your king, I won't object."

"Keep thinking that, stud, you'll go far. Help me out of bed, please."

"Do you think you should? You haven't been out of bed in three months. Let me call the nurse."

"Fine. You call the nurse, and in the meantime, I'll wet myself." Davi sat up and tried to swing her legs off the bed. "You have to help me so that I can get out."

Quinn got off the bed. "Tell me what to do."

He pulled the covers off Davi's legs. Davi brought her legs over the side of the bed and let them dangle. She could feel the blood rushing to her feet.

"Steady me while I try to stand. I think I can do it."

Davi let her feet touch the cold floor and got her balance.

"This isn't so bad," she said proudly.

Quinn wrapped his arm around her waist. "They'll kill me if you fall. Lean on me for support, Davi."

Davi moved her leg. She felt the stiffness instantly and grimaced. "Ouch. This is going to be tough."

Slowly, she shuffled her feet and headed towards the bathroom.

"You're doing great, love. We're almost there."

"I can't see my feet. I'm huge."

"You're beautiful. Don't think about it."

"I'm going to get bigger, you know."

"I know. I'll have more of you to love."

"You say that now. You might not get anywhere near me."

"I love a challenge."

"No, you don't. You like things easy and stress-free. That's why you picked me. You said I was easy. Remember?"

"Your love is easy. Everything else about you is a challenge."

"Not true."

"You scare the hell out of me."

"It's not intentional. I don't want to scare you. You might leave."

Quinn stopped. "I'm not leaving. Every time you scare me, it makes me love you more. I'm not saying I want you to scare me all of the time. But it sure keeps things interesting."

"We're here. Help me sit, please." Davi lowered herself onto the toilet. "This is so romantic."

Quinn squatted in front of her. He placed his hands on her knees. "I'm not leaving you. You could pass out or something. This is not the time to be modest."

"I don't think we've ever been modest with each other. We've seen everything, warts and all."

"I love your warts."

"I love your all."

When Davi finished, she stood in front of the sink and looked in the mirror.

"What are you doing?"

"I want to see where the dragon bit me."

"It's right here," Quinn said as he raised the silver hair covering her scar.

Davi still couldn't see it. "What does it look like?"

"You know Harry Potter's lightning bolt on his forehead?"

"Yes."

"It's nothing like that at all," he teased. "It's just a straight line, something like mine. We kind of match."

Davi pouted, hoping it would be something to show off. The line of silver hair would have to do.

"My arms are skinny. I've got to start working out."

"We'll get right on it."

"I'm tired," she said as Quinn took her back to bed.

"Go to sleep."

"Have you made the arrangements?"

"Arrangements for what?"

"Attending the Academy Awards."

"It's not for a few days. I'm still undecided. I don't want to go without you."

"Why don't you take your three best friends with you? I'm sure they'd love to go."

"You think so?"

"Just cover your ears when you ask them."

thirty-one

"It's starting," Sue announced. "This is so exciting!"

Under Sue's direction, Davi's hospital room converted into Oscar party central. Movie-themed decorations, along with a table of food and refreshments, and one sizeable flat-screen television to watch the Oscar award ceremony, filled the room. Davi didn't ask questions about how they got the tv or the reception for the signal. She didn't care. Her family was going to be on television, and that's all that mattered.

"Who's going to eat all of this food?" Davi asked in amazement.

"You just watch. The nurses and hospital staff will be dropping by all night. It will be gone before you know it."

"This has happened before?"

"Super Bowl Sunday. Now that was a party!" Jake laughed as he sat down on the bed beside Davi. He took her hand. "It's so good to see you awake and talking coherently. You scared the hell out of me, lovely lady."

Davi could see the sadness in his eyes. "I'm sorry. Don't blame yourself for any of this, Jake. It just happened."

"That doesn't cut it for someone who runs a security company, Davi. How do I explain a client getting kidnapped and shot? Sorry, it just happened. It should never have happened."

"But it did, and I'm fine. We're all fine. Don't torture yourself over it. Please."

"You're so forgiving."

"There's nothing to forgive. You're my protector. You did your job. You stopped Guy. Who knows what would have happened if you didn't get there? It could have been a lot worse, and you know it." Davi smiled at Jake. "No more sad eyes, Jake. Life's too short for that. Okay?"

"From now on, you don't go anywhere without one of my men or me by your side. Understood?"

"Understood."

"Are you two going to watch this or not? The commercial is almost over."

Jake supported Davi as she slowly made her way to the sofa. Sue covered her with a blanket, and then they settled in to see the show. They watched for almost an hour as celebrities arrived to walk the red carpet. They all commented on what the celebrities were wearing, especially the female stars.

"I can't believe someone let her leave her house wearing that dress. What was she thinking?" Sue cried out in disbelief. "She's a gorgeous woman. Why would she wear that hideous outfit?"

"And her makeup—did you see that? I don't think Sarah could do that if she tried. Her stylist must have had her eyes closed," Davi added to the commentary.

"I think she looks pretty hot," Jake said, unaware of the two women glaring at him in response.

"Where are they?" Sue asked impatiently. "What's taking them so long? We should have seen them by now."

"Haven't you heard of leaving the best until last?" Davi piped in. "Quinn was supposed to be a no-show. Maybe they're making him wait it out to surprise everyone."

"He's coming," Jake said with conviction. "Give him a minute."

Davi and Sue turned and looked at Jake.

Davi laughed. "You're connected, aren't you?"

Jake tapped his ear. "Yep. I'm not letting anything get by me tonight. Quinn says he loves you and to keep your eyes on him."

"What else is she going to do? There he is!"

Quinn appeared on-screen, exiting his limo. Cat, Tigger, and Rich followed behind him. The crowd cheered while the television commentators tried to conceal their excitement. They had no idea he would be attending the awards ceremony. Quinn flashed his best Hollywood smile at the cameras. The commentators spoke briefly on Quinn's nomination.

"He's so sexy." Sue sighed. "So damned sexy."

"So what does that make me?" Jake asked her.

"All mine," Sue answered. "Look at the kids! Wow!"

Davi smiled with pride as she watched her beautiful daughters and her handsome son walk with Quinn. Quinn walked slightly ahead of them, with Rich between the girls.

"Were they told to walk like that?" Davi asked, already knowing the answer.

"He can't have the girls too close to him, Davi. The press will jump on it."

"Bastards," Jake growled.

"This way, it looks like he's out with your family. It's safer."

"They're his family, too," Jake retorted.

"It's okay, Jake," Davi said calmly. "They're closer to him in age. I don't want the girls gossiped about, not over tonight especially."

Quinn stopped to talk to the interviewer.

"Quinn Thomas, congratulations on your nomination for best actor. We didn't expect to see you here tonight."

"I know, but my plans changed."

"You have been through quite the ordeal in the last few months. Are you with your wife's family?"

Quinn looked at the woman with disdain. "They're my family, too." Quinn nodded to the kids to follow him.

"Wow! Did you see how he shot her down? Quinn's hot tonight!" Sue clapped her hands. "Go, Quinn!"

Jake, Sue, and Davi watched with anticipation, waiting for another glimpse of the foursome. When the awards show finally began, the cameras panned the front row. There they were, Rich, Cat, Quinn, and Tigger sitting together.

"What is he doing?" Sue asked in disbelief.

"He's holding the girls' hands, Sue. It's for support," Davi answered. "You aren't going to begrudge them that, are you?"

Jake laughed. "Quinn doesn't give a rat's ass what anyone thinks. After that comment on the red carpet, he's playing by his rules now."

When Marcus sang one of the theme songs from a nominated movie, then pointed to Quinn and the girls, Davina shook her head. "We'll never hear the end of this."

Davi was surprised when Jocelyn Love's name wasn't among the nominations for best actress.

"Quinn made her look good, Davi. He does that with all of his costars. I thought you knew that," Sue said casually.

"She was good, Sue. It had nothing to do with Quinn. I thought she'd get nominated."

Sue looked at Davi with concern. "Have you forgotten that you hated that movie?"

"I haven't forgotten that, but I thought both Quinn and Jocelyn were amazing."

Sue turned her attention back to the television screen. "Well, there's no topping Meryl, Helen, or Jessica this time around."

Finally, the time came for the awarding of Best Actor. A headshot of each nominated actor appeared on the screen, followed by a clip from the film.

"I like him. He was good," Davi commented on the first nominee. "I didn't see that movie. Was it any good?" she asked during the second nominee's clip.

"No," Sue answered her. "The movie was boring."

The third nominee popped up on the screen.

"I've never liked him. I don't know why."

"He's not your type. You like them young and macho," Jake teased.

Davi laughed. "That's true, but that's not it. It's his brand of comedy. It never appealed to me."

Quinn's name came last. Sue took hold of Jake's hand and squeezed it hard. Davi stared at the screen as the camera zoomed in on Quinn's face. His face was calm, but his eyes sparkled. Davi smiled. As much as he tried to downplay his attendance, her man was now excited to be there.

"And the winner is Quinn Thomas for *Lovestruck*."

Sue screamed while Jake pumped his fist in the air. Davi sat quietly and watched as both Tigger and Cat wrapped their arms around Quinn's neck and kissed him on the cheek. Rich stood up and offered his hand to Quinn to congratulate him. Quinn stood up and hugged Rich, ignoring the hand. The camera followed Quinn as he made his way to the stage, accepting congratulations from various celebrities.

Quinn shook hands with the host and the presenters, received his award then stood at the podium. The applause went on for a very long time.

"It's because of you, Davi. They're showing him their support."

Quinn began to speak, "I wasn't going to come here tonight. In fact, I had taped my acceptance speech two weeks ago. It wasn't a reflection on the Academy or my fellow nominees. I just didn't have the heart to celebrate, but since then, things have changed. My wife came out of her coma this week."

Applause and cheers rang through the theatre. Quinn waited for the noise to quiet down before he spoke again. He acknowledged the support of the audience.

"Thank you. I want to share with you what my wife said to me when she awakened. Now, if this were a typical Hollywood romance where my wife came out of the coma and saw me for the first time, she would have cried out my name, and we would have had a loving and tearful reunion. The typical Hollywood drama would have had my wife wake up and ask me, 'Who the hell are you?' However, when Davi opened her eyes, the first thing she said to me was, 'You're going to the Oscars. No discussion.'"

There was laughter in the audience.

"And so I'm here accepting the award for Best Actor for *Lovestruck* not because I want to be here but because the woman with whom I am eternally lovestruck told me that I had to be here. Davi said, 'Be proud of your work because you made a great movie. You told a lovely story. Celebrate what you've done, even if you don't win, but you are going to win.' My wife is always right.

"When I agreed to be a part of this movie, I thought it would be a fun movie to make, showing how a man tries everything to make a woman love him. However, this film turned out to be a soul-searching journey for me. I put my heart and soul into it because I genuinely believed that it was essential to show how difficult it is to find love and win another person's love.

"And then I met Davi, and she turned my whole world upside down. Love is easy when it's meant to be. It's life that sometimes makes it hard. I am truly lovestruck when it comes to my wife. Loving her is the easiest and most challenging thing I've ever had to do.

"I'd like to thank the Academy for this honour. As a nominee among actors who I admire and respect, I am truly humbled. I'd also like to thank everyone involved in making this film—from the producers and director right down to every member of the cast and crew. Without you, I wouldn't have been able to give my best. To my Davi, I thank you for your love every day and for being my rock. I'll love you forever. Thanks for coming back to us. I'll see you tomorrow."

The audience broke out into applause, and then Quinn was escorted off the stage. Davi wiped the tears from her eyes.

"That was a great acceptance speech. I didn't expect anything less." Sue sniffed.

"What did he mean by loving you is the easiest and the most challenging thing he's had to do?"

No one answered Jake right away.

"Davi? What did he mean by that?" Sue finally asked her.

"He loves everything about me, and that's the easy part. The hardest part is the curveball that life has thrown at us."

"What curveball?"

"Guy Tremblant," Jake answered.

"He almost took it all away from us—three times. Quinn had to face the possibility of losing the twins and me. It was torture for him. It will take him some time to get over it."

thirty-two

Davi gave a heavy sigh as she sat down on the oversized sofa. The family room was warm from the fire burning in the fireplace and the afternoon sun shining through the large floor-to-ceiling windows. Quinn followed behind with two mugs of hot chocolate and a plate of his homemade chocolate chip cookies. He handed her a mug then sat down beside her.

"You're spoiling me."

"Good. It means I'm doing my job then."

Davi nestled into Quinn's side. "Let's watch a movie."

"Do you have anything in mind?"

"No. Maybe something's on the movie channel."

Quinn reached for the remote and turned on the television. He found a movie just starting. "How's this?"

"Good. Thanks."

They watched the movie in silence for a few minutes before Davi said, "Feel free to make any comments if you want to."

"Like what?"

"You can gossip about the stars or say anything that comes to mind. You can even make it up if you want to."

"You want me to talk through the movie?"

"I have a feeling this is a bad movie. Anything you can do for entertainment would be greatly appreciated."

"We haven't talked about Hollywood for days. Why the sudden interest now?"

"Well, after your Oscar win and your numerous television interviews, I thought you wanted a break from it all."

Quinn put the remote and his unfinished mug of hot chocolate on the coffee table. He turned to Davi and took her mug away from her, placing it on the table, as well.

"Out with it, Davi. What's on your mind?"

She couldn't resist his eyes, and he knew it. "What haven't you told me about *Second Harvest*? Nothing's been in the news about its death. I thought for sure there would be something announced over the last few months, but there's nothing."

"Did you check your bank account?"

"Quinn, it's not about the money. And yes, I did. There are a few extra zeroes in my balance now. Why has nothing been said about *Second Harvest*?"

Quinn gave her a mischievous smile then sat back against the sofa. "It's not dead."

"Why didn't you tell me?"

"It slipped my mind. I've been busy concentrating on you."

"Nothing slips your mind. What did you do?"

"I repurchased the rights for your book. I own *Second Harvest* now."

Davi leaned back against the sofa for support. Her mind raced with questions.

"Sarah was right. I owed it to you to fight for your movie. Taking a buyout was the chicken's way out."

"You didn't have to do that."

"I did. Now there's only one question remaining. Do you still have a crush on what's his name?"

Davi leaned towards Quinn and clasped her hands around his neck. "You're my only crush, Quinn Thomas. I don't care who stars in the movie as long as I've got you."

"Right answer, Davi Thomas, but I'm serious. He's yours if you want him."

"You won't mind?"

"No. I have no plans to be in the movie. *Second Harvest* is your past. I'm here for the now and happily ever after."

"What about you then? What are you going to do?"

"I asked for my work to be put on hold. Whoever couldn't wait moved on and cast someone else."

"Quinn! No!"

"Family is more important to me, love. I'm not leaving your side. Not for a very long time."

"I'll be fine, you know. I can manage."

"Oh, I know that, but this is my time with you. You can't stop me from having that."

"So what are we going to do? Sit around in front of the television all day and drink hot chocolate?"

"I have no objections." Quinn wrapped his arm around Davi and pulled her into him. "I can feed you chocolate-covered raspberries. We can make love. We have lots of catching up to do, three months' worth of hot sex."

Davi chuckled. "We'll never catch up, lover, but you hold on to that thought."

"I will, lover," Quinn answered back lustily. "You want it, too. Don't pretend that you don't."

"I'm not. It's just that I don't want to spend my spare time flat on my back. I've already done that for three months."

"You were in a coma. You won't be asleep this time. I promise."
Quinn leaned down and kissed her. Davi resisted the urge to run her
hands through his hair. She wanted to keep her thoughts on track. Davi
pushed away from Quinn.

"We should get ready for the twins while I still have the energy.
We haven't even thought about the nursery yet."

"It will get done."

"We don't have a nursery for our babies, but you went out and
bought a minivan. What were you thinking?"

"I researched them while you were in your coma. I bought the
safest one on the market. We'll need it for the twins. And the kids can
come along with us, too."

Davi laughed as she imagined them all in one vehicle. "We'll be
one big happy family."

"Yes, although I think the girls would have preferred that I bought
a limo for you instead."

"I can't think of anything more embarrassing."

"What do you mean?"

"Two babies, four relatively young adults, and me. I'll look like
the grandma, and the four of you will look like the parents."

"Don't."

"Don't what?"

"Don't put yourself down like that. You know you don't look like a
grandma. Everyone will know you're the babies' mom. Most importantly,
I will know that. I think you are the most beautiful woman alive." Quinn
stood up and offered Davi his hand. "Come with me. It's time for
some catching up."

XO XO XO

Davi enjoyed Quinn's caresses and soft kisses. She remembered this
Quinn who took his time and had complete control over her as he
claimed her. Davi didn't mind. She loved it when he did this to her.
Every inch of her tingled, while every part of her ached to be touched
and kissed. By the time he finally entered her, she was ready to fall off
the edge, waiting for that push that he always gave to her.

Davi fell asleep in Quinn's arms. Quinn held on to Davi and daydreamed. Being at home with Davi and knowing the twins were safe
and healthy excited him. They had three months to get the nursery ready.
Quinn's mind raced with the possibilities.

Unable to settle, Quinn slid out of bed carefully to not disturb Davi
and got dressed. He went across the hallway and walked into the guest
room that would become the nursery. Quinn closed his eyes and
imagined how it should look for the twins. He imagined two rocking
chairs over by the large window, one for him and one for Davi. He
would rock one baby as Davi nursed the other. Quinn saw himself
singing to his children and rocking them to sleep. His family with
Davi would soon be a reality.

"A penny for your thoughts?" Davi asked as she put a hand on his
shoulder.

"I was thinking about this room. We would have two rockers right
by the window there, and while you nursed one baby, I would rock
the other, and then we would trade. I can see where the furniture goes
and how it looks. I can see the colour of the room and everything we
have in it. It's amazing."

"You should do the nursery."

"What?"

"You heard me. You need a room that has your input, your mark. This house is ours, but there's nothing in it except for Oscar, your leather chair, and the clothes in the bedroom that say you live here. You should do the room. Put your mark on it."

"You don't mind?"

"No. I hate decorating, and I'd be happy to have you do it. It's only the babies' room. There's plenty of help and people to offer their opinion if needed. Go for it, Quinn. Do the twins' nursery."

"I have it all planned out in my head. It won't take much to make it happen."

Davi smiled. "You can make anything happen. I'm a believer."

"You can't see it until it's finished. No peeking."

"I promise. The nursery is off-limits until you say so."

thirty-three

"How can you sit here knowing your husband is upstairs decorating the nursery?" Maggie cried out in mock horror as she found Davi outside sitting on the patio, enjoying the fresh country air. "Have you gone crazy?"

Davi smiled at her best friend. "You know he has great taste and that he is quite capable of picking out colours and furniture for the babies. It's only a nursery, Maggie."

"It's my godchildren's nursery. I'll remind you."

"Which can always be changed," she teased. "Leave Quinn alone. Besides, I think he's going to finish today. He's adding the finishing touch."

Maggie sat down in the chair beside Davi. "How are you feeling? How are the little ones today?"

"I'm tired, and I haven't done anything. I feel like a beached whale, and I know I'm going to get bigger. Every time Quinn comes down to check on me, the twins kick up a storm when they hear his voice. I told him to stay away for a while."

"They kick for you too, though. It's not just Quinn's voice they react to."

"Oh, I know, but they kick up a storm when he's around. He just has to talk in that voice, and they're off." Davi rubbed her abdomen. "I had my doctor's appointment yesterday. Everything is fine. We're on schedule. Another two months to go, but they could come in the next month."

"But that's too early!"

"It is early, but they are big enough to make it on the outside."

"Promise me you won't do anything crazy. Sit in this chair for the next two months if you have to. I don't want anything other than normal when these two decide to enter the world."

"I can't promise normal, Maggie. You know Quinn doesn't do normal."

"I'm not talking about Quinn's normal. It's yours. Don't tempt the fates, Davi Stuart Thomas. Not this time, please."

"Maggie?" Davi asked suspiciously. "Are you reading your cards again? Is there something I should know?"

"I was going to tell you," Maggie said, clapping her hands. "I can read my cards again! No more visions of you popping in and messing with my head, I might add. But no, I don't know anything. I am speaking out of genuine concern for my godchildren."

"I will do my best. That is all I can do."

"Fine, then." Maggie stood up and kissed Davi on her forehead. "I think I'll go check on the nursery. There's still time for me to offer my help if it's necessary."

"Go ahead, be nosey. Just don't tell me what Quinn's doing. I promised not to snoop."

Maggie left Davi on the patio to enjoy the quiet. It was a rarity since she came home from New York. The girls were home full-time, and the house resonated from their endless chatter and laughter. They wanted to help look after Davi, even though Davi was quite sure she could look after herself, Quinn, and the large farmhouse. It didn't take long for Davi to change her mind. Being pregnant had never held her back before, but this time it was different. She was tired, and she felt huge. It was challenging to do the simplest of chores. Now the girls took over as housekeepers and cooks while Davi stayed out of the way, nestled into a comfy chair with a book and blanket.

XO XO XO

"Wake up, Mommy, there's something we want to show you," sweet cherubic voices sang into Davi's ears.

Davi opened her eyes.

Cat and Tigger stood on both sides of her. "Quinn's waiting for you. Come see what he's done."

The girls helped Davi out of her chair then into the house towards the stairway. Davi walked up the stairs with care. The extra weight made it difficult to climb the stairs gracefully.

The girls laughed with her as she cursed her bulk. "This is all Quinn's fault, you know."

"It takes two, Mom, that's what you always told us," Tigger teased.

"And that the woman should be the most responsible for birth control since she's the one who ends up pregnant," Cat added knowingly.

"I know what I said, and now you know why. Let your guard down, and this is what happens."

"Sorry, Mom, carrying Quinn's babies is not a good advertisement for safe sex. It just doesn't work."

"What doesn't work?" Quinn asked from the top of the stairs.

"Mom's advertisement for safe sex," Cat answered him. "She's got no credibility."

"Absolutely none," Quinn agreed happily.

"You're not supposed to be on their side," Davi whined playfully. "It's supposed to be us against you."

"But I have to be on their side when they are right. And right now they are."

Quinn reached out for Davi's hand and led her to the nursery, where a yellow ribbon stretched across its doorway.

Quinn handed Davi a pair of scissors. "Please make the official opening, Mrs. Thomas."

"I now declare this to be the nursery for Jack and Stevie Thomas," Davi said as she cut the ribbon. She handed the scissors back to Quinn. "I shouldn't walk with these."

Tigger put her hands over Davi's eyes as Quinn opened the door and led her into the middle of the room. Tigger removed her hands and stood back.

"Oh, my," Davi gasped in wonder as she looked around her. "It's amazing, Quinn, simply amazing."

"You like it?"

"I love it."

Slowly, Davi turned as she took in every detail of the entire room.

"I wanted a nice neutral tone, a soothing atmosphere, so I chose grey for the walls and cream for the trim. The dark wood, cream, and grey look great, don't you think?"

Davi looked at the wood trim and floor. Quinn had stripped them and restored both to their original colour. A cream-coloured area rug lay between the two matching antique replica cribs. The window covering was a simple blind. Two chairs sat in front of the large window. One was an antique rocker, the other an overstuffed armchair. A table sat between them with a small lamp and two books on its surface.

Davi walked over to the books and picked up the first—an old book of nursery rhymes. She opened the cover. Inside was an inscription with Quinn's name and his birth date.

"My grandmother gave that to me when I was born. My mother read it to me every night until I could read it on my own."

Davi recognized the second book. "Sleepy Puppy," she said softly. "This was my favourite."

"And ours, too," the girls piped in. "Stevie and Jack will love it just like the three of us did."

Davi put the books down on the table.

"Two change tables and two sets of drawers?" she asked.

"Why not? There's room, and then the kids can have a set when they're ready to have kids. We shouldn't need nursery furniture by then."

Davi opened one set of drawers to find it full of pink baby clothes for Stevie. The other dresser belonged to Jack.

"You've looked after everything."

"I did some shopping, yes. The girls helped me."

"But, I'm supposed to nest before the babies come. What am I going to do to get ready?"

"Everything's got to be washed, Mom. We left that job for you."

"Good. As long as I can do something."

Davi gazed up at the small prints hanging over the change tables. Quinn had framed everyone's baby footprints.

"Where did you get these?" she asked in amazement.

"I have my ways," he replied.

"Quinn's mom sent us whatever baby stuff she had of Quinn's. When we saw his footprints, we knew that you had a copy of yours in the baby book along with ours, so we decided to frame them individually. When Stevie and Jack arrive, we'll do the same with their prints. They'll go right here." Cat pointed to the empty frame on the wall.

"And over here," Tigger continued, "is a Quinn original. It makes the room, don't you think?"

Davi cried when she could see the picture up close. "That's our story."

"I know." Quinn walked up behind Davi and hugged her. "I drew this when I was in high school. I gave it to my mother for Mother's Day. I didn't know she had kept it, and I'd forgotten all about it. I dreamed about you back then, Davi. You've always been with me."

Davi wiped away her tears as she gazed at the framed picture. Quinn had drawn with exact detail a knight in shining armour on a black steed standing in front of a castle. From the knight's saddle hung a dragon's head. A maiden stood in one of the towers, waving at the knight. She had brown hair and blue eyes. She had a remarkable resemblance to Davi.

"Don't worry about the dragon's head, Mom. We'll have the little brats craving horror stories and science fiction in no time. They'll be immune to blood and gore and scary things. They'll think having a severed dragon's head in their room is cool."

"Is that the kind of bedtime stories your mother read to you?" Quinn asked in horror.

"And we turned out just fine. It's Rich who's still afraid of some things."

"That's right," Quinn agreed. "Clowns." Then he pointed at Tigger—"spiders"—then at Cat—"mushrooms."

"I'm not afraid of mushrooms, idiot. I don't eat them. I'm not afraid of anything, at least anything that I'll tell you about."

"You did a great job, Quinn. You should be proud of this. You've got great talent."

"Thank you. Now, all we have to do is wait for Jack and Stevie."

"And deliver them." Davi sighed.

"Can't help you there, Mom." Cat smiled.

"Nor me," Tigger chimed in.

"You'll be fine, Davi. Maggie says you don't have labour. You just pop them out."

"I haven't had twins before, Quinn. I don't think they just pop out."

"There's always a first time."

"Be careful what you wish for, husband. You never know."

thirty-four

"Come on, Mom, we're going to be late!" Cat called to Davi as she waited by the kitchen door.

Davi held her finger up to Cat to indicate she needed a moment. "Quinn, I have to go. Cat's getting rather impatient with me," Davi said quickly into the telephone. "Call me tonight when you get back to the hotel. I can tell you all about my party."

"What kind of party is it again?" He was purposely doing this— keeping her on the phone when he knew she had to say good-bye. Quinn missed his wife, especially the sound of her voice.

Davi answered, tamping down her frustration at being late, knowing all too well that she missed him, also. "Boudoir and baby. It's the latest thing for baby showers—sex toys and lingerie for mom and baby stuff for the baby."

"What about dad? Doesn't he count?"

"I'm sure dad reaps the benefits from mom's toys. Quinn, I really have to go. Maggie's going to be sending out a search party for us."

"I miss you."

"Me, too. We can talk later."

"Have fun and hug Maggie for me. Later, Davi."

"Break a leg, Quinn. I love you." Davi ended the call then looked over at Cat. "I'm coming," she huffed.

"How are things in New York?" Cat asked as she started the car's ignition.

"He's having fun, but I don't think he wants to admit it. Not that it was a good thing for Chas to get sick, but filling in for him has been a godsend for both Quinn and me."

Davi thought back to a couple of weeks ago. With the nursery finished, Quinn found himself with nothing to do. He had scripts to read through and correspondence to answer, but they didn't hold his interest for long. Chas Elliot, a friend of Quinn's and current boyfriend of Cat, had come down with strep throat while in the last month of his contract for the musical *Wicked*. His understudy had backed out from filling in for him, and Chas immediately thought of Quinn, who had a fantastic singing voice, a photographic memory, and loved to work on the stage. Immediately, Quinn declined the offer, but Davi convinced him to take it. Quinn had been at home for two months, and Davi knew that deep down, he needed to do something more constructive than nest as he waited for the twins.

"Go for it, Quinn," she told him. "You're not far away, and I know you'll be great. I have always known you could sing. Now you have to show the rest of the world what you can do on stage."

"Are you sure? I promised you I'd be here for you."

"And you've kept your promise. It's only for a few weeks, and the twins are due well after that. We have time. You should go."

"I could embarrass myself, you realize."

"No, you won't. Chas wouldn't have asked you if he thought that was even remotely possible. Make me proud. Go."

"I miss him, but I'm glad he's out of the way for a while. My body is suffering from Quinn overload."

"Mom!" Cat admonished her.

"No, not that," she said thoughtfully. "Quinn's always around me. I didn't have the heart to tell him to give me some space after all he'd been through."

"He loves you, Mom."

"Oh, I know."

"Ladies," Maggie said as she held up her glass, "I'd like to welcome you here tonight to celebrate Davi's recovery and the impending arrival of Jack and Stevie. Davi, you are so near and dear to our hearts. We can't imagine what you or anyone in your family went through these past few months. Please know that our thoughts and prayers were with you."

"Thank you."

"So tonight, we have a boudoir and baby shower for you. We have gifts for the babies, and we have gifts for you."

"And Quinn," someone called out.

"Yes, and for Quinn, which we know you will both enjoy."

Davi began opening the gifts. "I haven't had a baby shower in over twenty-five years," Davi said, embarrassed when she had to ask what some of the baby items were.

"They don't do it the same way we used to, Davi," Maggie said with sadness. "Gone are the good old days of generic baby creams and baby shampoo and disposable diapers. Everything has to be natural now."

"I think our kids turned out okay. No one sprouted a third limb."

"I know, dear, it's just the way it is. You'll catch on."

The twins received plenty of toys. Cat gave them two plush Holstein cows. It was a family tradition to give stuffed cows to the newest members of the family.

"Dragons?" someone asked when Davi pulled out two stuffed dragons from a gift bag.

Davi read the card aloud, "Remember to start them early—love Tigger." Davi smiled. "Dragons are part of our story with Quinn. It's a family thing."

Davi could feel the heat from her blushing when she opened a gift bag and found a sexy negligee. "Oh my," she said softly. "I like this." She took the black negligee out of the bag and held it up against her large belly. "What do you think?"

"It's called Forever Love, Davi. I saw this and thought of you and Quinn. That's what you've promised each other, and that's what we all hope you have."

"Look at how delicate it is," a guest remarked, "with the roses bordering the waistband then along the halter top. It's beautiful."

"Quinn will love this, Mom. Roses are his favourite flower, aren't they? He's always giving them to you."

Davi put the negligee away carefully in the bag then moved on to her next present.

"Massage oil and body lotion."

"You can give each other a massage. It's a great way to reconnect when you're exhausted from looking after the babies."

"You think she'll want him touching her after she has the twins?" someone asked.

"It's Quinn Thomas. She'll want him touching her."

"Excuse me!" Davi put up her hand. "His wife is in the room, and if there will be any touching, it will be me touching him."

"Davina Thomas!" Maggie exclaimed, embarrassed. "Your daughter is in the room."

"Don't worry, Maggie." Cat chuckled, enjoying Maggie's embarrassment. "I've heard worse. Just don't get Mom talking about Star Wars."

XO XO XO

"One more night without you," Quinn said lustily over the telephone. His warm voice sent shivers through Davi's body.

"I think you'll manage. How did it go tonight?" Davi asked sleepily. The party had worn her out, and she struggled to keep awake despite her need to hear Quinn's voice. She sat up in her bed and turned on the bedside lamp.

"Great, but it's so damned exhausting. I'm having a soak in the tub. You should be here with me."

Davi laughed. "I don't fit in the tub with you anymore, remember? The last time I joined you, there was no water left in the tub. It took days for the floor to dry."

Quinn laughed with her. "I don't quite remember it that way."

"You never remember it the way you should. It's those rose-coloured glasses again."

thirty-five

Davi woke and looked at the bedside clock—8:00 a.m. She was exhausted. The twins had been overly active all night long, keeping her awake. Someone had told Davi that there would be less kicking as the twins grew because they had less room to move in. They lied.

Davi struggled out of bed and made her way to the bathroom. Her belly felt unusually low and heavy. She sat on the toilet and waited. Davi held her head in her hands as her arms rested on her stomach. The flow came slowly. Anytime now, she told herself, anytime. "Finally," she said aloud as the flow stopped and her bladder was empty.

Her pregnancy was going well. Her blood pressure, blood sugar, and weight were all within the normal range. The twins were growing according to schedule, and if all went well, Davi expected to deliver them next week, but not today.

Davi stood up and looked in the bowl. She looked for the cervical plug, a sign that the babies would be on their way and labour would be starting soon. Davi didn't expect to see anything, but knowing how early and quickly her other deliveries had been, she monitored her bodily functions, just as she did the cows'. She didn't want the plug to show up today. Quinn wasn't home and wouldn't be until late tonight. The plug sat on the bottom of the bowl. Davi didn't mistake it for anything else. Cows and humans, it didn't matter—the gestation period was the same, and so were the signs of labour. Nine months, nine days for pregnancy and that damned cervical plug. Davi checked for it all the time with her cows and for herself. She'd been pregnant three times before, and three times, she saw the plug and delivered a child the same day.

"Jack, Stevie, we talked, remember? While Daddy is away, we don't come out. We stay inside where it's safe and warm. Tomorrow, you can come out, but not today."

Davi had a warm shower. The twins kicked up a fuss when the water was cold, just like their father. She had to admit the warm water was nice, especially for lovemaking. The last time she'd made love with Quinn was in the shower, and that was—Davi tried to remember. Two weeks. Had it been that long?

Today was Quinn's last day in the show. He was scheduled to be a guest on *Kimmy*, perform in the final evening performance then catch the midnight flight to Toronto. Everything was going to plan until now.

Davi finished her shower then got dressed. She tidied up her bedroom then checked out the nursery. Everything was ready for the twins. Their baby clothes laundered, soft bedding in the cribs, and diapers at the ready.

"Soon," Davi said as she closed the door before walking down the stairs.

Davi felt a contraction. It was light, just a slight twinge. She looked at her watch. It was quarter to nine. Hold off, she thought. For a while, please. She made herself a cup of herbal tea and toasted a blueberry bagel. By the time breakfast was ready, *Kimmy* was about to start. Davi sat in her armchair and turned on the tv already tuned to the right station. She sipped her tea while she listened to Kimmy banter with the audience. She laughed as Kimmy joked about her crush on Quinn.

Davi finished her bagel while Kimmy introduced Quinn. Davi could feel herself getting excited, the same excitement she felt as a lovestruck teenager, the way she always felt around Quinn. Some things never change.

"Daddy's on television, babies," she said excitedly.

Quinn came out on the stage. Kimmy kissed Quinn on the cheek. He pulled back, took her in his arms then kissed her lightly on the mouth. The audience cheered wildly then Quinn released Kimmy from his embrace.

"Why did you do that?" she asked as her face revealed a heated blush.

"Because you wanted me to, Kimmy. You fantasize about it, don't you?" Quinn asked as he gave her his best Hollywood bedroom eyes.

"You're awful," Kimmy said. "What would your wife say?"

"She'd think it was funny. She trusts me, Kimmy."

Davi laughed then felt another contraction. They were half an hour apart and could continue throughout the day. She wasn't going to take any chances. She'd call Quinn and leave a message for him.

Davi picked up her phone and dialled Quinn's number. She heard it ring on *Kimmy*.

"What's that?" Kimmy asked.

"My cell phone. Maybe Davi didn't like me kissing you, after all, Kimmy."

"Answer it, Quinn. Let's hear what she says."

"Hey, Davi," Quinn said.

Davi hesitated before responding, "I'm sorry. I thought you would have turned off your phone. I wanted to leave you a message."

"Can Kimmy listen in? We're on the air right now."

"I can see that, Captain Obvious. I'm watching the show. Hi, Kimmy."

"Hey, Davi, what's up?"

"Not much. I'm phoning to let Quinn know that I'm in labour. The contractions have just started. You may want to come home now, Quinn."

Davi watched the reaction on Quinn's face. She saw the tears come to his eyes.

"Today?"

"Feels like it."

"For sure?"

"Quinn, I've been through this before. Get home if you want to see the birth of your babies."

"Did she say babies?"

"We're having twins, Stevie and Jack. Stevie's the girl."

"Quinn, you better go."

Quinn rose from his chair. "You're right. I'd better go. Sorry." Quinn raced off the stage and out the back door where Jake waited for him in the limo with the engine running. "Jake."

"I heard," he said. "Sue just called me. She's booked a flight for you. We've got half an hour to get you to the airport. Got your passport?"

Quinn patted his inside jacket pocket. "Always." Quinn pulled out his phone and called Luke. "Luke, I'm bailing out on tonight, man. Davi's in labour. Jake's driving me to the airport. Look after everything. I'll call you later. Thanks."

"Did he pick up the phone?" Jake asked, laughing.

"He said hello."

XO XO XO

Davi's phone rang. "I'm on my way over. How are you?"

"I'm fine, Maggie. I've called the girls and Rich. Quinn's on his way home now."

"And the contractions?"

Davi felt another and looked at her watch. "Thirty minutes apart."

"Don't move. Just sit. I'm almost there." The phone went dead.

"Hold off for Daddy, okay, babies? Let's not do this without him."

Davi's phone rang. "Hey, Daddy. How's it going?"

"I'm a mess. I just spilled coffee down my jeans, and I'm flying commando."

"That's not good. Are you burned?"

"No, but I'm having a hard time keeping the hostess from dabbing at my crotch. No more commando."

"I like commando on you."

"I'll go commando at home then, but not in public. There's only one woman I want dabbing at my crotch. How are you?"

"We're good. I'm sitting in my chair, listening to Kimmy talk about us. Your exit made quite an impression. Where are you now?"

"They've just made the boarding call. I'll be home in two hours. Can you hold off until then?"

"It's not up to me, love." Davi sucked in her breath as another contraction came. She looked at her watch. "Quinn?"

"Yes, love?"

"Take a taxi to the hospital when you land. I've just had another contraction. I don't think they're going to wait for you."

"Who's with you?"

"Maggie's car just pulled in. She'll look after us. Don't worry. We'll be fine."

"I love you."

"I know. I love you, too. See you soon, Daddy."

XO XO XO

"You don't have to speed, Maggie. The hospital's just a few minutes away." Davi laughed as she clung to the armrest of the passenger seat.

"I'll speed if I damn well please," Maggie said, bristling. "I'm not having any baby born in my car."

"These aren't any babies," Davi teased. "They're a Quinn Thomas and Davina Stuart production."

"That may be, but we're not having their premiere in the front seat of my Audi."

"Fine. Speed away then." Davi looked at her watch. The contractions were down to ten minutes apart. The twins were eager to make their arrival.

"You know, I wouldn't be speeding if you didn't insist on having me paint your toenails."

"They looked awful. I promised Quinn I'd always have red toenails for him. When I'm straddled in those stirrups giving birth, I want him to see those red toenails."

"I don't think he'll even notice."

"Oh, he'll notice."

XO XO XO

"Just breathe, Davi," the delivery nurse coached her. "You're doing fine."

"I know I'm doing fine. I've done this before. I just want to slow it down a bit. Quinn will be here in half an hour. I want to wait for him."

"We can't slow this down," the nurse said.

"I've done it before. I can wait."

"You better not slow down," Maggie mumbled.

"Where's your sense of adventure, Maggie?" Davi panted as she breathed through another contraction.

"I left it at home. Just like your hospital bag. How could I forget that?"

"We both forgot it. It doesn't matter. I don't need anything from it yet. The kids will see it by the kitchen door. They'll bring it."

"They should be here by now."

"They'll get here. Quinn will get here. It's all good."

"You're very calm," the nurse remarked.

"She doesn't give birth," Maggie snapped. "They just pop out. Why would she get excited?"

"Ignore her," Davi teased. "She had it rough. We don't talk about it." Davi started to pant through a contraction. "That was a good one."

"They're down to three minutes. I'll call the doctor."

"How much longer until Quinn gets here? Call him, please."

Maggie pressed Quinn's number on her cell phone. "Quinn? It's Maggie. When will you be here? She won't deliver until you get here, and she's starting to piss me off." Maggie smiled at Davi. "Ten minutes? Fine. We'll see what we can do. Hurry."

"He's almost here," Davi panted. "I can wait."

"Yes. Mr. Hollywood is just around the corner, making the home stretch."

"Are you comparing my husband to a stud, Maggie?" Davi's eyes twinkled.

"No. I meant a racehorse. You're the one who used the word stud."

"But that's what they do with racehorses. They use them for stud."

"That may be, but I was only thinking of a horse running. You're the one thinking of a horse having sex."

"Oh. You're right. I'm always thinking of sex." Davi breathed through another contraction. "I wonder why?"

"Do you want me to smack you on the side of the head?"

Davi laughed. "You're grumpy. You'd think you were the one having the baby."

"And you're silly. Who thinks of sex while having a baby? Who gets their toenails painted red? No sane woman would think of such things. Are you sure you're not on any drugs?"

"Quite sure. All I've had is this glass of ice chips." Davi breathed through her contraction. "I miss him, Maggie. It's been two weeks. I miss my kiss. You'd miss it, too, if he kissed you that way. Admit it, Maggie, you like my husband."

"You know I like your husband."

"No, you really like my husband."

Maggie laughed. "Now you're crazy. He's gorgeous, and he's manly, but he's yours. I don't think of him that way. I would never think of him that way."

"Never? Never is an awfully long time. Come on. Tell me you've thought of him, Maggie."

"Why?"

"Because I know you have. It's okay. I don't mind. You can tell me or keep your little fantasy all to yourself."

"I don't fantasize about him. It's just that he's—"

"He's what?" Davi asked before breathing through another contraction. They were closer now.

"He's so infatuated with you. Everything about him oozes his love for you, and you're the same. It makes me love being in the same room with you. Your love is contagious. It makes all of us feel good."

"It's just not the sex, you know."

"I know it isn't."

"But the sex is amazing."

"So you've told me many times."

"I have not."

"Right now, it feels like it. Hurry up, Davi, have the babies. Maybe you'll have some sense by the time they arrive."

"I can't. Quinn's not here."

"What? You can't be sensible until he gets here, or you can't have the twins until he gets here?"

"Both," Davi panted.

The door opened. Davi's doctor walked in, with Quinn following close behind.

"I found this man out wandering the halls, looking for his wife. He said she'd have red toenails. Does he belong to you?"

"He's mine," Davi answered with a smile when she saw Quinn's face. "I've been waiting for him."

"I got here as soon as I could. How are you?" Quinn took Davi's hand and kissed it.

"She's been talking about nothing but sex. I was getting ready to smack her on the side of the head if she didn't shut up."

Davi breathed through the contraction. "It kept my mind off the contractions. I had Maggie going." Davi winced. "Jack's coming. I feel the head."

"You know it's Jack?" the doctor asked as she examined Davi.

"He's the eldest. He arrived in our dreams first."

"When did you figure he'd be first?" Quinn asked her with bemusement.

"I don't know. It just feels as though he'll be first."

"Okay, Davi, the head is crowning. When the next contraction starts, give us a push." She looked at Quinn. "Dad, do you want to watch your baby come into the world, or do you want to be with your wife?"

"Quinn, watch if you want to. I'm okay."

Quinn moved beside the doctor. A nurse stood beside her as well.

"I'm with you, Davi. I don't need to see where it comes from," Maggie said as she squeezed Davi's hand.

Davi took a deep breath then pushed.

"Way to go, Davi. Keep pushing."

Davi watched the deepening emotion on Quinn's face as he witnessed his child make its way into the world. She could see the tears start to form. Davi started to cry.

"Hello, little man," the doctor said as Jack made his appearance. "Your mom was right."

Davi put her head back against her pillow. Quinn watched as the doctor quickly inspected his son.

"Care to cut the cord, Dad?"

Quinn took the offered scissors and cut. Tears ran down his face.

Davi listened for Jack's first cry and smiled when it came. "How is he, Quinn? Ten toes and ten fingers?"

"He's beautiful, Davi, and he's got everything he's supposed to have."

"He is perfect, Davi, and he's got a full head of black hair. He's definitely Quinn's son."

"Was there any doubt?" Davi asked.

"Rest, Davi, until the next contraction starts. You may have a minute or two."

The contraction came on quickly.

"She's not waiting," Davi announced.

Maggie helped her to sit up.

"Push when you're ready."

Davi pushed.

"Good try, Davi. This one's not in so much of a hurry. Push harder with the next contraction."

The next contraction came, and Davi put everything into it. Stevie made her appearance one minute and thirty-three seconds after her brother, Jack. Quinn cut her cord and cried the entire time. By the time the babies were cleaned up and handed to Davi to hold, Quinn was a blubbering mess.

"You're something else," Davi teased as Quinn kissed her on the forehead. "Don't worry. I won't tell a soul." Davi kissed her babies. "They're perfect."

"Just like their mom," Quinn said proudly. "You've done it again."

"Done what?"

"Made me love you more."

"You should do it all at once. It's not as hard on the system, you know."

"Maybe for you, but I like it this way."

"Let's take a picture of the new family. Quinn, Davi, look at me." Maggie took a picture of them with her cell phone.

Quinn handed his cell phone to Maggie. "Take another," he said. "I've got some bragging to do."

XO XO XO

Davi sat up in her bed, nursing Jack.

"He's hungry. I think he's going to keep me busy."

"Stevie's not such a glutton," Cat remarked. "She's going to be a little lady." Cat kissed her forehead as she held her little sister. "She's beautiful, Mom. You and Quinn did great."

"Was there any doubt?" Quinn asked as he stroked Stevie's cheek with his finger.

"We know what Mom's track record is, Quinn, but your stud record kept us all guessing."

"I'm ignoring you tonight, Cat. Nothing you can say will get me to rise to the bait."

"Don't worry. I'm leaving."

She handed her sister to Quinn. Tigger and Rich had already left the room, but Cat was taking her time in going.

"We'll see you tomorrow, Mom. Quinn, we'll leave the kitchen door open for you. You should come home and sleep. They'll probably kick you out soon anyway." Cat kissed Davi on the forehead. "Good night, Mom." She kissed Quinn, "Good night, Dad."

"Good night, Cat," Davi said as Cat left the room.

"How's he doing?"

"He's finished and fast asleep." Davi looked up at Quinn. "You should go."

Quinn sat down on the bed beside Davi. Davi handed him Jack to hold in his other arm. Quinn gazed lovingly at his children. He memorized everything about them. Their black hair, their furrowed brow, and the way they both pouted in their sleep. Stevie's tiny fingers curled around her thumb while Jack kept his thumb free. Quinn memorized every wrinkle and every dimple. Quinn inhaled their baby scent and kept it in his lungs. He exhaled reluctantly, wanting to keep the memory of their smell with him forever.

Davi watched as Quinn made his memory of his newborn children. His lips lightly brushed the top of their heads. When Quinn looked up with tears in his eyes, Davi knew, and so did Quinn. The moment that Davi had always warned Quinn about had happened. Unexpectedly and without warning, Quinn Thomas had fallen deeply in love.

"You've walked around the corner," Davi said softly.

"Did you know it would be them?"

"No, but I'm glad it's them."

"Me, too. I can never see myself leaving you, Davi. Never. You still have me. You'll always have me, but now I know what you meant about that special someone who would win my heart without warning. I knew I would love them. But, this feeling is so overwhelming. They have grabbed my heart and soul, just like you. I'm theirs and yours completely. I made a promise to love you always, and now I promise to love them, too. Forever."

epilogue

Davi could see him from a distance. There was no mistaking that bare chiselled chest or the muscled arms as he easily picked up the large bales of hay and threw them onto the bale elevator. His battered Stetson covered his thick brown hair, the hair she loved to run her fingers through and pull. She gazed at his faded jeans. A naughty smile formed on her lips.

"Daddy!" Stevie and Jack called out from their car seats, bringing Davi out of her lusty thoughts immediately.

Davi pulled her pickup truck alongside the hay wagon and waited for Quinn to finish unloading the hay bales. It wouldn't take him long. He was now an expert at unloading hay, cleaning out pens, feeding cattle, and milking cows. Her Hollywood heartthrob was now a full-time farmer.

She rolled down her driver's window as Quinn approached the truck. "Hey, farmer, how's it going?"

"Man, it's hot out today," he said as he wiped the sweat from his brow with the back of his hand. "I'm glad that's the last load for a while." Quinn leaned in and kissed his wife.

"Daddy!" the twins called out to him.

"How are my kiddies?" he asked, giving them his best smile.

"They've just woken up from their nap. They want to spend some time with you. Are you free to go visit the calves?"

Davi handed Quinn an ice-cold bottle of water. He drank from it greedily.

"Luke called again. You aren't returning his calls. He wants to know when you're coming out of retirement. He thinks three years has been long enough. The studios want you back. He said that you could name your price."

Davi gazed into his eyes. His eyes told her everything she needed to know.

Quinn leaned towards her, his lips barely touching hers. "I can be bought, but you're the only one I'd sell to."

"Still?"

"Yes."

"He thinks I'm keeping you hostage."

"Aren't you?"

"Quinn!"

"You have my heart, Davi. Here is the only place I want to be."

"He says you're wasting your talent."

Quinn laughed. "Did you tell him what I've been up to?"

"Yes, but he thinks you can still do your charity work, farm, and make one or two movies a year. He doesn't understand why you'd give up your acting career."

"My heart's not in it anymore. It's here with you and the twins."

"Cows!" the twins shouted, impatient to go visit them.

Quinn smiled. "And it's with the ladies and your crazy kids. This farm is where I belong, Davi. I'm supposed to be here."

"As long as you're sure."

"From the moment I sat next to you on that flight to LA, Davina Stuart Thomas, I knew I would be spending the rest of my life with you. I have never been more certain of anything else in my life. I want to be here with you raising our family. I promised you forever, love, and I keep my promises."

Book Club Questions

1. How did the book make you feel?
   - Were you amused, bored, intrigued by Quinn and Davina's story?
   - Are you glad you read it?

2. What did you think about the main characters?
   - Were they believable?
   - Which character did you relate to the most/least?
   - Was Davina's reaction to seeing Quinn's sex scene believable? Was she justified to react the way she did?

3. Which parts of the book stood out to you?
   - Are there quotes, passages, or scenes that you found particularly compelling?
   - Were there scenes that you thought were unique, out of place, thought-provoking or disturbing?

4. What themes did you detect in the story?
   - What were the main points you think the author was trying to make?
   - Was there symbolism that you noticed?

5. What did you think about the ending?
   - Were you satisfied or disappointed with how it ended?
   - How do you picture the characters' lives after the end of the story?

6. What is your impression of the author?

- What do you think of the author's writing style?

- What do you think of the author's storytelling ability?

- Would you read another book by the same author?

7. What changes/decisions would you hope for if the story were made into a movie?

- Which sections would you cut?

- Who would you cast to play the main characters?

8. How does this book compare to other romances you've read?

- Did you like it more or less than *Forever Love*?

- Do you want to read more in the series?

Turn the page for a taste of Book 3 in the Davina + Quinn series

one

They gazed into each other's eyes as passers-by made their way around them on the crowded sidewalk. Her heart called out to him. *Kiss me.* He stepped toward her. He was so close to her that she felt the sweet warmth of his breath caress her face. Her bottom lip quivered in anticipation. After all these years of longing and regret, he was finally going to kiss her. She raised her chin to him as he lowered his face to hers. She closed her eyes and held her breath. His lips pressed against hers with a soft kiss. She liked this kiss. He'd never kissed her like this before.

She felt her knees weaken when he grabbed her and pulled her against his hard body, his sculpted chest pressing against her breasts. Her hands gripped his shoulders, letting him know she wanted him to hold her tighter as she rubbed her aching breasts against him. The dampness between her legs reminded her of how much she had missed him. She didn't need reminding. She thought of him every day and every lonely night.

Kiss me harder. Her mouth pressed against his, her tongue mating with his tongue. He allowed the invasion and continued to kiss her. Her hands left his shoulders and ran through his thick hair, pulling on the long dark strands that framed his chiselled face. His soft moan vibrated through her mouth in response. Emboldened by his reaction, she let her fingers find his ear lobes and caress them.

He groaned as he broke their connection. "Come on, Rene, we discussed this. No playing with my ears. French kiss me if you want, but leave my damned ear lobes alone."

"Cut," the director barked. "Rene, what the hell are you doing? That kiss was perfect until you screwed it up."

Rene Adams looked at the famous director, giving him her best sex-kitten eyes. "Clint, I couldn't help it. It felt like the right thing to do." Then she batted her eyelids at Quinn. "Sorry, honey, there's something about your ears that I just can't resist."

Quinn Thomas stepped back from Rene as he shoved his hand through his perfect mess of shaggy brown hair. Nine takes for a damned kiss. Everyone knew what she was doing.

"Okay, let's try this again," Clint called out. "Rene, keep your hands off his ears."

Quinn leaned toward Rene and spoke in a low and threatening tone, "Fuck this up one more time, and you'll get my stand-in."

"You wouldn't!" Rene hissed. "He doesn't look anything like you, and his breath stinks."

"I don't give a damn. Keep this up, Rene, and I'll leak it to the press that I refused to kiss you in front of the cameras because you have halitosis."

"Two can play this game, Quinn."

"Try me, Rene, and I guarantee you'll lose."

about the author

Deborah Armstrong hit the big 50, and became restless and couldn't concentrate on much. Her favourite escape was to read. Instantly, her daughter's romance novels became the ultimate magnet. Hours were spent devouring them.

That was then ... this is now. Deborah turned her restlessness into writing hot and spicy contemporary romance with a touch of country.

Deborah lives with her husband and five hundred cows on their dairy farm in Ontario, Canada. When she's not writing or working on the farm, she enjoys reading, travelling, watching movies, and spending time with friends and family, especially her grandchildren. She also proofreads and edits for fellow authors. Her writing muse tends to run on the liquid side: strong coffee, chocolate milk, and single malt scotch in no particular order.

Thrice each week, the local gym beckons. Cardio means book thinking time for unravelling plots and conversations for her current work in progress.

When Deborah's characters talk, she listens. Not surprisingly, they decide when and how to tell their story, talking to her at the strangest times. When she's driving, working out, or trying to fall asleep, they whisper in her ear and say, "this is what needs to happen next."

Other books in the series

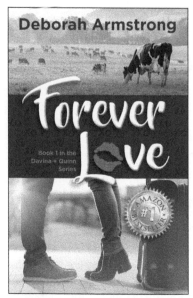

Book 1

Book 3

Book 4

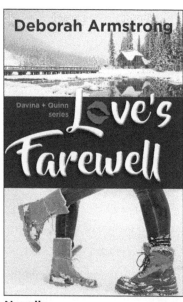

Novella

Also by Deborah Armstrong

stay connected

Deborah Armstrong is a storyteller, creating fantasies and weaving them for your reading delight from her farm in Ontario, Canada.

If you are in a Book Club, bring Deborah to yours via Skype, Zoom . . .or in person! Whether it's a hot and steamy summer day or one kissed with a wintry landscape, have your Club gather their favourite snacks and beverages and discover the Davina and Quinn series. Deborah invites her readers to follow her on social media and to contact her by email. To work with her, visit her website and subscribe to her newsletter.

Website: DeborahArmstrong.ca

 WriterDeborah

 deboraharmstrongauthor/

 DeborahArmstrongAuthor

 deborah_armstrong_author/

 author/show/6467157.Deborah_Armstrong

Lightning Source UK Ltd.
Milton Keynes UK
UKHW010731170621
385673UK00001B/117